Playing with Fire . . .

"Do you not think it would have done you better to remove your clothing rather than put on more?" He paused abruptly when her eyes narrowed on him. Grimacing, he said, "Well, mayhap you could at least take one or two of your gowns off? Surely one gown, or even just your shift is clothing enough?"

"Nay, I want to look nice for the consummation," she said simply. "Do you not think I look nice?"

His mouth twisted. "I think you look hot."

Kyla was not just hot, she was boiling, but she wasn't going to tell him that. "Actually, I am a touch chilled," she lied glibly. "But if you are warm, mayhap you should beat down the fire a bit."

Her thoughts died abruptly as his plaid hit the floor and he stood before her in only his shirt. It was soft and white and draped his muscled body almost lovingly, reaching halfway to his knees. And somehow, the pureness of it seemed to emphasize the strength and width of his shoulders. Kyla admired them briefly, then glanced down at his legs. Hard and strong and nicely shaped, and GOOD GOD— What was she thinking of? If he took that top off, she'd be lost.

By Lynsay Sands

Historicals

Argeneau Novels

LYNSAY SANDS

Sweet Revenge

AVON
An Imprint of HarperCollinsPublishers

This is a work of fiction. Names, characters, places, and incidents are products of the author's imagination or are used fictitiously and are not to be construed as real. Any resemblance to actual events, locales, organizations, or persons, living or dead, is entirely coincidental.

AVON BOOKS
An Imprint of HarperCollins*Publishers*
195 Broadway
New York, New York 10007

Copyright © 2000 by Lynsay Sands
Excerpt from *The Immortal Who Loved Me* copyright © 2015 by Lynsay Sands
ISBN 978-0-06-201981-3
www.avonromance.com

First Avon Books mass market printing: December 2014

Avon Trademark Reg. U.S. Pat. Off. and in Other Countries, Marca Registrada, Hecho en U.S.A.
HarperCollins® is a registered trademark of HarperCollins Publishers.

Printed in the U.S.A.

10 9 8 7 6 5 4 3 2 1

To Chris K.
Thank you.

Chapter 1

KYLA was the first to see them.

Lying on her stomach in the back of the horse-drawn cart, she was dozing in and out of a fitful sleep when a leaf fluttered onto her forehead. Frowning slightly, she reached out from beneath the furs covering her and brushed the item away. She then tried to settle back into the warm cocoon of healing sleep again, but found discomfort would not allow it.

Forcing her eyes open and blinking as the furs she lay upon came hazily into focus, she shifted slightly, trying to find a position that would ease the awakening pain in her back. It was a mounting, burning pain and was a miserable way to start the day, she decided unhappily, her mind immediately turning to thoughts of Morag's miracle salve. The stuff smelled as putrid as a privy on a hot summer day, but it made the pain in her back disappear immediately after it was applied. Temporarily at least. The effects lasted for only a few hours, then the foul balm had to be reapplied to beat back the white-hot agony. She could do with some of its lovely numbing effect now, she thought with a sigh, shifting carefully onto her side to peer hopefully at the woman who slept beside her.

A drop of what she thought to be rain landed on

her face as the fur slid aside and she wiped it away, surprise replacing her irritation as she felt the grittiness on her finger and looked down to see that it wasn't rain but a small bead of mud. Eyes raising instinctively, she gaped at the shapes that hovered in the branches overhead. Silent and still, they hid among the trees, watching tensely as the procession moved along beneath them.

Kyla had just opened her mouth to shout a warning to her escort when a long, loud wail filled the air. Bloodcurdling and ferocious, it set the hair at the nape of her neck on end. The first voice was joined by what seemed like a hundred others, and the mounted party came to an abrupt halt.

Grabbing for the side of the conveyance to steady herself, Kyla watched in amazement as a man dropped lithely from the branches above to land between her and Morag in the cart. Her eyes widened as a ray of sunlight speared through the trees, glinting off of the sword he held and turning his red hair to fire. Her gaze dropped over the plaid he wore. At this angle and with it flapping in the early afternoon breeze, she had an exceptional view of his naked legs all the way up to his thighs. And a fair pair of legs they were, too, she noted with an interest wholly inappropriate to the situation. Shapely ankles, muscled calves, nice knees, and strong thighs distracted her—until he let loose another long, loud wail that drew her eyes upward. He raised his sword high in one hand.

Truly, had she not seen him, she would have thought his wailing the shriek of the dead rising up from the pits of hell. It was loud, long, and ear-piercing, and it seemed to stab right through her skull to her brain, making it throb in contest with her back. It didn't help when his voice was joined by the others still in the branches above. And when the others suddenly began dropping from the trees as well, bedlam broke out in the clearing. Startled warning shouts and bellows of pain rose up around Kyla like the springtime flood waters in the river by her home, and the fellow standing at her feet suddenly leapt off the wagon and out of sight.

Gritting her teeth, she closed her eyes briefly, then pushed herself to her hands and knees. Her arms shook, weak from that small effort, and the bottom of the cart seemed to swim before her eyes, but she took a deep breath and managed to ease back to sit on her haunches. Raising her head determinedly, Kyla peered around as the clang of metal against metal joined the shouts and shrieks already filling the quiet glade they had been passing through.

The miserable burning in her back and her pounding head were immediately forgotten as Kyla took in the activity around her. They were under attack. What made her mouth drop open and her eyes widen incredulously was the unbelievable fact that the mad savages attacking her chain-mailed escort actually appeared to be winning!

Several members of her escort had already fallen from their mounts. The rest were attempting to urge their horses closer to the wagon to form a tight circle around it to defend from, but their attempts were hampered by the panicked rearing of the now-riderless horses that suddenly seemed to be everywhere.

Swallowing the fear tightening her throat, Kyla peered slowly around the glade with a sort of stunned apprehension. Her men were dropping like flies at summer's end. Already a third of them lay injured or dying on the muddy ground.

A roar drew her eyes as a great mountain of a man slammed into the back of the cart, struggling with one of her men-at-arms. With no time to prepare herself for the jolt, Kyla was sent sprawling onto her stomach again in the bottom of the wagon, her chin slamming hard into the floor of the cart despite the cushioning furs.

Cursing, she started to push herself back to her haunches again, but had barely lifted her head when one of her escort rode up to the side of the cart. He forcefully shoved her down again, ordering her to be still before riding off into the fray once more.

Frowning and muttering under her breath, Kyla did as she was told . . . for all of a heartbeat. She popped back up into a sitting position again.

"What's about?"

Remembering the woman who had been resting beside her throughout this journey, Kyla tore her gaze reluctantly from the fray and sank slowly back into the wagon. Rolling carefully onto her side, she peered worriedly at the wrinkled, old face of the woman who had been a maid, nurse, and mother figure to her for as long as she could recall, then lied, " 'Tis all right. 'Tis nothing. Go back to sleep."

A bloom of pale color tinged wrinkled old cheeks with anger and Morag's black eyes narrowed. "Yer lying, girl. Ye never could fool me."

The maid began to rise, determined to see for herself, but Kyla quickly pressed her back down. "Nay, do not rise."

"Then tell me!" she ordered sharply. "And the truth this time."

"Aye." Kyla sighed, searching briefly for a way to lessen the old woman's imminent terror, then shrugged. There was none. "We are under attack."

"What?!" Gasping in horror, Morag began to struggle upward again.

Kyla was trying to push the woman back down into the safety provided by the sides of the cart when a second jolt gave pause to them both. Stilling, they spun to stare at the warrior now standing on the back of the wagon. He was the same man who had first landed in the cart and as she had before, Kyla found herself memerized by the sight of him. Tall. Strong. Magnificent. He stood poised for a moment surveying the battle, the sweat on his body gleaming in the sunlight, then, just as suddenly as he had arrived, he lunged off the cart again, sword swinging ferociously.

"Gor!" Fanning herself with her good hand, Morag collapsed back against the skins in the bottom of their cart. "Savages!" she muttered crossly. "Highlanders. And 'tis one of them yer Catriona is wedding ye to. Yer dear departed mother must be rolling in her grave."

"Aye," Kyla agreed, then scowled as Morag pushed herself back up so that she could peer over the side of the cart.

"What are you doing?" Kyla hissed, sitting up to pull her back.

"Watching to see if we win."

Kyla opened her mouth to say that it mattered little—even if Catriona's men won, she would not be the winner—but before she could comment on that, two battling Scots crashed into the side of the wagon sending both women tumbling sideways against the far wall. Just as Morag would have raised herself again to continue her watch, a sword swung over their heads, then caught in the wood of the wagon. A man cried out in agony.

The Scot who had landed briefly in the wagon earlier peered over the side at them, a fierce glare on his face. "Keep yer heads down, ye lack-witted harpies!" he bellowed in Gaelic.

When Kyla's eyes widened in confusion, the man then repeated the order in English. Obviously he'd thought she had not understood the order the first time, but in truth, her confusion was due to the fact that he had given it at all. He was not one of her escort, but one of their attackers. What the devil did he care if she lived or got herself killed?

Frowning, she peeked over the edge of the wagon again, dismay overwhelming her as she saw that every single one of her mail-armored escort had fallen. Not one still stood among the battling men. Even the driver of the wagon was now sprawled on his seat, bleeding badly from a shoulder wound. The only warriors between herself and capture were the Scots her betrothed had sent to meet them at the border. There seemed few of them left.

Peering around at the fighting men, she estimated that perhaps fifteen of her escort still stood. Fourteen, she corrected as another man fell. Thirteen.

"What's about?" Morag rasped anxiously. Kyla bit her lip as she glanced down at her companion. Once the last of their defenders were slain, the attackers would no doubt turn their attention to them.

Kyla was not willing to contemplate what would happen then. These savages bore no resemblance to the knights of her brother's court.

Muttering under her breath, she ignored Morag's question as well as her own aches and pains and began to move. Climbing over the lip of the cart, she crawled onto the seat beside the slumped driver, grabbed the reins from his slack hands, then gave them a sharp snap. Unnerved by the smell of blood and the battle that raged around them, both animals were more than happy to fulfill her silent order. After a brief spate of snorting and wild rearing, the beasts set out, hooves tearing into the moist earth beneath them as they drew the cart quickly away from the melee.

Movement to her side brought Kyla's eyes around in time to see the previous driver tumble from the bench seat, dislodged by the lurching motion of the wagon. She winced at the thud as he hit the ground, but set her teeth and snapped the reins over the horses again, urging them to greater speed.

"Damnation!" Pushing herself up weakly, Morag peered out the back of the cart. Behind them, their attackers seemed not even to notice their escape.

Kyla scowled and reached back to push her gently down onto the floor of the cart. "Stay down, Morag. You are not well."

The woman snorted at that, but sank down among the furs willingly enough, though not before muttering, "Oh, aye, but ye are, I suppose?"

Disregarding the sarcastic comment, Kyla concentrated on steering their cart through the trees they had entered. They hadn't gone far when she spotted the horses. About twenty of them. No doubt belonging to their attackers. She was just worrying over the idea that they may have left someone to mind the animals when Morag's earsplitting scream rent the air from the back of the cart. Kyla turned just in time to see a figure drop from a tree branch.

He was huge. A veritable mountain that made the whole wagon shudder as he landed in the back of it. Kyla's gaze found the shiny blade he held in one hand and she panicked. With a broken arm and cracked ribs, her nurse maid was helpless against such a brute.

Dropping the reins, she stood, turned, drew her own dirk from her waist, and lunged—all at once. It was really quite amazing that she hit her target, but not only did she hit him, she sent the attacker backward right off the cart.

It had been an incredibly stupid thing to do, Kyla realized. With nothing to hold on to but the person she was tackling, she went tumbling off the wagon with the man. Driverless, the cart continued on its merry way, Morag screeching frantically from the back.

The savage's body cushioned Kyla from the worst of the fall. Yet despite this bit of luck, her landing was jarring and, for a moment, she could only lie atop the man, trying to regain her breath. It was the shine of sunlight reaching delicately through the summer leaves overhead to touch the tip of the blade she had dropped that moved her to action. She had just managed to grasp the dirk when the brawny man she lay on suddenly released a loud roar and rolled her onto her back, a move that sent all of the air rushing out of her lungs.

Gasping in agony, Kyla blindly jabbed her knife at him. Much to her relief, the great bear cursed and moved off her at once. Taking advantage of that, Kyla rolled quickly away from him and onto her stomach, sighing as the pain that had been ripping at her immediately eased a bit. Still, her vision wavered slightly as she eyed him where he now sat, gaping at her with amazement as he grasped the wound she had made in his side. It really wasn't much of a wound from what she could see; once he got over his surprise at her aggressive action, he would no doubt come at her again.

Turning her head, Kyla peered about, her gaze fastening on a good-sized fallen branch a few inches away from her right hand. It was leafless and pale brown from time spent in the elements. The bit nearest her was obviously the tip, but it widened out as it went, growing until it was thicker around at the end than her upper arm. Stretching, she closed her fingers over it, dragging it toward her even as she began to struggle to her hands and knees. Then, grasping it in both hands, she used it to help lever herself back to her feet.

The man recognized her intent the moment she lifted the stump of wood in her trembling arms and turned toward him. He immediately started to rise, but Kyla was already swinging for his head. The wood connected with a crack, the dead branch snapping in half as it slammed into his head. For a moment, Kyla feared all she had managed to do was anger the man further, then, a gurgle of surprise slipped from his lips and he sank back to lie in the leaves and grass.

Kyla felt nausea rise up inside her, then Morag's screams reached her through her dismay. Turning away from her enemy, she hurried after the fleeing cart, her heart nearly stopping when another figure dropped from the trees directly in front of the wagon. Spooked, the horses reared, the cart tipped, and Morag tumbled out with a cry that turned Kyla's blood cold. The cart righted itself and the horses stopped, stomping fearfully at the ground.

All she could see was Morag's frail body lying on the ground as she rushed forward. Forgetting the other man, she rushed to her maid's side, the knife slipping from her limp fingers as she dropped to her knees and gently touched one leathery cheek. "Morag? Morag!"

The flickering of those old, white eyelashes seemed the most beautiful thing in the world to Kyla. Releasing a gasping sob, she hugged the frail body close and silently offered up a prayer of thanks.

It was only then that she recalled the other barbarian. Glancing up, she saw with some surprise that he was a mere boy. And that he wasn't paying her the least bit of attention. He was looking past her.

Following his gaze, she immediately understood his lack of concern. The battle was over. The warriors were approaching, expressions grim.

Laying Morag quickly back down, Kyla snatched up the dirk she had dropped and got to her feet, moving instinctively between the prone woman and the approaching men. But, like the boy, the warriors paid her little heed. Instead, they hurried to their fallen comrade and encircled him, hiding him from view.

Clenching the dirk tighter in her sweaty hand, Kyla set her gaze darting about the area. It seemed obvious there was no escape, for she could not leave without Morag. Standing and fighting was her only option. In truth she wished it were not. She had never thought to die this way. Nor so young.

The men began to turn their attention to her now. Expressions forbidding, they moved forward, forming a half-circle in front of her as they took in her stance and the dirk in her hand.

Kyla expected an immediate attack, men coming at her all at once. It was a bit unnerving when they merely continued to stare at her, then began to discuss her in Gaelic, unaware that she understood the language.

"Bonnie," one commented, drawing her wary gaze to him. He was tall. Good God, they were all tall. She was of average height herself, and these men seemed giants. They stood, looming like a forest of trees before her. Broad-chested, solid, strong, and terrifying.

"Aye. Bonnie. But wee." The man who said that seemed to be the leader. She had noticed that the others had deferred to him as he led the way to stand before her. He was the red-haired man, the same one who had stood on the back of the wagon, then called her a harpie and ordered her to keep her head down. He was one of the tallest of them. He also seemed to be one of the brawniest, though the man directly beside him, the one who had originally called her "bonnie" was a good deal larger. Good grief, that man could be mistaken for a small building from a distance, she thought, frowning briefly at him before turning her attention back to the leader. She realized that the men were agreeing with him and not very flatteringly.

"Aye. Puny."

"Pulin'."

"All bones."

"Frail-lookin'."

"Pale as death, too and swaying on her feet. I be thinkin' she won't survive the trip home, let alone our harsh winters."

The leader nodded at that observation and they all eyed her gloomily. A dark-haired man behind the leader brightened. "Mayhap 'tis not her. Mayhap we attacked the wrong party."

Those words brought a round of hopeful looks from the other men, but the leader shook his head. "Nay, Duncan. 'Twas the MacGregors we fought with the Sassenach. I recognized at least two of them."

Kyla's sigh of disappointment joined that of the men. For a moment she had glimpsed freedom; surely if they had erred, they would have let her go. Alive? But, aye, it was the MacGregors that had been escorting their party. Twenty of them had met them at the border. It had been an added precaution, though Kyla had thought it unnecessary at the time, since forty of Catriona's men had already been escorting her. Now she saw how wrong she had been; the English men-at-arms had been slow and awkward in their mail. They had fallen quickly against these savages, leaving the MacGregor men alone to protect her. She supposed she was who these men were looking for, though she could not for the life of her figure out why. Unless the entire betrothal had been a ruse to get her away from the castle and assassinate her. That was a possibility. And not beyond her sister-in-law's nefarious mind.

"Well, we'd best be collecting her and moving on," the leader commented finally, drawing her attention back from her thoughts. He did not seem eager to accomplish the deed. In fact the only move he made was to shift his feet as he eyed her. Still, even that was enough to make Kyla stiffen warily. She would not go down without a fight.

"Careful of that blade of hers. 'Tis verra sharp. She gave me a fair nasty scratch with it."

Her gaze turned at once to the speaker, the man she had noted could be mistaken for a building. Shock covered her face now as she took in his features rather than his bulk; he was the one she had stabbed, then knocked out. The man was now standing tall and strong, no discomfort on his face and little to show that she had hurt him except for the blood on his shirt and plaid. And there was not very much of that either, she noted now with disgust.

Mouth tightening, Kyla braced her feet farther apart and bent her knees slightly in the manner she had seen her brother take during hand-to-hand combat.

Tipping his head to the side, the leader eyed her briefly, then suggested in English, "Ye'd best be dropping the blade, lassie, ere ye hurt yerself."

Kyla's only response was to lift her chin grimly. When the leader moved calmly forward, she was ready for him. Or so she thought.

He took two steps in a slow, meandering pace, then suddenly lunged. Grabbing her wrist in one hand, he forced it into the air, snatched the knife from her fingers with embarrassing ease, then tossed it to the man she had stabbed.

Screaming in frustration, Kyla kicked at his legs. She screeched even more furiously as she found herself picked up and slung over his shoulder like a sack of wheat.

"Calm yerself!" The stern order was accompanied

by a slap on the behind that shocked her into silence. "We'll not hurt ye or the old witch."

Cursing roundly, Kyla thumped her fists ineffectively against his wide back, then paused to watch anxiously as one of the other men stooped to survey Morag. She nearly sobbed with relief when the fellow seemed to realize the woman's fragile condition and took care to lift her gently before following the man carrying herself.

When the barbarian transporting her suddenly paused, Kyla knew instinctively that they had reached the wagon and that he would most likely drop her into it. She tried to brace herself for what was to come, but no amount of preparation on earth could have readied her for her landing in the back of the cart. 'Twas not that he was unduly rough. Simply that he knew not of her injury and set her flat on her back in the bottom of the wagon with a small bump. It had the same effect as if she had been dropped on a wide board with nails poking out of it. The pain took her breath away, leaving not even a small gasp for her to cry out with. Lights danced briefly before her eyes before everything went black.

Chapter 2

"THE old woman is in a bad way."

Galen raised his eyebrows at the man who had ridden up beside him, Tommy MacDonald. His First, as well as his cousin. "What makes ye think that?"

"I took a good look at her ere I carried her to the cart. She's nursing a broken arm and a cracked rib or two."

Galen frowned over that. "Ye'd be telling me this for a reason?"

His cousin nodded slowly, expression thoughtful as he surveyed the trees they were passing. "'Tis normal for a servant to ride in a wagon. But titled ladies are usually mounted. Unless they be ailing or injured."

When his laird's expression darkened, but he did not respond, Tommy added, "The old woman had the smell of weeds about her. Some sort of medicinal herb I would warrant. I was wondering if the lass did as well."

Galen stiffened at that in some surprise. "Aye. She did."

He nodded. "She be sleeping now. Has been since ye set her in the cart."

"And?"

"I be thinking 'tis an odd reaction for a lass who has just been captured and her soldiers defeated. Especially when she showed such spirit earlier."

"Spirit?" His eyebrows rose in surprise at the word.

"Aye. It takes a great deal of spirit and courage to confront thirty warriors alone with little but a blade," Tommy pointed out.

"Aye, that's true." The MacDonald chief perked up slightly at that. He had only noticed how puny she was, not that, puny or not, she was standing her ground and trying to defend the old woman. "She has spirit," he said, realizing it was the first sign of hope he had known since seeing his would-be bride. 'Twas a relief to be sure. Especially since he had spent the last few hours berating himself for this escapade.

It had made sense when he had planned it out. His wife and the wee bairn she had been carrying at the time had been killed by the MacGregor some nine months earlier. Galen's soul had cried out for vengeance, as had his men, but he had bided his time. Then the news had come of MacGregor's coming remarriage—to an Englishwoman of all things. Galen shouldn't have been so surprised. The MacGregor was half-English himself.

Still, English or no, Galen could not justify simply attacking the party and killing the woman. What had happened to his wife and child had nothing to do with her. She was as much an innocent as his own wife had been. Yet he still sought vengeance. So, to satisfy his need for retribution, along with his sense of fairness, he had decided on stealing and marrying the wench himself. He had even managed to convince himself that he would be doing her a favor. Everyone knew the MacGregor was rough with women. There was even some question as to why his first wife had died. Had it been from child birth, or from the beating that had brought on the early labor during which she died?

Stealing MacGregor's bride had seemed the perfect solution to Galen at the time. He would get a wife, heirs soon enough, and his revenge on Mac-Gregor in one tidy little raid.

Aye, except for her being English it had seemed the perfect solution . . . right up until he had seen how puny and frail she appeared. Then he had begun to think he may have made a grave error. Tommy's pointing out that she had shown some spirit back there brought him welcome relief from the barrage of self-reproach he had been indulging in. Small she may be, but if she had spirit . . . Well, at times, spirit could go a long way toward making up for a lack of size and physical strength.

"Ye ken, me laird. I think he be right."

With a start, Galen glanced at the man who had been riding on his other side all afternoon. He had forgotten all about Duncan's presence.

"Aye," the second man agreed now. "She has spirit." He, too, was cheering visibly and that only served to show Galen how deep they had all been in worry. Who he married would affect all his people.

"Who has spirit?" Angus urged his horse up to Duncan's side, his expression curious as he caught the words.

"The Sassenach." When the other man looked doubtful, Duncan pointed out what Tommy had noted. "She thought to take us all on with naught but a wee knife back there. She stood her ground to defend the old witch. And she stabbed Giant Robbie."

" 'Twas naught but a scratch," Robbie rumbled, urging his horse forward so that they rode five abreast. Several of the other men crowded their horses closer to hear the discussion as well.

"It bled," Duncan pointed out, undaunted. "She had blood all over her hand. Ye even have some on yer shirt."

Robbie glanced down at himself with a start and cursed. "Aelfread will be fair froth over that. She'll work herself up something fierce before I can assure her 'tis naught."

They all smiled slightly at that comment, finding it amusing that a man so large could find a five-foot female's temper worrisome. But his wife was a fiery one.

"Ye may be right," Angus murmured thoughtfully now, disregarding the larger man's complaint. "It may be spirit the English was showing. I thought 'twas jest plain stupid, but mayhap 'twas spirit."

"Well," Duncan said uncertainly after a silent moment, "mayhap 'twas stupid, but 'twas brave, too."

At their murmurs of general, if unenthusiastic, agreement to that, Duncan rallied. "Aye, 'twas brave. 'Twas brave of her to try to escape in the cart, too. From what I hear, most English ladies would have sat about crying 'woe is me.' "

When the agreement to that was a bit more enthusiastic, he added excitedly, "Aye, she be a spirited lassie. In fact, from all I have seen, 'tis sure I am that at any minute now, the wench'll try to escape again. She may be doing so even as we speak."

At that, every last one of the men brought their

horses to a halt and turned to peer back toward the approaching wagon expectantly. Even Galen.

Expression curious, the man driving the cart slowed it, bringing it to a halt as he reached them. When they immediately circled the wagon to peer down into it, he craned around on the bench to look as well, bewilderment on his young face at the disappointment obvious all around as they took in the two sleeping figures.

"Well. Mayhap all her bravery earlier wore her out," Duncan murmured after a moment, wincing at the disgusted looks tossed his way at that. Then, Tommy suddenly leaned down into the wagon and pressed a hand to the woman's forehead with concern. It was only then that Galen noticed the flush to her cheeks.

"Fever?" he asked worriedly, recalling Tommy's hinting earlier that she may be injured.

"Aye." The other man straightened on his horse, then swung his leg over the edge and dropped into the wagon. The old woman awoke at once. Her eyes widened as she noted all the faces peering down into the wagon, then her gaze slid to her charge. Dismay crossed her features as she noted the man bent over the girl.

"Leave her be, ye filthy wretch!" she snapped, struggling to rise despite the pain it caused her.

"Don't fash yourself, old woman. I mean no harm." Tommy didn't even bother to glance at the servant, his concern taken up with examining her mistress. The girl's face was as red as an English rose and felt afire. She was in the throes of a fever and a bad one at that. "She's ailing."

Wincing as she gained a sitting position, Morag

felt the girl's forehead herself. "Get me my bag of medicinals."

"Where is it?" Galen asked, dismounting to join them in the open cart.

"In the corner there."

Tommy was closer to the bags stacked in the upper corner of the wagon. As he turned to begin searching through them, Galen knelt beside the girl and felt her forehead for himself, frowning over the heat pouring off her. "What ails her?"

The witch's answer was forestalled when the girl opened her eyes and peered up at him through glazed, feverish eyes. "Johnny? Johnny. It hurts so much. It burns. Make it stop."

Galen stared into those tormented eyes for a moment, then turned angrily on the old woman. "Who the hell is Johnny?"

"The salve's worn off," Morag murmured worriedly, cursing herself for not thinking of it before when they were both awake. "Turn her on her stomach."

Galen hesitated, then did as instructed, leaving his questions for later.

"Have ye found the damn thing?" she snapped as Tommy opened the last bag to peer in.

"Aye."

"Open her dress," she ordered, reaching for the bag.

The two men exchanged a glance, then with a shrug, Galen pulled a small knife from his boot. Hands quick and sure, he slit the back of the gown open, eyebrows rising when he saw the thick bandages he had revealed.

"The bandages," Morag muttered, digging through her bag as Kyla groaned.

Moving more carefully, Galen cut away more of the dress, then turned his attention to the bandages. They covered the whole of her back, running all the way around her body. The only way to remove them without lifting her to a sitting position was to cut them away as he had the dress. He did so without hesitation when the girl beneath his hands groaned again, then he sat back with a horrified curse at the wound that was revealed to him. He was vaguely aware that the men about the wagon were exclaiming in dismay as well, most of them dismounting to move to stand against the wagon to get a better look, but his attention was mostly taken up with the injury he had revealed.

A long, deep, angry-looking gash ran from her left shoulder down to the right side of her lower waist. It was obviously a sword wound. And one that should have killed the sliver of a girl lying before him, he thought a bit faintly as his gaze slowly slid over it, taking in the countless stitches of thread through her porcelain-white skin. The wound looked to be a couple of weeks old. Some healing had begun, but not enough for her to be traveling about. She certainly should not have been rushing around, dagger in hand, trying to defend an old lady. It was amazing to him that none of the stitches had burst.

"It must have hurt like a bugger."

Galen glanced at his First at those words, then at the men still gathered about the wagon. They were all nodding in a sort of awed agreement.

"Well. Now we ken why she isn't trying to escape again," Duncan murmured with a sigh.

"Aye." Angus nodded. " 'Tis a wonder she had the strength to try the first time."

"It wasn't strength. 'Twas stubbornness," Morag informed them shortly, struggling to open a small leather pouch she had retrieved from her bag. " 'Tis the same thing that kept her alive when she was struck down. Sheer stubbornness, God bless her. She got it from her mother. A Ferguson," she added proudly.

"She's no' English?" Tommy took the bag the old woman was struggling with and opened it for her before handing it back.

"Half. Her mother was a Ferguson. As am I. Lord Forsythe was English."

Galen's eyes widened in surprise at the injured girl. So, she was not wholly English, but half Scot. A lowlander Scot, but Scot just the same. That was a plus. It was better to be half lowlander than wholly English. His gaze slid over her flushed face again and it suddenly occurred to him that he did not even know her name. He had attacked her party and basically kidnapped her, all with the intention of making her his wife, and he really knew not a thing about her, not even her name. All he had known was that she was an Englishwoman on her way to marry MacGregor. And even that wasn't wholly true. She was only half English. "What's her name?"

"Kyla. Here."

Turning, he stared blankly at the leather pouch she held out to him.

"Mix a bit of this with some water, then pour it on the wound."

Galen took the bag and peered inside, his nose wrinkling at the smell that wafted out to him. "What is it?"

"Salve. It'll clean the wound. 'Tis infected. I warned

that this might happen," she added grimly almost to herself. "You can clean and bandage a wound up much as ye like, but it does little good doing so when you're camping in three feet of mud. But that English viper wouldn't listen. She cares little if my little one lives or dies, she just wanted her out of the way."

"Who wanted her out of the way?" Duncan leaned further over the edge of the cart, handing his water jug to his laird to mix the salve. All the men were dismounted now and jockeying to get closer to the wagon and a better look at the wound.

"Lord Forsythe's new wife."

"Kyla's stepmother?"

"Nay. Both her parents are dead. Johnny, her brother, is lord now. So long as he lives," she added grimly. "If the viper has her way, that won't be long."

"Johnny?" Kyla's eyes opened, a moan slipping from her lips as she turned her head at the sound of her brother's name. "Johnny?"

"Nay, lass. Sleep. He isn't here." The old woman reached out a hand to soothe the girl, but she would not be soothed.

"We must help Johnny, Morag. Catriona will smother him in his sick bed ere he can heal," she fretted weakly.

"There is naught ye can do for him just now. Rest. We're going to clean your wound." Her gaze moved to Galen who was holding both the salve and the water, but had done nothing with them. Retrieving a small wooden mixing bowl from her bag, she shoved it at him and ordered, "Get to it, boy. The wound needs cleaning." She waited until he had started to do as instructed before digging in her bag for a second pouch and bowl which she handed to Tommy. "Mix that with some water as well. 'Twill numb the pain once the cleaning's done."

"Shouldn't ye numb her ere ye clean the wound?" One of the men asked a bit anxiously. " 'Twill sore hurt."

"Nay. Clean the wound, then numb her back," she said firmly, then pulled a strip of thick leather out of the bag and eased closer to her charge's mouth. "Kyla, child. We have to clean your wound again."

The girl's eyes opened slowly, confusion in them until she recognized the strip of leather Morag was trying to press into her mouth. Realization dawned then, with fear, before resignation entered her face and she opened her mouth for the leather to be inserted.

Straightening awkwardly, Morag glanced about to make sure all was ready, then nodded.

Galen hesitated. The salve she had had him mix was going to hurt like sin. He knew that. He'd had similar concoctions poured on enough of his own wounds. The idea of inflicting that kind of pain on a woman was unthinkable to him. Unfortunately, it had to be done. Sighing resolutely, he took a deep breath, then poured the liquid along the length of the injury.

He had expected hysterical screams. He had expected to have to hold her down to keep her from thrashing around, and he was not the only one. Tommy had positioned himself in such a way that he could help restrain her, as had the other men around the wagon. All of them stood, leaning over the sides of the cart, hands half outstretched, ready to lend aid. However, they were all wrong. His little English prize stiffened, her body going as hard and stiff as the blade that had wounded her, but other than a small whimper and the groan of leather beneath the pressure of her teeth, she made not a sound or movement.

Galen would have preferred it otherwise. It was almost unbearable to watch such silent suffering. Screams and thrashing would have at least kept them all too busy to imagine the agony she must be enduring. Instead, all they could do was watch helplessly as the liquid soaked into her wound, burning out the infection.

A bare half-second after Galen finished pouring the cleansing salve on, Tommy moved to administer the numbing one, but the old witch stopped him with an upraised hand. They all sat back, swallowing bile and waiting what seemed hours as the seemingly frail woman struggled with her pain. Her face blanched white, then gray, then almost blue as she suffered. Sweat beaded on and slid from her face. Her hands were clutched in the cloth beneath her, near rending it with the strength of her pain. It was an agony to watch. They all sighed in relief when Morag finally motioned for Tommy to go ahead.

Leaning forward at once, he tipped the container of salve over the wound. Whatever the concoction was, it seemed a powerful medicine. A bare breath after Tommy poured it, Kyla sagged with relief, her face dropping back into the cloth, cushioning her head as a small sob escaped her. Her body was now as limp as a cloth doll's.

"Here." Morag held out fresh wrappings to Galen and instructed him on binding her, then had him leave the girl lying on her stomach, a blanket pulled up to cover the bandages and torn dress she wore.

"What about you?" he asked once he had done all he could for the girl.

Morag appeared surprised by his solicitude, no matter that it had been offered in a gruff voice. Shrugging, she settled back in the wagon. "All I be needing is rest."

He stared at her silently, then glanced toward the woman lying prone beside her. She looked to have fallen asleep. "How was she wounded?"

"What are your intentions toward her?"

Galen scowled at the question. " 'Tis not yer place to be asking that."

Morag merely shrugged and turned her head away, making it obvious that were he not to answer her question, neither would she answer his.

He sighed impatiently. "She'll come to no harm. I mean to marry her."

Eyes widening, Morag looked him over carefully. He was tall. Well-built. He had a fine form. His face held fine features that were strong and attractive. Of course, his hair was a mite too red for her to think him handsome. Morag did not like red hair. But, all in all, her little one could do worse. Especially if he was who that startling fiery hair made her think he was. "Are ye Galen the Red?"

He stiffened at the question, then lifted his head arrogantly. "I am Galen MacDonald. Chief of the MacDonald clan."

The old woman nodded her head slowly, concern playing about her lined face. "I presume, as laird of the MacDonalds, ye needn't steal another's bride to find a wife. That would mean ye chose Kyla for a reason?"

Galen scowled briefly, then said coldly, " 'Tis a marriage for revenge. The MacGregor caused my wife and child's death, so I shall steal his wife-to-be and bear my children by her. Children that should have been his."

Morag sighed at that, Highlanders were known for their feuds, and it seemed Kyla had been dropped into the middle of one. Still, from what she had heard of the MacGregor and his cruelty, the girl was better off with the MacDonald. . . . So long as he didn't take his revenge out on the girl by being cruel to her. She would have to think of some way to ensure he didn't.

The MacDonald's sudden impatient shifting told her that she had delayed as long as he would allow. Leaving for later the problem of how to get him to leave Kyla alone until they sorted out things, Morag plunged into the tale of her ward's bravery. "Kyla, her brother, and his new wife went for a picnic in the woods outside Forsythe. They were attacked. Johnny was run through, and Kyla received the wound ye saw and some bruises."

"And the new wife?"

"Completely untouched," Morag said dryly, then paused before adding. "Kyla may not have been injured either, but she ran to aid her brother when he was wounded. He had received a dangerous injury already, but still they were going to cut his head off. She threw herself across him. 'Twas how she received the injury to her back. They were both left to die. I think she *would* have died, too, but after she was struck down, she remained conscious long enough to see those evil vipers approach Catriona, Johnny's wife. She thanked them for their service and paid them off with a nice fat sack of coins."

Galen and Tommy both cursed at that, but Duncan goggled from Kyla's unconscious form to the old woman. "The wife paid to see them both dead?!"

"Nay." The answer was uncertain at first, then the old woman frowned and shook her head firmly. "Nay. Not both of them. Only Johnny. Kyla was not supposed to be with them that day. 'Twas Johnny who'd invited her along at the last moment. And 'tis lucky for him that he did. If he lives, 'twill be thanks to her."

There were murmurs of agreement as all eyes turned to the woman on the floor of the wagon. Each one of them was recalling the sight of the now-covered wound on her back and imagining an unknown man's head rolling across a clearing.

"She saved his life and no denying that," Robbie rumbled.

"Aye. 'Tis amazing she survived, though," Angus muttered. "She's surely got spirit enough for ten men to manage it."

" 'Twas stubbornness," Morag repeated. "Her anger alone kept her alive when she realized Catriona had planned the entire thing."

There was silence for a moment, then Galen asked, "And yer injuries?"

Morag sighed. "Catriona rode for the castle once the deed was done and sent men back to collect the bodies. She was in her room picking out her mourning clothes when they returned. I had them both put into Kyla's room so that I could tend to them easier. We were all so rushed with tending them, that I didn't think to send someone to inform Lady Forsythe that her husband was still alive. When she finally asked where he had been put, she was just told that he was in Kyla's room. It came as quite a shock when she walked in and found they both still lived," she told them dryly. "Lady Forsythe despises surprises."

"She beat ye." Duncan shook his head in disgust as he guessed that.

"Nay. 'Twas no beating. She simply pushed me. But in her anger and frustration, she pushed me hard enough I crashed over a chair. Me bones are not as strong as they used to be. And I was not prepared for that reaction. Had I known that she'd been the one responsible, I would have known to watch her reaction, but I did not even suspect until Kyla told me on the way here."

Galen was silent for a minute, then, "So, this Catriona arranged Kyla's marriage to MacGregor to keep the girl from telling anyone else what she had seen?" he surmised.

Morag shook her head. Catriona doesn't ken that Kyla saw her pay off the attackers. She simply wanted her out of the way, injury or no injury. Whether she died on the way was not important. I suspect Catriona cares little either way. Besides, it will be easier for her to kill her husband without Kyla around."

"And you allowed this?" Duncan blurted. "Ye'd see her just kill yer laird?"

"I knew naught about it until the second night of the trip," Morag snapped. "Kyla remained unconscious until then. By the time she regained her senses and could tell me, we were too far away to do anything. Catriona had sent her own men as escort, men she had brought with her to the marriage. They were loyal only to her. None of them would have listened to what Kyla had seen and heard, let alone have turned back to warn Lord Forsythe."

"Is there someone you could send a message to who could help?" Galen asked quietly.

Morag considered that briefly. "Lord Shropshire. He is a good friend and lives nearby. He could go and keep an eye on things if he were told. If 'tis not too late already."

Galen nodded, then glanced down at his unconscious soon-to-be bride. "I will need something of hers that he will recognize."

"What for?" Morag asked with a frown.

"She's in no condition to write a message and while I have spoken to Shropshire a time or two at the English court, he has no reason to believe the claim without some proof at least that the message is truly from Lady Kyla. We shall have to send him some personal item to prove 'tis not some trick or trap."

Morag was still for a moment, her expression thoughtful, then she leaned down and pushed the girl's unbound hair out of the way so that she could remove a locket from about her neck. "He will recognize this. She has worn it near all her life. 'Twas her mother's. 'Tis precious to her, though, so it must return to her."

"It shall return," Galen assured her quietly and the vow was backed by the murmurs of his men.

"I'll take the message, me laird." Duncan faced him solemnly. "And ensure the necklace returns safely."

Nodding, Galen handed the locket to him. He glanced briefly at the injured woman he would soon marry, then turned away and got out of the cart. "I shall prepare a message for you to take with it."

Chapter 3

"THE old woman's wanting a word with ye."

Galen frowned at Tommy's announcement and glanced back toward the wagon following them. It had been three days since they had taken the Mac-Gregor's bride-to-be, and still they were not yet home. They had traveled far more slowly than normal to avoid jostling the women about. They had also stopped often to tend their wounds. In fact they had stopped a mere half-hour back for that purpose. Galen had hoped it would be the last stop. They were a mere twenty minutes from the coast and the ship that would take them to their island home. Certainly once he had her at his keep, the girl would mend.

She had been out of her mind with fever for most of the trip. Galen had tended to her needs himself during that time, listening to her moans and feverish babblings as he did. Most of that time she had seemed to think he was her brother Johnny and she was re-living a memory. In the last three days she had swam in the river with him, bested her brother at a game of chess, and run a race with him on horseback ... all without even regaining consciousness.

Galen found himself charmed by her wit and spirit. As had most of his men, all of whom seemed to spend an extraordinary amount of time around the wagon, watching over their would-be mistress. He had overheard enough of their conversations to know that while they admired the fire and courage she had shown, they were also beginning to fash over her well-being like a bunch of old women.

It was a distressing tendency he himself was not immune to. For instance, this very minute he was fretting. Her fevers had been up and down for the last three days, and up more than they were down. That was why Galen was relieved to note that they were so close to home. He had told the old witch that, as well. He felt his heart speed up. If Morag wished to see him now, it could only mean that her charge was worse.

One glance down at Kyla when he reined in beside the cart was enough to tell him that he had been right.

" 'Tis the fever," Morag told him unnecessarily.

"She looks like she's fair freezing," Angus muttered as he and the other men converged on the wagon. "Should ye no cover her up better?"

"Nay. We needs must cool her down, not warm her more, and right away—else I fear, if she lives, she won't be quite right in the head." As the men began to mutter in dismay, she added wryly, "Not that she was all there to begin with."

"What?" the MacDonald snapped, his eyes wide. Morag nearly smiled; this was the idea she had come up with for protecting her little one. What man would wish a madwoman to wife? Who would want to beget his heir by a lunatic? It seemed perfect. This way, the MacDonald would leave Kyla alone until she was well enough to decide what she wanted to do. Morag had no fear that the MacDonald or his men would treat the girl badly in the meantime. She had already come to realize that courage was prized by these men above all else, and they were already impressed with Kyla's bravery—both while facing them down and in saving her brother. Nay, this was the best way to deal with it. And if the girl decided later that she wished to marry the MacDonald, Morag could always clear the matter up then.

"What do ye mean that she was not all there to begin with?" MacDonald asked sharply now. Morag put on an expression of feigned reluctance. "Well now, madness does run in her family. The father's side, of course. Weak English blood," she added. "Her grandmother went quite mad by the time she was thirty, but she showed signs long before that, even whilst as young as Kyla. I fear the girl has shown a sign or two of going that way herself. No doubt all of this has just rushed it along."

"What of her brother?" Duncan asked suddenly, "Is he mad too?"

Now Morag hesitated. Claiming Kyla mad was one thing, but calling John Forsythe, Morag's own lord that, was quite another. Shaking her head at last, she said, "Nay. 'Tis an affliction passed down only to the women."

There was silence for a moment after that, until a moan from Kyla drew their gazes. Mouth tightening grimly, the MacDonald laird asked, "What do ye need to cool her?"

"A bath. Water as cold as ye can find."

Head raising, he glanced at the land surrounding them. He could smell the ocean, they were so close. While it would take twenty minutes to reach it at the speed they had been traveling, it was only five minutes on a fast horse. His gaze moved to Tommy as the other man suddenly dropped from his mount into the cart to feel Kyla's forehead.

"She's burning up," he verified grimly.

"Hand her up to me," Galen ordered at once.

Nodding, the man lifted her carefully up to his laird's waiting arms. Galen wheeled his horse around at once, fear coloring his expression as he felt her heat radiating through her clothing. "I shall meet ye at the coast," he called, spurring his mount to a run and leaving the others to follow as quickly as they could.

It was only a matter of moments before he reached the shoreline. Holding her close, he leapt to the ground and strode quickly into the cold, salty surf of the calm bay. The chill liquid lapped at his feet, his calves, his knees. The first slap of it against his thighs made him gasp and grit his teeth. Pausing there, Galen glanced down at Kyla's flushed face, silently offered an apology for what he was about to do, then gritted his teeth, bent his knees, and lowered them both into the frigid water.

She was instantly awake. Her eyes shot open and she cried out, shuddering and clutching instinctively at him. Grunting, Galen peered down into the vast green depths of her eyes with surprise. He had not noticed their color before, nor how large they were, or the fact that they were framed with long, dark lashes. They were glazed with fever just now and filled with dismay as the cold water enveloped her—but lovely just the same.

"Whyst, sweetling," he soothed as she struggled against his hold. " 'Tis unpleasant cold I ken, but we needs must get the fever down."

"C-cold," she murmured faintly, her teeth clattering together.

"I ken. 'Tis—*arrgh!*" he cried out as she suddenly caught at his ears with both hands and pulled on them hard, using them as handles as she tried to pull herself out of the water. It was then he realized, eyes open or not, she knew not what she was about. In fact, he began to suspect her so feverish she thought herself a cat as she dug her toes into the flesh of his thighs and, pulling on his ears, tried to climb atop his head to escape the frigid water.

"Sweetling," he muttered, catching at her hands, then cried out again as she dug one foot into his groin to lever herself upward.

Cursing, Galen pulled her back down into the water with him, then stumbled and slid onto his behind, the liquid reaching his neck and covering her up to her lips. Kyla began to struggle in earnest then. He fought to hold her still, but it was an impossible feat with her thrashing about as she was. Afraid she would tear out her stitches, he caught her close, wrapping his arms tight around her.

" 'Tis too c-cold, Johnny," she cried, twisting against him in the water.

Sighing at this further proof that she was not really aware, Galen held her fast and assured her. " 'Twill warm up in a bit, sweetling. Don't fash so."

They grappled silently for another few minutes, then she twisted in her struggles and cried out in pain. Realizing she was doing damage to her injury, he gave her a shake and snapped, "Ye must stop this thrashing!"

It did not have the desired effect. Rather than calm her, his sharp order simply set her to thrashing harder, a shrill wail streaming from her throat and piercing his ears. Within seconds the sound seemed to be scratching its way inside his brain and tearing away at his nerves.

Galen was at a loss as to what to do and had about reached the end of his patience when a hand suddenly stretched in front of his face and popped a rolled up piece of cloth into her mouth, choking the sound off at once. Glancing up with a start, he gaped at his Second. "Gavin! How did ye ken I was—"

"The men were watching for ye. We recognized ye soon as ye reached shore and headed over to see what was about. Is this her?" He gestured to Kyla who seemed to have dropped back into unconsciousness in his arms.

Frowning at her sudden pallor, Galen was just wondering if she hadn't choked to death on the gag Gavin had placed in her mouth, when the bit of cloth fell out and began to sink in the water. "Aye," he admitted with a sigh.

"Well." Reaching up, the other man scratched at the skin behind his ear, perplexity on his face. "I ken her screaming was fair annoying, but I thought the plan was to marry the lass, not drown her."

"Aye." Galen sighed again and shifted her slightly in his arms. She had twisted to a position where she lay with her back resting against one of his arms as they had struggled. No doubt that was what had caused her screaming, he realized now with a grimace. He glanced over her face again, noting with relief that her color was a little better. Dunking her was actually working at bringing the fever down. " 'Twas not drowning her I was attempting. She has a fever."

"What be the matter with her?"

"She was wounded ere she left for Scotland. It was healed some but now 'tis infected. She's burning up from the inside." Standing in the water suddenly, he moved past Gavin and the six men he had brought, wading toward the small sailing boat they had used to reach him. It seemed they had chosen speed over size when they had set out from the island. Normally they would have crossed the water in one of the larger ships. One big enough to carry the returning men, the horses, and the wagon back.

"Have one of the men stay here with my horse to await the others," he ordered, spying the larger boat now slowly crossing the water toward them as he reached the smaller craft. Clambering aboard with Kyla cradled close, he settled on one of the small bench seats as all but one man reboarded and pushed off.

It took several minutes to cross to the island. Galen spent the time filling Gavin in on everything that had occurred. Seconds after the boat ran aground on the island, he was striding grimly up the path to the castle, Kyla in his arms.

Warned of his arrival, the villagers had poured down to the shore to meet him. All were eager to get their first glimpse of the woman that was to be their mistress. Now they lined the path to the castle. Rather than smile and cheer, however, they were all silent, their dismay obvious as they saw the pale, limp form of the woman he carried.

This was not how his new bride had been meant to arrive, he thought unhappily as he reached the keep and mounted the steps where the servants were gathered. They parted like curtains for him, worry evident on their expressions as they craned their heads to glimpse the woman he held.

"Is there anything I can do?" Gavin asked, trailing him into the keep.

"Aye. Have a bath brought up to my room," Galen ordered.

"Me laird!"

Pausing, he turned to scowl at the priest rushing toward him. "Aye?"

Father William paused and shifted uncertainly, almost wringing the Bible he held. "The wedding, me laird? Ye said—"

"Hell!"

The priest stiffened at his curse, disapproval crossing his jowl features, but Galen ignored him, his gaze on Kyla's face as he silently debated the situation. Did he really wish to marry her? The old woman claimed she was mad. Well, actually, she had claimed the girl's grandmother went mad at thirty and that this woman had already shown some of the first signs at her tender age, just as the grandmother had before her. Which meant a good ten years mayhap. . . . And the possibility of female heirs going the same way. But not male heirs, he reminded himself. They'd be sane. Of course, he'd probably have to lock their mother up in the tower in ten years for her own safety, but in the meantime, he'd have his revenge. And the girl would be safe from the MacGregor.

"Aye. We'll get it done," he decided grimly, turning back. " 'Tis no sense delaying. But make it quick, father. She's burning up even as we speak."

The priest glanced worriedly at the woman in his laird's arms, then nodded resignedly and turned toward the doors. "Outside, me laird."

"Outside?" Galen grumbled, following him. "Can we no'—"

"Ye ken 'tis right. All should witness this . . . grand event." He said the last dubiously, for truly the woman did not look as if 'twould be a long marriage.

Stepping out of the keep, the priest paused at the top of the stairs and eyed the people milling uncertainly about. They had been told a wedding would take place as soon as their laird returned with Mac-Gregor's girl, but seeing how pale and still she was, they had some obvious question as to whether the wedding was still on. Truthfully, there were some who doubted she was even still alive. She looked more a corpse than anything. For those that believed her still alive, there was no joy in Galen's marrying her, for she'd surely be dead by nightfall.

Of the same opinion himself, the priest made his introduction of the apparently unconscious bride quickly, then immediately moved on to the ceremony. When he came to the part where the bride had to speak, he paused and frowned at the unconscious woman. "She has to repeat the vows."

Eyebrows rising, Galen pointed out dryly, "She's unconscious, Father."

"Aye, but she must speak the vows," the priest repeated firmly.

Cursing under his breath, Galen glanced toward his Second. "Fetch me some ale, Gavin," he ordered, then eased his bride's feet to the ground and held her up by the arms. "Kyla? Kyla. Lass?"

She was slow to stir, and when she opened her eyes, Galen was sure she knew not where she was. Still, he must continue. He had decided ere heading out that he'd marry the girl as soon as he returned with her. It was necessary to quash any thought that the MacGregor might have about stealing her back—for that was truly a concern. So long as she lived, she was in danger of being forced to marry the ham-fisted bastard . . . unless she were already married.

"Say 'aye,' lass," he murmured, peering into her face and trying to infuse her with his own strength. She *would* get through this.

"Aye?" she asked in confusion.

"That's it." He turned to the priest. "Finish it up, Father. Thank ye, Gavin," he added, taking the tankard of ale the man had returned with. He urged it to his bride's lips as the priest reluctantly continued with the vows. He was still nursing the liquid into Kyla's parched mouth when the priest cleared his throat expectantly.

"Aye," Galen muttered without glancing up.

"Ye don't even ken what I said," Father William protested at once.

"I have been through this before, Father," Galen reminded him grimly.

The priest calmed at once, resignation entering his voice. "Aye, lad. Ye have. Can she sign the papers?"

Galen peered at Kyla uncertainly. She was much more alert now, but she was still feverish and confused. "Kyla, lass? Can ye sign yer own name?"

"My name?" she whispered faintly. "Aye."

"Good." Turning, he held a hand out to the priest who tugged the papers from the voluminous folds of his gown. Galen peered at them blankly, then glanced toward his Second. "Gavin?"

"Aye." The man knelt on one knee before him and Kyla, bending his back slightly to make a writing surface for them.

Galen set the paper on his man's back, then glanced about. "I need a quill, Father."

"Oh, aye." He turned to glance over his shoulder and a waiting servant rushed forward carrying a quill and small container of ink. The priest took the quill, dipped it into the ink, then turned back to hold it out.

"Thank ye," the MacDonald murmured, taking the item. Placing it in Kyla's hand then, he urged her toward the paper. "Can ye sign here, lass?"

"Sign?"

"Aye. Just sign the paper and ye'll be safe."

Understanding seemed to sparkle briefly in her eyes then. "Johnny?"

"He's being looked after. Now sign the paper, sweetling."

She did as she was told, her hand trembling with weakness so that 'twas a messy scrawl, but legible.

Nodding his satisfaction, Galen plucked the quill from her fingers, handed it and the paper to the priest, then scooped her up and headed back into the keep.

Taken by surprise at the speed of it all, his people were a bit slow to realize it was over. He was nearly through the door before they regathered their senses and burst out in uncertain cheers. Gavin and the priest chased after him.

"But *you* haven't signed, lad! You must sign, too!" the priest cried.

"I'll do it when I return below," Galen answered, then reminded the servants about the water and carried his bride quickly up to his own room.

Kicking the door of the chamber open, he hurried to the bed, set her down, and began rapidly stripping her. Once the last item of clothing dropped away, Galen swiftly removed the sodden bandage that had sagged down around her waist, then turned her to lie on her stomach and reached for the blankets to tug them up. He had just grasped the corner of the material when his eyes finally focused on all the naked flesh before them. He had tended her many times over the past several days, changing bandages, cleaning her wound . . . But never had he seen more of her than the expanse of her naked back. Now he paused, his gaze drawn reluctantly over her body.

She was slender and delicate in form. He'd always preferred more robust women, but her figure was not in the least disappointing to him. His eyes slid across the curve of her back, gliding over the angry-looking wound, and down to the silky white cheeks of her behind, noting the upside-down heart they made. They had a nice curve to them and her legs were long and well-muscled from riding. She had most likely lost some weight due to the fevers and her injury, but still she was well-formed and strong. She was rather like a young colt in build.

She lay, head turned to the side on the pillow, and his gaze lifted to her profile, running over the cheeks pink with fever, the straight, noble nose, and the generous lips. She was an attractive woman. They would have handsome children.

The sound of clomping footsteps in the hall warned of someone's arrival and Galen finished drawing the bedclothes up to cover her to the waist, leaving the injury uncovered as the door opened.

"The others must have been closer behind than ye thought," Gavin announced, closing the door. "They're boarding the boat even as we speak."

Galen grunted at that and moved to the chest at the foot of the bed to get a dry shirt and plaid.

"My God!"

Stiffening, he whirled at Gavin's exclamation, then relaxed as he realized the reason for it. The other man had just got a look at the wound on Kyla's back.

" 'Tis amazing she lived," his Second murmured as he regained himself.

"Aye," Galen agreed bleakly, dropping his wet plaid to the floor and tugging his shirt off.

"And ye say she tried to escape you?" There was disbelief in his voice.

Tugging a fresh shirt on, Galen nodded. "Aye, and stood up to us with but a wee dagger."

Gavin shook his head. "I don't believe it." There was no insult intended in the words, merely amazement. Realizing that, Galen did not respond, but attended to putting his plaid on. A knock sounded at the door.

Moving reluctantly away from the bed, Gavin opened the door. Two men immediately entered bearing an empty tub. They were followed by several servants carrying buckets full of water. Every single one of the servants was busy stretching their necks toward the woman in the bed; there was no mistaking their shock on seeing the long ugly wound on their new lady's back.

Galen ignored their questioning glances, too tired to bother explaining. They would learn soon enough what had happened. No doubt the entire crew of the boat bringing back the rest of his party had already heard of Lady Kyla's adventures. It would spread through the castle soon enough.

Finished donning his new plaid as the last of the servants deposited their burden and left the room, Galen moved to sit on the side of the bed. He reached to feel her forehead, an action he performed automatically after three days of tending her. Usually his hand met a heat that was frightening in intensity. This time was no different. While she had seemed a bit cooler in the boat, he decided now that that must have simply been the effects of the cool sea breeze. Her skin was nearly as hot now as it had been when the witch Morag had sent him off with her in search of a cold bath.

Cursing, he got to his feet and lifted her quickly into his arms, carrying her directly to the tub. Setting her in it, he immediately began pouring a pail of cold water over her. He dropped the pail when she suddenly began to thrash again.

Bending to his knees beside the tub, Galen tried to hold her in place with one hand and pour the rest of the water with the other, but it was rather like juggling a pair of elephants. It was a relief when Gavin came to his aid, leaving him to hold her in place as he poured bucket after bucket over her.

"Cold only."

His Second nodded and avoided the steaming buckets as he worked. After several minutes Kyla lapsed back into unconsciousness, her head dropping over the lip of the tub. Galen took that opportunity to assist Gavin with the pails of water, quickly dumping the last of them in. By the time they had emptied all of the buckets, the tub was half full, the bath reaching Kyla's waist.

Dropping back to his knees, Galen grabbed up the shirt he had discarded earlier and dipped it in the water, then began running it over her fevered skin. Despite the seriousness of the situation, he found the chore somewhat erotic. He watched the drops of cool liquid slide down her throat and across her heated flesh; one drop skimmed across her left breast, reaching the tip of a nipple, only to hang perilously there. He found himself unable to look away, suddenly overcome by the most vivid image of himself leaning forward and licking that drop away.

"Will she live?"

Galen glanced up at his Second with a start. He had quite forgotten the man's presence. Gavin was standing at his side, looking terribly uncomfortable—he avoided looking at Kyla.

"Aye. She'll live," he said, willing it to be so. Scowling suddenly, he glanced toward the open window. "How close is the ship with the others?"

Moving across the room, Gavin peered out. "It's about to land."

"Fetch the witch to me as soon as it puts ashore."

"The witch?"

"Her maid. She has a knowledge of herbs. She may ken something useful."

Nodding, Gavin exited the room with relief. In the next instant, the splashing of water drew Galen's eyes back to the tub to see that Kyla had regained her senses somewhat and was struggling to get out. She was already half-standing. Jumping to his feet, he caught her arms. "Nay, lassie. We need to cool ye down."

Catching at his arms, she swayed against him. Galen caught her to his chest for a minute, feeling her heat through his clothes.

"We must cool ye down," he repeated worriedly as she tried to pull free. He let her tug herself a few inches away, unable to stop his gaze from dropping over her body as it glistened damply in the sunlight coming through the window. He was distracted enough by looking at her that when she jerked in his arms, he lost his balance and stumbled forward, banging his knee on the side of the tub.

"*Cold.*" It was almost a wail of despair. Galen felt his heart melt in sympathy, then stiffened in surprise as she suddenly wrapped her arms about him.

"Lass?" he murmured uncertainly, unsure of what she was about when she suddenly wrapped her legs about him as well. For a moment he thought that, in her feverish state, she was making improper advances toward him—though he supposed they could not be considered improper since they were now married.

Married! Good God, how had he forgotten that? Well, he supposed he hadn't forgotten, he just really hadn't thought of what it meant. It meant that she had every right to crawl upon him as she was. Hell, he even had every right to crawl on her. His manhood, which had been yawning and stretching in anticipation for days now, rose to throbbing life at that thought. Then, as she shuddered and trembled against him, he realized that she was simply trying to climb out of the cold water. He was ashamed of his own wayward thoughts.

Sighing with regret at what he had to do, Galen tugged her upper body a few inches away and peered down into her feverish face. " 'Tis sorry I am, sweetling, but we needs must cool ye down."

"P-please," she begged and he hesitated, staring down at her wide feverish eyes and flushed cheeks. Her breasts were pressed firmly to his chest, her legs and arms clinging to him like ivy, her groin rubbing against him, making him more than aware that the only thing between them was the material of his plaid. When she tightened her arms about him and shifted for a better grasp on his body with her legs, Galen groaned himself and gave in to the urge to kiss her soft, hot mouth.

He had meant only to sip of her sweetness, but when she opened her mouth on a mutter of surprise beneath his seeking lips, he could not resist taking more. Slipping his hands down to cup her behind, he plunged his tongue into her mouth, moaning his satisfaction when he discovered her tongue. It danced away at once, seeking to avoid his, but when he pressed his advantage, unconsciously grinding his pelvis against hers, it halted its retreat and withstood his probing, then began to explore on its own, her body shivering against him.

When he tore his lips away from hers to kiss a trail down her throat, she cried out in his arms and threw her head back instinctively. Already unsteady on his feet, Galen stumbled forward against the edge of the tub again, but this time with enough impetus that he tumbled them both into it.

The icy water was an unpleasant shock. Galen immediately began cursing and trying to disentangle himself, but found his attempts hampered by Kyla as she screamed, clutched at him, and tried to climb over him all at the same time.

"What the Devil is about here?!"

Head whipping around, Galen peered at Morag as she surveyed them from the open door. Extracting himself from both the tub and the woman in it, he faced her, irritation plucking at his features from the guilt he was experiencing. This was his castle and she was his bride, he reasoned to himself defensively.

He had nothing to feel guilty about. Of course, some might say he had been busily taking advantage of an ailing young woman, but hell, he had been nine months without a woman and— Mayhap that was why she affected him so, he thought suddenly and was filled with immediate relief. In retrospect, his complete lack of control of a moment ago had been sorely distressing. The woman was ill, for God's sake!

Realizing that his own inner arguing was making absolutely no sense, Galen glared at the woman, then turned to scoop Kyla up into his arms again to carry her to the bed. "I was trying to cool her off and I fell into the tub."

"Did ye get her bathed at all?" Morag asked worriedly, following him.

"Aye. I dunked her in the water at shore 'til the boat arrived, then put her in the tub soon as we got her up here."

"Hmmm." Bending over the girl as he straightened from setting her down, Morag felt her forehead, her lips tightening. "She isn't much cooler."

"Should we put her back in the tub?"

Morag hesitated, then glanced at him. "Did she regain her senses?"

"Nay. I lost mine," Galen muttered.

"What was that?"

"Nothing. She did come about a bit," he admitted reluctantly. "Do ye wish to bathe her again or not?"

"Nay. Not just yet. I'll watch to see what happens for now."

Nodding, Galen turned and headed straight for the door. "I'll be about me business then. Call me if there is any change. My servants are at yer disposal."

Morag waited until the door had closed before allowing the laugh she had been holding back to flow. Fell in the tub, indeed! He was no better a liar than her girl was. His lips had been red and swollen and his manhood had been poking his wet plaid out so far she could near look beneath it.

Shaking her head, she turned to glance down at the naked woman on the bed, taking in the signs on her of what had transpired. Kyla's lips too were swollen and rosy, as were her breasts, which were still erect as she lay in silent slumber.

"Wore ye out, did he?" she commented dryly, then sighed and sank onto the side of the bed to brush the hair from her ward's sleeping face. "Let us hope he fires ye so when yer alive and kicking, else we may have a problem on our hands." She shook her head. "He forgets I am Scottish if he thinks I don't know he wed ye soon as the ship landed. 'Tis all they're talking about down there. So much for my plan to keep ye free of such a bond til ye were back on yer feet. Yer married, lass. Like it or no, our course has been changed. Let us hope the seas here aren't as rough as the waters into which Catriona would have tossed ye."

Chapter 4

KYLA stared at the bed drapes overhead and sighed impatiently. She had awoken earlier with a horrendous headache, a terribly dry mouth, and feeling as weak as a puppy. Morag had been bending over her at the time, a relieved smile on her face and a wonderfully cool tankard of meade in hand for her. A bland broth had followed and Kyla had swallowed every last spoonful, then dropped back into an exhausted sleep.

Now she was awake again and had been for an hour. Only this time, Morag was sound asleep on a cot beside the bed. Kyla was loath to wake her. Judging by how she felt, she knew she had been dreadfully ill and that meant her maid had probably been nursing her and most likely getting very little sleep herself.

Morag had given up her position as lady's maid to Kyla's mother when Johnny was born and devoted herself to the chore of nursemaid. From then on she had fretted over first Johnny, then Kyla, too, like a mother hen over her chicks. She had tended various childhood injuries, seen them through myriad illnesses, held them as they sobbed out their sorrows, soothed their worries, and always had satisfactory answers to childish questions like, "*What holds the sun in the sky?"* Unfortunately, at the moment Kyla had quite a few questions she was dying to get an answer to. Where she was, for instance, but Morag was not awake to answer.

She peered about her for the hundredth time and ground her teeth together. This was not her room. Even more confusing, it was not any of the rooms in Forsythe keep. She had no idea where she was. She also had no idea why she had been so ill. What illness had she had? Was Johnny struck down with it as well? Those were only a few of the questions whirling in her head. She had at least a hundred more and every second that Morag slept brought her another. Kyla had half a mind to get up and find out the answers for herself.

That, she decided suddenly, was a fine idea. Pushing the linens aside, she slid her feet off the bed, pushed herself to a sitting position, then eased herself slowly to the floor, grabbing at the wall as the room swayed dizzily around her.

She used the wall for support until the room stopped it's mad spinning, then used it to brace herself as she walked to the chests resting a few feet away. She had recognized them as her own on first awakening and was reassured by their presence. Wherever she was, she had her belongings with her. Quite a few of them, too, she noted now, quickly counting the chests. Good God! It looked as if she had brought everything she owned.

Pausing by the larger of the chests, she opened the lid, then knelt to rifle through it. Most of the gowns were too wrinkled to even consider, but she chose the best of the bunch, a dark blue one with a cream trim. She considered taking the time to find a fresh under-tunic and accessories to wear with it, but decided she was too weary for such effort and the under-tunic she had awoken in would have to do. That decided, Kyla eased onto the edge of the bed and began struggling into the outfit. She actually worked up a sweat simply getting dressed. That was distressing. It showed just how weak she truly was.

Her gaze moved to Morag, a frown briefly tugging at her lips. If her weakness had not suggested to her that she had been desperately ill for a length of time, Morag's exhaustion would have. For as long as she had known her, the old woman had been the lightest of sleepers, awaking at the slightest whisper of sound. However, Kyla had done a great deal of huffing and puffing while trying to dress and the woman had not even stirred. Morag was dead to the world.

Kyla glanced toward the bed, briefly considering giving up this foolish escapade and collapsing back into it's welcoming softness. Then she shook her head and made her slow unsteady way to the door.

Her first sight of the hallway outside the chamber told her a great deal . . . and very little. One look assured her that she definitely was no longer at Forsythe. She'd thought that perhaps Catriona had redecorated one of the rooms of the castle and had had her placed in it to convalesce—Catriona had changed a great many things since marrying Kyla's brother. That was not the case, however, for the hall was not one she recognized.

Biting her lip, she hesitated briefly, then slid cautiously out of the chamber she had been sleeping in. She quietly eased the door shut before heading toward the end of the hall at a slow shuffle. A moment later, she found herself at the top of a wide set of steps leading below. Pausing there, she listened to the noise rising up to her, slightly reassured by various spurts of lighthearted laughter and bits of jovial conversation. Then she realized that the bits and pieces of discussion she was listening to were in Gaelic; worry drew her brows together again.

What the Devil was she doing in Scotland?

Or was she?

Mayhap she was listening to the conversations of Scottish visitors in an English manor, Kyla thought, but discarded the notion at once. She had been standing there for several minutes now and had yet to hear one word of English. It was more likely that she had finally set out to visit her mother's family.

Aye. That made more sense, she decided. It would even explain why she had brought so many clothes with her. The muscles in her shoulders relaxed somewhat at this explanation. She had been planning such an outing since she was a little girl and had always intended on staying for an extended visit. She had simply never gotten around to going.

Kyla had been thinking about it a great deal lately, though, what with Johnny being newly married. She had felt to be crowding him and his new bride, a feeling that was aggravated no doubt by the fact that she found she did not care overly much for her new sister-in-law. The woman was pushy, overbearing, and just plain nasty. But she was also sneaky enough to hide these less attractive traits from her new husband. Unfortunately, Kyla was not as skilled at prevarication as her new sister-in-law; Johnny had seen right through the friendly facade she had tried to present. He had been quite hurt, and it had put them at odds of late.

Catriona, she thought now on a sigh. Even the name sounded bitchy to her.

Pushing such uncharitable thoughts aside, Kyla ignored the twinge in her back that had begun as she was dressing and pasted a smile on her face as she started down the stairs. She was determined to enjoy this visit. She had looked forward to meeting her mother's family all of her young life. She had started a correspondence with her uncle, the chief of the Fergusons, and his wife when she was twelve. Ever since receiving their warm response to that letter, she had been daydreaming about a visit with them and how it would go. Oddly enough, not in one single dream had she imagined spending the first part of it in a sick bed.

Determined to turn this visit around, Kyla managed the stairs at a slow pace with one hand merely trailing along the wall. She was halfway down before she saw anyone and that was just a servant rushing in the front door and hurrying past the staircase to disappear from view into the unseen part of the room below. After a couple more steps, Kyla spied another person. This time it was a man-at-arms, and he saw her as well. His reaction upon spying her was as shocking to Kyla as her presence apparently was to him. He took one look at her, froze in his path to the keep doors, crossed himself, and turned to bellow toward the part of the room Kyla could not see. That shout was enough to bring all conversation in the room to an immediate halt.

Despite his reaction, Kyla continued down two more steps until she could see into the rest of the great hall. It was the nooning hour and the trestle tables were crowded with people sitting down to eat, but not one of them was eating just now. They were all staring at her with varying expressions of shock. Some, like the man-at-arms, looked quite dismayed. Others looked simply startled. She was just becoming a bit concerned by that fact when they all seemed to rise as one and move toward her.

Kyla had the sudden urge to turn and flee back up the stairs. Unfortunately, she did not think she could manage them in her weak condition. Just descending them had made her frightfully tired. Her head was spinning, her stomach roiling, and her back seemed to sting more with every passing moment. That being the case, the only option open to her was to face these people dead-on.

Determination buoying her up, she raised her chin and managed two more steps before pausing again, too discomfited by the very stillness of the staring people before her to continue. They hardly seemed to be breathing, she noted with a frown as she peered over the crowd, taking in their long hair and plaids. She was definitely in Scotland. That much was obvious. Unfortunately, she had no idea what her aunt and uncle looked like, so had no idea if they were present.

"Good morrow?" she said at last when her nerves seemed stretched as tautly as the silence around her.

"Good morrow," they answered as one.

Shifting uncomfortably, Kyla hesitated, then descended the last three stairs to stand on the floor. She released the wall as she did lest they see her weakness.

"Mistress, shouldn't you be abed . . ." someone asked fearfully.

Kyla started toward the trestle tables, her gait as unsteady as a drunkard's. The crowd pressed a step closer, seemingly eager to catch her should the necessity arise.

Kyla noticed that everyone had moved nearer, worry on their faces. Their collective behavior was making her distinctly uncomfortable. It was almost as if they were all privy to something she should know but did not. Doing her best to ignore these discomfiting thoughts, she straightened her shoulders and continued toward the table, concentrating on keeping her gait steady and straight.

She was weaving like a drunken doxy. Robbie was just wondering if he would be overstepping himself to pick her up and cart her to the table, when she stumbled. Several people reached out quickly to steady her, but he himself drew her arm through his own and half supported her the rest of the way to the table.

"Thank you, sir," Kyla murmured as she settled on the bench.

"Robbie."

Kyla peered up at that. "Robbie?"

" 'Tis my name."

"Oh, aye. Of course." She smiled at him uncertainly, acutely aware of the sudden murmuring that had now started up around them.

Casting a silencing glance toward the others, Robbie shook his head. It would not do for her to overhear the speculation the others were openly indulging in regarding her presence of mind. Or lack of it, as the case may be, he thought on a sigh. He wished Galen were here to handle this situation. Had Lady Kyla waited a bit longer, or even had she come down a few minutes earlier, mayhap he would have been. But just a few short moments before her appearance, Gavin had sent word that Duncan had returned from taking the message to Shropshire and had arrived on the mainland shore. Galen and Tommy had gone down to await the boat Gavin had taken over to pick the other man up.

Leaving him in charge, he supposed with a sigh as he turned back to peer curiously at his new mistress.

"Do ye no' remember me?" he asked expectantly after a moment. Kyla raised her eyebrows, a slight frown curving her lips.

"Remember . . . ?" she queried uncertainly.

Nodding, he prompted, "I be the one ye stabbed."

Her jaw dropped at that, partially due to what he had said and partially due to the way he said it. He had spoken as if announcing a sacred honor.

Thinking she must have misunderstood, Kyla shook her head faintly. "I . . . I am sorry. What did I do?" she asked in disbelief, frowning as the murmuring around them became a buzz and Robbie's expression became worried.

"Ye stabbed me, my lady. Right here."

He was gesturing to his chest and Kyla paled, unsure what to say to that. But when she shook her head in denial, he nodded at once with firm certainty.

"Aye, ye did. With yer dirk. Don't ye remember?" he asked, definitely looking worried now. "Ye jumped me," he prompted. "Knocked me right off the cart, ye did, and plunged yer dirk right here." In his distress, he jerked his shirt out of his plaid, displaying a rather nasty, jagged wound that was unbound and still healing.

At his words Kyla was on her feet at once, but the sudden motion simply set the room to spinning and forced her back to her seat. "I am sorry," she said faintly at last, unsure what to do or say. She had no recollection of what he was claiming she had done and simply could not understand why, rather than being upset, the man seemed pleased as he imparted such information.

"Nay. No need to apologize, me lady. 'Twas an honor."

Kyla's head began to swim at that announcement. Trying to retain her composure, she finally asked, "Where are your laird and lady?"

"Yer our lady, me lady."

She turned in confusion to the man who had spoken.

"I be Angus, me lady. Do ye remember me?"

"I . . . Nay . . . I-I am sorry," Kyla repeated, her mind still stuck on the confusing claim that she was their lady. She was sure she had misheard him, but before she could clarify what he had said, the keep doors burst open.

For a moment, with the sunlight pouring in behind them, Kyla could not make out who was entering. It was just long enough for her to grasp at the hope that the newcomers might be her aunt and uncle and that they would bring some semblance of sanity to this situation. Then the door closed, her eyes readjusted, and she saw that those entering were both men and far too young to be her uncle. The one in front was tall with an angular face and long, fiery red hair. He also, Kyla noted, had wide shoulders and well-formed legs. She found him oddly appealing.

Frowning, she glanced toward the shorter man, quickly noting his equally healthy physique and that his hair was dark before they both spotted her and slowed. They had nearly stopped walking altogether when the shorter man's face suddenly became animated with something akin to worship. Rushing forward, he crossed the great hall quickly and dropped to one knee before her, holding his hands out as if offering a wondrous treasure.

"Yer necklace, me lady. I guarded it well. Yer brother is safe."

Frowning, Kyla reached for the gold he offered her, her other hand going to her throat as she recognized her jewelry. "My locket."

"Aye." The man before her smiled widely. "Lord Shropshire recognized it and went at once to Forsythe. He sent a messenger back to tell me that yer brother still lives. He promised to see that it remains so—and that all is sorted out."

Kyla peered at the man in confusion, his words not really making any sense to her. Johnny? Safe? From what? She swayed on the bench slightly, then eased back to lean against the table for support. But pain immediately shot up her back and she stiffened, a rush of scenes flashing through her head. She could hear the clash of metal against metal, see swords glinting in the sunlight as they met. Her brother's scream of agony ripped through her head, accompanied by an image of him grabbing a sword that lanced him through his chest. A blade rose in the air over his fallen body, the ground rushed by beneath her feet, then the searing pain in her back worsened a thousandfold.

Crying out, Kyla tried to reach behind her to stop

the agony, but there seemed to be no muscles left in her arms . . . nor the rest of her body for that matter, she realized. She slid toward the floor.

"Is she all right?"

His face tight with concern, Galen pushed his way through the crowd to his wife's side as that question was repeated by seemingly one and all. He had seen the memories return to her and realized only then that she had not recalled them on awakening. He had started forward at once, but by then it was too late. She had already been crying out and sliding from the bench to lie in the rushes on the floor.

"She came below all on her own, me laird," Robbie told him anxiously, moving out of the way as Galen reached his side.

"I don't know where she got the strength," Duncan murmured. Kneeling on her other side, he picked up the necklace from where it had fallen to the floor.

"She didn't recall me," the bigger man added reluctantly now, worry obvious in his tone. "Ye don't think the witch was right and the fevers rushed . . . it along, do ye?"

"I don't know," Galen muttered grimly as he checked her swiftly for injury. Reassured that she bore no new wounds from her adventure, he lifted her gently.

"We shall have to watch over her," someone murmured. " 'Tis plain she doesn't know what's good for her."

"Aye. She should have stayed abed."

" 'Twas brave of her to try it on her own," Duncan said defensively.

"She is too brave for her own good," Angus

muttered. There were many murmurs of agreement to that, but Galen ignored them as he carried his wife from the room.

"Damn me, I knew she would do something like this," Morag paused in her headlong rush as she spotted Galen carrying her charge up the steps.

"Where were ye?"

The maid flushed under the accusation in those words, shame filling her voice as she admitted, "I fell asleep."

Galen opened his mouth to berate her, then recognized the exhaustion lining her face. She had sat awake with Kyla for a good week now. Swallowing back his condemnation, he merely strode past her and down the hall.

"The fever broke in the middle of the night," Morag told him, hurrying past him to open the chamber door.

"Aye. I know. Guin told me."

"Guin?"

"The serving wench who brought the broth," he rumbled, carrying Kyla into the bed chamber.

"What happened?" Morag asked as she closed the door behind them.

"She leaned on her back."

The old woman clucked over that. "Aye, the salve would be wearing off about now. I shall apply more."

Grunting, Galen eased Kyla onto the bed and set about undressing her again. He had removed her gown and had started on her under-tunic before he told the maid, "She didn't seem to recall what had happened. I think she remembered when she hurt her back, though."

"Hmm." Morag did not even peer up from her bag of potions at that. " 'Tis not unusual to be confused on first awakening."

"Is she any worse than she was before the wound, do ye think?" Morag glanced up at his question, eyes sharp as she took in his concerned expression. She glanced at the woman on the bed. "I don't know," she said carefully after a moment. "She hardly spoke a word the first time she woke. I filled her with broth and meade and watched her back to sleep. We shall know more when she wakes again."

Galen nodded at that, but did not meet the old woman's eyes again as he finished slipping his bride's under-tunic off and dropped it to the floor. Reaching for the blankets, he drew them up to her waist, leaving only her back in view. A sigh slipping from his lips, he bent forward to brush her long, dark tresses away from her face, contemplating her peaceful expression.

There was still intelligence in that face, he assured himself grimly now. She would not be addled. And if she was? It made little difference, he supposed. He had already carried out half of his revenge by simply stealing and marrying her, and he could still beget an heir off her. The witch had said the males were not affected by the madness. Whether she was addled or not would affect nothing really. The servants had looked after things here since his first wife's death and could continue to do so.

Still, he thought, that would be a shame. She had shown herself to have a sharp wit. He had noted it when she had relived conversations and babbled to him in her fevers. Even out of her mind with illness, she had seemed keen and bright. He would regret losing that part of her.

"Here."

Turning away from his thoughts, Galen glanced at the salve the old woman was holding out to him.

"Rub it on her back," she instructed, moving to the door. "I needs must fetch fresh bandages and herbs."

Galen watched her go, then turned to peer down at the woman he had married. Had he made a mistake? Nay. As he had already pointed out to himself, addled or not, her fever would not have made her sterile. She could still bear him heirs. The problem was, that he wanted more than that from her now.

His hands slid across the angry wound on her back, rubbing in the salve, but his eyes were elsewhere. Those hungry orbs were sliding over the lily-white flesh surrounding the wound, trailing down to the base of her back, then taking in the beginnings of the upward slope of her behind that was just revealed before the blanket began.

The sight of her like this brought back vivid images to him. Pictures of the first day when he had brought her home. For a moment he was lost in the memory of the taste and scent of her, and it was not the first time that had happened since their arrival home a week ago. Her sweet face and heated moans had haunted him both in his waking hours and dreams, torturing him with their few shared moments of passion. Just as they were now, he thought with a sigh. He felt his body tighten with the beginnings of hunger.

A moan from Kyla brought his eyes back into

focus to see that as he had sat lost in memory, his hands had caressed their way down her lower back, pushing the bedclothes before them until he now sat cupping the sweet curves of her behind.

Muttering under his breath, he pulled his hands away and quickly tugged the bedclothes back into place, then jumped guiltily to his feet when the door abruptly opened and the old woman re-entered the room.

Catching his guilt-flushed expression, Morag raised her eyebrows questioningly, but the MacDonald merely muttered an unintelligible excuse under his breath and hurried past her out of the room.

"Highlanders," Morag muttered, shaking her head as the door closed again.

"Morag?"

"Aye, loving?" The maid hurried to her side now. "How is yer back?"

"Numb," was the weary reply, then in a confused voice, "So is my bottom."

Morag stiffened at that, her gaze becoming worried. "I don't think I heard ye right, lass. What else is numb?" she asked, but received no answer. Kyla had already slipped back into sleep's gentle embrace.

Chapter 5

"WHAT be yer name, child?"

"What?!" Kyla frowned at that question from Morag. She had awoken just moments before, this time to find her maid awake and sitting by the bed.

"Yer name. What is it?" she repeated with quiet urgency.

Kyla grimaced with disgust and shifted to rise.

"What are ye doing?" The old woman moved forward at once, standing directly beside the bed and blocking her from standing.

"I am getting up."

"Nay. Yer too weak."

"Now, Morag—"

"Do not 'now Morag' me, young woman."

Kyla raised her chin defiantly. "I am your mistress. If I say I shall get up, then get up I shall." Shoving the bedclothes aside, she sat up and stared in amazement as the room suddenly swayed before her eyes.

"I told ye that ye were too weak to be getting up," Morag muttered triumphantly, urging her back into the bed and tugging the covers up about her.

"Aye, you did and you have told me little else

since I woke up this morning," Kyla responded testily.

"I'll answer yer questions, soon as you answer mine."

They had a short war of glares, then Kyla slumped in defeat. "Fine. My name is Kyla."

"Kyla what?"

"*Lady* Kyla Forsythe."

"What was your mother's name?"

Kyla shifted impatiently. "Lady Iseabal Forsythe, née Ferguson."

"Do ye recall what brought ye to be here?"

Kyla paused at that. Truly she had to think for a moment before any memories came back to her, then anxiety immediately covered her face. "Johnny!" She started to rise then and Morag immediately put out her good hand to hold her in place on the bed. Weak as she was, the one hand was all that was needed.

"All is well. Lord Shropshire is with him."

"Gilbert?"

"Aye. He's vowed to keep Catriona away from Johnny until he is well enough to hear what ye saw."

Kyla sagged back against the bed in relief, then her brows drew together in confusion. "But how did he . . . ?"

"The MacDonald sent a message to him."

"The MacDonald?"

Morag frowned at her blank expression. "You don't recall how we got here? The trip in the wagon? The—"

"Attack!" Kyla sat up at that and this time even Morag was not able to keep her down. "We were on the way to . . ." She frowned, recalling Morag explaining something to her in the back of the wagon as they had traveled, but unsure what she had explained. "Where were we headed?"

The old woman frowned over the question. "Ye don't remember?"

"Nay." Biting her lip, she searched her mind desperately for the bits of information it seemed to be missing. She could vividly recall the picnic with her brother now, the attack, throwing herself forward to protect Johnny. But all of her memories after that seemed to be a jumble of pain and fever.

She vaguely recalled waking in her room as they had lain her brother beside her. Then she had some spotty recollections of waking in a wagon and Morag bent over her whispering about Scotland and someone called—"MacGregor," she murmured. "Are we in the MacGregor keep?"

Morag's brow puckered with worry. "Nay. We were on our way to him, but the MacDonald attacked the escort and brought us here to his home."

"The MacDonald?"

"Tall laddie? Well-built? Hair as red as fire?"

A sudden image of a man standing proud, the wind whipping his hair about and buffeting a rather minuscule loincloth about his hips popped into her mind.

"I see ye recall *him* at least," Morag muttered dryly, taking in her blush.

Kyla grimaced slightly. "Why did he interfere?"

Morag hesitated, then admitted, "The MacDonalds and the MacGregors are feuding; lucky for us."

Kyla's head tilted curiously. "Why is that lucky?"

"Because the MacGregor's a brutal bastard. I've heard some nasty tales about him liking to hurt women, lass. Yell not be wanting to go to him."

Kyla's eyes widened at that, a slight suspicion rising inside her. "Why was I going to him in the first place?"

Morag shook her head, worry furrowing deeper on her brows. "Ye were to be wedded to the scoundrel."

"Wedded?" Kyla stiffened at the word. "Me wed to some beastly Highlander who— Nay! Johnny would never arrange such a thing. Never! He—"

"Settle yerself," Morag soothed. "Catriona arranged the wedding. Johnny would never send ye to such a fate. 'Sides, it matters little what she planned, those plans are awry now. The MacDonald saw to that."

"Oh . . . aye." Kyla relaxed somewhat with a sigh. "He attacked our party."

"Aye."

Kyla began to frown as her memories dribbled back. "Our men were slain—"

"Nay. The men weren't killed. Just injured. Knocked unconscious for the most part is all."

Kyla calmed as images entered her head, supporting that claim. Men falling senseless from their mounts. Then she recalled the groups of half-naked men fighting on the ground around the wagon and she frowned. "We had Scots escorting us as well."

"Aye. Well. They didn't fare so well," Morag admitted reluctantly. "But then they were MacGregors."

Kyla shrugged, her mind already moving on to another memory. "I tried to take us away from there . . . I *did* stab that man!" she exclaimed with dismay as she remembered the mountainous warrior showing her his wound below stairs. Then she glanced sharply at Morag. "Are we prisoners here?"

"Nay," Morag assured her, but was unsure what else to say so said nothing.

"What of the MacGregor then? Am I to be ransomed to him?"

"Nay."

Kyla sighed in relief. So long as the MacDonald did not plan to hand her over, she was safe. Once Johnny recovered, he could deal with the illegal marriage contract. It had to be illegal. Catriona was not her guardian, therefore couldn't legally arrange anything. In the meantime, for whatever reason these MacDonalds had interfered. At least she thought that was who Morag had said were their attackers . . . or rescuers. She supposed it depended on how you looked at it.

"How does yer back feel?"

Kyla grimaced at that question. Her back was burning something fierce. It was what had woken her up and now that her immediate questions had been answered, the pain was becoming more unbearable by the moment.

Her expression was answer enough for Morag. Getting to her feet, she shuffled to the table beside the bed and set to work mixing the herbs she had left there. Within moments she was turning back to the bed.

Pushing the linens aside, Kyla sat up and started to unwrap the bandages, only to have Morag wave her hands away and tend to the job herself. Moments later her back was blessedly numb once more and a fresh swath of bandages had been wrapped around her. Still, Morag sat at the side of the bed. Kyla could almost hear her hesitation in the silence.

"What is it?" she asked at last.

"How be yer bum?"

"What?" Kyla stared at her in amazement.

"Never mind, I must have misheard ye," Morag muttered, getting to her feet. "Are ye hungry? Shall I fetch a tray up to ye?"

"Nay. I would get up." Kyla slid her legs off the bed even as she spoke.

"I feared as much." Shaking her head, she shuffled around the bed to fetch a gown and under-tunic for her. "The MacDonald won't be pleased."

Kyla's eyebrows rose at that, then disappeared under the tunic as Morag dropped it over her head.

"Why?" The question was muffled by the soft material as she took over tugging the gown on herself to prevent Morag from trying to use her broken arm.

"Because ye've been sore ill. He won't like ye being up and about so soon. Again."

Kyla grimaced over that. "I am perfectly fine now. A bit weak perhaps, but I shall be careful not to overdo it. Besides, I am curious."

"And curiosity has ever been yer worst attribute," Morag muttered dryly, handing her her gown.

Kyla shrugged at that. "My memories of this morn are fuzzy, but the MacDonalds seemed nice enough. Odd mayhap, but nice."

When Morag quirked one eyebrow up at her words, Kyla smiled crookedly and shrugged. "That fellow I stabbed—the one who jumped on the cart?"

Morag nodded to show she knew who she spoke of.

"Well, he reminded me that I had stabbed him. He actually seemed pleased at the announcement."

Her bewilderment over that was obvious and Morag turned away to hide an amused smile as Kyla finally started to put her gown on.

"He thinks ye showed spunk."

Kyla blinked at that, then shook her head, unable to fathom the idea. Her feelings for the man that had injured her were directly opposite of Robbie's apparent pleasure at having been assaulted by her. She could not comprehend his reaction. Mayhap he was a mite slow in the head. Or a touch crazy. If that were the case it might be best to keep her distance from him. Come to that, who knew how the others would react. Mayhap his friends and kin would not be so good-humored over the injury. She actually had second thoughts about going downstairs as she considered that possibility, but then waved those thoughts away. She had ever been curious about Scotland—now that she was actually in a real Scottish castle, she had no intention of missing an opportunity to explore.

Kyla finished with the lacings of her dress, then stood, only to pause and grab at her throat with dismay as she recalled the man presenting her locket to her.

"Here." Seeing her actions, Morag picked up the locket she had set on the bedside and handed it to Kyla.

"Oh." Kyla took the necklace with relief and quickly fastened it, then pressed the locket to her chest with one hand. "That man . . ."

"Duncan," Morag supplied.

"Aye. He had it. He said something about bringing it back safely?"

Morag nodded. "The MacDonald needed something of yours that Shropshire would recognize so that he would ken the message he sent was true."

"What message?" Kyla asked and Morag frowned at the question, sure they had discussed this already. Mayhap there had been some damage done by the fever after all, she worried. Morag pushed the thought away and answered her question when her ward shifted impatiently and stood to move toward the door.

"Of the trouble that had befallen ye. The MacDonald sent a message telling him of it, and yer claims and a request that he go to yer brother and see him safe."

"Oh." Kyla nodded, surprise evident on her face. " 'Twas kind of him."

Morag nodded. "He seems a fair and honorable man. A much better choice for husband than the MacGregor."

"Why, Morag," she teased, moving toward the door again. "I never thought to see the day that you would start acting the matchmaker. He must indeed be a fine man. I shall have to consider him carefully. Mayhap I could trade in one Highlander for another."

"The chances are better than ye think," Morag muttered under her breath.

"What was that?"

"Nothing," she murmured, opening the door for her and offering her arm should she need support. It was not her place to inform the girl of her marriage. As far as Galen knew, Morag herself was not even aware of it. Let *him* explain what he had done, she thought as they traversed the hallway to the stairs.

" 'Tis dinner time," Kyla murmured with surprise

as they started down the stairs and the hall came into view.

"Aye."

Frowning at Morag's easy agreement, Kyla paused and turned toward her to say, "But when last I was awake it was only nooning time."

Morag shrugged as she watched an angry-looking Lord MacDonald stride toward them. "Ye've been ill. Ye needed the rest."

"I suppose," Kyla murmured, then gasped in surprise as she was suddenly swept off her feet to rest cradled against a very large, wide, strong-looking chest.

"Her back?" Galen asked grimly.

"I put some salve on. Though mind ye don't rip her stitches swinging her about like that."

Nodding, Galen turned and started back up the steps.

Kyla gaped from her unconcerned maid to the man carrying her, shocked that Morag would allow anyone to behave so without raising a protest, then quickly began to protest herself. "Nay. Put me down. I would join the table."

"Ye need yer rest," came the implacable response.

"I needs must eat, too!" He paused at that, hesitating halfway up the stairs and she added, "I am very hungry."

Galen peered down at the pitiful expression she was giving him and sighed. "All right. But ye'll not be walking about. I'll not have ye falling over and hurting yerself some more," he told her sternly. Turning to retrace his steps to the table, he added, "Ye shouldn't even be up. So don't plan on gallivanting about. Once yer sitting, yer sitting and no argument about it. When ye grow weary, yer to tell me and I'll see ye back to yer room. Understood?"

Kyla briefly considered telling the man to go stuff himself. After all, he really had no right to tell her what she could or could not do. As grateful as she was for his preventing her from having to marry the MacGregor, not to mention his sending Lord Shropshire to her brother, that did not give him the right to control her life or her behavior, and she almost told him so, but then thought better of it and merely nodded. This was his home. She supposed that gave him some rights. Enough that she would simply bite her tongue and accept his orders until she was well enough to travel again and could return home.

Although that could be a problem in itself, she realized now. She would need an escort home. Unfortunately, that meant she either had to wait for her brother to recover and send another escort for her, or she would have to rely on the kindness of her benefactor and hope he would supply her with one.

Truthfully, she supposed she would feel safer with a MacDonald escort. After all, they had made short work of her other escort. Doubtless they would be able to give her the protection she needed to arrive home safely. But she didn't relish being further indebted to the burly Scot carrying her. That meant she would most likely be stuck here until her brother could send his men . . . which would just indebt her further, since she would have to rely on MacDonald's hospitality.

She was frowning over the tangle she appeared to be in when the solution suddenly popped into her head. The Fergusons. Surely were she to send word of her predicament to them, they would be moved to send an escort for her? That was at least something to think about, she decided, then pushed these thoughts aside and murmured a thank-you as she was set upon the bench seat at the head table.

Shifting to a more comfortable position on the seat, Kyla set about brushing the creases out of her skirt, then glanced curiously around at the other people in the room as space was made for the man who had carried her.

If her expression was curious as she peered around her, the people she faced showed both that emotion as well as obvious and intent worry. The curiosity was to be expected, she supposed. The worry, however, was a slight surprise. She understood that their fear was for her well-being, but was surprised by the extent of it. They were virtual strangers to her, after all. A little concern and consideration for her would not have gone amiss, but most of the people in the great hall were eyeing her with unmistakable anxiety.

Kyla smiled nervously at the room in general, then glanced down at the trencher the man who had carried her suddenly plopped before her. It was only then that she realized that she had not a clue what his name was. She knew he was the MacDonald chief from his position at the center of the head table—not to mention his highhanded behavior—but that was all she knew about him.

Realizing now that she should have spared the time to ask a few more questions of Morag, Kyla sighed unhappily. She searched her waist for her dirk to eat with, but became flustered as she realized it was no longer there. She had forgotten to collect it on dressing, she realized. She muttered her thanks when one was placed in her hand. Kyla raised it to stab at a hunk of meat on her trencher, only to pause when she saw that the dirk she was using was her own.

Raising her head, she peered at the man who had given it to her. She gasped. It was Robbie, the man she'd stabbed.

"You were in no state to hold on to it on the journey, so I took the liberty of holding it for ye, me lady," the man murmured and Kyla tried to swallow past the sudden lump in her throat, then offered a sickly smile and glanced toward the man who had carried her to the table. While everyone else in the room seemed to be smiling and nodding at her, he was eating and paying her no mind.

Kyla turned back to Robbie. She had not been mistaken about the man's attitude earlier in the day. He truly did not mind that she had stabbed him. And judging by the smiles everyone else was giving her, they didn't either. It seemed she was in a castle full of crazies. To her, there could be no other explanation for such a ridiculous attitude. They were all insane, she decided.

"What was that?" The MacDonald laird peered at her suddenly, one eyebrow raised and Kyla flushed as she realized she had been muttering her thoughts under her breath. It was a bad habit she had, and one she wasn't even aware of most times. Sooner or later it would land her in deep trouble.

"Nothing," she croaked, then cleared her throat and forced a smile.

The MacDonald frowned at her briefly, then gestured toward her trencher. "Eat. Ye need yer strength."

Nodding, Kyla ducked her head and began to eat.

The man seemed in a surly temper and there was no sense in aggravating him. After all, she did need to regain her strength to leave here. Travel could be wearing on the healthy, let alone someone just getting over an injury. And Kyla now intended on traveling away from this castle of lunatics at the first opportunity. She would write a message to her Ferguson uncle as soon as she was back in her room, she resolved.

With that thought in mind, she set determinedly to work at the food in her trencher. It was tasty fare. Stewed beef of some sort. But Kyla hardly noticed as she chomped away. Her mind was racing, puzzling over how to phrase her letter so that her uncle would understand her urgency and not refuse her request. When she began to feel full, she peered down at the contents of her trencher, disappointed to note that she had only managed to eat half the food placed before her. She briefly considered forcing herself to continue eating, then decided against it. Healing could not be forced.

Sighing as she came to that conclusion, she pushed her dish away and sat back on the bench to peer around the room again. Morag had found herself a place at one of the two side tables and seemed deep in conversation with a woman sitting beside her. Kyla wondered briefly who the woman was. She and Morag seemed to be the only people in the room, besides the MacDonald himself, who were not staring at her. The rest of the diners were still gawking, even as they ate, she noticed. It was terribly discomfiting. They all watched her with mingled speculation and concern. Here and there she saw a face or two filled with displeasure and doubt, as well. Kyla wasn't sure what to make of it all. Her gaze fell on the fellow who had carried her necklace and a message to Shropshire. When he beamed on her brightly as her gaze met his, Kyla managed a small smile in return.

"Are ye finished?"

Startled at the sudden question from the Mac-Donald laird, Kyla turned sharply and managed to nod, then cried out in surprise when he suddenly rose and scooped her up into his arms.

She started to protest at once, then shrugged inwardly and gave up. She was too tired to bother arguing over his high-handed behavior. Besides, she supposed she had learned one thing about Scotland. Clan chiefs were a law unto themselves who seemed to think whatever they wished was the way it would go. She supposed her brother was not unlike that himself. Give men a little power and it did seem to go to their heads.

Sighing again, she relaxed into his arms as he mounted the last of the steps and strode toward the door to her chamber. The last time he had carried her, she had been too dismayed at the idea of being returned to her room so abruptly to enjoy the sensations that being lugged about by him engendered. Now she was much more relaxed and hard-put not to notice.

The man had massive shoulders. Their very size made her feel safe, while the gentleness with which he held her made her feel small and delicate. Odd how pleasing those sensations were. Kyla was a particularly independent young woman, an unusual trait for a female, she knew. Her brother and father had shaken their heads in dismay over that flaw when she was younger. Only her mother had encouraged it. Lady Forsythe had been a particularly independent woman herself. She, like Kyla, would normally have struggled against any behavior insinuating she needed assistance . . . such as being carted about as she was now. Oddly enough however, Kyla didn't feel any desire to fight the MacDonald's present kindness. She pondered that briefly, then frowned as they reached the door to her bedchamber and— rather than set her down and wish her a good night— her host simply shifted her, reached out to unlatch the door, and pushed it open.

It seemed her host was slightly lacking in knowledge about proper protocol and behavior becoming toward a lady, she thought wryly, wondering if she should comment on the faux pas or let it slide. The question remained undecided, her attention taken up by more important issues when her host carried her directly to the bed, set her on the side of it, and immediately began tugging at her laces.

Kyla slapped at his hands at once. "What do you?"

"Helping ye to bed." He spoke in a perfectly reasonable tone of voice that left her gaping.

"I can tend to it on my own, thank you," she managed at last when he continued worrying at her clothing.

Shrugging, he let his hands drop to his side and took a step back, then simply stood there.

Kyla scowled, then raised her chin slightly and announced, "A gentleman would have left me at the door."

He gave an unconcerned shrug. "I'm no' a gentleman."

Kyla's nose rose at that. "Well, *I* am a lady and 'tis not proper for you to be here. So if you would not mind . . . ?" When he simply stared at her blankly, she ground her teeth together in frustration. "I would like you to leave my room."

"My room."

"What?"

" 'Tis my room."

Flushing at that, she stood abruptly. "Well then *I* shall leave *your* room."

"Nay, ye'll sleep here." Pushing her back to sit on the bed, he tilted his head to eye her curiously. "Do ye still possess all yer faculties?"

"What?" She gaped at him in bewilderment.

"Do ye recall how ye came to be here?" he asked now and Kyla sighed with exasperation.

"I have been through all this with Morag. I was on the way to the MacGregors to be married. You attacked our traveling party."

Grimacing, he shook his head and corrected, "Nay. Ye were being transported to a murdering bully of a coward and me and me men rescued ye."

Kyla's gaze narrowed at that. "Murdering bully of a coward?"

"He beat his last wife to death," he informed her calmly, adding for good measure, "She was pregnant."

Kyla stiffened at that. She should have realized that Catriona would not have been overly concerned over the suitably of this MacGregor as a husband. After all, the woman had tried to murder her own husband. Still . . .

"Do ye remember the time yer brother pushed ye into the mud in yer brand-new gown and ye got him back by making his bed with manure?"

Kyla blanched. "How did you know of that?"

"Ye told me."

"*I* told you?"

"Aye. While ye were with fever."

What else had she told him, she wondered with horror, then stood abruptly. "I am most tired, my lord. I assure you my faculties are all intact, but I am most tired. So . . . if you would kindly leave me be I'll disrobe and retire."

"Hmm." He tipped his head to the other side, then sighed himself and nodded. "Aye. I'll leave ye be to rest. I'll find out soon enough if yer addled."

Chapter 6

SHIFTING in the chair that Duncan had placed by the fire for her, Kyla glanced unhappily toward Morag and Guin. They had been her constant companions for the past three days.

Three days? Was that all it had been? It felt more like three years since the MacDonald had left. The minutes had crawled by like hours and the hours like days since the morning after he had carried her above stairs. Kyla had found out from Morag he was gone as she helped her dress the next morning. She had mentioned her intention to send a message to the Fergusons and her maid had said it would have to wait; the MacDonald had headed out at dawn and would likely be gone for days as he was tending to outlying business. Whatever that was.

Morag had then added that he had left certain orders regarding Kyla herself. Firstly, Morag and/or Guin, the servant who had apparently assisted in nursing her back to health, were to be with Kyla at all times. Secondly, she was also to have at least one guard with her at all times. He had left Angus, Duncan, and Robbie behind to see to that. The final order was that she was not to leave the castle, not even to go out into the bailey, until he returned.

Kyla wasn't sure whether she was angry about this or simply frustrated. She did hate to be told no. She had not been pleased to find her way barred each time she had tried to leave the keep since then. Despite the MacDonald's order, she had twice gotten up now and tried to simply exit the keep. Both times she had waited until her guard had seemed distracted, then calmly got up and headed for the door. Unfortunately, her guards took their job seriously. Distracted or not, they always seemed to know where she was and were quick to escort her back, explaining politely that she could not go out. " *'Twas for her own good.*"

As far as Kyla could tell, every last person in this place was preoccupied with her "good." Too much so. It was positively smothering.

While officially the only orders he had left were that she was not to be left alone or leave the castle, her jailers had taken their own translation of this. In their translation she was not allowed to actually *do* anything. Should she try to pick up something, there was immediately someone there to do it for her. The only thing they allowed her to hold on to was her needlework.

Embroidery. Kyla detested embroidery. She did it badly and despised the doing. It was a punishment for her to be forced to rely on embroidery to fill her time. Here she was in the Highlands of Scotland, a land she had pondered over for many a year now and she was restricted to the castle. Castles were the same the world over. She wanted to see the land and meet the people. However, it seemed she would not be allowed to do so until the chief of the MacDonald clan returned. So, for that reason and that reason alone, she wished he would return. Well, that and the fact that she could not send her message to the Fergusons until he returned. Other than that there was little reason for her to wish for his homecoming, she assured herself. She hardly knew the man and what little she knew was not very impressive. He was bossy, arrogant and ... Well, he did have a nice figure and quite the loveliest red hair she had ever seen, she allowed thoughtfully. She pushed all thoughts of him aside and feigned a yawn.

"Oh my, 'tis fair wearing to work at this all day," she murmured.

Morag and Guin both glanced up at that comment, suspicion rife in their expressions. And no wonder, Kyla decided with a sigh. After all, she had hardly touched the sampler in her lap. Still, they could have shown a little more respect and kept their suspicions to themselves, she decided irritably.

Trying not to show her annoyance at their expressions—and the wary stiffness it immediately produced in Duncan as he caught their facial casts— she rolled her embroidery into a ball and set it in the basket beside the chair, muttering, "Or mayhap 'tis just too boring. Whatever the case, I am fair worn out."

Morag relaxed at that and Kyla smiled at her.

"I think I shall retire for a nap. Mayhap you could wake me for the sup?" She waited until Morag and Guin nodded, then turned and moved toward the stairs, smiling sweetly at Duncan as she passed him and forcing herself to move slowly and calmly as she went. It would not do to rush about after claiming exhaustion. She would never escape that way. And Kyla had every intention of escaping this dull keep ... She had a plan.

Desperate to get out for a bit of fresh air, Kyla had wracked her brain for two days for a way to give her guard the slip and make her way outside. In the end, she had come up with her idea after accidentally mistaking her host's chest for one of her own.

Kyla had retired early the night before. She had grown tired of being stared at by the hordes of Scots in this place. They did seem to enjoy gawking at her, and having all eyes fastened on her for so long was terribly wearing. It made her self-conscious and nervous, her movements becoming awkward and jerky. She had dropped more food on her lap than in her mouth the night before under those stares and every time she had, the people in the room had seemed to glance at each other meaningfully and shake their heads a bit sadly. That had only made her more nervous, causing more spills. Kyla had been more than eager to escape such scrutiny and flee to her room by the time the agonizing meal was over. Only, once there, she had quickly become bored and restless.

After pacing about for a bit, she had decided to retire. In search of a fresh under-tunic to wear to bed, she had popped open the chest at the foot of the bed. It had taken a mere glance for her to realize her mistake. The chest's contents were obviously a man's. Curious, Kyla had rummaged through it briefly anyway, examining the two plaids it held, the small sword, the animal hides . . . It was her host's chest, of course, and Kyla hadn't been able to make herself look further. She hadn't wanted to pry. Besides, Morag had come into the room then and interrupted her.

After helping her find an under-tunic and assisting her to change, the servant had slid silently out of the room once more, leaving Kyla alone to ponder what she had found. The plaids she had seen in the chest had tickled her mind for hours as she had lain awake in bed, eventually giving her a plan.

It was a relatively simple plan, the success of which hinged on whether Duncan would stand guard at her door. He was following her up the stairs now she knew, but she hoped that after standing about outside her door for awhile, he would grow bored and move back to the great hall where he could watch both the stairs and the door in comfort. Then she would merely have to wait for her chance. The moment his attention shifted even briefly away, she would make her exit. Of course, should he see her, he would stop her . . . if he recognized her.

That was the crux of her plan. Kyla had considered various ways of giving her guards the slip over the past two days, but knew she could not get far dressed as she was. Because of her long English gown she stood out, but she had seen no way to change that until she had spotted the plaids in the chest at the foot of her bed. She just might blend in a little better and make good her escape if garbed in a plaid as all the other women wore. It seemed worth a try. She would borrow one of the plaids and slip out for a bit of fresh air.

Reaching the bedchamber, Kyla slid inside and eased the door closed, then moved quickly to the chest at the foot of the bed. Opening it, she reached for the plaid, a frown plucking at her lips as she shook out the huge strip of cloth and peered at it unhappily. It looked just like a blanket, she thought with a mixture of worry and disappointment.

What she hadn't considered, she realized, turning the material in her hands, was that while she had seen Morag don the plaid several times over the years, she was not at all sure she could replicate the act herself. At least not satisfactorily enough to pass as a Scot. She had a vague recollection of the maid laying it out, folding it into creases, laying on it, then bringing the edges about her body to fasten it in some way that she could not readily recall just then.

Well, she thought with a sigh, there would be no success without trying.

Duncan frowned unhappily at the closed door to his laird's room, then moved to the head of the steps to peer below. The old woman was seated by the fire nattering away to Guin. The rest of the hall was empty, though. Angus and Robbie were out in the yard just now, no doubt spending their time bemoaning the fact that their new mistress was English, weak, frail . . . and mad.

The word had spread of course. You couldn't keep something like that quiet. Now, one and all were looking for any signs that Lady Kyla's fevers had rushed along the heriditary madness that supposedly plagued the women of her line—and they were finding them in everything.

They pointed toward every little thing she did. Foolish things even. Some claimed she looked at them all with a suspicious sort of gleam in her eye, an odd gleam, for what did she have to fear in the home of her husband? Others pointed to her lack of agility, and Duncan had to admit she did appear to be uncommonly clumsy. Even he had noticed the way she kept dropping her food the last three days, and it was something that seemed to be growing worse with each passing meal. Last night she had left more food on the floor than she had managed to get into her mouth. Even the dogs had noticed. Rather than roam the length of the table in search of the occasional spill or drop of food, they now positioned themselves firmly at her feet where they could lap up the constant flow of droppings from her trencher. Aye, she was clumsy.

Still, that was not a sign of madness in his mind, no matter what the others claimed.

Not that anyone treated her badly because of it. Everyone had been extra patient and friendly with her. Well . . . all but Robbie's wife. Aelfread. She was still steaming a bit over Robbie's being stabbed and whacked up the side of the head by the lass. As the man had feared, his wee wife had taken a right fit upon seeing the wound, then had gone on to hold a grudge. No amount of talking on Robbie's part seemed to change that, and he had refused to allow her anywhere near the keep lest she go out of her way to insult their laird's new wife.

Duncan shook his head mournfully. Women were a difficult breed.

And it wasn't as if Kyla hadn't given them reason to fear for her sanity. For instance, the more friendly everyone was to Lady Kyla, the more nervous she seemed to grow. Added to that, she had developed the distressing habit of talking to herself. It had begun after the first time she had disregarded the laird's orders and tried to leave the keep. Got up, she did, and walked right out of the keep, calm as ye please. Robbie had been watching her the first time she did it. He swore that he thought she was heading above stairs. Instead, she had walked to the door and tugged it open. He had hurried after her, only barely catching her arm as she tried to slip out. Robbie had been polite about it, but he'd informed her firmly that he could not allow her to leave and reminded her that the laird had ordered it.

Duncan shook his head now as he thought. Lady Kyla did seem to have difficulty remembering that order. The very next day, while Angus was watching her, she had tried to leave again. Angus had responded much the same way as Robbie, stopping her, explaining that she was to stay indoors, then escorting her back to her seat. According to him, Lady Kyla had dropped back into her seat with a huff and taken to muttering to herself under her breath. She had been muttering to herself off and on ever since.

Still, Duncan was positive that if Lady Kyla would just show another example of courage and intelligence, this talk of madness would die down. The people didn't want to think her mad, they just expected to. Unfortunately, the woman who sat glaring at the embroidery in her hands, muttering to herself, then acted so nervous at the supper table, was not helping. Duncan wanted to see again the woman who had charged off in a cart, her back sorely cut, then bravely faced down the entire MacDonald raiding party with naught but a dirk. There was a fiery lass who would never just sit back and listen to Laird Galen's commands.

Nay, he thought now glumly. He was sore unhappy to have to admit it, but that Lady Kyla had been laid low by the fever. It seemed her senses had been stolen along with her spirit. He would give much were it not so, but even he was unable to argue the point. Duncan had hoped she would rally against the orders Galen had left, to escape. The woman who had rambled on in her fevered state about wanting to run barefoot through a stream was not a woman to be caged up like a bird. But other than trying to walk out the door under the very nose of her guard, she had not even attempted escape.

He had expected more from her. He still did, in fact. Mayhap he had expected too much. And perhaps he was a fool to do so.

He glanced over his shoulder at the click of a door down the hall. Seeing a servant slip out into the hallway and turn her back to him to close the chamber door, he started to turn away once more, but paused as her image stuck in his mind.

It was the state of her dress that had his eyes narrowing blindly on the floor below as he reviewed her image in his head. It was the sloppiest attempt at wearing a plaid that he had ever seen. The item was lopsided, its creases varying in size from wee to huge, then back to wee. Worse yet, it was well littered with bits and pieces of rushes; they stuck out from both her hair and the material of the tartan she wore as if she had rolled on the floor in it.

It was not a true Scot wearing the weeds, Duncan knew, for no Scot would be caught dead garbed so. Recalling the door the woman had come out of, he realized it was the laird's bedchamber. He stiffened where he stood. There was only one person in the laird's chamber.

Lady Kyla! Duncan nearly whirled around at his realization, then caught himself and paused to ponder what she was about. The answer seemed easy enough. The spirited lass *was* trying to escape.

He nearly crowed aloud at that, but caught it back and sent up a prayer of thanks instead. A show of spirit was just what he had been pleading for and here it was. She was boldly attempting escape. At least, he hoped she was. The possibility that she may simply be trying on Scottish garb arose and he frowned unhappily, then shrugged the unpleasant thought away. Nay. She was attempting to flee. He wondered what to do. Should he stop her here and now, it would be sorely demoralizing to one and all. Every man, woman, and child in the keep was aching for a sign that their mistress was more than just a madwoman. All were hoping that her old witch-woman of a maid was wrong and that their new lady was worth the battle fought to capture her. Mayhap this attempt would be a sign to them that she was sane. It would certainly show that she had spunk and was clever. Or at least it might if she had done a better job of donning the plaid.

But she hadn't done a better job, and this was a bad attempt. A good idea, he had to admit to himself, for if the plaid had been well set and unlittered by rushes, he should not have known it was her and most likely would have paid her little heed. But that was not the case—and anyone she passed would know at once that something was amiss. Then she would be discovered and everyone in the clan would be convinced once and for all that she was as daft as the day was long for even trying it.

He would have to help her escape, he decided resolutely. It would prove to one and all that she was not just an English, fancy with nothing between her ears but what boiled brains the fevers had left her. First, however, he had to find a way to fix her up a bit so that no one else would discover her. He would somehow have to seem not to recognize her, while still managing to straighten her plaid and de-rushing it. It would not be an easy task.

Kyla quietly closed the door, keeping her back deliberately to the man at the end of the hall. She had been working carefully at donning the plaid when she had heard his footsteps move away from the door. Her first reaction had been relief that her plan was going so well. But then she had considered the possibility that he had not retired below to watch the stairs and door, but had simply left briefly to use the privy or to fetch himself a beverage.

That possibility had sent her into something of a panic and she had completed donning the plaid as quickly as she could. Unfortunately, in her haste, she feared she had not taken as much care as she would have liked and she was now quite distressed at the state of the garb. It did not seem nearly as pristine and well done as Morag's had been, but, more than aware that her guard might return at any time to bungle her plans, Kyla had decided well enough would have to do. She had spared a bare moment to try to straighten it the best she could, then she had quickly let down her hair to further her disguise before hurrying to the door.

Peering out to see her guard standing at the top of the stairs had been a distressing discovery. But, fearing he would not move much farther away than that, she had decided to risk discovery and make the attempt anyway. Taking a deep breath, she had slid out into the hall and turned her back to the man—ostensibly to close the door, but really to shield her face from his view as much as possible and gain a moment for a steadying breath.

Kyla had just managed to close the door when she heard him approaching from behind. Her heart squeezed its way right up into her throat at the sound of his footsteps and Kyla unconsciously clenched her fingers, her mind in a panic.

"Ho there! Leave her ladyship alone. She rests."

Kyla nearly sighed aloud at those words, relief pouring through her like cool water through a dry river bed. Bobbing, she turned, careful to keep her head bowed as she directed herself toward the end of the hall. "Aye, sir. Sorry, sir."

"Look at ye. Ye've hay all over ye, lass. What have ye been doing? Rolling in the stables with the stable master's son? Ye should be ashamed."

Kyla gasped in surprise as her arm was taken firmly in one hand and Duncan began brushing her down with his other.

He removed the worst of the rushes for her and managed to straighten her plaid a bit without being conspicuous. It was just enough, he hoped, that at a glance no one would notice the poor job done in the donning.

"Be on about yer business," he ordered then and Kyla charged down the hall without even a nod, her face flaming under the tendrils of her hair.

Duncan waited until she had started down the stairs before allowing his amusement to show in a wide grin. She was back. Their courageous little English miss. Yes sir, he'd told them she—

His joy stalled when he realized that he had let her escape. It was grand that she still maintained her courage and some wit—and that he could prove it—but it was a sore trial that he had allowed her to show it by letting her escape. Galen would be fair angered at him for it. What a quandary. Catch her and let everyone keep thinking her daft, or let her go and be in trouble himself?

Mayhap he should follow her. Let her escape so far, then catch her back. Bringing her back would redeem him for letting her escape, he decided. Aye, it would prove to one and all that she had courage, yet keep him out of trouble.

Mind made up, he hurried after her.

"Ye don't think they're right, do ye?"

"What?" Robbie glanced at Angus. "That she's not quite right in the head now? No." He shook his head, but with less conviction than he would have liked. He could not forget the odd way she acted around him. Sometimes she appeared alarmed to be near him and other times he spied something akin to pity in her gaze. It was as if she could not make up her mind whether he were to be pitied or feared.

Sighing, he leaned back against the rock wall surrounding the bailey and glanced toward the keep doors as a woman hurried out. She seemed in quite a rush, he noted absently and started to turn away, only to pause to watch her when she suddenly halted on the steps, an air of uncertainty about her.

"I don't think so, either," Angus said with about as much conviction. "It'd be a real shame if it turned out she was."

"Aye," Robbie murmured absently, his gaze trained on the woman's face. She seemed familiar, but he could not place her. Starting to move again, she suddenly set off at a much slower pace than the one in which she had exited the keep and headed across the bailey toward the gate.

Shrugging inwardly, Robbie started to turn away when the keep doors opened once more and Duncan stepped out. The other man let his gaze run briefly about the bailey until it settled on the woman now making her way toward the castle gates, then he started down the steps after her.

"I'll be damned," Robbie murmured under his breath, straightening away from the wall as he was suddenly able to put a name to the woman's familiar face.

"What?" Angus glanced around curiously.

"Look there."

He peered toward where Robbie pointed, eyebrows rising when he saw Duncan hurrying across the bailey. "What the Devil is he about? He's supposed to be guarding Lady Kyla."

"Aye." Robbie moved his finger further along the path. "Now look there."

Angus shifted his gaze to the woman Duncan was following and frowned. "Who is that? I don't think I recognize her."

"Nay, neither did I 'til I saw Duncan."

Angus raised his brows. "It isn't that lass he's sweet on, is it? What's her name? Alice? Nay. Her hair's red. Is it— By the saints!" he exclaimed suddenly. "Yer not thinking that that there is Lady Kyla?"

Robbie hesitated briefly, then nodded. "I think so. I'm no' sure. I didn't get a good look at her face, but what I did see seemed familiar. 'Sides, who else would Duncan be following?"

"By Jesus, yer right." Straightening away from the

wall, he grinned widely as he strained to see her better. "It just may be. Damn me. Isn't that grand!"

When Robbie raised an eyebrow at that, Angus gave a laugh and said, "Well now, all those fools claiming she's daft will have to take their words back. The clever little wench is escaping." Admiration clear on his face, he added, " 'Twas damned crafty of her to don a plaid to escape in. I never would have looked at her twice." He shook his head now and leaned back against the wall once more. "Damned crafty. They won't he able to say she's daft now."

"Nay, they'll say we are for letting her escape," Robbie commented dryly.

The other man's amusement came to a dead halt. "Say! Ye don't think— I mean, well, Duncan will bring her back, he—"

"Couldn't catch a hare were it sitting on his chest?" Robbie supplied, one eyebrow cocked.

"Damn me!" Angus straightened abruptly. "Well, come on, Robbie. Should Duncan lose the wench, Galen'll have our hides."

Chapter 7

KYLA peered about at the people she passed, taking in their expressive faces and returning the few curious smiles of greeting sent her way as she meandered along through the village and continued down the path. She had been walking for several minutes when she came to a fork in the path. She followed the divergent road without hesitation. It was a lovely day. The air was fresh, the sun shining, the way edged by wildflowers, and she paused to pick one or two as she strolled along. When the road finally ended, she found herself on the edge of an empty beach. Stopping, Kyla glanced out over the sand and the wide open water it led to, briefly breathing in the smell of the sea with pleasure before moving forward again.

She had taken several steps onto the beach before realizing that it was not as empty as she had first thought. There was a woman seated on the shore, sitting so still that Kyla had not even noticed her. Fingers tightening nervously around the flowers she held, Kyla was about to turn and leave unnoticed, when the woman suddenly turned her head and peered toward her. Her first instinct was to flee, but before she could, the woman offered a smile of greeting and got slowly to her feet.

Biting her lip uncertainly, Kyla glanced back the way she had come, fear of being recognized nearly sending her sprinting back up the path. She had managed her escape up to now only because no one had gotten a very good look at her. She very much feared that if anyone got more than a passing glance, her disguise would not hold. Fleeing, however, did not seem a viable option. The woman was already moving toward her and would surely be made suspicious should she suddenly turn and flee back up the path as she wished. Sighing, Kyla moved forward, hoping her disguise, such as it was, would hold for her.

"Oh, hell," Robbie muttered as he recognized his wife, then rubbed at his nose when a sprig of grass tickled it briefly. He and Angus had caught up with Duncan shortly after leaving the bailey. The man had immediately tried to explain himself, claiming he was unsure whether the woman they followed was their laird's wife or not. Robbie and Angus had merely rolled their eyes at that and gestured him to silence as they continued to follow the wench, keeping a respectable distance to prevent her realizing she was being trailed.

That distance had nearly been their undoing. The fork she had taken was midway between two bends in the main path. Had Robbie not happened to glance to the side as they passed the offshoot, he would have missed the glimpse of the green and blue plaid she wore and they would have continued on down toward the docks, truly having lost their mistress. But luck had been with them. He had seen her, and they had followed her down this small path to the beach, grinning foolishly at each other as they had watched her pick flowers, test their scent, and continue on. When she had reached the beach, they had found a nice little patch of high grass into which to drop and watch her. And none too soon, for she had peered back just after they had reached the cover where they now lay on their stomachs, the three of them spying on her through the grass curtains hiding them.

Robbie's first worry about what was to come did not crop up until he spied the second figure on the beach and recognized his wife. Of all the people Kyla might have run across on this little excursion, Aelfread was the worst. His wee wife was not above holding a grudge and was still quite angered at the small wound he had gained in stealing Kyla from the MacGregors. No matter the wound itself had all but entirely healed, Aelfread's outrage at Kyla's attack had not. Now, here the two women were, face-to-face. His only hope was that, having escaped from the keep, Kyla would have the sense not to reveal her true identity. Aelfread had only been at the keep herself a short while and did not know everyone yet; she would most like accept any false name Kyla offered. But should the woman say who she really was, Aelfread would leap upon her like a cat on a mouse.

"Mayhap we should catch her now," Angus murmured uncertainly as he watched the women approach each other.

"Nay. Not yet," Robbie rumbled in response.

"But, if Aelfread recognizes her—"

"She's ne'er seen her up close. I don't think she'll recognize her."

"Well, what if Lady Kyla tells her her name? Aelfread'll—"

"Let us hope that, despite her madness, she has the good sense to lie about who she is," Robbie interrupted grimly.

"Lady Kyla lie?" Duncan looked outraged at the very idea.

Robbie rolled his eyes at that. "She is escaped, Dunc. Would ye confess who ye were to the first person ye came across were ye escaping?"

"Oh . . . aye. I mean nay," Duncan murmured, turning back to peer at the two women.

The woman greeted her in Gaelic.

Kyla returned the greeting, surprise now lighting her face. Like the MacDonald, this woman was a redhead, her hair a veil of crimson that whipped about in the slight breeze off the water. Now that there was only a foot of space between them, it was hard not to notice that she was also extremely petite. Kyla would have placed her age at somewhere around eighteen, yet the top of the woman's head barely reached her own chin, putting her at a height of perhaps four and a half feet, no more. Despite her lack of height, she was a shapely little thing, both buxom and well-heeled of a hip. The waist between narrowed to an impossibly small span, Kyla noted with a touch of envy, then she raised her eyes again, aware as she took in the woman's heart-shaped face and wide green eyes that the other woman was giving her the once-over as well.

"I be Aelfread MacDonald."

Kyla hesitated, then offered her mother's first name, which also happened to be her own second name. "I am Iseabal." She deliberately withheld the offer of a last name, not wishing to lie more than she must to someone who might prove to be a friend.

" 'Tis a pleasure to meet ye, Iseabal."

Kyla nearly sagged in relief at the easy acceptance, her smile widening far enough to near split her face before she whirled nervously to peer out over the open water. " 'Tis a lovely spot."

"Aye." Smiling herself, the woman turned to glance over the sparkling sea, then moved back to where she had been sitting, picking up a small basket. "I came to fetch some weeds, but stopped to rest a breath or two and enjoy the air first."

Galen strode grimly out of the stables and paused to glare around the bailey. Being unsure where to look next, it was a relief when he spotted Tommy and Gavin rushing toward him. He could tell from their expressions that they had learned something. And that was the first spot of good news he had had since arriving home to find his wife, as well as her three guards, missing.

It helped his presence of mind little that the old witch seemed just as dismayed over Kyla's absence as he was. She had told him on arriving that her mistress was above stairs having a nap. When he had then asked where the men were, she had said Robbie and Angus had been "outside most of the day, it being Duncan's day to guard her," and that Duncan had stepped out shortly after Kyla had retired. She had thought he'd gone to the privy. But a quick check had proven the bedchamber empty and the bailey to be absent of any sign of Duncan or the other men.

That was when Galen had really started to worry.

He had immediately sent Tommy and Gavin to question anyone and everyone they could as to the whereabouts of the missing four, while he himself had sought out the stable master to see if he knew anything or if there were any horses missing. The answer to both questions had been no, much to his consternation, so it was with relief that he hurried to greet his First and Second as they approached. "What news?"

"No one has seen Kyla, but Roy's guarding the gate and says he saw Duncan, Angus, and Robbie walking toward the docks. He thought mayhap they had gone to meet the boats."

Galen frowned over that. "But they didn't arrive at the boats. And we didn't pass them on the way up."

"Aye." Tommy nodded at that. "Mayhap they took one of the paths."

Not sure whether to be worried or angered, Galen shook his head. "Why? Where would they have been headed? They are supposed to be guarding my wife. Why would they be out gallivanting about on the beach paths?"

"Well—" Tommy glanced at Gavin before pointing out—"They generally take their responsibilities seriously . . . Robbie especially. Mayhap they realized her ladyship was missing and went off in search of her."

"Without calling an alarm?" Galen shook his head again, frustration beginning to clench his stomach. "Nay. Were they to realize her missing, they would have had the whole castle looking for her."

"Then mayhap she isn't missing," Gavin suggested thoughtfully, bringing sharp gazes from both men.

"What are ye saying, Gavin?"

"Well, Roy did mention a woman leaving just ere Duncan, Angus, and Robbie. He—"

"Kyla?" Galen interrupted sharply.

"Nay." Tommy frowned at the other man for getting their laird needlessly excited. "He said they walked out behind a woman, 'tis true enough, but he said she was a Scot. At least he said she wore a plaid."

"Mayhap Lady Kyla has donned a plaid and escaped."

Galen stiffened at his man's phrasing. "Escaped? Escaped what? This is her home now. We are wed," he pointed out indignantly.

"Aye, but . . ." Gavin grimaced. "I would wonder if ye had the time to tell her that ere yer leavetaking?"

Galen blinked at the question, then let his breath out on a half-grunt, half-groan. "Damn me, I didn't, either. There was no time . . ."

"Well me laird, 'tis sure I am there wasn't ere now, but soon will be. Let us find her so ye can give her the grand news."

Galen nodded uncertainly at that but did not move. Instead he peered at the ground, deep in thought and worry, the expression on his face saying more than his silence that he did not relish the telling. "Do ye think so?" he asked finally.

"Think what, me laird?" Tommy asked after exchanging a look with Gavin.

"Think she will find it grand news?"

There was silence for a minute as both men considered that. It was hard to answer. Women were such a queer lot. Who could say how she would react to such news? Any *man*, upon finding out that rather than having to marry a vicious, murdering bully like MacGregor, they had already been wed to the MacDonald, would be well-nigh ecstatic. After all, Galen was wealthy, a good fighter, and fair as a leader. But women rarely reacted as men would, something neither man was wont to tell their laird.

"Of course she will. How could she not be?" Gavin said reassuringly.

"Aye," Tommy agreed. "I would be fair grateful for the news, were I a woman. Ye did her a favor stealing her from MacGregor and marrying her yerself."

"Aye," Galen nodded on a sigh. "I did her a favor."

"That ye did. Most like saved her life."

"Aye. I did. I saved her life." Regaining some of his confidence, he straightened his shoulders. "She will be grateful."

"Most like, aye."

Galen stiffened at that addition from Gavin. "What mean ye, *most like*?"

"Well, women are an odd breed," he pointed out, deciding a bit of caution would not go amiss.

"And?"

Gavin shrugged. "Who can ken the way their brains work, me laird? She may be grateful. Then again . . ." Hesitating, he glanced toward Tommy before finishing. "She may need to be told how she *should* be grateful."

Galen sighed at that, then straightened his shoulders again and turned toward the stables. "Come. We will take our mounts. There are a dozen or so paths to check and I would find her quickly."

"I don't think she gave her true name," Angus murmured. The women had been talking for several minutes and had not yet come to blows. That seemed to indicate that Aelfread did not know it was Lady Kyla she addressed.

"Aye, she must have," Duncan insisted firmly. "I simply can't see the brave and courageous lass that stood up to us in the woods lying about her name. Even to prevail in her escape."

Angus rolled his eyes at that, then said soothingly, "Mayhap she hasn't given a name at all."

Duncan perked up at that possibility and the three men continued to watch their mistress as she joined Aelfread in sitting on the sand.

"What do ye think they are talking about?"

Robbie shrugged. "What do women ever talk about? Men. Gossip. Chores."

"Nay, I disagree," Kyla said firmly. "The knight and the bishop are the most valuable players in chess. 'Tis true the queen can move more freely, but next to the king, she is the one an opponent is most eager to gain. They almost always forget about the bishop and knight. A smart player takes advantage of that."

Aelfread considered that then grimaced. "'Tis a shame we have no board here to play with. I would enjoy a game of chess."

"Aye." Kyla sighed. "'Twould have been grand."

"Ah, well." The woman peered out at the water, then glanced toward her hopefully. "I don't suppose ye like to swim? Do ye?"

"Nay. I don't think she's daft."

Both Robbie and Duncan glanced at their friend as he continued.

"'Twas quite crafty of her to don a plaid for her escape. Were we not so vigilant and had she had a bit more luck, she may well have made good her escape. She did a fair job of donning it as well."

"Aye, well . . ." Duncan sighed, then admitted, "I assisted with the plaid. In truth, she did a fair lousy job of donning it herself."

Both men gaped at that and he frowned at the expressions on their faces. He spoke quickly to dispel any notions of impropriety.

"She came into the hall covered with rushes and her pleats all aruck. I pretended to think her one of the servants. I straightened them and removed as many of the rushes as I could without her realizing that I knew who she was."

Angus sighed. "Pity. When I saw her escaping I thought—"

Robbie grunted and interrupted, " 'Tis not much of an escape anyway. She'll not get far sitting about on the beach."

"Aye," Angus agreed grimly. "She's daft. Just think on how she kept trying to walk out of the keep when we had told her already that she was to remain indoors. Well, at least she still maintains her courage," he added, ignoring Duncan's indignant glare. " 'Twas brazen of her to at least try to escape. Aye. She maintains her courage."

"Foolish courage," Robbie rumbled now. "Made more so by the addling her brains have taken."

Angus sighed, then nodded in solemn agreement. " 'Tis a shame, really. She's a pretty lass. And she seemed so sharp, too, ere the fever."

Robbie raised an eyebrow at that. "Ye didn't ken her ere the fever."

He shrugged that aside. "She did a lot of talking

while in the fever's grip. She seemed sharp when she spoke of events ere her wound."

Duncan frowned at them both. "Now don't go labeling her daft again. 'Twas a sound plan. I near did not recognize her meself. She needs a little practice at donning the plaid ere she escapes again is all. Were it not for the rushes and bad pleats, she truly would have slipped past me."

"Thank God for rushes and bad pleats, then."

Heads whipping around, the three men gaped at the man who had crept unnoticed up behind them, then rose as one. "Laird!"

"So she donned a plaid, let her hair down, and slipped from the castle?" he asked, his gaze sliding to the women on the shore. He thought at first that they intended on leaving the beach, then realized his mistake. His eyes widened when they both began to disrobe instead. It seemed they had a quick dip in mind.

"Come," he muttered, gesturing for his men to follow him back through the trees as his wife's plaid slid from her body to reveal a short tunic beneath it.

He'd left Tommy and Gavin to try the other paths and he'd agreed to meet them on the main path. He would send Angus, Robbie, and Duncan back to meet them, then he would tend to his wife.

Reaching the path where he had left his horse, he paused. The men walked to his side, worry on their faces. He knew they were concerned at how he would react to their letting her escape. He waited for one of them to speak.

As the one left in charge, it was Robbie who broke the silence to report. "All was quiet while ye were gone until today," he started out, only to be interrupted by Angus.

"Well, except for her trying to leave ere this."

Galen stiffened at that. "She tried to escape before?"

"Not exactly," Robbie answered reassuringly. "She simply . . . er . . . tried to leave the keep." When Galen began to frown, the large man sighed. "I told her yer instructions about staying inside, but she . . . er . . ."

"She seemed to have trouble remembering," Angus filled in helpfully.

"Aye," Robbie sighed. "In truth she did. After the nooning meal on the first day, she got up and just . . . well, she started to walk out of the castle. I thought she was headed above stairs and didn't ken what she was about until she was near out the door. But I caught her then and explained again about yer orders and she sat quietly by the fire the rest of the day."

"She did the same thing yesterday while I was watching her," Angus informed him sadly. "Right after the nooning meal, she got up and started to walk out of the castle." He shook his head. "She just doesn't seem to be able to keep the instructions in her head. In fact, mayhap she wasn't trying to escape at all today, mayhap she just—"

"Forgot my instructions," Galen finished with disgust.

"Nay," Duncan argued at once. "She didn't just walk out today. She donned a plaid and—"

"Tried to walk right past ye? As if ye wouldn't recognize her?" Angus said doubtfully, his eyebrows arched.

Duncan frowned at the other man. " 'Twas a clever

plan. In truth, she would have pulled the wool over me eyes except for—"

"The rushes and pleats," Galen filled in dryly, and Duncan sagged in defeat.

"Aye."

Galen glanced from one to the other slowly before asking, "Why didn't ye stop her ere she left the bailey?"

"We decided not to apprehend her until we knew what she was about," Robbie admitted. "And in truth, I don't think she was trying to escape at all. I think she was simply looking for a bit of fresh air. The beach is hardly the place to go to escape."

"Unless she planned to swim for it," Angus interjected suddenly. When the others peered at him as if he had lost his mind, he defended his comment. "Well and sure enough 'tis a long way, but if the woman is daft, she may try it."

The others nodded reluctantly, not noticing how stiff Galen had gone. He was recalling the fact that his wife and Robbie's had been disrobing to swim as they had been leaving. He doubted very much if Aelfread would try to escape, but Kyla may have suggested the swim as a way to get herself out into the water. Once there, she might simply swim for the mainland and never turn back.

"Gavin and Tommy should be along shortly. Return to the castle with them when they do," Galen ordered, mounting his horse and galloping back along the path toward the beach.

" 'Tis nice to find someone to swim with. Most everyone else takes only quick dunks in the water. They seem to think swimming will make them ill."

"I would agree with them at this moment," Kyla muttered dryly, pausing in the water as soon as it reached her waist. It had been three and a half weeks, all told, since the injury to her back and while Morag's salve had sped her along in healing, she didn't wish to do herself damage by getting her back wet. Which was sad really, for Kyla loved to swim, and she probably would have warmed up faster in the water were she fully submerged. As it was, the icy water seemed to flow right through her short tunic and was clutching at the white, goose pimpled flesh of her legs with icy hands.

Aelfread suddenly gave a happy laugh, then lay back in the water to float on her back with a sigh. "I love the water."

Kyla smiled slightly at the other woman. "The way you say that makes it sound as if you do not get to enjoy it often."

"Nay. I used to spend a lot of time at the water's edge on the mainland. My clan depended on fishing for survival. I was down on the shore all the time," she laughed slightly. "That is where I met my husband. My cousin's wife is kin to him. He was visiting. He says he fell in love with me on sight and I suppose I did, too. He offered for my hand that night, but I told my Da to make him wait. A man never values what he can get cheaply."

Kyla smiled at the other woman. She could see Aelfraed's love for the great mountain of a man on her face and hear it every time she spoke of him. "How long did you make him wait?"

"Oh," she grinned. "Six months. It seemed like forever though. He visited as often as he could. My cousin was fair sick of his face and *begging* me to take him by the time I did. We married, I moved here, and we spent many a sweet day here on this beach," Aelfread's smile disolved, her mouth straightening into a flat line of displeasure. "Until that Sassenach wench came here."

Kyla blinked in surprise at the bitterness in the other woman's voice. "The . . . er . . . wench?" she asked curiously.

"Aye. His laird's new wife," she muttered with a disgust that spoke volumes on her opinion of the woman and simply made Kyla's curiosity deepen. Kyla had yet to meet the woman in question. She had actually come to the conclusion that the MacDonald laird was still single, yet now Aelfread was telling her the man was married. Where was the lady? Why was she never at table?

"Ever since she came, my husband is too busy— either looking after her, or filling in for one of the other men while they look after her—to spend any time with me during the day. He used to get away early three or four times a week to take a walk or swim with me ere she came," she muttered with resentment.

Kyla eyed her curiously. "Why does she need looking after?"

Aelfread whirled in the water to stare at her with disbelief. "Yer jesting? Where in bonny Scotland have you been that you don't know about that?"

"Oh, well . . ." She frowned slightly. "I have been away," she finished lamely.

"Hmm." Aelfread seemed to accept that easily enough and relaxed back in the water again. "Well, you can't have been back long, if you don't know about it." Sighing, she twirled in the water slowly.

"She has to be looked after because she's daft as the day is long."

Kyla's eyebrows rose, interest suffusing her face. "Really?"

"Aye. She nearly killed my husband, you know."

"Nay!" Kyla gasped, shocked at the idea that there was a murderous madwoman hidden somewhere in the keep she had just left.

"Aye." She shook her head. "It's a sad tale to be sure. Our laird surely deserves better than this after all the loss and tragedy he has suffered."

"Hmm," Kyla murmured, afraid to say or ask anything that might give away the fact that she knew nothing of these tragedies. She was supposed to be a member of the clan. A clan member would hardly be as ignorant as she was of what the other woman spoke.

"I think he should set her aside. The last thing we need is a madwoman as our lady. I mean, what kind of children is he like to get from a mad woman?"

Kyla shook her head sadly in answer. If the laird's wife had always been mad, she was likely to produce children who would grow up to be mad as well.

All of this news was making her feel a bit more kindly toward her guards and their laird. She began to see that they had probably been watching her so closely and restricting her movements in an effort to keep her safe from the lady of the castle. It made her grateful that she hadn't run into *that* woman here on the beach.

A sudden sigh drew Kyla's gaze to her companion as the woman quit her floating and regained her feet in the water. "As much as I would enjoy continuing this, 'tis growing late in the day. 'Twill be time to sup soon. I suppose we should get out."

"Aye," Kyla murmured quietly and had started to follow Aelfread out of the water when her new friend suddenly gave a squeal and charged across the sand to her plaid. Glancing about, Kyla froze. There, astride his horse, the MacDonald waited upon the path. At first, she was so consumed with the fear of discovery that it took her a moment to realize that she was standing there wearing naught but her under-tunic.

Flushing brightly, she charged after Aelfread toward her own plaid as he started down the path toward them.

"Me laird." Aelfread had her gown on and a pained smile on her face by the time he reached them. Kyla, unable to pleat and don the thing quickly, had merely drawn it around her shoulders. She quickly scattered her damp hair with her fingers so that it hung half across her face, then she turned to meet the man whose hospitality she had been attempting to flee.

"Laird." Kyla dropped her head in pretended obeisance to hide her features.

"Ladies. 'Tis a fine day for a swim, but I fear now that I have returned, Robbie will be looking for ye, Aelfread."

Kyla glanced from beneath her lashes in time to see the petite woman blink in surprise, but then her gaze narrowed and her mouth tightened. Lifting her head, Aelfread gave him a stiff smile. "Aye, me laird. Yer right. Thank ye for telling me. Iseabal and I'll just be heading back, then."

Kyla nearly sighed aloud at that. For a moment

she had feared the other woman would abandon her, leaving her alone with the MacDonald, to make her own excuses—a dangerous situation she was sure. She could hardly have continued to stare at the ground as she spoke and even had she done so, there was still the chance that the man would recognize her voice. Aside from that, the very sight of him seemed to have scared all thought right out of her head. She wasn't at all sure she could have thought up a viable excuse to leave. Her relief was short-lived.

"Iseabal, is it? Well, 'tis a pleasure to meet ye, Iseabal," he murmured, then glanced back at her new friend. " 'Tis no need to wait for her, Aelfread. I'll be seeing her back meself."

Aelfread frowned over that and opened her mouth to try to extricate the girl once more but the hard glint in Galen's eyes made her think better of it. Nodding resignedly, she turned away, her anger growing with every step she took up the path. She had never thought to see the day that she would think badly of Galen MacDonald. Robbie had sung his praises to her since she'd known him and she had listened and accepted all he said. She would have a word or two to say on that subject now, however. Her dear Robbie was going to get an earful when he came home that night. Iseabal was an innocent young lass and the look in Galen's eyes as he had eyed her wet shift had been nothing short of lustful. And if he took advantage of that girl . . .

Chapter 8

Silently cursing her luck, Kyla stared at the sand by her feet with feigned fascination as her friend left. She felt as bereft as an orphaned pup. A moment later she had no room for such emotion, panic filling her as the MacDonald chief urged his mount closer. "Shall we head back to the keep?"

"Oh, n-nay, I—" Kyla began nervously, only to gasp in surprise as she was suddenly plucked from the sand and hauled up before him on the horse. "All right," she squeaked, grasping frantically at the pommel of his saddle to balance herself as he turned the horse back toward the path he had taken to the beach.

"Iseabal."

Kyla stiffened as he murmured the name consideringly.

"A lovely name for a lovely lass."

"'Twas my mother's name, too," she muttered uncomfortably, shifting slightly in an effort to put a little space between herself and him. It was an impossible feat with them both sharing his mount. His legs were solid behind her thighs, his arms around her to hold the reins before them, and while her back wasn't touching his chest, she could feel the heat of his nearness through her damp shift and the plaid wrapped around her.

"Hmm. 'Tis fair amazing to me that I have no' noticed ye ere this, Iseabal. 'Tis sure I am, yer a fresh, shiny coin among so many dull and plain ones here."

"Oh, well, I do not get out much, my lord—laird," she said quickly, then heaved a sigh. For it was true. She did not get out much. Thanks to the very man at her back and his blasted rules. Or perhaps it was due to his wife's madness. Kyla frowned over that and shifted again, attempting to put a little more space between them without seeming obvious. He was as hot as a Midsummer's Eve fire. The flesh of her back was tingling something fierce in reaction to his heat. And he wasn't even touching her!

"Stop wiggling about," he instructed not ungently.

"I am not wiggling about," she said quickly, sitting a little straighter before him.

"Ye are."

"I am not," Kyla insisted firmly, casting a glare at him over her shoulder to let him know how rude he was being by even suggesting such a thing.

Galen frowned right back. "Aye, ye are."

Kyla pursed her lips and gave him a dirty look. " 'Tis obvious that you know nothing of good manners, my lord. A true gentleman would not deign to point out a woman's discomfort."

"I think I already told ye I'm no' a gentleman," he muttered, but this time he seemed irritated to have to make the admission.

Giving a harrumph, Kyla turned to face forward again, then whirled quickly back, her mouth a round "O" of dismay.

"What is it?" Galen asked with amusement.

"You know who I am," she realized aloud as his words sank in. The last time he had told her that he was no gentleman was when he had carried her up to his room. As Kyla.

Irritation covered his face briefly. "Of course I know who ye are. Did ye really think donning a plaid would fool anyone?"

Kyla flushed, but sat a little straighter before him. "It fooled your men," she pointed out stiffly, and he rolled his eyes.

"Nay. They weren't fooled."

"They were so," she insisted. He scowled at her. Rather than be intimidated, she scowled right back, then glanced away in confusion when his lips began to turn upward in a reluctant grin of amusement.

"My men knew it was you. They followed you down to the beach and kept an eye on you until I arrived."

Kyla frowned at that announcement, her back stiffening a bit more at the idea of having been spied on the whole time she had been enjoying her freedom. Damn these Scots anyway, she thought with sudden irritation. She could not wait for the arrival of her relative's men, whether it was her brother's men or her uncle's she would be happy to wish this place a "fare thee well."

Then she recalled the terrible troubles the man who rode behind her had and was ashamed of herself. The poor man had a madwoman for a wife. And he had assigned his men to guard Kyla only to keep her safe from that woman. Kyla was being terribly ungrateful over it, and troublesome to boot, by trying to escape the protection he offered.

On the other hand, he could have simply told her

why she needed protection instead of just denying her freedom and setting guards on her. But then, men had never been known for sharing such vital bits of information. At least her brother and father had tended to keep such details to themselves, preferring to merely give orders and expecting them to be obeyed. Besides, she supposed it would be humiliating for the man to admit that his wife was deranged.

Clearing her throat, she glanced back at him and even managed to squeeze out a smile. "I am terribly sorry to be such a burden," she murmured. "I realize now that I should have stayed at the keep."

"Aye. Ye should have."

Kyla's good intentions fled under his easy agreement and she snapped. "Well, mayhap I would have had you troubled to explain yourself."

"Explain myself?" he rumbled ominously.

"Aye." She sighed in exasperation, then tried for a conciliatory tone again. "It must be difficult for you. . . . Having an ailing wife, I mean," she clarified, sensing his confusion and trying to explain what she meant without offending him. When he stiffened at her words, she glanced back to see amazement on his face.

"You know?" he asked.

"Well, of course, I know." Her lips twisted slightly. "Did you really think I wouldn't hear about it?" She suddenly worried that she might be getting her new friend into trouble by revealing what she had been told. After all, if the men had followed to spy on her, they would know that Aelfread was the only person she had spoken to and therefore the source of the knowledge.

"Not that Aelfread told me, mind you," she said

quickly, trying to protect the woman. "And even if she did, 'Twas only because she thought I knew—which I would have if you had troubled yourself to tell me, my lord." Her attempt to protect her friend turned into a lecture again as her irritation returned. "Really, my lord, you should have told me."

"Aye," he began on a sigh, but she continued right over him.

"I mean I can understand your reluctance to share such a shameful admission—" She saw his eyes widen incredulously at her words and quickly tried to amend their harshness. "Not that marrying a madwoman is shameful, mind you, especially if you didn't know about the madness ere the marriage—and I'm sure you didn't know else you surely wouldn't have gone through with the wedding, but really . . ." She paused briefly, taking in his expression with a frown. It had changed from surprise to upset to dismay, and now his features had settled into a sort of bemused stare as she babbled at him.

Considering the burdens he lived with daily, she felt her anger slip away, settling into sympathy again. "It must be hard for you. Never knowing when your own wife may again try to murder one of your men or a guest." She shook her head sadly, oblivious to the way he had stiffened in shock, then realized that they had ridden back through the gates and were now paused before the keep. "Oh, here we are. I should go inside and prepare for the sup, my lord." She slid off his mount as she spoke, then whirled back to flash him a brilliant smile. "Never fear my lord. Now that I know what is about, I shan't try to flee my guards again. Good day to you."

Then she was gone, skipping cheerfully up the

steps to the keep and leaving a rather stunned Galen in her wake. What had she just told him, he wondered. That she knew about their marriage? Yes, it seemed Aelfread had told her, though she had obviously tried to protect her friend. Of course, there was nothing to protect her from; if anything, Galen was relieved that the burden of informing her had been removed. Nay, he was glad to be rid of that chore. He had expected hysterics, upset, mayhap even anger. But nay, she appeared not the least upset by the news. But what had she been talking about when she'd mentioned the burden of a mad wife? Did she fear she was mad? And that part about his never knowing when she might take it into her head to try to kill one of his men or a guest, had that been a threat? Good Lord, she wouldn't, would she? Nay, of course not. She wouldn't have dared warn him of the possibility were that the case . . . unless she *were* mad.

The men converged on Galen with questions the moment he reached the stables.

"Did ye tell her? What did she say?"

"What did Aelfread do when she realized who Kyla was?"

Galen waited until the stable master had moved off with his horse before turning to survey men that had ridden with him since he himself had been but a boy. In the end, he addressed Robbie's question first. "Aelfread doesn't know yet that the woman she spent the afternoon on the beach with was her mistress."

"She doesn't?" They all looked amazed at that announcement, but none more so than the giant. "How? Why not?"

"Because she gave Iseabal as her name and I didn't give her away."

"She lied!" Duncan appeared crushed by the discovery.

"I told ye she would have to lie," Angus said smugly.

"She didn't lie," Galen defended, though the Lord knew why. There was nothing wrong, in his mind, in giving a false name to gain escape. "Iseabal *is* her name. Her second name. I saw that when she signed the marriage decree."

"Hah!" Now Duncan looked smug. "*I* knew she wouldn't lie. Not entirely."

Angus rolled his eyes at that, then turned back to Galen. "So ye let her keep her secret until after Aelfread left," he concluded. "What did she say when ye let her know ye knew who she was and then told her she was yer wife?"

"I didn't."

"Ye didn't what?" Gavin asked slowly. "Tell her yer wed, or that ye knew who she was?"

"Tell her we were wed," Galen muttered, turning to move toward the keep.

"But why?" It was Robbie's voice rumbling to life as he and the other men rushed after him. "Do ye no' think it might have been better to tell her whilst the two of ye were alone? 'Tis no' me place to tell ye how to handle yer wife, but after three months with Aelfread, 'tis my experience that women tend to think 'tis fair important they learn things like this at the first possible opportunity. In fact, they tend to get quite testy should that not be so."

Galen paused at that and turned as his friend continued. "Why, I told ye about how she reacted when she found out about that little scratch yer wife gave me. I thought to spare her an upset, but when she found out, she fair near killed me with her screaming alone. First she was howling over the fact that I didn't tell her, then she was howling over the wee scratch itself."

"Mayhap yer wife just likes to howl," Tommy suggested with amusement.

Robbie considered that briefly. "Aye. That may be so. Aelfread tears a strip off me ear if I don't tell her even the most pesky of little things. Why, the other day she set up a'hollering over the fact that I hadn't mentioned 'twas me day of birth. Still, I can't help but think ye'd best be telling her alone."

"There is no need. Aelfread had already told her."

The men gaped over that, then shifted around, glancing at each other briefly before Robbie cleared his throat. "And just how angry was she over finding out that way?"

"She wasn't."

There were more glances exchanged, then Angus murmured, "And you'd be sure about that, me laird? I mean you don't think she may have been hiding her upset?" When Galen began to scowl at that, he added quickly, "I only ask because, well, me sister, God bless her, I don't think she'd take news like that too well. I mean, I'm sure hearing it from a stranger would not please her one bit. If you see what I mean?"

Galen's expression turned thoughtful as he considered that. "Well, she seemed not to be upset. But then she did say that bit about killing one of you men."

There was a moment of shocked silence, then the men burst out, all trying to talk at the same time. Galen held up a hand for silence. "She didn't mean it, I'm sure. She just said that it must be hard having an ailing wife and never knowing when she might take it into her head to try to kill another one of me men." Leaving his men to chew over that, Galen turned and continued on toward the keep.

Pushing through the heavy keep doors, Kyla ignored the few people milling about the great hall, rushed up the stairs to the bedchambers, and into the one she had been using since awaking from her fevers.

"Thanks be to the saints!" Morag cried, pausing in her worried pacing to rush forward and embrace Kyla. "I thought ye'd up and fled."

"What?" Kyla pulled back slightly to frown at her. "And leave you behind? I would not do such a thing."

"Nay. I know you wouldn't." Releasing her, she stepped back to look over her plaid. "So *that* is how ye managed it."

"Aye." Kyla glanced down at the damp wrinkled garment wrapped around her torso and grimaced. "Not that it worked," she added grimly, then sighed and began to remove the damp material.

"Well, it must have worked a bit—it got you out of here. And the laird was fair furious to find ye gone, too, I can tell ye. He searched the entire keep and bailey, roaring and snapping with worry. It didn't help that the men he left to guard ye were missing as well. He—"

"He is not angry anymore. It seems the men disappeared because they were following me," Kyla announced dryly as she let her plaid drop into a damp heap on the floor.

"Well—" Morag grabbed up the plaid and began to tend to it as Kyla set to work on her shift— "They could have let me know what was about," she muttered a bit irritably. "Duncan left shortly after ye retired. I thought he had gone to the privy, but he never returned. Then, there was no sign of him when the MacDonald arrived and you were discovered missing. There was no sign or word of the other two, either. You could have let us know what was about."

Kyla avoided her reproving glance for a moment, then sighed. "I am sorry you were worried. I guess I didn't really think this outing through. I just— I—"

"Ye just wanted to get out from under the thumb of yer guards fer a bit," the old woman finished for her calmly, setting the plaid aside and digging out a fresh shift for Kyla to don. "Ye aren't used to being restricted and I could tell ye were fretting under the burden of it. I should have realized what had happened as soon as it was known that ye were missing." Sighing, she turned back to dig through the chest again, straightening a moment later to study two gowns she now held in her hands. "Do ye wish to wear the gold or the green?"

Kyla shrugged slightly. "The green, I suppose," she murmured, then eyed the other woman solemnly. "Well, no matter the case, I am sorry you were worried. It won't happen again. Now that I know about this Lady MacDonald business, I shall stick close to my guards and not try to flee them."

Turning away and moving over to the fire to brush her still damp hair, she didn't notice the way Morag stiffened at her words or the burning look the nurse turned on her.

"This Lady MacDonald business?" Morag queried carefully.

"Aye." Kyla glanced around in surprise. "Surely you have heard about the MacDonald laird's wife?" When the maid merely stared at her mutely, uncertainty in every line of her body, Kyla gasped in amazement. "You have not heard? Oh, my! Well, apparently he has one, and she is quite mad." When Morag's eyes widened incredulously, Kyla nodded emphatically. "It's true. Why, Aelfread says she actually tried to kill one of the MacDonald men."

"Aelfread?" Morag echoed faintly.

"Oh, she is my new friend. I met her on the beach today," Kyla explained. "From what she said, it sounds as though Lady MacDonald is quite dangerous. I mean, trying to kill one of her own men? Can you imagine? 'Tis lucky I am that I did not run into her today unawares. Why, I might have said something to set the woman off and had her trying to kill me." She paused then, her head tilting slightly as she listened to the faint sounds filtering through the door and into the room. Laughter, talking, and shouting. People had begun to fill the great hall below.

"Child—"

Kyla jumped from her seat and rushed forward. "Come, we must hurry. They are gathering for the sup." Reaching Morag, she snatched the green gown from her and began to tug it on, muttering, "My hair is still damp but there is no help for that, I shall have to just tuck it up in a bun. Or mayhap I should just leave it lie flat to dry. What do you think?"

"I think we needs must have a talk," Morag said unhappily. "I should have told you sooner, but I felt it was his place to say so, so I let it go, but now—"

"Now whatever it is shall have to wait," Kyla said impatiently, finishing with her laces and quickly tugging to be sure everything lay right. "You know what mother use to say about being late to sup. 'Tis terribly rude."

"But—"

"Come along, Morag. Let us go. I'm rather hoping Lady MacDonald will be at table tonight. I do not suppose she will be, but I am terribly curious to see her." Leaving her hair lying damp down her back, she hurried out the door leaving Morag to follow with a shake of her head.

Kyla took a sip from her mug and set it back on the tabletop, trying to ignore the rude stares of the people around her. Lady MacDonald was not at table. It was not a big surprise, but Kyla would have liked to have seen her. In her head she had a rather vague picture of a thin, waifish woman, her hair all wild. Distracted by that thought and her curiosity for the woman, Kyla had been able for a while to ignore the rudeness of the Scots staring at her. Not that the MacDonald laird was one of them; if anything, he seemed rather distracted as he methodically made his way through the food in his trencher. But everyone else seemed to be watching her with a constant wariness that made her wonder what the devil was wrong with them. It was as if they expected her to leap to her feet at any moment and do something mad such as plunge her dirk into their laird's chest.

Mayhap having a madwoman as mistress here made them wary of all noble women, she thought, then glanced curiously to her side when the Mac-Donald finished the last of his meal and stood suddenly, raising his mug. The room went silent.

"I would make a toast to my wife."

Kyla's eyes widened briefly, then warmed with approval. What a wonderful man he was, to toast his poor, mad wife even in her absence. It was a shame his spouse was not in a state of mind to appreciate such kindnesses, she thought. Ah well . . .

Lifting her glass, Kyla glanced toward the others in the room, relieved to see that they, too, were supporting their lord with raised glasses and smiling faces, even if some of the smiles were doubtful.

"Ye all ken the circumstances leading up to the presence of Lady Kyla being here," he began, and there were solemn nods to that from his people, while Kyla merely blinked at him in confusion. He had said he wished to toast his wife. So much for that.

"And ye all ken of her injury and her recovery which, while it has been remarkable, has also taken time." He paused to allow another round of solemn nods. "I have been away these past days, tending to business, which has also delayed this eve. But now, all is out of the way and I wish to make a toast."

Turning suddenly, he took Kyla's arm, urging her to her feet. Once she stood beside him, he raised his mug higher. "To Lady Kyla MacDonald. My wife. May our marriage be long and prolific and may yer life here on this island be happy. Yer husband and yer people welcome ye."

Offering a smile, Kyla nodded briefly. "Thank you, my lord. I—*What did you just say?!*"

Galen arched one eyebrow mildly. "Welcome?"

"Nay. Ere that."

His eyebrows rose slightly. "About hoping our marriage is long and happy."

Kyla stared at him blankly, her thoughts in a whirl. The reason behind her rescue from marriage to the MacGregor had been gnawing at the back of her mind since recovering from the fevers. Morag had said it had something to do with the MacDonald wishing revenge on the other clan chief. Kyla had foolishly thought he had satisfied himself by merely preventing that marriage. Now she saw that she had not really been rescued at all. She had been plucked from one unwanted marriage only to be forced into another. Why? That was the first question to pop into her head. The MacDonald surely had no need to marry her simply to effect his revenge. Ransoming her would have achieved that. Wouldn't it?

It mattered little, she decided suddenly. She would not be married to him.

"Never," she announced coldly. "It shall never happen, do you hear me?"

The MacDonald's eyebrows slid even nearer his hairline, then he glanced around uncertainly, cleared his throat, and said, "Aye . . . Well . . . Ye see, 'tis no' that I was saying we *would* marry. I was drinking a toast to the fact that we already *are* married," he explained carefully, apparently bewildered by her reaction.

Kyla's mouth tightened, then she shook her head. "Impossible."

The MacDonald seemed baffled by her words, and he looked thankful as the clan priest hurried from his position further down the table.

" 'Tis true," the cleric assured Kyla anxiously. "I presided over the ceremony meself. 'Twas all nice and legal. A lovely ceremony, too," he added, as if he thought she might care. "We held it soon as ye arrived, on the steps for all to witness."

He glanced toward the room at large and Kyla followed his gaze, taking in with a sinking heart the shared nod of the entire room. "But I was ill on my arrival and for weeks afterward. I could not have possibly attended a wedding—"

" 'Tis true ye were sick even then, but we felt 'twas better to hold the wedding right away so the Mac-Gregor wouldn't plot to steal ye back and marry ye."

"Was I conscious?"

The MacDonald winced at her sarcasm, but left it to the priest to answer.

"Aye, my lady. Ye even managed to stand for a bit. And ye signed the contract," he added, turning toward his laird who gestured toward Gavin. His First leapt to his feet and hurried from the great hall, returning a moment later to hand a scroll to the priest. Taking the document, the man quickly unrolled it, then turned it for Kyla to see.

There it was. Her signature. Sloppy, even shaky, but recognizable as hers nonetheless. "Bloody hell," she breathed, dropping onto the bench with dismay.

"Well, where the Devil were you?!"

"On the boat," Morag explained calmly, seating herself on the edge of the bed and sighing as she watched Kyla pace the length of the room again. She had known the lass was not taking the news well when she had remained so quiet through the rest of the meal. After seeing the contract, she had sat there on that bench with a glazed look in her eyes that had said more to Morag than any amount of ranting and raving could have. The room had quieted then, all eyes remaining trained on the head table as the Mac-Donald had reclaimed his seat and sat peering about uncomfortably, looking as though he had not known quite what to do next. After several minutes, Morag had finally made her way to the head table and led Kyla above stairs.

The young woman had followed docilely, not snapping out of her nearly catatonic state until the bedchamber door had closed behind them. Then she had turned on Morag in fury.

" 'Twas done ere I arrived at the island," the old woman explained. "The MacDonald had traveled ahead with ye, to bathe ye in the sea and bring down yer fever. When we arrived at the coast, he had already sailed across to the keep with ye. By the time I arrived on the island, 'twas done. There was naught I could do about it."

Kyla paused in her pacing to snap, "And you did not think I might like to have this information?"

" 'Twas not my place to— What are ye doing?" she asked in dismay as Kyla suddenly bent to a chest and began to push it toward the door.

"What does it look as if I am doing? I am barricading the door. If he thinks he will simply saunter up here and—" Straightening abruptly, she glared at her servant. "Come help me."

Shaking her head, Morag rose to join her. "I daresay he won't be pleased by this," she pointed out dryly, putting her back to the chest and helping to shove it across the floor to brace it against the door.

"I do not care if he likes it or not," Kyla informed her grimly, leading her to another chest. "And *you* should not, either. *I* am your mistress. If I were you, I would be more worried about how angry *I* am. You should have told me."

Grimacing, Morag bent to assist her with the second chest, wincing at the loud scraping sound it made as it moved across the floor. Straightening once it rested against the door, she sighed and said, "Ye were too ill to tell aught to at first. Then, while ye were recovering, I didn't wish to upset ye."

"That is—"

"And," the old woman interrupted, "marriage to the MacDonald seemed a safe refuge for ye."

Kyla stilled at that, amazement on her face as she straightened from the chest they had just moved. "Safe? From what?"

"From Catriona and her plottings. If Johnny should die—"

"He will not die!" Kyla yelled, then took a breath and said more calmly, "Shropshire is with him. He will not allow Catriona to—"

"I hope yer right. I hope that she and all of her people are kept far and away from him, but he may still die. He suffered a terrible wound."

Kyla paled at those words. Morag knew more about healing than the king's healer. To hear her doubt Johnny's chances of survival was a horrible blow. It sent fear coursing through her in waves. "No worse than mine, surely?"

"Mayhap not, but 'tis a miracle ye survived. I have little reason to count on two such miracles. 'Sides, yer surviving was due in part to your own stubbornness. Ye saw that Catriona hired those villains and were determined to live to tell that. Johnny has no such knowledge to prop him up."

Sighing, Kyla sank onto the chest they had just moved, her heart suddenly leaden as she accepted the old woman's words. Her brother could die despite Shropshire's presence. He might already be dead.

"The MacDonald is strong, young, wealthy, and honorable."

Kyla snorted at that. To her mind it was hardly honorable to marry an unconscious woman. And she didn't care what they claimed, she could not have been conscious when she married him; she simply would not have done so. She supposed she should be grateful that he had not consummated the deed while he was at it. At least she still had a chance to have the marriage annulled.

That thought made her sit up a little straighter on the chest. He hadn't consummated it, had he? Surely she would know if he had? She would feel different somehow or something. Wouldn't she? Scowling over these thoughts, she turned on Morag sharply. "How long was it between when he reached the island and you caught up to him?" she asked suspiciously.

"The marriage is unconsummated, if that is what ye are asking," she said after a moment. Kyla relaxed, then leapt to her feet.

"And it shall remain so," she announced firmly, moving to another chest. "I will have this marriage annulled."

"Why?"

Pausing, Kyla frowned at her. "Why?"

"Aye. Why? He is a good choice in husband. Strong. Not too young but not old. A good leader . . . I have been asking questions these last weeks while you healed. His people are healthy, happy, and loyal. They think much of him. And the MacDonald is prosperous. He will be a good husband."

"Oh aye, if I wish to be locked in the castle and known as the mad Sassenach, I should be perfectly happy." Hearing those words slip out of her own mouth, she closed her eyes and groaned as she recognized their source. Aelfread, she realized. The woman from the beach had described her laird's new wife as "the Sassenach wench." She had also said that she had tried to kill her husband.

She, herself, was the Sassenach wench, Kyla realized with a moan, then wondered when she had tried to kill poor Aelfread's husband. Had she attacked someone else besides that big man, Robbie? Surely he wasn't Aelfread's husband? Nay, he was far too large to be a match for the petite girl. She must have attacked someone else, too. Good Lord! Those fevers had made her terribly aggressive, had they not? And—

Pausing abruptly, she sank down to sit on the chest again with bewilderment. But why did they all think she was mad?

"Aye, well . . ."

Morag's mutter made Kyla realize that once again she had spoken her thoughts aloud unintentionally. But it was the guilty grimace on the woman's face that made her eyes narrow on her suspiciously. "Aye, well, what?"

Morag sighed heavily. "That would be because I told them you were."

"What?" Kyla was off the chest at once, her eyes wide with horror.

"Why?"

"I was trying to protect ye," Morag said quickly. "I thought surely he wouldn't wish to marry a madwoman."

"You thought wrong," Kyla snapped, and Morag made a face.

"Aye, it would seem so . . . Unless he didn't believe me."

Kyla turned sharply toward the old woman at

that, her mind grasping desperately at that idea. Mayhap he hadn't believed her. Surely no man would wish to marry a madwoman? Nay, she thought, lowering herself to the chest again. He must not have believed her, else he surely wouldn't have married her. But what if she could convince him it were true? Surely he would want the marriage annulled. Wouldn't he?

Despite the weight in front of it, the bedroom door suddenly began to push open, startling Kyla to her feet as the chest she was on slid across the floor several inches. Whirling, she was just in time to see the MacDonald laird frown at the chests before he slid into the room. When he raised his eyes to hers, she was surprised to see uncertainty flicker across his face. It was quickly covered by a stern mask. "We could hear the racket you were making all the way down in the great hall. What is about?"

"I was rearranging the room," Kyla lied glibly.

His eyes narrowed slightly, but he said nothing, merely turned his scowl onto Morag. The nurse muttered something unintelligible under her breath and fled the room, leaving Kyla alone to face her husband.

Chapter 9

KYLA watched warily as the man who was apparently her husband moved across the room to the bed, her mind racing as she sought a way to convince him that she was mad and therefore a bad prospect as wife. She was still searching wildly for ideas when he paused beside the bed and turned to eye her diffidently.

"Did you plan to stand by the door all night, or will you come to bed?"

"What?" Kyla choked out, then turned wildly to the side and blurted, "Oh, do be quiet! I can hardly hear him with you nattering at me."

The idea had struck her suddenly. Kyla didn't know many mad people. There had been only one person at Forsythe who had shown the least sign of mental illness and that was Crazy Mary. The woman wore mismatched and tattered clothes, wandered the Forsythe woods at night, and served ale to the warriors at the Forsythe table during the day. Kyla's mother had first given Mary the job. Out of pity, Kyla had always thought, and her mother had turned a blind eye to the fact that Crazy Mary was as free with her body as she was with the ale she served. On her good days, Mary just seemed a bit loud and loose. On her bad days, the woman spoke to people who simply weren't there, holding forth whole conversations and even yelling furiously at non-existent persons. It had always made everyone just a tad nervous.

"Er . . . wife?"

Kyla stiffened at that word, but turned a pleasant, slightly questioning face to the man who had married her. "Aye?"

"Who is it ye'd be talkin' to?"

"Why, my friend, of course. Surely you can see that," she said lightly, then turned quickly to the side again and nodded. "Aye, you are right, it is a bit chill. I shall just put another log on the fire, shall I?"

Bustling over to the room's small fireplace, she snatched a log out of the basket beside it and tossed it onto the flames. Grabbing up the iron rod that leaned against the wall nearby, she began poking energetically at the fire in an effort to avoid going anywhere near the bed. She kept up a steady stream of chatter the whole while, babbling away nonsensically to her non-existent friend about the fine weather that day, the nice visit she'd had to the beach, even what was served at supper—all as she beat the fire vigorously. Then the MacDonald laird was suddenly there beside her, snatching the poker from her fingers with a pained smile.

"I think the fire is quite strong enough," he said dryly, quickly flicking a couple of burning branches that had flown out of the fireplace from her wild stoking back onto the pile, before setting the rod aside and turning to eye her.

"Mayhap, ye could . . . er . . . introduce me to your friends?" he suggested carefully after a moment and Kyla's eyes widened with dismay. "Wife?" he murmured with concern, but she continued to stare at him blankly.

Snapping out of her frozen state, she stammered, "Oh, a-aye, of-course. How rude of me. Well, this is . . . er . . . er . . . Nestene. Ernestene," she got out at last, pulling the name out of the air.

Nodding solemnly, the MacDonald laird gave a slight bow. "A pleasure to meet ye, Ernestene. Howbeit, ye'll have to be leavin' now as my wife has been very ill and need's her rest to recover."

"She does not wish to leave," Kyla said grimly, gritting her teeth in frustration. What the Devil was the matter with the man? Here she was giving him the perfect excuse to annul the marriage and he wasn't taking it. She would have to take it a step further, she realized, eyes narrowing on him. "In fact, Ernestene wants me to sing."

The MacDonald blinked at that. "Sing?"

"Aye. Sing. And play her a lovely soothing tune on my harp to send her off to sleep."

"Oh." He actually looked relieved, the ninny. It seemed he wasn't as eager to carry out his husbandly duty as she had believed. Well, mayhap there was hope for her plan yet, she thought on a sigh. "Well," he said. "A tune would be nice."

"Aye." Smiling at him sweetly now, she rushed forward, caught his arm, and urged him over to the chairs by the fire. Settling him there, she whirled away to survey the chests in the room. She hadn't asked as yet if her harp had been sent with them from Forsythe. She certainly hoped so. If it had, it wouldn't fit in any of the smaller chests. But— Ah! That one, she thought, hurrying to a great one in the corner. It could only fit in that one.

Bending before the box, she opened it, and rifled through the clothes inside until her hand hit on something hard. Following the shape to discover that it was indeed her harp, Kyla released the breath she had been holding. It had been packed in among the clothes so they would cushion it during the journey. Clever Morag, she thought, shifting through Crazy Mary's songs in her head while tossing gowns and tunics willy-nilly in an effort to unbury the instrument. Once she had, she straightened, lifted it out, then lugged it across the room to the empty chair opposite her husband. She set the harp down with a discordant crash of vibrating strings.

Smiling innocently at her husband's wince, she then settled in the chair, rucked her skirt up, spread her legs in the vulgar way Mary liked to sit, then tugged the musical instrument between them and plucked a couple of strings. It was, of course, hopelessly out of tune after the journey and weeks of unuse.

Fiddling with it briefly, Kyla tightened a string here and there as she settled in her mind on a song to sing. It was a difficult task, for while all Mary's songs were rude or suggestive, being a lady, Kyla had rarely paid enough attention to remember all the words. Eventually, she came up with one, unsure though whether it was actually one song, or a combination of two.

It mattered little, she supposed, so long as it did the trick.

Galen shifted in his seat, trying not to look at his "wife" as she tuned her harp. Her hair was a mess from her search for the instrument and that combined with the way she sat, perched on the edge of

her chair, knees spread wide, skirt pulled up and
dangling between them leaving her ankles, calves,
and knees bared as they cuddled the harp, was a bit
distressing. She looked like a tavern wench, nothing
like the delicate noble woman she was supposed
to be.

He was relieved when she cleared her throat in
preparation to begin. Then she plucked a note, its
soft sound vibrating in the air as she tilted her head,
opened her mouth, and suddenly began to shriek at
the top of her lungs.

"Ohhhhhh, aaaaaa keg of rum, a keg of rum!
Ask me sirs and I'll bring ye some!
Ask for me, you can have that, toooooo!
I'll do the things your wife won't do!"

Galen gaped at the woman before him, his face
flushing, his hands clenching, and his eyes wide with
shock. She paused in her discordant braying to smile
at him sweetly. Then she plucked another string, filling the room with its brief sweet trill before she
tilted her head, opened her mouth, and continued to
belt out her song.

"Ohhhh, hohhh, on me knees or on me back,
I'm the best there is and that's a faaaaact!"

She paused to give him a lusty little wink there as
he began to make gasping, choking sounds, then
plucked another cord.

"I'll spread me legs and make ye welcome!
And even let ye squeeze me melo—"

Galen let out a squawk, lunging to his feet in dismay, but when he opened his mouth to say something—
anything—to stop her, he found himself choking and
coughing as the words stuck in his throat. His wife

was on her feet at once and at his side, thumping his back energetically. A little too energetically in his opinion.

"Are you all right, my lord? Do you need a drink? Shall I send for . . . ?" Her voice trailed away as he shook his head, clearing his throat as he straightened.

"Nay, nay I—"

"Good!" Giving him one last thump, she returned to her seat, hitched her skirt back up, and cuddled the harp again, then paused, muttering. "Now, where was I? Let's see . . . A keg of rum . . . la-da-de-dum, dum-de-dum, de-la, welcome . . . Ah! Aye, here we go!" Smiling at him charmingly as he sat reluctantly back in his own seat, she plucked another lilting note and continued,

"Ohhhh, I'lllll call ye love, I'll call ye ducky
And sure enough, ye can even—"

"Enough!" Galen roared, surging to his feet again, this time with his voice intact.

Kyla plucked another cord, and finished innocently, *"Pluck meeeeee!"*

Closing his eyes, Galen sank weakly back into the seat, his head shaking slightly back and forth as he wondered, with horror, what exactly he had done by marrying the wench. She was mad. No doubt about it. At this moment she even *looked* mad with her hair all wild, her cheeks flushed red with what he could only think was excitement, and her eyes sparkling with a sort of lunatic anticipation as if awaiting his praise!

"Well," she prompted suddenly, sounding impatient, and Galen sighed.

"Thank ye for the song," he managed to get out in a calm voice. "Mayhap we should retire now."

She looked as if he had struck her at those words, and Galen regretted that he had not managed some sort of praise for her attempt to entertain him. Still he simply didn't have it in him to do so. He wasn't much for lying, even if meant as a politeness.

"Fine!" she snapped, letting her harp thump back to the floor with a jangle of strings. Standing, she stepped around it and stomped over to the bed. She hesitated there, muttered something—he presumed to her imaginary friend—then threw herself across the width of the bed and rolled over so that she lay fully clothed across the bottom of the mattress staring at the ceiling.

Frowning, Galen moved slowly to the foot of the bed to peer down at her. "Do ye not think ye might wish to prepare first?"

She stiffened at that, then smiled at him sweetly. "Aye, of course! I do not know *what* I was thinking."

Launching off the bed, she moved to the nearest chest and began digging inside. Shaking his head, Galen turned away and moved back to the fire, pretending to stoke it in an effort to give her a moment of privacy. He could hear the rustle of clothing as she undressed. It went on and on and on. Just when he was beginning to lose patience, he heard the chest slam closed, the patter of her feet crossing the floor, then the whoosh of her dropping into bed once more.

Setting aside the iron, Galen straightened with relief. He turned to face the bed, frowning in confusion when he saw his wife there, lying flat across the bottom of it once more. She was not undressed, not stripped down to just her tunic even, but was apparently wearing more clothes than she had been the first time she had laid down. Now she had on one or two gowns more on top of the one she had been wearing earlier.

Moving to the end of the bed again, he scowled at her. "What are ye doing?"

"Awaiting you, of course," she answered dryly, then turned her head to the side and muttered *sotto voce,* "Nay, he's not dense. No denser than most men anyway. 'Tis not dense to ask a question."

Galen stiffened at that, and said a bit sharply, "Do ye not think it would have done ye better to remove your clothing rather than put more on?"

She turned back to peer at him in surprise. "Why, my lord, surely you know that the Church forbids consummation while naked?"

"Aye, well the Church can—" He paused abruptly when her eyes narrowed on him. Grimacing, he said dryly, "Well, mayhap ye could at least take one or two of your gowns off? Surely one gown, or even just your shift is clothing enough?"

"Nay."

"Nay?" he growled.

"Nay. I want to look nice for the consummation," she said simply. "Do you not think I look nice?" When he hesitated at that, she added, "Ernestene thinks I look lovely."

"Ernestene." His face twisted with disgust, then he muttered: "Well, I think you look hot."

Kyla grimaced slightly at that, because she was indeed hot. It was summer, and she had stoked the fire to an infernal level, and then he had gone over and stoked it some more in a really rather nice effort to give her privacy. Which *really* had nothing to do with the situation at hand, she berated herself, then sighed. She had donned not one, not two, but four more gowns. She would have put on more, but none of the other outfits would fit over top of the five she already wore. She was not just hot, she was boiling, but she wasn't going to tell him that. "Actually, I am a touch chilled," she lied. "But if you are warm, mayhap you should beat down the fire a bit."

Her husband's answer was to lean forward and place his hand to her forehead as if checking for a temperature. Apparently not finding any, he straightened, frowned at her with displeasure, then began to work at his own clothes.

Kyla watched him, her mind not really on what he was doing, but quickly sorting through all the rest of the rules that the Church had about when sex was forbidden, hoping to come upon one that would delay things at least long enough for her to find a way out of this marriage. According to the Church, sex was forbidden during Lent, Advent, Whitsun week and Easter week . . .

No help there, she thought with a sigh, then continued on with feast days, fast days, Sundays, Wednesdays, Fridays, and Saturdays. Today, unfortunately, was a Thursday and was neither a feast nor a fast day. She sighed unhappily, then continued to tick the forbiddens off on her fingers. Never during daylight, never in a church, never for any other purpose than to produce a child, and never when the woman was either bleeding, pregnant, or nursing . . .

She paused on that thought, briefly considering telling him that it was her woman's time, but that seemed a bit cowardly to her. In fact, now that she thought about it, pretending to be mad was rather cowardly, too. He seemed a nice, reasonable sort of fellow. Surely if she simply explained that she didn't wish to be married to him, he would allow her to—

Her thoughts died abruptly as his plaid hit the floor and he stood before her in only his shirt. It was soft and white and draped his muscled body almost lovingly, reaching halfway to his knees. And somehow, the pureness of it seemed to emphasize the strength and width of his shoulders. Kyla admired them briefly, then glanced down at his legs. Hard and strong and nicely shaped, and—GOOD GOD—What was she thinking of, laying there ogling him like that, she berated herself as he reached for the hem of his long shirt, to take it off.

"The Church says—" she bleated now, positive that if he took that top off, she would be lost.

"Aye, I ken," he sighed wearily. "Intercourse is forbidden whilst naked. But I swim naked, bathe naked, and sleep naked—and it seems silly to keep my clothes on to consummate this marriage, then get up to remove them afterward." Despite his words, he apparently decided to leave the shirt on for a moment more. Shaking his head, he climbed onto the few spare inches of bed she had left him, then scowled at her. "Do ye not think we could at least lie the right way?"

"This *is* the right way," Kyla answered nervously, scooting slightly to the side in an effort to put space between them. She suddenly found his nearness terribly distracting.

Apparently, thinking she was making room for him, Galen spread himself out on his side beside her, and peered over at her with a sigh.

Eyes wide, Kyla watched him nervously, then when he reached out to grasp the lacings of her top gown, she opened her mouth and let loose a shriek. When he immediately withdrew his hand in surprise, Kyla's mouth closed, ending her wail.

He gaped at her uncertainly for a moment, and Kyla managed a sweet smile. But when he reached for her lacings again, her mouth opened on another keening cry. His hand was again quickly removed, and her mouth closed, her shriek silenced once more.

This time her smile had no effect.

"What are ye doing?" he asked between gritted teeth.

"Nothing."

"Ye were screaming."

"Nay."

"Nay?"

"That was Ernestene practicing her singing," Kyla murmured calmly.

He didn't appear to know what to say to that, and Kyla was just congratulating herself that she had finally struck on a way to convince him she was mad and therefore to annul the marriage, when he reached for her lacings again. Eyes widening, Kyla popped her mouth open, another cry ready to issue forth, only to have his other hand suddenly plop over her mouth, silencing her as he worked one-handed at her clothing. She didn't fight. She had no right. He was her husband, unfortunately. But she did glare at him over the hand on her mouth as he fumbled at her lacings. It took him several moments, but he did finally manage to undo them. Then he began to try to tug the first gown off of her shoulders, but it was a difficult task, made more so by the fact that she lay on her back and he only had one hand to work with.

It took her by surprise when he suddenly removed the hand from her mouth. So much so that he had sat up and tugged her into a sitting position beside him before she remembered to continue shrieking again. The moment she began, though, his palm covered her mouth once more and he scowled.

"Nay," he said. When she arched her eyebrows in challenge, his own brow furrowed back at her. "If Ernestene cannot be quiet, I will have to ask her to leave," he threatened. Kyla ground her teeth in frustration. He was supposed to wish to annul the marriage, not humor her!

Her irritation was replaced with surprise when he suddenly stood, tugging her along with him. Then he began to again work at her clothes. He did so with the same gentle attention a mother would give undressing a child. There was nothing sexual in it, nothing in the least provocative. He merely unlaced the top gown, tugged it over her shoulders, down her arms, around her waist, then over her hips and pushed it down to pool around her feet. Then he did the same with the second gown. Kyla was as stiff as a board by the time he got to her last dress, her eyes wide, an odd tension building inside her and making her breath come in shallow bursts despite his gentle nonchalance.

When he straightened, Kyla didn't wait to see what he would do next. She whirled away, crawled onto the bed, then flipped onto her back again, spread-eagled, to stare at the ceiling blindly. She heard Galen release a sigh, then a rustling drew her gaze around to see that he had walked to the foot of the bed and was now shrugging his shirt off over his head, leaving him naked. Completely naked. Totally naked. Manhood-swinging-in-her-face naked.

Good Lord! Kyla had been told the facts of life quite bluntly long ago by Morag. She also had a brother, whom she had seen naked on several occasions when they were just children, but still, despite all this she nearly gasped aloud at the sight before her. Her brother Johnny had never stirred her like this. She had never thought his warrior's form especially attractive to look upon like that of this man. Her gaze devoured the MacDonald's wide, muscular shoulders and powerful arms, heating as it slid over his chest, taking in the way it gleamed in the amber glow from the fire, and how his flat stomach rippled as his arms moved. He was, quite simply, beautiful to behold. And the very sight of him was having an effect that was most detrimental to her well-being and the plan she had been trying to carry out. It was bad enough that he was prosperous and a good, strong leader, that his people were happy and content, that, so far, he even seemed relatively nice. But looking at him now was making her question whether she really had any reason not to wish to marry him.

Then her gaze dropped to the limp member waving in her face, and disappointment overcame all her wonder and, yes, even lust, of a moment earlier. She knew enough, about the facts of life to be able to see that the poor man had no more interest in consummating this marriage than she'd had when he'd first entered the room. Which left her to wonder what on earth they were doing.

"If we do not consummate, it could still be

annulled," she blurted as he started to climb onto the bed beside her once more. That made him pause, his eyes finding her face and settling there rather blankly.

"What?"

"I said, if we do not consummate it, this marriage can still be annulled. On the grounds that I am addled."

"I suppose it could," he agreed slowly, appearing to consider it briefly before shaking his head. "But that'd hardly be a fitting reward fer yer courage would it?"

Kyla's eyes widened in amazement. "What do you mean?"

"Well, it would hardly be just of me to set ye aside fer something that wasn't yer fault."

"It would not be unjust at all since that is what I want," Kyla announced with a scowl.

"But since yer addled, yer not really capable of deciding what's best for ye, and that leaves it to me to decide for ye. And I *know* ye would be safer and happier with me than ye could possibly be with the Mac-Gregor, so I could not possibly annul this marriage." Smiling at her gently, he took her hand and patted it like a father soothing a child or old woman. "Never fear, m'lady wife, I'll look after ye with care. Ye'll be guarded at all times and I'll do what I can to ensure yer happiness."

Kyla's eyes widened in horror at that assurance as she realized what she had done. While she had certainly succeeded at convincing him that she was indeed mad, he was not intending now to annul the marriage. No. All she had managed to do was to ensure that she would be treated like a child, guarded against her own insanity at all times, and given no freedom at all. Desperation welling up in her, she cried, "But, surely you can not wish to be married to me?"

"Nay."

She blinked in surprise at that, a certain amount of effrontery rising up within her. "What do you mean, nay?"

"Well and sure enough I'd hoped for more in me wife than this," he admitted honestly. "I'd hoped for a partner, a helpmate. A woman who'd stand beside me and help me rule my people. Not a madwoman I'd have to protect my people from . . ." He sighed sadly. "And I had that briefly, ere the fevers rushed yer madness along."

Kyla blinked, rather surprised to find the idea of standing and ruling beside this man attractive. Most men wished to rule all, including their wives. Then she frowned slightly. "What do you mean, you had that briefly before the fevers rushed my madness along?"

He looked surprised that she would even ask. "Well, ye were all I could have wished for in a wife ere they did their damage. Intelligent, witty, courageous." He sighed again miserably. "Aye, ye were the perfect wife."

Kyla felt another pinch of regret that she had convinced him that she no longer was those things, then asked suspiciously, "Now, how would you know what I was like ere the fevers? We met after they had taken hold."

He smiled slightly with memory. "Ye talked a lot on the way here. Actually, ye talked nonstop." He shrugged apologetically at the dirty look she threw him. "Some of it even made sense, and what didn't make sense, yer old hag explained. She told us tales of yer growing up, of yer skills and abilities, of how ye bested your brother repeatedly over the years with yer sly intelligence, of how ye charmed all with yer wit, of how ye saved yer brother . . ." He shook his head sadly. "I warrant each and every one of me men was just a little bit in love with ye by the time we arrived here."

Kyla stared at him, charmed by this confession. He had a lovely smile and his eyes were gentle at the moment, crinkled with wry humor. He had a nice face. He was a nice man, and the more time she spent with him, the harder it was for her to remember just why it was exactly that she didn't want to be married to him. Had there really even been a reason? Or had she just resented it because she'd had no say in it? That was probably closer to the truth, she acknowledged to herself. She had no reason to turn this man away, to wish this marriage annulled. In fact, with every passing moment in his presence, Kyla became more certain that she could have a good life with him. A happy life. Ruling at his side. Helping him to tend to the daily troubles of being laird here. Bearing his children . . .

Lots of children. At the moment, that idea was uppermost in her mind. His face was nice, his hair nice, but he had a beautiful body. Just being close to him like this was building an incredible excitement within her. She wanted to touch him, wanted to press and feel her naked body against him. Have his strong arms close around her and cuddle her close. She wanted *him*.

Reaching out, she ran her fingers gently over his cheek, feeling the stubble of a day's growth. She saw his eyes widen in surprise at the touch and smiled slightly. If he had expected her to be shy, he had been mistaken. Kyla was nowhere near shy. Her brother had taught her to fight for what she wanted with anything and everything she had at hand. And she now wanted this man.

Lifting herself up on her elbow slightly, she pressed her lips to his, rubbing them curiously back and forth, enjoying the feel of their lips meshing. A smile of triumph curved her mouth as she felt him suddenly growing against her hip where he was nestled. He, too, was finally showing some interest in this endeavor. In the next moment there was no doubting his interest as he took over the kiss, his tongue surging out to part her lips and dive inside her mouth. Kyla tilted her head, her mouth opening wide, her own tongue slipping out to duel with his. She turned slightly, pressing her body to his, wishing her undertunic were not between them as his hands slowly began to move. She felt one hand on her outer leg, then it swept its way upward, riding beneath her gown to her hip, even as he tried to caress her with his other hand. She felt the tips of his fingers brush lightly over the under curve of her right breast and shuddered, but knew that he was hampered by the need for his elbow to remain in place on the bed to hold him up.

When he suddenly made a grunt of frustration in his throat and started to pull himself into a sitting position, she followed automatically rather than give up his lips. She felt him smile against her mouth with his own moment of triumph at that, but didn't care as he began to tug on the collar of her tunic. Reaching up to help him, Kyla pulled the gown to the edges of her shoulders, then wriggled her arms and shoulders helpfully as he tugged it downward.

An excited shudder ran through her as she pulled her arms out, and it dropped around her waist, leaving her upper body bare. She quickly pressed herself against him, moaning into his mouth as the hairs on his chest tickled the tips of her nipples. Then she felt one hand slide between their bodies and curve itself over her breast like a second skin.

Tingling under his touch, Kyla arched against him, her breathing becoming rapid as his other hand slid around to cup her buttocks. He kissed her until she was moaning a plea into his mouth. Only then did he grasp her more firmly, urging her upward onto her knees before him. She did as he urged, her head bending down, trying to maintain the kiss, but then he pulled his mouth away and she groaned in disappointment, only to gasp in the next moment as he pressed a kiss between the breasts now before him, then turned his head to catch and lave one nipple.

Clutching at his shoulders for balance, she tilted her head back and arched into the caress, a tortured moan slipping from her lips as his mouth suddenly left her breast, leaving it moist and cold in the open air. But as his lips closed over her other breast, she moaned again with pleasure and peered down on him, finding watching what he was doing even more erotic. His eyes were closed, his lips pursed around her nipple as he suckled.

As if her gaze were a physical thing he was aware of, his eyes suddenly popped open and he met her glance. He let the nipple slip from his lips, and, still watching her face, he slid his tongue out and deliberately laved the erect tip. Kyla felt like a log he had set a torch to. Dropping back onto her haunches, she claimed his mouth again, her own tongue coming out aggressively, demanding attention. She heard him chuckle deep in his throat but found no time for self-consciousness. She wanted his kisses, she wanted him, she wanted it all.

Kyla had become so engrossed in devouring his mouth and arching her body into his that she didn't at first notice when he began to urge her backward onto the bed. She merely tightened her arms fiercely around her neck, keeping him where she wanted as she arched into him. In fact, she didn't notice until he caught her hands in his and drew them relentlessly away from him, forcing them down onto the bed on either side of her head. Then he tore his mouth away.

Panting as if she had been running, Kyla glared at him briefly, then gasped and moaned as his lips dipped down to one ear and began to explore there. She had never noticed her ears being especially sensitive before, but now nerves there were screaming with excitement, making her almost mindless.

She stood it as long as she could, her hands clenching beneath his where he held them down, her toes curling. She cried out and stretched her neck, wanting to evade and prolong the sensation at the same time. But he was already moving on, his lips skimming her throat, her collarbone, cresting her breast. He stopped for another lick there, then dipped further, sliding provocatively over her stomach and setting it quivering in reaction as he continued downward, pushing her tunic before him.

He had released her hands by now, but she wasn't really aware of it. Her fingers were now clenched into the linens on the bed, her nails digging into and through them right into her palm. She noticed neither, though, as her senses followed his trail down over one hip. He raised himself up slightly, quickly and efficiently slid the gown the rest of the way off, and knelt between her legs. He paused then to glance toward her face, and Kyla held her breath, her own gaze meeting his before dropping boldly to the evidence of his arousal, and there was no mistaking his interest now. Her eyes were still fixed there when he shifted backward a bit on the bed, dropped to his stomach, urged her legs further apart, and suddenly lowered his face between her thighs.

Kyla nearly bucked right off the bed, her body going tense, arching upward as he did things she had never imagined anyone doing. Good Lord, she wasn't even positive *what* he was doing, but she liked it. . . . It felt so good.

That was her last coherent thought as she rode the wave he set her on, her body arching and tightening and quivering until she suddenly cried out, her shoulders rising up off the bed as her body convulsed with such intense pleasure that she could have sobbed from it.

Consumed by the sensations overwhelming her, Kyla wasn't really aware of his moving until he was on top of her. Her arms moved automatically around his neck, her mouth pressing against the salty skin of his shoulder as she felt something nudge against her still spasming flesh. Then he surged into her with an abrupt thrust that made her gasp.

Freezing fully inside her, Galen dropped his head to her chest and they both lay as still as granite for a moment. Then he lifted his head and peered at her cautiously. "I'm sorry," he shifted slightly, testing their fit and shook his head slightly. "Damn, yer tight. Are ye all right?"

"Aye," she breathed, shifting carefully to wrap her legs around his hips in an effort to ease the discomfort she was experiencing.

Galen caught the wince that flashed across her face as she moved and narrowed his eyes in concern. "Yer not all right."

"It isn't what you think, I—" She sighed unhappily. " 'Tis my back. The salve has worn off. But 'tis not so very bad," she added pleadingly, then held her breath as he continued to simply frown at her. That breath slid out on a sigh of disappointment when he withdrew himself and ordered her onto her stomach. Doing as he asked, Kyla turned on the bed, thinking he meant to tend to her back, ending this sweet torment. Confusion filled her when, rather than removing her bandages, he ran a hand lightly over her rounded buttocks.

"We must be careful," he announced and Kyla nodded jerkily, her attention focused on the hand caressing her, teasing her briefly before slipping between her legs to find the spot that had so aroused her earlier.

Kyla bit the bunched up bedclothes beneath her face, her legs easing apart to offer him better access as he continued his caress.

"That's it, sweetling," he murmured as she wriggled against his touch, then frowned as his gaze slid to her scar. He had thought to spare her back by positioning her like this, but was now afraid of hurting her with his own weight. He considered the problem for a moment, then slid his other hand beneath her stomach and pressed upward.

Confused, Kyla shifted onto her hands and knees on the bed and glanced over her shoulder curiously, her eyes turning round as her husband knelt behind her. Catching her expression, he grinned, and slid into her from behind with no more ado than a light grasping of her hips.

Fingers digging into the bedclothes beneath her, Kyla experienced the sensation of him filling her, then gasped again and stiffened as his hand slid back down and past her stomach to find the core of her once more. Still holding her by the hip with one hand, he began to urge her back into him and away with that hand while the other continued fondling her in a way that had her gasping and crying out. Within moments, her body was shuddering, her muscles convulsing around him.

Galen waited until she had stilled, his aroused flesh buried deep within hers, then began to fondle her again as he eased himself out. Kyla shuddered violently under his touch, shaking her head in denial, then moaning as he eased back into her, amazed to find a fire she had thought dead bursting back to life.

"Is it not done?" she gasped in surprise.

"Do you want it to be?" he gasped from behind her, and Kyla shook her head violently. Nay, she didn't want it to be over. At that moment, she never wanted it to end.

And it didn't until she found release again. This time, he arrived there with her.

Chapter 10

"WHAT?" Kyla gaped at Morag where she sat doing needlework by the fire, hardly able to grasp what the woman was saying.

"Ye heard me. He's out."

Kyla sank weakly into the chair across from her old nurse, oblivious to the waiting stares of the few people in the hall. Morag's friend Guin was silent and still, as were the two servant women who had been scrubbing diligently away at the trestle tables when she'd come below. The only other person present was Robbie, her guard for the day.

Robbie stood a few feet away, leaning against the hearth and peering into it as if lost in thought. In truth his ears were cocked and awaiting her reaction. He had no idea what it might be, but suspected it would not be good. New brides tended to expect attention from their husbands the day after consummating a marriage, and judging by his laird's wide smile that morn, he had got more than strife from his wife yestereve—despite the inauspicious beginning to the evening at supper. No doubt, Lady Kyla would take exception to his leaving her to her own devices today. Besides, his morning had been fairly lousy so far; he could hardly expect the pattern to change now.

Actually, things had been going that way since the day before when he had returned to his small cottage to find his wee wife in a foul temper and slamming things about. It seemed she had taken exception to their laird's behavior on the beach, thinking he had intended on seducing that poor *innocent* Iseabal she had met—"and him married and all."

Robbie had had quite a time getting her to be silent long enough to tell her that the lass she had befriended on the beach was none other than their laird's bride. Aelfread had been flummoxed by that information, and in truth she had not accepted it well. Staring at him as though he had suddenly sprouted another head and dropping into the nearest seat with amazement, she'd begun raving about the sneaky ways of the English and fie on that Sassenach wench for fooling her that way. By the time she was done and he had been able to drag her—protesting all the way—to the keep, their laird and lady had retired to their room.

He and Aelfread had had to hear secondhand of what had happened when Galen had toasted the marriage. Much to Robbie's surprise, where only moments before his wife had been cursing the Englishwoman, on learning that the lass had had no idea of the marriage—Robbie had forgot to mention that bit to his wife—Aelfread had changed allegiance at once.

In truth, he had avoided saying anything about the lass, since any mention of the woman who had given him the wound in his chest had sent his wife into fits. That being the case, Aelfread had had no idea that Kyla had been so ill at the time of the marriage that she had not even recalled it upon awaking. Upon learning that, Aelfread had then concluded that her sickness had likely induced her attack of Robbie as well; Kyla was forgiven. It all seemed clear, she said. Everything was Galen's fault.

Where before she had cursed their laird's new bride as a foolish Sassenach who knew not when to be grateful for such an honorable man's interference, she had turned to denouncing Galen for mishandling the whole situation. She now sympathized vociferously with Kyla's dismay and outrage.

Robbie shook his head now at the very memory. Women were a daft breed and impossible to understand at the best of times. Any man who thought differently was a fool. The moment you reckoned you had them figured out, you may as well cock up your toes in preparation for burial, for your very arrogance was sure to get you killed.

Realizing that the silence had dragged on quite awhile, Robbie glanced over his shoulder to see Lady Kyla still staring rather blankly into space. Frowning slightly at her reaction to a situation he had felt sure would infuriate her, he glanced toward her maid and cocked an eye in question. Morag shrugged.

"Lass?" Kyla peered up forlornly at Morag when her raspy voice caught her ear. "Be ye all right?"

Sinking back in her chair, she forced a nod. In truth, she was far from all right, but had no intention of letting that be known. The people here already thought her a silly fool incapable of looking after herself. She did not wish them to know just how foolish she really was. And she was coming to the conclusion that she was most definitely a fool of the first order.

Last night had been . . . Well, for her it had been a beautiful, exciting, eye-opening experience. She had come alive in the MacDonald's arms, experiencing

heights she had never imagined possible as he had
loved her throughout the night. She had gone to
sleep lying on her stomach upon his chest, her head
cushioned in the crook of his shoulder, her mind lulled
by the feel of his hands gently caressing her arms. She
had dreamed of a joyful life filled with laughter, children, and her husband.

She had awoken to an empty bed in a chill room,
thinking at first that her night of passion had been
imagined. But the bedclothes had been in a tumble
and her body had borne enough aches and pains to
assure her it had not been a dream.

Still, unable to keep back the smile that had been
bursting over her face, she had washed herself at the
basin by the bed, her mind drifting to memories of
the night before. She had remembered her dreams, as
well, of the long life and happiness she felt sure she
could find with the gentle lover of the night before.
Surely someone so gentle in their bedchamber would
be equally caring and considerate outside it. She'd
enjoyed a shiver of anticipation for the life ahead of
her. Everything would be different now. She had a
partner to travel through life with, a mate to bear
and raise children with, a people to belong to . . .

It wasn't until then that she had realized how
lonely and out of place her brother's marriage had
made her feel. Until Catriona, Forsythe had been her
home, its people her own. She had run the manor for
Johnny when he was away, which had been most of
the time. The people she had grown up with had accepted her word without question . . . until Catriona
had arrived. As Johnny's bride, she became mistress
there, taking over all the little chores that had been

Kyla's domain until then. She had tried to pretend that she did not mind stepping aside, but every time someone had approached and made an enquiry of the new Lady Forsythe, Kyla had felt a part of herself cringe from the reality that was so hard to face. Forsythe was no longer her home.

Somehow, the exchange of a few vows between Catriona and Johnny had changed everything for Kyla. She had gone from being lady of the manor to being the master's sister, a burden, until she could be married off and had a home to call her own. It had seemed patently unfair to Kyla, despite her knowing that it was natural, and her heart had ached at the loss of what she had always thought of as her family. Oh, the servants and villagers had not been cruel about it, nor had Johnny, nor even, in truth, Catriona. Her new sister-in-law had been neither overly cruel nor overly kind and considerate regarding the takeover, merely matter-of-fact.

Everyone else, however, had been exceedingly kind in all their dealings with her . . . and that had been the worst of it. Where she had once felt kindness and even affection from these people, she had suddenly sensed vague apologies and pity as they had glanced at her uncomfortably before turning to Catriona. Last night and this morning on arising, Kyla had thought that all changed. She had a home now thanks to this marriage. A home and people.

In a burst of enthusiasm, she had hurriedly dressed and rushed below stairs with some vague idea that her husband would be sitting at the table. He would glance up at her arrival, smile sweetly, kiss her gently, and wish her a good morrow, then urge her to sit with him and discuss her plans on this the first day of her role as Lady MacDonald, mistress of the manor. Such had not been the case.

She had realized before she had reached the bottom of the stairs that she had misjudged the time, that it was far later than she had thought. That had been her first disappointment, but she had rallied, thinking her husband would be about the keep somewhere and would be pleased upon her arrival wherever he was. Only that did not appear to be likely, since the man was off with his men in a boat, seeking lobsters or some such thing.

Well, she thought with a sigh, recovering some of her earlier mood, mayhap there would be no sweet kiss good morn or discussion of her plans for the day, but that did not mean that she could not at least set those plans into effect. This was her home now. It was well past time she took the trouble to look into its running, see if there were any things that could be improved upon, discuss meals with the cook.

Aye, meals. She would have a special feast arranged for this eve. It would be a belated celebration of their marriage. A grand—

"Ere ye start dashing about setting those plans I see festering in yer poor, woolly mind to action, ye should ken the MacDonald left orders that ye were to rest. Yer not to do anything while he's gone except needlework."

Kyla stiffened at that, wide eyes shooting to her old servant's wrinkled face. "What?" she asked with disbelief.

"Ye heard me. Needlework."

"Blast that!" she snapped after a prolonged pause of dismay. "I am mistress here now and there are things that will need my attention." Whirling on her heel, she headed directly toward the kitchen, aware that the giant Robbie was hard on her heels. It seemed things were not as different today as she had thought, much to her chagrin. She still had a guard, but was determined to ignore him. She was mistress here now. No doubt the man had been left to . . . Guard the madwoman, she realized suddenly, her steps slowing. Damn, she had not thought to clear that up last night. She frowned over that briefly, then straightened her shoulders and continued determinedly forward. Well, that didn't matter. She would clear that up tonight. In the meantime, she would just ignore her guard and go ahead with making a place for herself here.

So she thought. More the fool her, she realized with a sigh some half an hour later as she sank wearily back into the chair by the fire, defeat hanging over her like a cloud. She had accomplished absolutely nothing. Cook had smiled at her pleasantly, offered her food and drink to break her fast with, and listened politely to her questions until she had asked who ran the manor. He had glanced at Robbie then, and when Kyla had turned to the giant expectantly, he had murmured that Galen had always given the orders. When Kyla had then asked who this Galen was and if she might have a word with him, there had been a dead silence as the cook and Robbie had exchanged blank glances. Then, turning back to her with a wary, though somewhat pitying expression, the cook had suggested she return to her needlework.

Kyla had frowned over the obvious dismissal and had changed tactics, leaving the questions for now to announce her desire to have a celebratory feast that night. Cook had raised his eyebrows, then said that this Galen he'd spoken of had mentioned naught of that. Once again, he'd suggested she rest.

Realizing she would get nowhere with the man, Kyla had given up and stomped from the room, Robbie hurrying to keep up with her. In the great hall once more, she had hesitated, then approached the women working at the trestle tables. She had taken care to be polite and friendly but firm as she had asked them if they might tell her who this Galen was that been acting as chatelaine. Once again she had been met with dead silence for a moment, then they had ignored her question and suggested she rest, reminding her as they did that it was their laird's wish.

It seemed she would rest today, like it or not, she thought with irritation, her gaze shifting to the cold hearth of the fireplace. She sighed. She supposed it was all her own fault. She should have cleared up the issue of her sanity last night. Then, too, her expectations had perhaps been unrealistic. Her husband had given her no power as of yet here, not openly, and the servants were only attending what they saw as his wishes—but she wished they might have at least answered her questions ere ignoring her. Having been forced aside by her brother's wife, she had no wish to do so herself to someone else. She wished to meet and speak to this fellow who had borne the chore of running the estate for her husband. She wanted to compliment him on a job well done and assure him that he would always have a place and be needed here even as she made a little space for herself. But it seemed, as it stood, she had no need to reassure the man. The way things were arranged, she would have little chance of making room for herself.

Sighing, she stood abruptly and waited for Morag to peer at her. Once she had the woman's attention, she announced that since everyone insisted she rest, she would do so . . . in her room. With that, she swept above stairs and marched into her room, closing the door with a distinct slam as Robbie positioned himself across the hall.

The crash of the door made her feel a bit better . . . for all of a few moments. Then Kyla became restless. She wasn't tired. And she didn't much like being treated as if she had hit her head one too many times. She also didn't care for having her illusions shattered. But shattered they were. All her dreams of the night before had been just that, dreams. This was no love match, despite the passion of their joining. There was no reason for her to hold out any hope for happiness or contentment. She and her husband were strangers. More than strangers, she thought grimly as it suddenly occurred to her that she knew little about him. She had no idea if he had any family. For all she knew, this Galen might be a brother, or even an oddly named sister. Were his parents still alive? From which of them had he inherited his fiery hair? she wondered, sinking onto the side of the bed. And who—

Damn! She shot to her feet with dismay as she realized she had no idea of her husband's name even. Good God! What was the matter with her? At his mere touch the night before she had responded like a bitch in heat, and all to a man whose name she did not even know.

But he is your husband, some part of her brain reminded her, and Kyla shifted, then began to pace the room. Aye, my husband. It was acceptable to respond so to a husband, was it not? Even if she did not know his name. It was her duty even . . . Well, nay, perhaps not her duty. A wife was to suffer her husband's touch, true enough, but nowhere had she heard she was expected to enjoy it.

Sighing, she paused by the window, her gaze moving over the cloudless sky before dropping to peer at the small stretch of beach below. It was a long way down. The castle was built on a cliff and this side appeared to have been built directly on the edge of it. For protection, she supposed absently. It would be fair impossible to scale the cliff and then the castle wall itself. All in all, the small slash of a beach appeared to be a good hundred feet below her window.

Her gaze slid to the water and she sighed, silently pining to return to the simplicity of the day before. As tangled as her life had been then, between her worries for her brother and her concerns over what would become of her, she had all those concerns and more now. She felt positively enmeshed in problems. Yesterday she had escaped her worries, however briefly, and portrayed herself as a simple village woman with not a care in the world. And, briefly, she had felt that way. Today, she would give much for that feeling again.

And why could she not have it? she asked herself suddenly, stilling where she stood. She had escaped then, why could she not do so again? If she could slip past Robbie . . . Kyla grimaced at that. She had been lucky yesterday in Duncan's moving to the end of the hall, but Robbie was a solid soldier. Once at his post, he would not leave until someone else had taken his post. She knew that from her first day after the

MacDonald had left, Robbie had not left her side for a moment, not even to relieve himself.

But mayhap she could manage something, she thought with a smile as her gaze slid to the small bag on the bedside table that held the salve Morag had been putting on her back. It had been quite useful when her back had pained her so, but her back had been bothering her less of late. She only suffered pain now when she actually put strain on the wound by leaning on it, so had no real need for the salve. She suspected Morag knew as much, for the woman had not asked if she wished to have some applied when she had gone below stairs. Still, Robbie did not know that, which might work to her advantage.

Hurrying to the chest at the foot of the bed, she threw it open to grab up the plaid Morag had replaced the day before. One look at it was enough to make her grimace. She had not noticed yesterday, but the soft cloth was very badly covered with hay. What had she looked like yesterday?

Frowning, she rummaged through the chest again until she found the second plaid. Quickly unfolding it, she laid it out on the bed. With no reason to rush and after having seen the MacDonald pleat it for her the day before on the beach, she found it a lot easier to manage the garment now. Her pleats were not perfect by any means, but seemed good enough that she would pass for a Scot. That done, she hesitated, then moved to one of her own chests in search of the small chess set her brother had given her on her last birthday. Hooking it to her belt so that it hung half-hidden in the folds of the tartan's skirts, she took a deep breath, managed what she hoped was a pained wince and moved to the bedchamber door.

Robbie looked startled when she suddenly tugged the door open, then frowned as she poked her head out. "Is aught amiss, me lady?"

Expression pained, Kyla nodded. "I fear I forgot my back and lay upon it. Would that you could go below and send Morag to apply her salve?"

"Of course, right away." Turning, he headed quickly down the hall.

Kyla closed the door with a slight snap, then immediately opened it again, quickly unraveling her hair from its ornate coif upon her head as she waited. Once Robbie had descended the first few steps and disappeared from sight, she hurried down the hall as silently as she could. Robbie was only halfway down the stairs when she reached them, so she waited there a moment until he finished descending, then crept down, her eyes scanning the room as she went.

Positive she was awaiting her maid above, Robbie did not bother to look around as he made his way toward the fireplace. Guin's head was bent to her mending, and Morag was blocked from her view by Robbie's enormous girth. As for the two women by the trestle tables, they appeared deep in discussion as they worked and did not notice her slip silently out the keep door.

Unlike the day before, she did not hesitate on the steps, but moved quickly down them and straight for the gate, relieved to see that no one seemed to notice her exit from the castle. Once through the gates, she quickened her pace, heading for the beach where she had met Aelfread. She had no fear that

Morag would give her away. That woman was a trustworthy and smart servant. As soon as she saw the open chest with its missing plaid and Kyla's own gown tossed on the bed, Morag would know what her mistress was about and keep her secret. That meant that she had several hours to enjoy the fresh air and hopefully play a game or two of chess with her new friend before she must return to the castle. Needlework, indeed.

"The salve, ye say?" Morag frowned at the man blankly for a moment, then muttered under her breath and got to her feet.

Robbie waited until she had set her needlework aside, then turned to lead her back above the stairs, his own feet eating up the distance twice as fast as her smaller shuffling steps. Pausing at the door, he glanced back to see the woman still only halfway up the hall and silently urged her to hurry as he rapped lightly on the solid wooden door.

"Morag is here, me lady," he called, then awaited a response . . . and waited. Frowning, he turned toward the old woman, just catching an odd expression on her face before she suddenly picked up her step and hurried toward the door.

"I will see to her," she muttered, trying to hurry past him, but Robbie had an unpleasant suspicion creeping over him. He thrust the door open before she could get at it. The empty room confirmed his fears quite thoroughly. Growling a curse, he hurried back down the hall.

Aclfread was seated on the sand, sorting through a basket of weeds. She glanced up when Kyla's shadow fell upon her, then raised a hand to shield her eyes from the sunlight, her eyes widening as she realized who it was. Aelfread was on her feet at once. "Me lady!"

Kyla grimaced at those words, embarrassment covering her face briefly. "You know," she murmured unhappily.

Aelfread nodded. "Robbie told me last night ere we joined the table at sup."

"I did not see you at table last night," Kyla admitted, "but I fear I was a mite distracted at the time."

"Aye." Her expression tightened somewhat. "So I heard. We were late to sup. Ye and the laird had retired ere we arrived."

Kyla nodded again, then hesitated, her gaze dropping to the sand at her feet briefly before she took a deep breath and peered at the other woman. "I am sorry I lied. I mean I did not lie, *really*. Iseabal is my middle name, but I am sorry I did not give you my true first name. I only did so because I was not supposed to be out and I feared being forced back to the castle. I hope it doesn't stop us from being friends."

Aelfread shook her head, a shy smile slowly curving her lips. "Nay. Actually, I came down here today in the hopes that you might come by again. I enjoyed talking to you yesterday."

Kyla sagged with relief. Smiling widely now, she tugged the bag at her waist out for her new friend to see.

"I thought mayhap we could play chess. You said yesterday you missed the game and—"

"Don't tell me there is a board in there?" Aelfread

was eyeing the small pouch curiously, so Kyla opened it and tugged the little board out for her to see.

" 'Tis small so that it can be carried about easily. My brother had it made special for me." She tugged out a couple of pieces so the other woman could see the fine workmanship in the carving.

" 'Tis lovely," Aelfread murmured, then glanced about the beach with a frown. "But I wouldn't wish ye to lose any o' the pieces in the sand." Biting her lip, she glanced up the path briefly, then nodded as if coming to a decision. "Come. We will go to the cottage to play. We can have something to drink there and have no fear of losing any of the little men while we play."

Dropping the pieces back into their pouch, Kyla tightened the strings to close it, then let it drop to her side as Aelfread quickly picked up her basket.

"I will not be taking you away from anything important?" she asked, following as Aelfread started up the path.

The other woman tossed a smile at her over her shoulder. "Nay. Actually I came to the beach hoping ye might come along." Spying Kyla's surprise, the other woman admitted, "I don't have many friends here yet. I guess I'm not very good at making them. I hadn't realized how lonely I had become until yesterday when I met ye. Yesterday was a nice change fer me."

"And for me," Kyla admitted honestly. " 'Tis why I came out again today."

Aelfread glanced at her sharply. "Ye haven't slipped away again, have ye? 'Twas quite a stir over it yesterday, ye ken."

Kyla frowned at that. " 'Tis what Morag said as well, but my husband did not appear the least distressed at sup." Her lips twisting, she muttered, "If anything, I seemed the only one distressed."

Catching the half-whispered phrase, Aelfread slowed her steps as they reached the main path, glancing at her curiously. "It was said ye were fair upset when ye retired. They were taking bets when we arrived on whether ye would even allow his lairdship into the room, but he didn't return below . . ."

Kyla felt herself flush, but, clearing her throat, she merely said, " 'Tis true, I was none too pleased when I got above stairs. We had words."

"Words, hmm? I fear there would have been more than words to deal with had it been me," the wee woman announced. "I fear I have something of a temper. Still, 'twas wrong of them not to mention the wedding to ye."

"Aye. Even Morag did not mention it," Kyla informed her with a grimace.

The woman's eyebrows rose at that. "Yer maid? She knew and didn't tell ye?"

"Aye."

Aelfread fell silent as they reached the first row of cottages along the path. Smiling and nodding at an old woman seated on a bench outside one of them, she led Kyla to the third little hut in the row and ushered her inside.

Robbie hurried down the path to the beach and paused, frowning as his gaze slid over the empty stretch of sand. He had thought for sure he would find Lady Kyla here. He had been so sure, he had come directly here, not even pausing to call out an alarm and gather men to help him search. Now he peered over the abandoned shoreline and cursed himself for a fool. Galen would be furious when he found out he had lost his wife—for real this time.

Chapter 11

KYLA'S gaze slid around the cozy interior of the small cottage. A good-sized table seemed to be the centerpiece. There was a fireplace that appeared to be used for both heat and cooking. Two chairs sat before that, both plain but sturdy. One corner of the room was taken up with a bed. By itself, the room would have seemed cramped and gloomy, but Aelfread had added touches here and there that made it charming.

"Has she been with ye long?"

Kyla glanced toward the other woman. While she had been looking around, Aelfread had fetched two mugs and a pitcher of meade and was now setting all three items on the table. Kyla moved to the table now. "Who?"

"Yer maid. Ye said even she didn't tell ye about the wedding and I wondered had she been with ye long?" she explained, reminding her of the conversation they had been having before entering the cottage.

"Oh. Yes." Kyla sank onto the bench and began unhooking the bag at her waist as Aelfread took a seat across from her. "Morag. She is like a mother to me. She has been with me all my life."

Aelfread leaned forward to help Kyla set up the chess pieces on the board. "Why didn't she tell ye about the wedding?"

"She said she wished not to upset me," Kyla said dryly, then sighed. "In truth, I think she was waiting for me to get to know him better so that the news would not be such a blow. Only he was not around long enough for me to get to know. I have yet to even have a conversation with the man . . . that I know of."

The petite redhead set the last of her chessmen in place, then peered at her curiously. "What do ye mean, 'that I know of'?"

Kyla hesitated, then admitted a bit wryly, "Well, it seems I was a trifle talkative while down with fever. Too talkative. I told one and all of the time my brother Johnny ruined a dress of mine and I filled his bed with manure for revenge."

"I did that to me brother as well once," Aelfread told her, grinning widely, then her expression turned wry as she added, "He still hasn't forgiven me for it."

"As I recall, Johnny was none too pleased, either," Kyla laughed, then sighed unhappily as she thought of her brother and wondered if he had recovered or was now dead.

Taking in her expression, Aelfread remembered Robbie telling her about Kyla's brother's woes. She reached out to pat her hand. "Yer fretting over him?"

Nodding, Kyla stared blankly at the chessboard, then gave a harsh laugh. When Aelfread raised her eyebrows at the sound, Kyla merely shrugged and shook her head. "I was just thinking that this time yesterday I was praying he would hurry and get well so that he would send an escort to free me from this place."

"And now?"

"And now I know there is no escape," she muttered bitterly.

"Surely, 'tisn't so bad?" Aelfread murmured worriedly.

Kyla was silent for a moment, then glanced at her. "You asked me what happened when we retired and I said we had words, which is true, but after the words . . . we . . . er . . . consummated it. The marriage I mean."

"Did ye now?" Her gaze slid down to the board between them.

"Aye. Well, he seemed to think it necessary."

"O' course he did."

Kyla hardly noticed the dryness of the other woman's tone, her mind was on more upsetting matters as she whispered: "I do not even know his name."

Aelfread raised her head sharply, amazement on her face. "What?"

"I said, I do not even know his name," Kyla repeated grimly. "I am married to the man. Did things with him last night that I wouldn't even have done with . . . Well with anyone, yet I do not even know his name."

"*What?!*"

Seeing the total bewilderment on the other woman's face, Kyla clarified for her. "We were never properly introduced. Morag always refers to him as the MacDonald and everyone else calls him 'me laird.' I do not know his name."

Aelfread accepted that disclosure with a blink, then sank back on the bench, seeming at a total loss as to what to say.

Kyla nodded. "You can see what a spot I am in. Somehow I do not think this is the path a normal marriage takes. At least I am sure most women know their husbands' names, if nothing else, before indulging in such intimate . . . er . . . frolicking."

"The lack-witted oaf!"

Kyla's eyes widened in amazement and Aelfread waved her hand in disgust.

"M'lady, after these months of marriage to Robbie, it has become me sorry conclusion that men are God's most lack-witted of creatures. They charge about doing this and that, but never bother with the important stuff like actually *telling* someone about it . . . Or even introducing themselves." Shaking her head, she glanced toward the board again, muttering. "His name is Galen."

Kyla gave a start at that. "Galen? Well, *he's* been acting as chatelaine then."

"What?"

"Well, you see, when I got up this morn Galen was already gone. I thought to take on some of the duties as mistress and wished to speak to whomever was in charge of them now. When I asked who that was, everyone kept saying Galen, then when I asked who Galen was, the servants all seemed to get quite distressed." Amusement tugged at her lips now. " 'Tis no wonder they reacted so. They must have thought it odd for me to ask such a question."

"Oh, damn!" Aelfread leapt to her feet and began to pace the small stretch of floor on the other side of the table.

"Now what is the matter?"

"Don't ye see?" She asked, turning on Kyla with wide, distressed eyes.

"That will just be another incident that they will hold up as proof that yer mad," she pointed out grimly.

"Aye." Kyla sighed glumly, then blinked and peered up at Aelfread. "You do not think I am mad, do you?"

"Me?" She clucked her tongue and shook her head firmly. "Nay, of course not. But *I* have talked to you." She sighed dispiritedly and admitted, "I tried to tell Robbie that you weren't crazy last night, but he wouldn't even listen to me on the matter." She was silent for a moment, then murmured, "Robbie says the witch said—"

Kyla waved her to silence, a disgusted expression crossing her face. "Morag was hoping it would convince the MacDonald he should not marry me."

"I fear it did not work," Aelfread said, her lips tipping up with slight amusement.

"I had noticed that," Kyla muttered dryly, then moaned. "I am married to a stranger and mistress over people who think me mad. . . . Aelfread, what am I to do?"

Her friend looked uncertain, then sighed and admitted, "I don't know."

When Kyla began to chew on her lip worriedly, Aelfread patted her hand again. "I shall think of something. I'll think on it tonight and come up to the keep on the morrow. We will work it out, never fear. Now come, let us not think on it for now. Let's play chess."

* * *

It was a serious case of déjà vu. One that Galen was not happy to relive. "What do ye mean 'she is missing'?"

Morag winced at the MacDonald's roar and shook her head. "Just what I said. She is missing. She snuck out. She sent that great mountain of a man to fetch me and while his back was turned she slipped out. He's out looking for her now. I can't—" She paused as the keep door flew open and Robbie came in.

"Where is she?" Galen snapped, hurrying to meet his man.

Robbie had been told that the laird was back. He had not been happy to hear it; he was even less so now with the news he had to give him. "I haven't found her."

"*What?!*"

Robbie winced at that roar, but explained quickly, "I thought mayhap she had returned to the beach, but she wasn't there, so I rounded up some men and we've scoured every inch of the island. She is nowhere to be seen."

Kyla could tell the moment she reached the entrance to the bailey that something was amiss. The bailey itself seemed more crowded with people than usual and there was a buzz of tension in the air that set her on edge even before the men at the gate spotted her and started grimly forward. When the two men clapped hands on her arms and began dragging her toward the keep, Kyla immediately set up a struggle, aware of the silence that was spreading around the bailey as her arrival was noted.

"What the Devil is going on?" she asked with

amazement as she was propelled up the front steps, but the men merely continued forward. She was still struggling and muttering as they opened the keep doors and hustled her inside.

"Nowhere?! *Nowhere?!* My wife is damned well *somewhere!* I want her found!"

"We found her, me laird!"

For a moment, Kyla was too stunned by the distress obvious in her husband's voice as he had bellowed those words to realize that the men presently strong-arming her across the hall were claiming to have "found" her. Once their words sank in, however, she frowned and struggled free of their hold. "No one *found* me, I was on my way back into the bailey when these two—" Her voice died as Galen turned toward her and she caught the fury on his face. Goodness! He looked about to explode. Clearing her throat, she forced a small smile. "How went your fishing trip?"

Kyla could almost hear the rumble of thunder as the storm clouds rolled across his face. When he clenched his hands in rage and took a step toward her, nothing on earth could have kept her where she stood. Turning on her heel, she raced up the stairs to their bedchamber, crashed into the room, then immediately set about barricading the door with as many chests as she could move. She had no idea if her husband was prone to violence . . . and she had absolutely no intention of finding out just now.

She had just moved the last chest into place when a light tap sounded at the door. Stiffening, she peered at the panel of wood, cleared her throat, then asked, "Who is it?"

"Morag."

Kyla hesitated briefly, then: "Are you alone?"

"Aye."

Cursing, she shifted from one foot to the other briefly, then, muttering under her breath, began shifting the chests again. With the last one out of the way, she tugged the door open cautiously and peered out, stepping aside to let the old woman in when she saw that she was indeed alone.

"What is he doing?" she asked, shoving the first chest back into place.

"He's gone to fetch Tommy to watch ye."

Kyla paused at that and straightened. "He has?"

"Aye."

She thought briefly, then, "What of Robbie?"

Morag raised her eyebrows. "What? Are ye deaf now? He dressed the man down something awful. Called him a fool, amongst other things, and sent him home. Said he couldn't watch a kitten worth beans."

Kyla bit her lip at that, guilt assailing her for getting the man in trouble. She had heard Galen roaring away below, but had paid little attention to what he was saying as she had hurriedly been shoving nearly the entire contents of the room against the door. Sighing, she let her shoulders sag. "He is very angry, isn't he?"

"Oh, aye. I'd say so," Morag said dryly and moved back toward the door.

"Where are you going?" Kyla asked, following her anxiously.

"Out of harm's way. I just came to warn ye he'll no doubt still be angry when he returns with Tommy."

"You are leaving me alone?" Kyla cried with alarm as she opened the door.

"Ye got yerself into this one, child," she said calmly,

then seeing the fear on Kyla's face she relented a bit and patted her arm. "He's a fair man. Ye'll get no more than ye deserve."

With that, she slid from the room. Kyla stood briefly, staring at the door with dismay, then hurried to the chest to fetch her other plaid. Draping it over herself like a shawl, she hurried to the door and slid out into the hall. His giving her no more than she deserved was a bit less than reassuring at that moment. In his anger, who knew what he might think her deserving of?

"*She's* daft? *She* is?" Aelfread glared at her husband furiously.

Kyla had left only a few short moments before Robbie had stomped into the cottage. Banging the door open, he had charged in, then crashed about the cottage, muttering under his breath. Aelfread had been gaping at her usually placid husband in amazement when he had suddenly turned on her to announce in something close to a roar, "*That silly bitch the laird married is as daft as the day is long and will be nothing but trouble 'til the day she dies.*"

Having just spent the afternoon being demolished at chess by that "*daft*" woman and now counting her as friend, Aelfread was a little less than impressed. She had no problem letting her husband know it, either. "It seems to me 'tis *ye men* that have gone soft in the head!"

Whirling around in shock at those words, Robbie glared at the small redhead now facing him, hands on her hips. "And what would ye be meaning by that?"

"Not a thing," she said dryly, then snapped, "Did

it never occur to all ye *fine* men to introduce her to the man?"

"What?!"

"Ye heard me!"

"Aye, I heard ye! But I don't have any idea what the bleeding hell yer talking about!"

Pausing to take a deep breath, Aelfread exhaled slowly, then explained, "She was here today—"

"Here! Right *here? This* is where she was?" The veins in his throat began to bulge at this news. He had searched everywhere on the island for that woman and all that time she had been right here in his own home.

"Aye. We played chess."

"*Chess?!*"

Ignoring his mounting fury, Aelfread nodded. "Aye. And talked. And Kyla told me she didn't even ken Galen's name ere today."

Robbie peered at her blankly at that, then grunted in triumph. "There ye are then! She's daft. Soft in the head. Looney as—"

"Ye never introduced them!" Aelfread interrupted with frustration.

"Who?"

"Lady Kyla and Laird Galen!"

He peered at her as if she had gone mad. "Why the Devil would I be introducing them? They're man and wife."

"Well, I've no doubt ye introduced yerselves. Could ye no' take the trouble to introduce the man she'd married? The poor lass didn't even ken his name."

"Now who is it gone soft in the head?" He snorted with derision and plopped onto one of the benches that lined the table. "Didn't ken his name? Indeed! If she didn't ken it, 'twas because she couldn't keep it in her head long enough to remember it."

"I tell ye, she wasn't told his name!" Aelfread snapped furiously.

"Everyone knows his name," Robbie snapped back.

"Everyone calls him *me, laird!*" Aelfread roared. "And I've no doubt, from all I've heard of this sorry tale, that none of ye fine men thought to introduce him."

Robbie looked stunned for a moment, then rallied to bluster, "Well, 'tis sure I am, the laird—"

"Him?" 'Twas Aelfread's turn to snort in derision. "He didn't even bother to mention that they were married until last night." Sighing, she took a deep breath. "She isn't daft, I tell ye. The old witch just said that to keep the laird from marrying her. I've spent many an hour talking with her now and she's as swift of mind as any. And ye'd ken that if ye'd stop thinking so much and start listening."

Robbie stared at his wee wife blankly as those words registered, then slammed his dagger onto the table. "Well, hell!" he roared in frustration, then rocked to his feet and stomped toward the door. Jerking it open, he froze, eyes wide as he stared at the man standing there, hand raised to knock. "Me laird!"

Aelfread whirled about at that surprised cry from her husband, her own expression mirroring his as she spied Galen standing in the door. The chief of the MacDonald clan had not set foot in this cottage since the day she had married Robbie. Most of the time Robbie was up at the keep and the laird had no purpose to come to their humble home. It seemed now he did. Ironic, Aelfread decided dryly, for this was the first time she did not feel like offering him a welcome. Grabbing her basket off the shelf, she pushed past the two men without a word and crashed out of the cottage herself.

Galen tried to get out of the way as Robbie's little wife stormed toward him. He took a hasty step to the side, but there was a small tree stump with an ax in it blocking his path. He nearly tumbled over that stump as Aelfread bumped him on the way by. Only Robbie's hand snaking out to steady him kept him from landing in the dirt along the front of the house.

"Aelfread!"

If she heard her husband's enraged roar as she beetled off down the path, she ignored it. Robbie glanced apologetically toward Galen, then ushered him into the cottage. " 'Tis sorry I am, me laird. Aelfread has a foul temper when aroused and once her sails are up . . ." He shook his head. "I fear she thinks little ere acting."

"Aye . . . Well." Galen cleared his throat, his gaze shifting around the cottage, hardly taking in what his eyes were seeing. His mind was caught up with the apology he had come to offer. Galen did not like to make apologies. But when he owed one, he gave it, and right now he owed Robbie. His behavior upon discovering Kyla missing had gone beyond the pale. There was no excuse in his mind for shaming one of his men in front of his comrades, and he explained all of that to Robbie now in a rush. The man shook his head at once.

"Nay, me laird. Ye had every right to yer anger. I let her escape."

"Aye, but ye are one of my best men. I know ye didn't slacken yer vigilance. 'Sides, 'twas not all yer fault. She took advantage o' yer concern for her."

Robbie stopped shaking his head at that and started to listen, so Galen continued, "Any one of the men would have gone below to fetch the old witch had she asked it and Kyla knew that. In truth, she tricked ye."

They both blinked as those words slipped out, then Robbie began to grin. Despite Aelfread's words, he'd retained some doubt about his new lady's sensibilities. Now it seemed Aelfread may be right. And wasn't that a relief? "Aye, she did, didn't she? Damn me, that isn't the action of a daft woman, now is it?"

Relief broke across Galen's face in a grin as well as he realized himself that Kyla had shown cleverness and daring in escaping that day.

"Damn me, Aelfread is right. She isn't soft in the skull."

Galen smiled and nodded, then sighed and shook his head. "I can tell from Aelfread's leave-taking she isn't pleased with ye, and if 'tis because she heard of me set down earlier I—" He paused at the sudden change in his friend's expression.

Robbie pursed his lips briefly, then met his gaze. "Well, now. I haven't even told her about that yet."

"Ye haven't?" His surprise was obvious.

"Nay," he admitted slowly, then paused consideringly before saying, "I be thinking a nice mug of ale would hit the spot just now."

Galen shook his head. "Thanks, but nay. I couldn't find Tommy and left Angus guarding the door. I must—" His voice ended abruptly as Robbie's massive hand clamped on to his shoulder to direct him toward the table.

"I be thinking yer *really* going to be needing this mug, me laird."

One hour and several mugs of ale later, Galen marched determinedly toward the keep. His mind was near buzzing with all that he had to say to his wife. He repeated it to himself under his breath as he mounted the stairs to the room they shared. Angus greeted him on his arrival and Galen nodded in response, then opened the door and stepped inside— only to pause and gape, everything he wanted to say slipping away as he stared around the empty room.

"Angus!"

Only a step away from the door, the man was inside at once, a question on his face that was answered the moment he saw the vacant room. "I haven't left the door since ye posted me there," he said at once.

Galen's mouth worked briefly, then he shook his head and turned away.

"She must have been gone ere I arrived," Angus murmured.

"Aye," Galen muttered grimly.

"While ye were fetching me, most like."

"Aye."

He followed Galen down the stairs, offering quietly, " 'Twas clever of her."

Halting, the MacDonald chief, whirled and bellowed, "Me wife is not daft!"

"Nay, me laird," Angus agreed at once.

"Do ye ken the poor lass didn't even ken me name?" The man looked blank and Galen's frown grew. "We didn't even introduce me to her. Her own bloody husband and we didn't even tell her me name!"

Frowning now, Angus appeared doubtful. "We didn't?"

"Nay." He scowled at the man. "Do you recall introducing me?"

"Nay . . . But everyone knows yer name, me laird."

"And everyone calls me 'me laird.'"

"Oh. Aye." Angus looked amazed as he realized the truth of that.

"She is me wife and mistress here and we are all strangers to her."

"Nay!" Angus protested at once. "Why we ken her as well as—"

"But she doesn't ken us, Angus," Galen pointed out firmly. "Aye, we learned a lot about her while traveling here. But she was feverish, she recalls nothing of the trip, and she recalled none of us when she awoke. We told her she was married now, and we were her people and that was that."

"Aye," Angus nodded slowly, then raised a confused face. "That would explain her not knowing yer name, me laird, but what of her trying to leave the castle after Robbie had explained about yer not wanting her to leave?"

Sighing, Galen shook his head and continued down the stairs once more. "Do ye remember when ye took the sword in the side by that Lynsay last year?"

"Aye." The pain of recollection was obvious in his voice.

"Well, as I recall, after a week in yer sick bed, nothing on God's green earth could keep ye from making yer way out into the bailey for a bit of fresh air."

"Aye. I was fair going crazy locked up inside all that long time— Oh! I ken! Yer saying she was suffering the same thing."

Nodding, Galen led him out of the keep. They were both silent as they crossed the bailey. It wasn't until they entered the stables that Angus asked, "Still, if the lass isn't daft, why would she be foolish enough to run off again? Doesn't she ken that the MacGregor could try to steal her back?"

"Did ye tell her that?" Galen asked dryly after ordering the stable master to fetch his mount.

"Nay."

"Well, neither have I," he admitted, then sighed. "There is much I haven't said to her that I should have." Shaking his head in self-disgust, he moved impatiently down the row of horses to take over the chore of readying his mount.

"Surely ye talked to her some yestereve? She must have had a question or two when ye went above stairs?" Angus queried, following his laird's lead in preparing his own mount.

"Nay. I had things on me mind other than talk yestereve," he admitted. " 'Sides, I fear I . . . Well, in truth I think I have been avoiding talking to her at all . . . I didn't want to know it if she *was* daft."

"Then how did ye learn she didn't ken yer name?"

"Robbie told me. Aelfread told him today."

"Ahh."

About to mount his horse, Galen paused and glanced at the other man suspiciously. "What does that mean?"

"Women," Angus answered with a shrug, mounting his own animal. "They always seem to ken things ere we do. I often think that if they were running things—"

"We'd all be wearing skirts and running in circles trying to understand each other rather than killing each other."

Angus blinked at that as Galen mounted his stallion, then started to laugh. " 'Twould no' be so different I suppose . . . Except, less men would die."

"Which would mean more mouths to feed. Death serves as much purpose as birth in this life, me friend, and never doubt it." On that note, he whirled his horse toward the entrance and set it moving before glancing back to shout, "I'll check the beach. Ye start at the dock and make yer way back."

Chapter 12

'T IS lovely."

"Aye," Kyla agreed on a sigh. Standing in the waist-high water now that her body had adjusted to the temperature, she started wading farther out into the ocean. She had been quite surprised when Aelfread had come upon her on the beach. Having left her friend at the cottage not that long ago, Kyla had thoroughly expected the woman to still be there. She had even considered going there to pour out her woes, but realizing that Robbie most like would have headed there after Galen had dressed him down and dismissed him, she had headed for the beach instead. She had not been there long when the other woman had arrived, an empty basket over her arm and the flush of anger on her cheeks.

They had spent quite a bit of time relating what had happened since leaving each other and commiserating on the stupidity of men. Then they'd decided to forget all about it briefly and relax in the water with a swim.

"Damn me."

Kyla whirled in the water at that exclamation, her face reddening as she saw the shock on the other woman's face. She had worn one of her older under-tunics today. One Morag had been trying to get her to throw out for ages, but it was one of Kyla's favorites and she wore it often. Too often. It was worn near threadbare and was no doubt as useless as wearing nothing at all when wet. It was obvious now by the other woman's expression. She sighed at her decision that morning not to bother having Morag bandage her back, so that it could get some air. Aelfread had obviously just got her first look at the scar she knew crossed her back. The woman confirmed her suspicion with her first words.

"I had heard 'twas a vicious wound, but good God! It looks as if they tried to slice ye in two," she exclaimed, wading through the water toward her.

" 'Twould be straight across my back, not from shoulder to waist, were that the case," Kyla murmured uncomfortably.

"Aye, but . . ." Pausing beside her, the other woman took her arm and urged her around so that she could see it again. Kyla turned reluctantly, uncomfortable in the silence that followed as Aelfread examined her injury through the cloth of her tunic. She was more than relieved when she finally had seen enough and waded back around to face her. "It still looks raw."

Kyla shook her head. "It bothers me little so long as I do not rest directly on it." She watched the other woman's face closely, then asked, "Is it very ugly?"

"Ugly?" Aelfread appeared surprised at the question, but considered it seriously before answering, "Nay. No' ugly. No' pretty either. 'Tis just there."

Kyla frowned at that response and tried to rephrase her question. "Aye, but do you think Galen would be repulsed were he to see it?"

Her eyebrows rose at that. "Were he to see it? Surely ye ken he has seen it already? Ye told me yerself that ye had consummated the wedding last eve."

"Aye. Well, this is the first time I have been without my bandages and he has not seen it yet."

"I see," she murmured, then said, "Robbie told me the laird helped tend ye on the way here and when ye first arrived, my lady. He has seen it many times." Pausing uncertainly at Kyla's suddenly stricken expression, she asked, "What is it?"

"You called me 'my lady.'"

"Aye." She tilted her head in bewilderment. "And so ye are, me lady."

"Aye, but—" Kyla began, then paused as the other woman's glance suddenly shifted past her. The stiffening of her body and tightening of her lips told Kyla that they were no longer alone. She turned swiftly to see Robbie coming down the path. He had nearly reached the beach itself when Galen suddenly appeared on the path behind him on horseback. Hearing him, Robbie paused and awaited his laird. They spoke briefly, then Galen dismounted and the two men continued forward together.

Recalling the state of her clothing, Kyla bent her knees, lowering into the water until only her head stuck out.

Her own tunic made of far sterner stuff, Aelfread remained standing, her hands raising to prop themselves on her hips as she watched the men pause on the shoreline.

"I thought I'd be finding ye here." Robbie's rumble rolled across the water to them with little effort.

Aelfread gave her head a shake that sent her long, damp tresses flying over her shoulder. She glared at

him, unimpressed. "Well and bully for you, husband."

Irritation flickered on the man's face briefly, then
he shifted where he stood and tried a smile. "Come
out of there. 'Twill be time for sup soon."

" 'Tis no' me who cooks yer sup. Whether I be
here or no', 'twill be ready at the same time since ye
insist on eating at the keep every night."

He looked terribly disappointed at that response
and quite suddenly took on the appearance of a great
mountain of a little boy. "Will ye no' join me fer me
repast, wife?"

Kyla stared at the man in amazement at the sudden transition, then toward Aelfread who was obviously softening. Shifting where she stood, the other
woman hesitated briefly, then tilted her head and
asked, "Did ye tell him?"

"Aye." He looked so proud and angelic as he said
that, even Kyla felt her heart soften toward the man.
No small feat that. She had found his very size in-
timidating since first meeting the giant.

"Well . . . all right then," Aelfread muttered, then
glanced toward Kyla. " 'Twill be all right, Robbie has
straightened Galen out," she reassured her quietly.
"I'll come up to the keep on the morrow and help ye
take the servants in hand."

She waited until Kyla had nodded, then started
out of the water.

Robbie was waiting on the edge of the water, plaid
in hand to wrap about his wife as she walked out of
the surf, but rather than help her into it, he simply
bundled her up and lifted her into his strong arms
before turning away. "I'll tell Angus ye've found her,"
he called as he disappeared up the path with his wife.

Calling out a thanks, Galen watched the couple out of sight, then turned to survey Kyla where she still knelt in the water. "Well?"

"Well what?" she asked warily.

"Do ye intend to stay in there all night, or are ye coming out?"

Kyla peered at her plaid that lay on the beach where she had left it, then back to her husband. "Will you turn your back?"

"Do ye no' have the courage to come out before me? I *am* yer husband."

Kyla hesitated briefly at that, then unbent her knees until she stood straight and proud before him. She couldn't help but blush, however, when his gaze immediately slid hungrily down over her body beneath the now-diaphanous gown. Goose bumps seemed to be springing out all over her body beneath the combination of his hot gaze and the cool breeze, but she raised her chin defiantly and strode out of the water, slowing when he stepped into her path on the edge of the water.

His eyes were shining with more than admiration as he gazed at her. Now that they were only two feet apart, she was sure that she could almost feel his gaze burn across her skin. She managed to stay still for a moment under that intense stare, but her eyes were drawn to his throat when he suddenly swallowed.

"Beautiful."

The word was a mere whisper on his lips, but Kyla caught it and felt her cheeks flush brighter. Dropping her gaze self-consciously, she saw what held him so enthralled and stiffened. The ties of her under-tunic had come undone in the water and the bodice of the thin gown now hung open, revealing one breast.

Gasping, she started to raise a hand to adjust the material, but Galen immediately caught her hand. "Nay!"

Startled by the harshness of his tone, she glanced at him sharply and was fascinated by the need on his face.

"Ye don't remember yer first day here, I know. But I do," he murmured, drawing her one step closer, but no more as he said, "Ye were burning up and needed to be cooled down immediately. I carried ye to our chambers to strip ye down and bathe ye. Ye were lying naked in the tub and I was washing ye down with the cold water and there was a drop of water just there . . . As there is now."

His gaze was focused on her naked breast and Kyla glanced down at herself, shivering when she saw the clear drop of liquid that dangled from her swollen, rosy nipple.

"I wanted so bad to lick that drop away, to taste ye like that." His eyes raised to her face now as he admitted, "That vision has haunted me ever since."

Kyla stared at him, amazed to feel a flicker of heat pushing through her embarrassment and a sudden tension sliding through her. She stood as still as stone, afraid to move or even breathe lest she stop whatever was coming.

"I'll have that taste now." Sliding to his knees before her so that his face was level with her breast, he opened his mouth and licked the drop away with one slow precise lash of his tongue.

Kyla nearly jumped out of her skin at that. He had done some amazing things to her last night, but none had raised as shocking and abrupt a fire in her body as that one lick did just then. Raising her hands instinctively, she braced them on his shoulders and stared down into his face as his tongue slid back into his mouth and he closed his eyes. He stayed like that for a moment, seeming to savor that one drop of liquid, then opened his eyes again to peer up at her solemnly.

" 'Tis as I feared. One taste just isn't enough," he murmured, then leaned forward, his tongue sliding out to lave the aureole again before it swirled around the engorged tip and drew it into his mouth where he suckled it hungrily.

Groaning, Kyla clutched at his shoulders, the chill damp air forgotten as he set to heating her up. When his hands finally left their lax position at his sides to grasp her by the waist and draw her closer, she went willingly, leaning into his mouth as he alternately nibbled and pulled at her flesh with his teeth.

When he raised a hand to tug at the lacings to make the gap in the front of the gown wider, she helped him, undoing them and tugging the damp cloth aside until both breasts were open to his view. The moment that was done, he dropped back onto his haunches and drew her down on the sand, urging her forward until her knees were on either side of his legs, then he slid his mouth hungrily from one excited breast to the other before drawing away and raising his head to kiss her. It was a long, hungry kiss that sent her head spinning as his hands gently urged the skirt of her short tunic up her hips. She was so excited and enraptured by that kiss that she nearly bit his tongue off in surprise when his hand slid between her legs.

She tried to draw away then, but he merely deepened the kiss, his tongue delving into her mouth as he plunged one finger into her body. Kyla stilled against him, her resistance dropping away like a well-used cloak as she began to move her body. It wasn't until he began to turn her to lay her on the sand that she put up any resistance. She began to struggle at once then, but it wasn't until she managed to tug her lips away and gasp, "My back," that he paid her any attention.

Unable to stop that abruptly, Galen turned at once so that rather than the two of them coming to rest on her back, they fell half on their sides, half on his back. Pausing then, he peered at her with concern. "Is it all right?"

"Aye." She flushed slightly under his concerned gaze, then explained, "But 'tis not bandaged any more and I thought 'twould not be good to get the sand on it."

He frowned at that, but nodded. "Aye, perhaps yer right. 'Tis good one of us is thinking," he added with a bit of self-derision, then suddenly turned to lie fully on his back and caught her beneath the arms to draw her up on top of him.

"There, that should do," he murmured, reaching down to urge her legs apart and down so that she sat straddling him.

Unsure of this new position, Kyla eyed him nervously as she braced herself with her hands at his chest, then glanced about the beach. "Mayhap we should—"

" 'Tis nearing the supper hour," he assured her, his hands sliding to cup her breasts as they swayed before him. "No one will come."

Her gaze slid reluctantly back to him as he caressed the flesh of her breasts, and she shifted her hips to find a more comfortable position, eyes widening slightly when she felt his hardness beneath her. As stiff as a sword, it lay flat against his belly, rubbing across her flesh as she moved.

"Oh, aye, loving, that feels good," Galen murmured, reaching down to urge her to move against him again.

Feeling awkward and unsure, Kyla shifted herself back, then forward again, swallowing as she felt his manhood rub against her once more. She did that another time or two, still too concerned with the doing to enjoy the feeling, then Galen caught her by the shoulder and tugged her down for a kiss. She sensed his hand moving down between them then, but was too caught up in the kiss to pay much attention to it. When he finally released her from the kiss and urged her back, it was to find his manhood not resting flat against his belly beneath her, but sliding into her as she moved.

Seeing the way her eyes widened as he slid into her, Galen smiled, one hand releasing the breast it held to dip down to touch her. "That's it, loving," he whispered encouragingly, his other hand leaving her breast now to move to her hip; it urged her to continue moving. "That's it."

Her movements awkward and even a bit jerky at first, Kyla began to ride him as he had done her the night before, her body eventually finding a rhythm she was comfortable with as she arched into his touch. It was an odd feeling being on top and in control, but it mattered little since her body was quite happy and was urging her not to stop.

It took a moment for the keening to catch her attention, then a moment more to realize that it was she herself doing it. Embarrassed, she paused in her movements and Galen's eyes opened at once.

"Nay, loving, don't stop," he gasped, the hand between them shifting to grasp her other hip, urging her to move again as he surged into her. After two more thrusts, he saw that he need not urge her on anymore and his hands moved to cup her breasts again, squeezing and kneading her as they moved together.

Kyla missed the caress between her legs at first, then found if she moved just so, she got almost the same sensation without his fingers. Her movements becoming quicker and more urgent, she pushed herself upward until she sat upright and shifted her hands to grasp his wrists. Holding him there to help her maintain her balance, she threw her head back and ground down into him, her mouth opening on a gasp of surprise as he thrust violently upward and stiffened as he erupted inside her. Shifting against him as he cried out, Kyla found her own release, her nails digging into his wrists as her body convulsed around him. Then she released her breath on a gasping sob and dropped to lay atop his chest.

Shifting sleepily atop her husband, Kyla yawned, then raised her head to peer at his face in repose. She had dozed off for a bit and was not sure quite how long it had been that they had lain there in shameless splendor, but the sun was setting now, bringing the day to a close.

Grinning at the smile on her husband's face as he lay beneath her, she reached out to smooth a strand of fiery red hair behind his ear, stilling when his chest rumbled under her. "Me name is Galen."

Kyla's eyes shot to his to find them open now and

intent upon her as he awaited her response. "Aye, my lord. Aelfread told me."

"She shouldn't have had to."

"Nay, she should not have had to," she agreed quietly, her gaze dropping to his chest. "But then ours was not the average courtship."

When he remained silent after she said that, Kyla peered up at him curiously, her eyebrows rising slightly when she saw the frown of uncertainty on his face. Then he pointed out carefully, "We didn't have a courtship."

"Afraid the fevers affected me after all, husband?" she asked, amusement twisting at her lips now, then she patted his upper shoulder reassuringly. "I realize we did not have a courtship, my lord, and that was my point."

"Ah." He relaxed slightly, then shifted under her and asked, "Are ye very upset to find yerself wed to me?"

Kyla hesitated briefly, choosing her words with care before saying. "If you are asking me if I would rather have married the MacGregor, the answer is no."

" 'Tis not what I am asking."

Sighing, Kyla began to pluck absently at the hairs on his chest, displeasure evident on her face. "How can I answer that? I hardly know you."

His eyes widened, the brows above them raising impossibly high on his forehead as he peered at her where she lay on his chest. Kyla rolled her eyes. "I did not mean in the biblical sense, my lord. Obviously I know you in that way." Blushing slightly, she shyly admitted, "In truth, I find more pleasure in that aspect of the marriage than I had ever dreamed possible."

"Really?" He puffed up like a bantam rooster at those words, his chest rising and lifting her with it.

Shaking her head, Kyla smiled slightly. "Aye. But other than that I know very little about you and that does trouble me."

Exhaling his breath slowly, he considered her briefly. "What would ye ken?"

Kyla blinked at that, her mind suddenly blank. It actually took a moment of searching to find a question she would like answered. "Are your parents alive?"

"Nay."

Kyla waited a moment for him to continue. When he did not, she prodded, "What happened to them?"

"Me father was killed in battle and me mother was taken by the plague."

"Ahh." She cast him a sympathetic glance. "How old were you when they died?"

His eyes moving past her shoulder to the sky above, he squinted briefly, then shrugged. "Young."

"I am sorry. My parents died when I was young as well."

"I ken."

She blinked at that. "You do?"

"Aye. Ye told me."

"When?"

"On the trip here. While down with—"

"Fever," Kyla filled in dryly.

"Aye."

Sighing, she shook her head. "I almost fear asking what else I told you."

"Everything," he answered promptly, and she laughed slightly at his certainty.

"Nay, my lord. I could not have told you all, else you surely would not have married me."

When he suddenly looked uncertain at that, she poked him in the ribs lightly. " 'Twas a joke, my lord."

"Oh." He smiled lamely. " 'Twas funny."

Eyes narrowing slightly at the obvious lie, Kyla murmured, "There is no need to humor me, my lord. I am not a daft wench who needs humoring."

Hearing the hurt beneath the teasing, Galen closed his arms around her and cuddled her closer as he reassured her, "I ken yer not daft."

"Do you?" she asked doubtfully.

"Aye. I'm no' saying I didn't have me doubts and fears earlier, but I ken now that ye were no' made daft by the fevers. In truth I begin to wonder if the rest of us are no' the daft ones to have misjudged ye so. Robbie told me the witch lied—and why."

Slightly mollified by that, Kyla leaned her head on his chest and smiled. "You took a risk marrying me when you knew so little about me."

"Nay. In truth I was lucky. I was expecting ye to be a peely-wally sow."

"Oh!" Rising up on his chest, Kyla struck out at his shoulders in retaliation for the insult, only to have him catch her by the shoulders and hold her still as he added, " 'Twas fair glad I was to find meself saddled with a fiery beauty any man would be proud to call wife."

As intended, she melted against him at once at the compliment, and Galen leaned up to catch her lips in a deep, sweet kiss.

Pulling her mouth reluctantly away a moment later, Kyla sighed resignedly and lay her head on his chest again as she murmured, "They will be sitting down to sup, my lord. We should return."

"Nay."

Head lifting in surprise, she peered at his now closed eyes. "Nay?"

Opening one eye, he asked, "Are ye hungry?"

Kyla considered that briefly, then shrugged. "Not really, my lord."

Nodding, he closed the eye again and relaxed. "Then, nay."

She considered his expression briefly, her fingers toying absently with the hair on his chest, then asked, "Are *you* not hungry?"

"Aye."

Fingers pausing, she frowned at him in confusion. "Well, then we should—"

"My hunger can't be satisfied at table. Though 'tis an interesting idea," he added as an afterthought. He suddenly rose to a sitting position, bringing her upright with him. Easing her to sit on the sand then, he got to his feet.

Kyla stared up the length of his body in a confusion that began to clear when his plaid suddenly dropped to the ground, followed by his shirt. In the next instant, he reached down and drew her to her feet before him. "Yer gown is dry."

"Aye," Kyla murmured, gasping in surprise when he suddenly bent to grasp the bottom of it and quickly drew it up over her head and off.

" 'Tis no sense in it getting wet again," he explained, dropping the tunic on his own clothes before sweeping her up into his arms.

"Are we getting wet again, my lord?" she asked with wry amusement.

"Aye," he announced, carrying her toward the surf.

"Why?"

"Well, ye see, loving. I have this vision haunting me—" He broke off to frown at her when she gave a small laugh. "Ye'd laugh at me?"

"Nay, husband." Kyla sobered at once and shook her head. "I find your visions most fascinating. Pray continue."

He eyed her a moment longer, then relented. "Well, on that first day—"

"The day I arrived."

"Aye. I was bathing ye."

"Purely for medicinal purposes."

"O' course." He cast a wounded glance her way. "Anyhow, I was bathing ye and ye suddenly lunged at me, throwing yerself around me like a trollop."

"I did not!" Kyla cried at once.

"Aye, ye did." Galen nodded his head firmly. "Soaking wet ye were— I like ye wet, by the by," he added with a wolfish smile that made Kyla flush. "Wrapped yer arms and legs around me and fair made me dizzy with wanting ye. I've thought o' little else but getting ye wet again ever since."

"You sir, are a rudesby," Kyla informed him succinctly, bringing him to a halt thigh-deep in the water.

"A rudesby?" he repeated with a frown. "What the Devil is a rudesby?"

Shrugging, Kyla turned her head away, her nose raising in the air. "A cad."

"A cad, am I?" He stared at her in amazement, then suddenly grinned. "Damn me, I guess I am." And with that, he opened his arms, dropping her.

Unprepared, Kyla could do little else but cry out in dismay as she sank into the water. She came out a moment later, sputtering and spitting water everywhere, then suddenly lunged at her husband, wrapping her arms about his shoulders and her legs around his hips as he had described but moments before.

Shouting at the chill of her damp flesh, Galen tried to untangle her limbs, but she was having none of it. Tightening her hold, she leaned up to bite his ear viciously, then asked, "Is this what you were wanting, my lord?"

Stilling now, Galen caught her buttocks in his hands and lifted her slightly until she rubbed against him. Pressing her tighter then, he groaned and dropped his head to her shoulder. "Aye, loving, this and a wee bit more."

The "wee bit more" proved an educational experience. Kyla hadn't realized that there were so many different ways to make love. Marriage was quite a learning experience for her. Kyla had always enjoyed learning.

Afterward, Galen carried her back to the beach and dropped to sit on the sand. He arranged her sideways in his lap before leaning his head on her shoulder as he waited to regain his breath.

Slightly winded herself, Kyla leaned her head against his and sat still for a moment or so, her hand moving absently up and down his back. Once her breathing and heartbeat had returned to normal, she sighed and slid the hand on his back up into his hair. "Husband?"

"Hmm?" he murmured, not raising his head.

"I think I am hungry now."

A laugh slipping from his lips, Galen briefly hugged her close, then lifted his head with a sigh. "Ye will be the death of me, wife. Where do ye find the strength?"

Kyla raised her eyebrows at that. "It takes little strength to be hungry."

"I would disagree with ye bitterly at this moment, woman." When Kyla remained silent at that, he sighed with resignation, then urged her to her feet. "Damn me, me legs are shaking with weakness," he exclaimed, following her up.

Lips splitting into a wide grin at that, Kyla moved to their small pile of clothes to retrieve her tunic. "Mayhap you are coming down with something, husband. I feel rather energetic myself."

" 'Tis the curse."

Tugging her under-tunic on, Kyla turned to glance at him. "Curse?"

"Aye," he muttered, moving to her side to retrieve his shirt from the sand. Shaking it out quickly, he tugged it on. "The curse of women. Every time a man spills his seed inside a woman, he is pouring a bit of his strength with it. She is stronger and he feels as limp as a damp plaid."

"Ahh," Kyla murmured, then shook her head with a laugh at his foolishness, and bent to retrieve the plaid she had been wearing. Shaking it out, she spread it open on the sand and knelt to fold the pleats. Moments later, she was standing beside him again, adjusting the pleats to her satisfaction.

"Ye've grown quite handy with that," Galen complimented.

"Thank you, my lord." Kyla murmured, then stilled when he suddenly caught her by the chin and tugged her face up to his.

"I ken ye like the beach, but ye must promise yell no' slip yer guard again."

Tilting her head, she considered the request briefly.

"May I come to the beach if I bring my guard with me?"

"Nay. But—" He added swiftly when she opened her mouth on a protest. "Ye may come here with me if I have the time to bring ye."

"But—"

"'Tisn't safe," Galen told her firmly. "The Mac-Gregor hasn't sought retribution yet. I'll no' have him stealing ye away. Marrying ye makes ye less likely a target, but I won't feel safe for ye until he has sought revenge in some other way. Promise yell no' come to the beach without me and ye'll no' slip yer guard again."

Sighing, Kyla tugged her face away. "It matters little, I suppose. Aelfread promised to come up to the keep on the morrow and help me take over the handling of the servants. I shall be too busy to come down here for awhile."

Relaxing, Galen nodded his head. "I'm sorry I didn't officially turn the castle servants over to ye ere this. But I'm glad to see ye interested in tending to them. It has been a strain at times, chasing after them as well as me soldiers."

"I am glad to be of help," Kyla told him honestly, a wide smile splitting her face as she leaned up to kiss him quickly.

Caressing her cheek briefly when she drew back after the kiss, Galen smiled at her softly, then took her hand in his and led her up the path. His mind was so full of the lecture he would give the servants on the morrow to ensure they followed Kyla's orders to the letter, that he was completely oblivious to the fact that she hadn't given any true promise not to return to the beach.

Chapter 13

KYLA moved her king's pawn forward one square, then waited for Aelfread to make her next move. But after several moments had passed, she glanced up to see what the delay was. The delay was that Aelfread was not paying attention. Her gaze was turned toward the men still seated at the trestle tables, talking and laughing over their mugs of ale: Galen, Robbie, Gavin, Angus, and Tommy. They were supposedly discussing the next day's plans and scheduling who was to do what, but the repeated bursts of laughter belied that. Kyla sincerely doubted that deciding who was to train the men, who was to oversee the watch, and who was to trail her around would be that amusing. They were gossiping and from their amusement, it was good gossip. Though of course, they would deny it to the death. "Men don't gossip, don't ye ken?" they would say.

Smiling slightly, she glanced to her friend, her brows drawing together as the other woman sighed. "What is it, Aelfread?"

"What? Oh, nothing." Forcing a smile, she quickly took her turn.

Kyla was silent for a moment, apparently contemplating the board, then she reached out to make her move, idly commenting, "Things are running rather well now. There was not a hitch today."

It had been a week since their last sojourn to the beach. As promised, Aelfread had shown up at the keep the morning following their swim to help her take the servants in hand. Kyla had been prepared to battle for the respect that was rightfully hers. Instead, she had found the servants all pleasant and attentive, even eager to do her bidding. Unaware that Galen had spoken to them, she could only think the drastic change in behavior mostly due to Aelfread's presence and support.

"Aye," Aelfread agreed now, taking her turn as well.

"I could not have gained the servants' respect without you," she added, sliding her bishop out from its spot. "Thank you."

Aelfread shrugged. " 'Twas not a difficult task to aid ye."

"Mayhap not, but it has taken you away from your own tasks and even your daily walks," she pointed out gently, finally getting to what she thought might be the heart of her friend's discontent. Kyla was grateful for her assistance, but suspected Aelfread was missing the fresh air and peace she was used to. She did not wish to see her friend unhappy. "There is no need for you to come tomorrow if you wish to do something else. I realize 'tis boring to be stuck indoors all day."

Her hand on her queen, Aelfread glanced up with surprise. "I haven't been bored," she assured her quickly. "I enjoy yer company, me lady."

"Kyla," she corrected quietly. "We are friends."

Aelfread smiled slightly. "Aye, we are."

"Anyway, bored or not, I noticed today that you were restless and while I enjoy your company, I know you are used to wandering the beach for a bit every day. I never intended for you to have to give that up. I would join you myself in a walk, were it not for my guards." Her gaze slid resentfully to the men at the table. While Galen had said he would accompany her to the beach, he had not yet found the time to take her. Between managing the men and his occasional trips to check on the mainlanders, he had very little time for anything. He was generally up and gone ere her rising and returned just in time for sup—which he often seemed to sit through in an exhausted daze. No matter how exhausted he was, however, he always found the energy to make love to her once they were alone in their room.

Afterward, he always dropped off into a dead sleep, though, leaving Kyla to frown and sigh at him. While she enjoyed their lovemaking, she found that afterward she had a desire to talk to him and get to know him better. But there was little chance of that when he was snoring loud enough to raise the rooftop. It was an uncomfortable predicament for Kyla. She quite liked what little she knew about the man she had married, but had had little chance to get to know him better. She still felt she shared her bed with a near stranger. Grimacing, she sighed aloud, glancing around in surprise when Aelfread's sigh joined her own.

"Aye. I ken well how annoying having a guard is," the other woman muttered grimly, reminding her of her own comment of a moment ago.

"What mean you by that?"

Her friend grimaced, "Robbie has set yer guards on to me as well."

"What?"

Aelfread nodded. "Aye, 'tis true. He's told the men that I'm to be kept here at the keep with ye all day until he can see to me. And with Galen's permission as well," she added with disgust.

Kyla blinked her surprise at that news. "But why?"

Aelfread looked uncomfortable for a moment, almost embarrassed, then admitted with quiet pride, "I'm carrying a bairn."

"Carrying a—" Kyla's eyes widened in amazement. "You are with child? Oh, but Aelfread that is wonderful!" she cried, jumping out of her seat and hurrying around the small table between them to hug the other woman. "That is grand news! You must be so happy."

Aelfread nodded, her face flushed with pleasure. "Aye."

"And Robbie must be so . . ." Her voice and smile faded slowly at the sudden expression change on her friend's face. "What?"

Aelfread sighed, her gaze sliding to the men still talking and laughing at the table. "Robbie is happy," she said carefully. "He would like a bairn or two as much as I, but he's been acting odd ever since I told him last week," she admitted on a sigh. "He doesn't want me cleaning or lifting. He doesn't even want me walking on the beach. He insists I sit up here, day-in and day-out and keep ye company. He acts like it's a favor I'm doing ye and the laird, but when I suggested last night that mayhap ye and I would please take a walk along the beach, he fair lost his brains. He set down the law, he did. Neither ye nor I was to leave the keep, he said. We would sit here and embroider, or some such thing, the day through like proper wives, and that was that. Angus wouldn't allow us out, he said. And he didn't, of course, as ye saw today when I suggested a walk and he overheard."

"Aye," Kyla murmured, recalling Angus and his blunt refusal of the suggestion. Kyla had felt bad at the time, thinking that her own restrictions were infringing on her friend's freedom, but now she saw that both husbands had gone a bit overboard in their attempts at protection.

Sighing, she moved back to her seat and dropped into it. "It sounds as though Robbie's just being protective. Like Galen. Mayhap both of them will ease up and give us a bit more freedom later."

"Not 'til I pop the bairn, I fear," Aelfread muttered with disgruntlement. "At least Robbie won't ease up his protectiveness on me until then. That should be in another six or seven months. . . . Mayhap Galen will ease up a bit on ye though," she added with forced brightness.

Kyla shook her head. "Not likely. I fear so long as the MacGregor lives, I'll have guards and be restricted." She smiled wryly. "I know 'tis a sin, but I am beginning to wish the man would die," she admitted cheerfully, not the least bit ashamed of admitting such a thing to her friend. As she expected, Aelfread accepted her words with calm amusement.

"I can see how that would be. Truthfully, I am beginning to regret being with child, though I have wished for a babe since marrying Robbie." Her gaze slid to her husband again and she sighed. " 'Tis because of his size, ye ken . . . his fear, I mean. He's a big man, as was his father ere him. They were both large babies. And like his father's mother, his own mother died in the birthing. He fears I'll go the same way."

Kyla's eyes widened at that possibility. The problem had not occurred to her. Her gaze slid to Giant Robbie now and worry began in her own head. As his nickname suggested, Robbie *was* a giant of a man . . . and Aelfread *was* a wee slip of a girl. Truly, she did not reach much above four feet. The idea of her bearing a babe of Giant Robbie's almost boggled the mind. It would surely rend the woman before her to pieces, she thought suddenly with dismay.

"Nay. Don't you start thinking like me Robbie," Aelfread warned grimly, catching Kyla's expression. "Me own father was a large babe. He grew to be over six feet and me grandmother was me size and she fared well enough. She said 'twas all in the hips, not the height. And when she met Robbie, she looked him up and down and nodded and said I would do well enough. I'll not have ye thinking his bairn'll split me."

"Of course not," Kyla agreed swiftly, forcing her fears aside. "Besides," she added with more hope than true belief. "Morag is a wizard with herbs and potions. No doubt she knows a thing or two that will help. 'Twill be easy."

"Hmm." Amusement plucked at her lips now. "I didn't say 'twas easy for me grandmother to bear me father. 'Twas hard work according to her and no mistaking it. But she survived, and I will, too."

"Of course you will," Kyla agreed firmly, deciding she would talk to Morag about it the first chance she got. She was not about to sit back and leave things to chance. Aelfread was quickly becoming the best friend she'd ever had and she was not taking any chances with her health. It was bad enough that she may have lost her brother. Kyla sighed at that thought. There had been no news yet from Forsythe. A fact that was beginning to bother her greatly. Did she not hear something from that quarter soon she would have to send a man there to find out for herself what was happening.

Aelfread suddenly cleared her throat, drawing her attention. "'Tis yer turn," she explained, gesturing toward the chessboard.

"Oh. Aye," Kyla murmured, glancing distractedly at the board and making a move as she contemplated the best way to approach her husband on the subject of sending a man to Forsythe. His behavior toward her was so odd sometimes, she was not sure what to say to him. He was as loving and gentle in their bed as any woman could wish, but out of it he was different. He was sometimes cool, sometimes friendly, but always in a standoffish sort of way. And sometimes he was just plain short with her, as if he were angry about something. She never knew how he would take her presence and to be honest, the uncertainty of his welcome was beginning to wear on her nerves.

"I ken it has only been a week, but it feels as if I haven't been to the shore in ages."

Kyla glanced at Aelfread at that, her mind pushing her thoughts aside. "Aye. It does seem a long time. I had no beach to wander on, but at Forsythe there is a river, and I often used to journey to it and walk along its edge. I have always felt there was something soothing about water."

"Hmm. 'Tis a shame we can't go. The morrow promises to be as grand as today. It would have been nice to have a picnic on the sand. Mayhap take a swim."

Kyla pursed her lips, her gaze sliding to the men at the table before returning to her friend. "Mayhap we could sneak away," she suggested doubtfully.

Aelfread shook her head at once. "Nay. We'd be caught. They're on their guard now."

"Hmm." Kyla frowned as she nodded over that, her mind searching another solution. After a moment, she came up with one. "What if we snuck out ere anyone else was awake? The—"

"Nay. They'd come searching for us right away and bring us back. 'Tis a small island and very little of it isn't watched. The only area unguarded is where the cliffs are. 'Tis too sheer there for anyone to attack . . ." Her voice faded away as she said that and she suddenly smiled. "I have it!"

"What?" Kyla sat forward in her seat.

" 'Tis too perfect."

"What?"

"We can slip away and no one would even ken . . . if we work it right."

"What?" Kyla asked, her voice rising with exasperation. "Tell me."

Aelfread hesitated long enough to glance toward the men across the room, then leaned forward across the table, waiting until Kyla had done so as well before explaining. "There are secret passages in the castle that Robbie—" she blushed—"showed me once."

Her eyebrows rose slightly. "Really? How interesting." She grinned. "There are one or two at Forsythe as well."

Aelfread smiled widely. "These ones lead down to a cave that opens out on the area of the island I said wasn't guarded because 'tis too sheer for anyone to attack from there. 'Tis nearly directly beneath yer bedchamber window. The castle is built on the edge of it."

Kyla nodded now, recalling the small stretch of beach her friend was talking of. The castle wall ended where the face of the cliff began. She could well understand why they would not bother to post guards on it. While a small boat or two might be able to land there, anyone in them would be trapped on the beachhead. The cliff face was nearly as straight and smooth as the castle wall itself.

"The cave is at the end of that small piece of cliff that juts out beside the little patch of beach. Robbie showed it to me when I first came here. 'Tis the escape route we're to take if the island is attacked and the defense isn't going well." She paused. "The cave entrance is open at low tide, but submerged at high tide. We could go down, take a boat around the corner to the beach, have a little picnic, wade in the water . . ." She sighed with pleasure at the very thought, then grimaced. "If we can think of some excuse for disappearing into one of the upstairs rooms for an hour or two."

When Kyla raised her eyebrows at that, Aelfread shrugged. "We can't simply disappear, else they'll have the whole castle looking for us."

"Oh, aye," Kyla agreed, glancing toward the men to see Robbie peering their way. There was passion, affection, and a touch of anxiety mingled on his face as he gazed at his petite wife, and Kyla was reminded of her friend's delicate state and the fears for her health it brought. Reminding herself that she intended on seeing to it that both baby and mother came through this healthy, she turned back to her friend suddenly. "Your delicate state."

Aelfread blinked at that and Kyla grinned as she explained. "I have heard it said that women who are with child tend to tire easily."

"Oh, aye," Aelfread muttered with a baleful glare toward her husband who was no longer looking their way, but caught up in some debate with his laird. "Robbie has told me that repeatedly since I told him that I am with child."

"Well," Kyla murmured with amusement. " 'Tis a handy excuse to use for this. You may claim that you grow weary. I will blame it on your delicate condition and suggest you go above stairs and rest for a bit. Does the room next to my bedchamber have a passage?"

"Aye." Aelfread sat forward again, delight illuminating her face briefly before she suddenly frowned. "But what of you?"

"After you have gone, I shall claim a nap sounds pleasant—"

"Morag will never believe it," Aelfread interrupted dryly, and Kyla frowned.

"Aye, and she is none too pleased with me at the moment. She got in trouble the last time I snuck out and is determined to obey whatever rules Galen gives her now. He threatened to return her to Johnny and Catriona should he catch her aiding me in any further escapes." Kyla wrinkled her nose with disgust, then paused to murmur, "We may be able to convince her, though. She might believe I truly wished a nap if she thought I was just bored because you are not around. And mayhap I could yawn every once in a while throughout the morning to let her think I was tired. If she asks, I can say Galen kept me up half the night."

Aelfread grinned at that. "With our luck, he just may do that."

Kyla blushed slightly, but shrugged the comment aside. "I will excuse myself for a nap and wait for you to come to get me."

Her friend nodded and grinned. "I can almost smell the breeze off the water and feel the sand beneath me bare feet."

"Aye." She grinned back. " 'Twill be a grand adventure."

"Ye've been yawning ever since ye came down this morn. Mayhap ye should have a lie-down."

Kyla blinked at Morag's unprompted words, her gaze shooting to Aelfread.

"Mayhap his lordship is working ye too hard of a night," her nurse teased, laughter in her eyes.

Kyla flushed brightly at that, the words striking too close to home for comfort. Not one of the sleepy yawns she had produced this morning had had to be feigned. They were real and Galen was indeed the reason for her weariness. He had kept her up so late the night before that the yawns were now coming of their own volition, and often enough to be bothersome.

"Mayhap Morag is right and ye should rest for a wee bit." Aelfread stretched with feigned weariness, one hand moving to her back as she arched it. "All this needlework is a strain on me eyes and I don't think a wee rest would go amiss meself."

Morag glanced up from her mending, her gaze moving over the other woman's stomach. " 'Twould not be a bad thing, considering yer condition."

Both of the younger women stiffened at that, surprise mirrored on their faces. Their whole plan was playing out now, but in a somewhat backward fashion. Aelfread had not yet announced her condition, and neither of them had had to suggest the rest; Morag seemed more than willing to do it for them.

"How did ye ken about me condition?" Aelfread asked the question both women were wondering and Morag rolled her eyes.

"Lass, I've been on this earth a long time. There is very little I don't know. I've known ye were with child for a week now, or at least suspected." She was silent for a moment as both women digested that, then she spoke again. "Ye've nice wide hips. 'Twill be a hard birth, but ye'll come through it."

Kyla felt herself sag at those words. If Morag said it was so, it was almost guaranteed. It was a relief to her. More surprisingly, it was obviously a relief to Aelfread if her own expression was anything to go by. It seemed obvious that, despite her words and bravado, the wee woman had not been quite as sure as she had pretended over how she would fare in childbirth.

"I be thinking ye both might benefit from a wee rest," Morag continued now. " 'Twould only benefit the babe ye carry, Aelfread." Her gaze slid to Kyla. "And while ye may be feeling well enough thanks to me potions and salves, yer back is still mending, child. Ye should be careful not to overdo it."

"Mayhap for a little while." Kyla's gaze slid to her friend. "I'll rest if you do."

Aelfread nodded.

"Rather than walk all the way back to your cottage, why do you not rest in the room next to mine?" Kyla suggested now as if the thought had just occurred to her. " 'Tis empty. That way Robbie will know you actually did sleep and did not sneak off to pick flowers or something once you were out of sight of Duncan's sharp eyes." She glanced teasingly toward Duncan who stood near the fireplace as she said that, her smile deepening when he made a face in response.

"If 'twould be no bother?"

"Nay. 'Tis no bother at all," Kyla assured her and got to her feet. "You go ahead. I think I shall just have a mug of meade ere I lie down."

Aelfread hesitated, then moved around her chair to join her. "I think I shall have a half a mug meself."

Smiling, Kyla turned and led the way toward the kitchen, almost feeling guilty at how easy it had all been. It was amazing how smoothly it had gone. It was almost as if Morag had known of their plans and set out to assist them, she thought with amusement as they passed through the doors into the kitchen and set about putting the second part of their plan into action: gathering food for their picnic.

It was not an easy task. Aside from cook, there were at least three other servants in the kitchen. Kyla's murmur that they sought a cup of meade immediately brought the three assistants away from their tasks to offer to fetch it. She quickly declined the offer and waved them back to their cutting and peeling, then set about the task herself in as slow a manner as she could manage as she set about lifting the necessary items for their feast.

With Aelfread to shield her, she managed to

pocket a small loaf of bread without anyone noticing as she passed the table where it was warming. A large hunk of cheese quickly followed, though Aelfread actually had to distract the girl that was cutting it for Kyla to do so. Then they finally moved to fetch the meade.

She was pouring the liquid into mugs, when Kyla happened to glance up in time to see Aelfread sidle a little closer to the next table, palm two apples and pop them into her top. It seemed the round, red orbs were a mite chill against her flesh—at least that was what Kyla assumed when the other woman grimaced and did a little dance. Her movements caught the attention of Cook who glanced curiously toward them, but he did not seem to notice Aelfread's now larger and somewhat lopsided chest. Kyla had to cough to hide her laughter as she turned away.

Aelfread was at her side at once, a moue of pretended sympathy on her face as she patted her back, muttering that she hoped she was not coming down with a cold. At that, Kyla was torn between another burst of laughter and a groan. The last thing she needed was for the people around here to think she was ailing again. They were just beginning to get over thinking her a weak and sickly Sassenach.

Shoving one of the mugs of meade into her friend's hand as cover, Kyla hissed a warning regarding the irregular state of her bodice. She then quickly drank from her own mug and smiled sweetly over the shorter woman's shoulder at Cook as Aelfread straightened her apples.

They both downed their drinks quickly, then fled the kitchen with their stolen booty, making their way straight above stairs. Aware that Duncan had followed them to stand guard in the hall, they murmured "good sleep" to each other as they each moved to their respective doors.

Closing the door behind her, Kyla immediately moved to the wall facing the room Aelfread now inhabited. This was where the entrance to the secret passage was supposed to be, but she could not see where it was exactly. It was well hidden. She was still silently examining the face of the wall when a portion of it suddenly slid inward directly beside the fireplace.

"So that is where it is." Kyla smiled at Aelfread as she poked her head into the room. "I tried to find it last night, but Galen came up ere I could discover it." Moving forward, she peered into the darkness of the tunnels.

" 'Tis hard to find." Aelfread was grinning like a child. "Are ye ready?"

"Aye—" Kyla began, then paused and turned in a listening attitude toward the chamber door. She stood still for a moment, ears straining, then waved Aelfread abruptly back into the tunnel, gesturing for her to remain silent as she slid the wall back into place. She had just done so and hurried across the room to the bed to pull back the covers when the door opened and Galen entered.

"So, 'tis true." His expression was surprised as he closed the door.

Kyla stiffened, wondering guiltily what exactly he was referring to, then smiled meekly. "What?"

"Morag said ye'd come above stairs to rest, but I didn't believe it."

Kyla relaxed slightly and shrugged, pulling the blankets back before sitting on the edge of the bed. "I am a bit tired is all."

He crossed to her side at once. "Yer no' ailing?"

"Nay," she assured him with a slight smile. "Just a mite tired. I have not been getting much rest of late."

Guilt covered his features at that and Kyla grimaced. " 'Tis not your fault; I have quite enjoyed the reason for my lack of sleep," she admitted with a small blush.

"Have ye now?" he murmured, sinking to sit on the bed beside her. "I came back with the intention of making good on me promise and taking ye to the beach, but if yer tired, mayhap a nap would be better. And mayhap I should have a wee one, too." His hand slid along her arm caressingly. "Mayhap I could help ye relax and drift off to sleep quicker."

Her eyes rounded at the tone of his voice. It was the tone that generally sparked a fire in her belly . . . among other places. Unfortunately, with Aelfread waiting on the other side of the chamber wall, that tone just now raised panic rather than passion in Kyla. She was frantically trying to find a way to change the direction of this interlude when Galen suddenly leaned forward and kissed her. She knew right away from the passion of the kiss that it was too late for any redirecting she might do. All she could hope for was a miracle as he pressed her back onto the bed, his hands sliding to her lacings.

That miracle came in the form of a tap at the door.

Sighing, Galen pulled reluctantly away from the embrace he had initiated and glanced toward the closed door. "Aye?"

"Gavin said to let ye ken there is someone on the mainland asking to see ye." Tommy called through the door. "He's taking a boat over to fetch him back."

"I'll be right down," Galen announced resignedly, then turned regretfully back to Kyla. "This will have to wait 'til later, sweetling," he murmured, kissing her gently before getting to his feet. "I shall make it up to ye tonight. In the meantime, have a nice rest." He paused long enough to tug the blankets up over her, then turned and left the room.

Chapter 14

KYLA barely waited until the door had closed behind her husband before throwing the covers aside and leaping out of bed. Redoing her lacings, she hurried to the hidden panel, grimacing apologetically at Aelfread when it opened and the other woman eyed her with amusement.

"Sorry," she murmured, following her into the tunnel, her nose turning up at the musty scent that assailed her.

"'Tis all right," came the wry response. "How fares the bread?"

"The bread?" Kyla frowned at the other woman's back as the panel slid closed behind them. Reaching down to her pocket, she realized that the loaf had been on the side on which Galen had half-lain upon her. Feeling the bread's now compressed shape, she grimaced into the narrow crawlspace, grateful that her friend had thought to bring a torch. She herself had not considered the necessity of one.

"'Tis flat," she admitted, then sharpened her gaze on the other woman's shoulders as she realized the only way Aelfred could have known that it would be. "You could see us?" she asked with dismay.

"There's a peephole," she admitted, then explained. "He was talking so softly I couldn't hear what was going on, so I looked in. I was about to return to the next room when the knock sounded at the door."

"He thought he might have a nap," Kyla explained lamely and was positive she heard a snort from her petite friend as they reached a set of stairs hewn into the rocks. Putting out a hand to brace herself, Kyla grimaced at the slimy feel to the wall, but kept her hand on it, afraid the steps might be just as slippery and she might lose her balance.

Both women were silent as they concentrated on negotiating the slick stairs and both sighed in relief when the tight walkway opened up into a large cavern.

"I'd forgotten how snug and spooky that secret passage was."

" 'Tis amazing that a man of Robbie's size can get through it," Kyla murmured, peering about the cave as far as the light reached. It was surprisingly large. They stood on a solid rock platform several feet wide. The rest of the cavern seemed to be made up of open water from what she could tell, though she couldn't even guess the width and breadth of that in this light. With the tide out, the water was a good ten feet below the top of the platform. Moving to the edge, she could see a set of steps hewn into the rock that led down to a second platform where several small boats bobbed. They were each moored to one of three poles that descended into the water directly beside the platform. The poles were smooth and the ropes tied loosely enough that they simply slid up and down with the water, allowing the boats to ride up and down unfettered.

"Well," she murmured, glancing back at Aelfread. "Is this not handy?"

"Aye." Setting the torch in a holder along the wall, she walked over to join Kyla, her own gaze moving to the narrow but high opening of the cave.

"The water rises that much?" she asked with disbelief.

"Aye, and lowers that much."

"But what do they do when the tide is in?"

"Robbie says if we needs must use the cave at high tide we must swim for the beach. They also keep boats there, hidden for just such a purpose. Someone checks on their upkeep every month to be sure they are seaworthy."

"Swim for it?" Kyla sounded as doubtful as she felt. "I do not think I could hold my breath that long."

" 'Tis no' that far. Ye can't tell because this passage curves to the left, but 'tis quite short really and the curve makes it near invisible from the outside—even at low tide."

Kyla merely nodded at that. It explained why she could see the beginnings of light, but the light did not illuminate the cavern. Grinning suddenly, she glanced toward Aelfread. "I do believe having you for a friend will be quite fun, though I fear our husbands will not agree."

Aelfread chuckled softly, then sighed. "We will be in trouble should they discover us not in our beds."

Kyla nodded solemnly. "Is a day on the beach worth it?"

Aelfread grinned. "To me 'tis, but then I haven't as much to lose as ye. The worst that could happen to me is that Robbie finds out and is angry with me."

Kyla started down the stairs toward the lower platform, waving her hand vaguely. " 'Tis all that could happen to me as well . . . Galen's finding out I mean."

"Nay," Aelfread argued, following her. "There is still the threat of the MacGregor for ye."

"Honestly, you are as bad as Galen. I do not understand why you all keep harping on about this MacGregor. There is naught he can do. I am married to Galen. 'Tis that simple. MacGregor cannot marry me now. If he is smart, he has forgotten all about me and found another poor, unsuspecting girl to wife."

"Scots don't forget, Kyla," Aelfread told her carefully. " 'Tis not in their nature . . . Or at least if they do forget, they don't forgive. Some feuds have gone on for six or seven generations. No one is quite sure how they started or what they be about, but they still hate their enemies."

Reaching the platform, Kyla turned wryly to her friend. "Well, I fear that just seems plain silly to me."

"Silly or not, the MacGregor won't simply accept yer being stolen away."

"Well he cannot marry me," Kyla pointed out reasonably.

"Nay," she admitted with a worried frown, but as Kyla started to turn away, she blurted, "He killed Galen's last wife."

"Who is it?" Galen asked Tommy as he reached the bottom of the stairs.

" 'Tis a party from Forsythe."

Pausing, Galen turned to frown at his First, noting

as he did that Morag had gone still where she sat by the fire. "Is Kyla's brother among them?"

"Nay. Neither is his wife." Shifting uncomfortably, Tommy glanced toward the servant. She was now straining to hear all they said. He murmured in a barely audible voice, "They are asking to see Lady Kyla, but I wasn't sure—"

"Ye did right. I would see who 'tis ere we inform Kyla," he assured Tommy quietly, then ignored the now obviously anxious woman by the fire and continued on to the trestle tables. Once both men were seated there, they each poured themselves a mug of ale and peered into them silently.

"'Tis most like 'tis not good news," Tommy muttered suddenly when the silence had dragged on. "Her brother would come himself should he be able."

Galen's only answer was to grunt.

Sighing, Tommy swirled the liquid in his mug glumly. "Lady Kyla talked about her brother an awful lot while feverish. She seems mighty fond of him."

"Hmm." The MacDonald nodded wearily.

"She will be sore distressed if he is dead."

"Aye," Galen sighed. The keep doors opened then, and he straightened as he recognized the man entering with Gavin, Angus, and Duncan.

"Lord Shropshire!" Morag hurried forward at once. "Ye were to stay with Johnny 'til—"

"He is recovering nicely," the English lord interrupted reassuringly. "I left my First and three men-at-arms with him until I return and things are sorted out."

Morag relaxed at that, relief evident on her face. She had briefly feared the man dead.

"I would speak with Lady Kyla," Shropshire announced.

Nodding, Galen turned to Tommy, but was forestalled when the old witch headed for the stairs.

"I shall fetch her."

He killed Galen's last wife.

Every hair on Kyla's body stood on end at that announcement. She could feel every inch of skin that covered her bones as if a small lightning bolt had somehow filtered down through the very rock surrounding them to shock her with its power. Turning back slowly, she met Aelfread's anxious gaze with blank amazement.

Seeing her expression, Aelfread released the breath she had been holding. "I feared ye didn't ken," she admitted with a sigh.

"Galen's *last* wife?" Her voice was husky with disbelief.

"Aye."

She was silent for a minute, her mind in an uproar, then it settled into dead calm and she raised hollow eyes to Aelfread. "Tell me."

"I ken only what I was told."

"Tell me."

"They were married only six months. She was pregnant. Galen had business at court, but Margaret— that was her name—Margaret was five months along in her pregnancy. Galen didn't want her to risk the babe by bouncing about on a horse all the way to court. She stayed behind. She became bored and restless after a week or two of his absence and wanted to go visit her cousin who had married one of the outlying MacDonalds."

"I thought Galen did not want her traveling and bouncing the baby about."

"Aye. I guess that was what Jamie said, too," Aelfread agreed with a sigh.

"Jamie?"

"Galen's cousin. He was First here then. Robbie thinks Jamie was sweet on Margaret, but whatever the case she begged and pleaded with him to let her go until he gave in. Since he was only crossing MacDonald land, he only took himself and his brother, Lachlan, and set out to visit Margaret's cousin. They were to be back the next day, but instead a neighbor of the cousin arrived with the news." She paused then to run her tongue around the inside of her dry mouth. "Margaret had been in the barn with her cousin, keeping her company while she milked her cow when a raid started. The MacGregors rode through, throwing torches on the house and the barn—"

"Why?"

Aelfread blinked at the interruption. "Why what?"

"Why would they set fire to the house and the barn?"

Aelfread shrugged. "'Tis generally what they have been doing lately when they raid. Set fire to the barn and house, then make off with the livestock. The people are kept busy trying to douse the fires and can't go after them right away. 'Tis slow to move cows, ye ken."

"I see," Kyla murmured with a sigh.

"Anyway, they set their fires, rounded up the cattle, and rode off. Had things gone as usual, Margaret and her cousin would simply have run out of the barn and all would have been well, but Margaret went into early labor from the scare. Her cousin came running out of the barn screaming for help, saying that Margaret couldn't walk. The barn went up in flames so quick that 'twas like one big bonfire when the woman came running out, but Jamie, Lachlan, and the cousin's husband charged in after Margaret anyway. None of them came back out. Eventually, the neighbors were drawn by the sight of smoke in the air. They found her cousin sitting on the ground between the burning house and barn in a daze. When they realized that their mistress had perished in the fire, they came straight away with the news."

"So, Galen returned from court to find he'd lost his cousins, his wife, and his babe," Kyla murmured sadly.

"Aye."

They were both silent for a minute, then Kyla glanced at her sharply. "He blames the MacGregor. That is why he attacked our party. A wife for a wife."

Aelfread nodded reluctantly. "That was the plan as Robbie told it to me."

She accepted that silently, neither angered nor injured by the truth. Kyla had not been foolish enough to believe that Galen had espied her from afar and fallen madly in love, desperate to have her. She had known their marriage was due to a feud. She just had not realized she was to replace a dead wife and child.

Did it matter? Kyla considered briefly, an image of her brother Johnny and his wife Catriona coming to mind and making her grimace. She had been much luckier in marriage than Johnny, for certain. Galen never tried to harm her—and he even treated her well and pleasured her in bed. She still had much to learn about him, but thought that what she had seen so far, she quite liked. It was no small matter that. There were many young women at court who not only disliked their husbands, but actually detested them, loathing their very presence in the same room, let alone their touch. Aye, she was lucky. Mayhap that was why she had not dug too deeply to find out the exact reason why Galen had married her. She had not wanted to be disappointed.

Now that she knew that reason, she understood his behavior a bit more. He had probably loved this Margaret a great deal, and if he sometimes seemed cool or detached with her, it was most likely because he was still aching from his loss. Mayhap in time he would grow fond of her, learn to love her. Her brother had always said she was the type to grow on a person.

Sighing, she glanced curiously at a worried-looking Aelfread. Giving her friend a reassuring smile, she asked, "How long ago did Margaret die?"

"A little less than nine months, I think. 'Twas about six months ere I married Robbie."

Kyla frowned at that news. That was not long ago at all. Her ghost would still be fresh in his mind.

"Do ye see now why he worries so?" Aelfread prompted.

"Nay." Kyla glanced up, wry apology on her face. "I fear I do not. Surely Galen realizes Margaret's death was not deliberate? The MacGregor could not have known she would go into labor. You said yourself that normally she and her cousin simply would have run out—"

"They most like didn't even ken she was there,"

Aelfread interrupted. "And Galen knows that. 'Tis why he didn't simply kill the MacGregor. Both sides have been staging such raids for decades. 'Twas a tragedy, not deliberate murder."

"Well then, I do not see why you all seem to think that the MacGregor is a threat to me. He did not kill Margaret deliberately. In fact, he most like feels awful about her death. He is hardly likely to come to kill me."

Aelfread peered at her as if she thought her daft. " 'Tis not to kill ye we think he will come, but to retaliate."

"Retaliate?"

"Aye. For Galen's stealing ye."

Kyla rolled her eyes at that. "How on earth could he retaliate?"

Aelfread shrugged. "Any number of ways. He may just ransom ye back, but if he took a shine to ye—"

"Aye?" Kyla prompted, when Aelfread cut herself off.

"He could use ye and send ye back shamed," she pointed out reluctantly.

Kyla stiffened at that suggestion, her face paling. "He would not."

"Ye were supposed to be his," Aelfread pointed out reasonably.

"Aye, but I am married to Galen now. We are *legally* married."

Aelfread shrugged. "Law doesn't mean as much to a Scot as right does."

"And 'tis right to rape a woman?" Her voice rose with disbelief.

Seeing that she was getting upset, Aelfread frowned. "Mayhap we should forget about a picnic on the beach and return to the keep."

"Nay!" Pausing, Kyla took a couple of slow breaths, then shook her head. "Nay. We will continue. It may be dark, damp, and gloomy in here, but 'tis sunny and lovely outside. A picnic, then a wade on the beach is just what I need right now." She said the last with grim determination as she turned to survey the small boats bobbing beside the platform. "Which of these shall we take?"

"Mayhap we shouldn't go," Aelfread repeated tentatively. "Now that we've talked about Mac-Gregor, I'm not sure 'twould be wise to go off on our own."

Kyla rolled her eyes in exasperation. "'Tis no less safe than 'twas when we planned it last night," she pointed out. "You said yourself that the beach is surrounded by cliffs that are impossible to scale. Why would MacGregor land there?"

"Aye, but—"

"Nay. No buts," Kyla interrupted firmly. "'Tis just the gloominess in here affecting you. You shall feel better once we are out in the fresh air. Think of the feel of sand under your feet," she added for incentive, then peered over at the boats again. "Why do we not take this one?"

Aelfread shrugged off her misgivings and glanced at the boat Kyla was pointing at. It was the one in the best shape, the paint nice and fresh. "Nay," she decided with a firm shake of the head. "The one on the end."

Kyla peered at the one Aelfread was now walking

past her to reach and grimaced. It looked in desperate need of painting. It was also the smallest of them all. Kyla had spent little time in boats, but was sure the larger they were, the less chance they would capsize.

"It may not be pretty, but 'twill be easier for us to handle," Aelfread argued as if reading her mind.

Kyla grimaced at the sound argument as Aelfread moved carefully to board the vessel, but silently drew on her courage and followed.

"What mean ye, she is gone?" The MacDonald stared blankly at Morag, forgetting entirely the Englishman now seated at the table beside him.

"Just what I said!" Morag answered him irritably. "I went to your room and she's not there. Aelfread's gone, too."

Robbie stiffened at that, worry filling his face. "Aelfread is gone, as well?"

"Aye. Both of them have flown the coop."

"But Aelfread is—"

"In the family way. Aye." Morag pursed her lips and shook her head. "Really shouldn't be gallivanting about in that condition. Neither should Kyla, what with her back and all. Mind ye," she added now, glaring at both men, "neither of them would be doing such and the like had ye allowed them some freedom and not treated them like a couple of Sabine slaves!"

"A couple of what!" Galen roared, rising to his feet.

"Ye heard me," she snapped.

"Should I send some men out to look for them, me laird?" Tommy interrupted, drawing Galen's attention back to the matter at hand.

"Aye." MacDonald wasted a moment to glare at Morag, then turned to Tommy. "Aye. Search the island. Everywhere. They can't have gone far."

"Where is the beach?" Kyla murmured, peering around. All she could see was open water ahead and a wall of rock at their back as they drifted a little further away from the mouth of the tunnel.

"Just around that rock there. 'Tis not even far to swim. Not for a good swimmer," she added honestly.

Kyla pursed her lips as she peered to the right, the direction Aelfread was pointing. "It does not look like a very large beach from my chamber window. They could not hide many boats I am sure."

"There's a cave there, as well. In the face of the cliff. Directly below yer window. 'Tis small, though. There's only enough room for one or two boats. But 'tis enough to take people to the mainland in shifts. Or they could wait and swim back for more boats at low tide if the cave isn't discovered."

Kyla glanced back the way they had come, a frown plucking at her brow. The cave entrance had already disappeared into the face of the cliff and they were only ten or fifteen feet away from it. "Where is the entrance?" she asked.

Aelfread peered back now herself. "Do ye see that pointed cliff? The one that looks almost like an arrow pointing upward?"

"Aye."

" 'Tis just at the base of that. Directly below it."

Nodding, Kyla shifted to the center bench beside Aelfread, to help power the boat. "I have never rowed a boat before," she admitted as Aelfread took up her own oar and was surprised by a sudden laugh from her friend.

"Neither have I, but I'm sure it can't be too hard. We shall manage."

Sharing a smile, they started out. It wasn't that hard a task . . . but not that easy, either. They got the hang of it quickly enough, though, and were soon managing to send the boat sliding across the water in the general direction they wanted. A few moments later, they slid around the outcropping of rock and the beach came into view.

"I think it would have been easier had we swum for it," Kyla murmured wryly as she surveyed the beach and the distance they had yet to traverse to reach it. She could have crossed that distance in a matter of moments swimming. By boat, it would probably take them three times as long.

Aelfread gave a breathless laugh beside her, her own gaze sparkling as she peered over the sandy patch of beach surrounded by rock and cliffs. "Aye, but think of the fun we would have missed. 'Sides, we are getting the hang of this. Who knows when such a skill may come in handy?"

Kyla snorted and took up her oar again. To her surprise, they were much better at the chore of rowing than they had been on first setting out, and it really didn't take that long to reach the beach. Still, she was relieved when the grating of sand along the bottom of the small skiff rang in her ears. Both women dropped their oars with relief at that sound and the jarring that accompanied it. Sliding the oars out of their slings, they set them in the bottom of the boat and shifted to disembark.

Kyla was the first to leap into the water. She did so just as Aelfread shouted her warning, but 'twas too late, by then she was discovering what the other woman was warning her of. The boat was deeper than she had realized and so was the water. Perhaps they'd skimmed a sand bar. Kyla released a startled cry as she found herself landing in waist-deep water. She had barely a moment to get over the shock of cold water up to her navel, when a second shout from Aelfread drew her attention. With her weight out of the boat, it had risen slightly in the water and slid off the sand. It was now drifting rapidly back out the way it had come.

Cursing, Kyla turned as swiftly as she could with her water-logged gown dragging at her and lunged at the boat, tugging on it to bring it back toward shore. It returned much more easily than she'd expected, sending her toppling backward in the water as it raced passed her and lodged itself in the sand once more.

Gasping at the shock of cold to her upper body now, as well, Kyla muttered a string of curses as she floundered toward the beach. By the time she reached shore, Aelfread had leapt to the sand with nary a drop of water on her and tugged the boat a safer distance up on land. Once that was accomplished, she turned and eyed Kyla, then burst into laughter as she slapped wetly out of the water.

When Kyla glared at her balefully, she tried to staunch her laughter, then shook her head. "I am sorry. 'Tis just that I never thought to hear ye speak such words, yer being a lady and all."

Flushing, Kyla shook her head, amusement tugging briefly at her lips until she gave in to it and grinned. "I learned them from my brother. He has quite a collection of words for such occasions."

Smiling, Aelfread propped her hands on her hips. "Well, ye'd best get out of yer dress and set it out to dry." Her gaze ran along the shoreline now and she frowned slightly. "Then we shall have to pull the boat further up the beach."

"Why?"

"The tide. 'Tis coming in."

"Now?" Kyla surveyed the water with dismay.

"Aye."

"But it will cover the entrance to the cave."

Aelfread nodded.

"But we shall be stuck here," she pointed out.

Aelfread smiled slightly at that. "For a bit, but we planned to have a picnic and mayhap a swim anyway."

"Oh, aye," Kyla murmured, the worry slipping from her face, only to be replaced a moment later by dismay. "Oh, hell!"

"What?"

"The bread." It was all she had to say. Understanding lit the other woman's face at once, followed by a groan of dismay.

"I daresay 'tis not just flat now," she said wryly. "I begin to think we weren't meant to eat bread this day."

"Aye," Kyla sighed.

"At least we still have the apples." The other woman dug them out of her bodice and Kyla laughed, then shook her head and turned her attention to undoing the laces of her gown.

Dropping the ripe, red apples into a pocket of her own gown, Aelfread left her to undress and turned away to explore the beach.

"Kyla!"

She had just stripped down to her under-tunic when Aelfread called her name. There was a worried sound to her voice. Setting her gown across the bow of the boat, Kyla turned and moved to join the other woman farther down the beach. Reaching her side, she peered down at the sand where Aelfread gestured, her eyes widening slightly as she took in the small bag lying on the ground before them.

"What is it?" Kyla asked, bending to pick it up.

"Someone has been here."

Raising her eyebrows at the fear-laden words, Kyla began to open the bag. "Mayhap whoever looks in on the boats dropped it when last checking on them."

"They check them at the beginning of the month. This is the middle."

"Mayhap they dropped it at the beginning of the month then and did not know where they had lost it," Kyla suggested with a shrug, then frowned. The bag had slid open to reveal oats inside.

"Nay."

Kyla glanced up at the quiver of fear in her voice.

"The tide reaches well past here when 'tis fully in. It would have taken the bag with it long ago. Someone has been here."

"And not long ago," Kyla murmured, picking out a handful of the dry flakes. Surely had the bag drifted onto the beach, the oats would be wet. That meant it had been dropped today . . . After high tide. Her gaze slid around the small beach now. "I do not see anyone."

"Do ye see the large tree against the cliff wall— Don't look," she hissed when Kyla started to peer past her. "I mean, try to look without appearing to."

She waited a moment as Kyla nonchalantly ran her eyes over the length of the cliff wall again.

"Aye. What of it?"

"There is a cave behind it, half-hidden. 'Tis where they hide the boats," Aelfread informed her quietly.

"If 'tis only half hidden, someone could have found it."

"And be in there now," Aelfread agreed grimly.

"We'd better get back to the boat," Kyla suggested tensely. "Whoever dropped this may have left already, but 'twould be better to go back, admit what we planned to do, and have Galen send someone to check the cave." Sighing, she glanced back at the small bag she was clenching in her hand. "It may be nothing. It could have been one of the men earlier. You said yourself there is no way to scale this wall."

"Aye," Aelfread agreed, her gaze moving blindly over the water. "But I have a bad feeling." Her gaze snapped back to Kyla. "We mustn't make it obvious that we suspect anything. Ye head back to the boat and act as if yer simply going to stretch out yer dress. I'll follow. Be ready to jump in and push off quick."

"Mayhap you should head over to the boat first," Kyla suggested worriedly. " 'Twill be harder for you to run if you have to in your full gown than it would be for me in my tunic."

"Aye, but I'm not the one they're after. I'm just your subject."

Kyla became indignant at that. "You are not a subject. You are the wife of one of my husband's best warriors. You are also my friend."

"Me lady, whether I work in the castle or simply live in the village, ye became me mistress the day ye married me clan chief and I swore an oath on me marriage to defend me laird and his kin with me life."

"What of your child's life?" Kyla argued stubbornly.

"The longer we stand here arguing, the longer we are vulnerable," Aelfread snapped. "'Sides, were it not for me we wouldn't be here. I'd never forgive myself should anything happen to ye. Now please . . . *Please* go to the boat."

Kyla glared at her briefly, then let her breath out on an exasperated sigh. "Fine, but I must say, Aelfread MacDonald, if my marriage does make you my subject, you are a poor one for daring to argue with me."

A small smile tugged at her lips despite the situation. "Aye, but then I never said I was a *good* subject," she murmured, then her smile slipped. "Go."

Reaching out, Kyla gave her hand a squeeze, then turned and headed calmly back toward the boat, swinging the small bag at her side in as nonchalant a manner as possible. She had only covered half the distance however, when she heard Aelfread's warning cry. Whirling in the sand, she saw the other woman running toward her, several men charging down from the trees after her.

Chapter 15

"RUN!"

The stark terror in the other woman's voice snapped Kyla out of the panic that had frozen her briefly to the spot. Letting the bag of oats slip from her hand, she spun back around and set out at a dead run.

It seemed to take forever to reach the boat. The harder she ran, the deeper her feet seemed to sink into the shifting sand, and the slower she seemed to go. Kyla was chanting a prayer under her breath as she moved—a prayer that got all jumbled with her apologies to God for sneaking about as she had done to come to this beach, and promises not to do so ever again. With each step she took, she expected to feel a hand grab her from behind or to be tumbled to the ground, but she made it to the boat unmolested. Once there, she did not even think, but gave the small vessel a sharp shove that sent it sliding back into the water, then caught it before it could go too far and glanced back toward Aelfread.

The other woman was still a good twenty paces away, her efforts to run hampered by her skirts as Kyla had feared. The men were gaining on her. Their long legs seemed to gobble up the distance twice as fast as Aelfread's smaller steps. The closest one would be on top of the woman in another moment, and Kyla began searching the ground frantically for something to throw at the man. A scream from Aelfread told her that she was too late. Glancing up, Kyla saw her falling beneath the weight of the first of their pursuers.

Cursing, she released the boat, grabbed the closest paddle off of it and charged forward. She lifted the oar over her shoulder in preparation to strike Aelfread's assailant, but the second man had reached the struggling pair on the ground by the time she arrived, and Kyla swung it at him instead. He went down like wheat before a sickle, but before she could bring the oar back to bear upon Aelfread's attacker, the third man shot forward to tackle her. His head down like a bull's, he slammed into her stomach, sending her crashing backward knocking the very wind from her.

"Kyla!"

She heard Aelfread call to her but had no air to respond. Rolling onto her side, she gasped for breath as the other woman shoved her captor away with disgust and crawled across the sand on her hands and knees to Kyla's side. Their captors stood, watching them silently.

"Are ye all right?" Aelfread asked, grabbing her shoulders and frowning worriedly as Kyla gasped desperately for air that simply did not seem to be there. "Calm," she soothed, brushing the hair back from her face. "Ye've had the breath knocked from ye. It'll come."

Kyla tried to nod, but could not stop gasping. Then the first small gust of air finally managed to force its way into her lungs, and she dropped back onto the sand with relief, dragging a second breath in as she did.

"Whist," Aelfread murmured, relief on her own face as she drew Kyla's head to rest in her lap while she recovered. Then her eyes froze over like the surface of a lake in the middle of winter and she raised her head to peer at the half-dozen men now surrounding them. "MacGregor, no doubt," she accused grimly.

"None other," the one who had tackled Kyla murmured, relaxing a bit as he saw that she had not been truly injured by his actions. " 'Twas unexpectedly kind of you to present yourselves here for us to collect. We expected to have to wait for dark to paddle around to a much more accessible, but guarded beach, then slip about the keep until we found you. You have saved us a great deal of trouble."

A groan drew his gaze to the man Kyla had downed and he grimaced, then turned back to add, "Though 'twould have been kinder had you not brained my man, Jimmy, here."

"*Ye* are the MacGregor?"

Kyla understood the surprise in her friend's voice. This man hardly looked a brutal, villainous bastard. Neither did he sound or look like a Scot. His accent was most definitely English, as were the braies he wore in place of the customary Scottish plaid. His hair was blond, his skin fair, his figure slender and long, and his dress meticulous despite having tackled her. He looked like a courtier, she decided, easing slowly to a sitting position.

"At your service," he answered, giving a mocking bow. Then he arched an eyebrow. "Are you out on your own, ladies? Or is the MacDonald following?"

Both women shared a glance but remained silent.

"No, hmm?" he guessed. "Well, mayhap we should return to our little hiding spot anyway. Bring the boat," he ordered his men, then turned and started back up the beach again, leaving his men to deal with the women and their vessel.

"What do ye mean ye can't find them?" Galen stared at Tommy blankly, then frowned. "Did the men search everywhere?"

"Aye, me laird. Every last inch of the isle has been searched."

Galen was frowning over that when Lord Shropshire suddenly stepped closer, concern evident upon his face.

"Am I to understand that you have lost Lady Kyla?"

"Nay!" Galen snapped, then calmed enough to add, "She is most like out for a breath of fresh air. She doesn't like being cooped up too long."

"Or mayhap she fled when she learned I had come to the island," the Englishman murmured thoughtfully. Galen peered at him as if he were daft.

"Why the devil would she do that?"

"Why do *you* not tell me?" the man responded calmly.

Irritation suffused Galen at those cryptic words. "Yer talking riddles, man. She doesn't even ken yer here."

Shropshire raised his eyebrows at that. "You are sure she does not?"

"Aye, I'm sure. Now sit down and tend yer ale. I don't have time for yer games now." Galen waved him away as if he were a pesky child and turned to Tommy. "Did ye check Robbie's cottage?"

"I had the men check *every* cottage, me laird. They aren't on the island."

"They must have gone to the mainland," Angus suggested now, perplexity on his face even as he said it. "But why?"

"Aelfread wouldn't go to the mainland without telling me first," Robbie rumbled, then shook his head in disgust and frustration. "Hell, she wouldn't go anywhere without telling me."

"MacDonald," Shropshire began slowly after one of his own men leaned forward to murmur something to him.

"Not now, man. I needs must find me wife."

"Could the MacGregor have—" Duncan began, then paused when Galen turned sharply on him. Swallowing uncomfortably under his gaze, he shrugged. "Well, we knew he wouldn't take the loss of her without some type of retribution. Mayhap he stole her back."

"From me own room? Under our very noses?" Galen's expression became ferocious at the thought.

Tommy shook his head at that. "Nay. No one went up or down those stairs after I went above to fetch ye, Galen. We would have seen them."

There was silence at that as all the men glanced uncomfortably at each other, then Shropshire opened his mouth again as if to comment. Morag interrupted him.

"Well, 'tis either that someone snuck them out under yer noses, or they did so themselves." Frowning now, she shook her head. "I thought sure they had both just tired of being mollycoddled and had slipped out for a saunter on the beach. Kyla always took to a walk along the river when she felt down or stifled at home. But if they are not on the island . . . Yer sure ye've searched everywhere?"

Tommy stiffened at the suggestion that he had not done his job properly. "Of course. Every inch. Except for the cliff beach," he added suddenly, his gaze going questioningly to Galen who shook his head at once.

"Nay, I had not got around to showing her that yet," he murmured.

"Someone else may have told her. Aelfread, for instance," Duncan suggested. They all turned to Robbie who had sunk down at the table and was now staring morosely into the distance, misery on his face and fear in his heart. He could not get Duncan's words out of his head. What if the two women *had* been taken by the MacGregor? Aelfread was such a wee lass. And she was with child. She was also a mere wife of a clan member. It was bad enough what might be done to Kyla, but Aelfread didn't have a title to protect her. She could be abused horribly, her wee body passed around the MacGregor men for each to use—

"Robbie!" Galen had to shout the man's name three times to get his attention. Once his friend had snapped out of whatever fears had grabbed ahold of him, Galen asked, "Does Aelfread ken about the cave?"

The giant blinked at the question, slow to realize the reason behind it. Then the horror slid slowly from his mind, anger taking its place and spurring him to his feet. "Damn!" he roared, stomping toward the staircase, Galen and the others, even the messenger, on his heels. "I'll kill the sneaking little wench!"

"The tide'll be in," Tommy pointed out as they raced up the stairs, his words slowing both Robbie and Galen until they paused at the top.

"Aye," Galen murmured thoughtfully. "But it wouldn't have been in earlier when they went above stairs. Still, we won't be able to follow." He hesitated, then glanced to Gavin. "Gather some men and take search boats out to the cliff beach. We'll check to see if they are in the cave or if there is a boat missing, then wait for ye on shore." Grimacing, he added, "'Twill give Robbie and me a chance to cool our tempers."

Nodding, Gavin turned away at once, descending the stairs and heading for the keep doors.

Galen did not wait to see him leave, but turned to lead the way up, pausing when he realized that Shropshire was following. "Ye'll have to stay here," he announced, then glanced to Duncan. "Keep him company." With that he continued up the stairs, to and through his chamber, to the tunnel entrance. Moments later he, Angus, Tommy, and Robbie were in the cavern, counting boats.

"Nine," Tommy murmured aloud as he finished counting.

"One is missing." Angus smiled with pride at that and Galen grimaced with disgust, deciding that his men's penchant for delighting in every little display of spirit or rebellion his wife now revealed was becoming most annoying.

"'Tis a shame," Robbie rumbled, bringing the other men's gazes to him curiously.

"Why?" Tommy finally asked.

"It means I shall have to kill Aelfread," he responded nonchalantly, then explained, "'Tis just punishment for this scare."

Galen bit back a smile and patted the man on the shoulder sympathetically. He'd had his own horrible demons chasing him for the past several minutes as he had considered the possibility that the MacGregor had his wife. He well understood his friend's odd behavior now. His own relief was making him giddy and in peril of saying or doing something incredibly foolish. That being the case, he thought it best he keep his mouth shut.

"Well . . ." Tommy shifted after a moment when they all simply stood there, contemplating the empty cavern. "I suppose we had best go down to the dock and await Gavin's return with them."

Heaving a sigh, Galen nodded and turned to lead the way to the steps, pausing abruptly when he spotted Duncan stepping into the cavern, the English lord directly on his heels. "What the Devil?"

"I ken ye wanted us to wait in the great hall," Duncan rushed out at once. "But I think ye'll be wanting to hear what Lord Shropshire has to say."

Pausing at the mouth of the cave, Kyla peered curiously at the MacGregor. He stood in the center of the small chamber, frowning over the other four boats that had already been crammed into the narrow space. It really wasn't much of a cave at all, from what she could see, just an eight-foot-square hole in the rock. With just the two boats Aelfread had told her the cave usually held, the space would have been snug, leaving a small area clear for someone to camp out should they be forced to during a storm. Now there were four boats leaning up against the walls. It left only a foot-wide and eight-foot-deep space for them to stand in.

Kyla assumed that the two extra boats were the MacGregors'. Their presence left very little room for anything, and she had to wonder how the six men had managed to be cramped in here while she and Aelfread had been on the beach. It would have been close quarters. Come to that, with two extra people and another boat, the situation would be impossible. She couldn't hold back an amused smile as she noted the MacGregor's frustration at the situation. It seemed things were not all going to go his way.

Turning toward the entrance of the cave, he caught her expression and his own tightened briefly, then he glanced past her toward his men. "You two, take that boat and hide it."

When his men merely peered at him blankly, his expression became annoyed. "Either take it back to the water and sink it, or dig a hole and bury it," he snapped. "There is no room in here."

Nodding, the two men turned back the way they had come.

"Be quick about it," he shouted after them as an afterthought, then turned his frown to the man who stood propping the unconscious Jimmy up. "Set him down and get over here, Willie," he snapped impatiently. He turned back to survey the cave again, his gaze moving over the roof as he waited for the man to do as he was told.

"We shall have to stack these boats upright," he announced when the man had set down his burden and joined him. " 'Twill make more room." He turned to glance at the man guarding Kyla and Aelfread. "You come help him, Roy. I shall watch the women."

Nodding, the fellow who had escorted them up from the beach released his hold on Kyla and Aelfread and shuffled into the cave as the MacGregor moved out of it. The clan chief positioned himself between them as he watched the men shift the boats so that they all leaned against the wall, standing upright with their bows in the air. It allowed them to set the boats side-by-side, two along each wall, leaving a small space in the center of the cave. It would be cramped with the eight of them, but much less cramped than it would have been before.

"In you go."

Kyla and Aelfread shared a glance, then moved resignedly into the new area as the men stepped aside to give them room. MacGregor followed as his men moved out to drag the unconscious Jimmy in and sit him up in the back right corner of the cave.

"Good, now go hurry the other two along ere they are spotted. And bring back Lady Kyla's gown as well," he added as the men left, bringing Kyla's attention to the fact that she was dressed in only a damp tunic. She had quite forgotten that fact during the excitement. Now that she was reminded, she was suddenly uncomfortably conscious of the way the thin material clung to her damp flesh.

Catching a sympathetic glance from Aelfread, Kyla forced a small smile, then turned back to the Mac-Gregor as he surveyed them. Her chin rose as his gaze slid slowly over her form under the thin tunic.

Raising an eyebrow at her defiant expression, the MacGregor gestured to the ground at their feet. "A seat, ladies?" he suggested with feigned gallantry. "Would that I could offer you a chair, but I fear the sand shall have to do."

Kyla hesitated, then sank to a sitting position on

the sandy floor of the cave, careful to be sure her tunic did not rise up as she did.

"What now?" she asked as Aelfread joined her on the sand.

"We wait," MacGregor responded with a grimace as he leaned back against the boat behind him. "I must admit that while I appreciate your making things so easy for us by coming here, 'twould really have been more convenient had you waited 'til later in the day to do so. I fear we cannot leave until darkness falls to give us cover, and I would not welcome the arrival of searchers looking for you."

"My apologies," Kyla drawled with some acerbity, then suggested sweetly, "Why do you not release us? If you do so, I promise we would return later."

His lips quirked sightly at that. "Bringing the MacDonald with you, no doubt." When Kyla merely shrugged, his smile widened. "Well, I must admit, surprised or not by your appearance, I am glad of it." When Kyla raised one disdainful eyebrow, he added, "I fear I was led to believe that you were a repulsive little wren. Yet here you are quite vibrant and attractive. Not beautiful in the traditional way, but quite appealing."

Kyla felt Aelfread stiffen and distinctly recalled her saying that should the McGregor take a shine to her, shaming her might be his retribution. Pushing that thought away now lest she not be able to think past her fear, Kyla cleared her throat. She murmured, "If you had been told I was so unattractive, why did you bother to come after me?"

"Ah, well, marriages are rarely based on the attractiveness of the bride, are they?" he answered easily. "And we *shall* be married. Though I must warn you, you will not find me as stupid as your present husband."

Kyla stiffened at that, but he merely shrugged at her indignance.

"Only a stupid man knows not where his wife is and I very much doubt that the MacDonald gave you permission to go puttering about in a boat with only a servant for company." He glanced at Aelfread now and smiled. "I must thank you for calling out your mistress' name. I confess I was not sure what I had on my hands when we spied your boat coming around the cliffs. I was a bit worried when you came ashore, but when I heard you call her name I knew the gods were smiling on me today." He glanced back to Kyla now to confess. "I fear I would not have known who you were without that."

She could almost hear Aelfread silently cursing herself, the guilt emanating off of her was so thick. Kyla opened her mouth to reassure the other woman, but MacGregor's words forestalled her.

"You will understand why I am so grateful when you realize that I might have killed you both rather than chance your reporting the bag I saw you pick up. Of course, once I knew who you were, killing you was out of the question."

"How fortunate," Kyla muttered, then tried to sound reasonable. "While I appreciate that you were originally intended to be my husband, my lord, I fear 'tis simply not possible now. Galen and I are married. Legally. Binding."

" 'Twill be annulled," he announced with a wave of the hand that seemed to say the marriage was of no consequence.

Kyla took a moment to control her irritation at his lack of concern, then said, "It cannot be annulled, my lord. It has been well and truly consummated."

He shrugged at that. "It will still be annulled."

"Are you not listening? I said—" She paused, then tried a different tactic. "My lord, I realize that my sister-in-law made some agreements and contracts with you, but she had no right. She was not my guardian. Still is not," she corrected firmly, hoping against hope that what she said was true and Johnny was still alive. "My brother is my guardian and as such he is the only one with any legal right to agree to my marriage and to sign contracts to that effect. The contract was not legal. You have no right to marry me."

"Neither did the MacDonald and yet it was done."

"Aye, but—" Kyla stopped in frustration, then said, "My lord, I shall be frank. I am quite happy in my marriage. I do not wish to change it."

"That is a shame, but your wishes notwithstanding, we will be married."

" 'Tis like talking to a rock," she snapped curtly.

"Aye, I have been told I can be stubborn," he agreed with mock sympathy, then shrugged. "Still, as my wife, you shall have to learn to live with that."

He actually laughed at her obvious rancor when she ground her teeth together. Then he stood and had the temerity to pat her head like a dog. "Relax. You will wear yourself out with your anger and I fear you shall need all of your energy later." Then he slipped from the cave.

"I'm sorry."

Kyla turned irritably on her friend at those words.

"Do not say it. 'Tis not your fault. You wanted to turn back, if you will recall."

"Aye, but—"

"Do not 'but' me!" Sighing, Kyla shook her head. "Rest," she murmured, glancing at the man they had propped up in the corner. He seemed still to be unconscious, but she lowered her voice anyway as she whispered. " 'Tis hours until darkness comes and we will need our strength then."

Aelfread hesitated, then whispered, "The cave?"

"Aye."

She nodded. "When?"

"When they take us out to the boats."

There was silence for a moment, then, "Do ye swim well?"

"Well enough," Kyla said grimly. "Can you find the entrance in the dark?"

Her silence drew Kyla's head around to see the uncertainty on her face.

"Oh, hell," she muttered darkly.

"I may be able to find it," Aelfread said quickly now.

Kyla sighed resignedly. "We shall have to try during daylight."

"Make a run for it? Oh, aye. That should be easy enough."

"I did not say it would be easy," Kyla muttered irritably. "Just that it had to be done."

"How?"

"I do not know. I shall have to think on it."

Aelfread opened her mouth to comment, then thought better of it and sat back, leaving Kyla to think in peace.

She only had a few moments to think before MacGregor returned to the cave, his men in tow. He held her gown in one hand, but it was the rope in his other hand that immediately caused a sinking feeling in the pit of her stomach. Pausing before Kyla and Aelfread, he peered at them silently for a moment, then slung her gown over his shoulder. Pulling a knife from his belt, he cut the rope into four pieces, then handed two lengths of rope to each of the two nearest men. When he ordered them to tie her and Aelfread up, Kyla knew they were doomed.

"My apologies," the MacGregor murmured, sinking onto the sand across from them as the men moved to follow his instructions. " 'Twill be uncomfortable I know, but 'tis several hours 'til dark and we were up all the night traveling here. We could only benefit from a rest and I shall rest better knowing you cannot escape. Not that I think you would try to," he added, with a smile that was all teeth. "I am sure you would not be so foolish. There is nowhere for you to go after all. Still, I will sleep better knowing you are tended to."

Kyla said nothing, simply glared at him as her hands were tied behind her back. He met her glare with a smile, then used his knife to start a tear in her gown as she and Aelfread were bound hand and foot.

"Once again, my apologies," he murmured, ripping a long strip of material from her gown. " 'Tis a lovely gown, but 'twould be better I think if"—he paused to hand the strip to the man who had tied her up—"the two of you were gagged," he finished as the cloth was fitted into Kyla's mouth and tied around the back of her head. "Just in case someone should decide to approach and search this cave, 'tis best you not be tempted to warn them of our presence."

Unable to answer, Kyla simply glared at him angrily as he ripped off another strip of her gown for Aelfread to be gagged.

He watched the process until both she and Aelfread were trussed to his satisfaction, then turned to the men. "We shall take turns watching the beach. One up while the rest of us sleep. Willie, you have first watch. Should anyone land a boat, give the alarm. The rest of you find a spot to lie down and get some rest. We will be traveling through the night again once darkness falls."

Galen felt a frisson of apprehension slide along his back at Duncan's words. Swallowing back the fear suddenly clogging his throat, he turned to Shropshire. "Tell me."

"It may be nothing," the Englishman cautioned. "Or at least not connected to your difficulty in finding Lady Forsythe—"

"MacDonald," Galen corrected with a snap. "She is Lady MacDonald now, and what may no' be connected to her being missing?"

"Lady MacDonald," the man conceded, then said, "When we reached the shore on mainland, we came across a cottage. There was an old man inside. With a beard to here." He gestured to his waist.

"That would be Scatchy," Tommy murmured.

"He was dead," Shropshire announced almost apologetically. "Throat slit, I fear."

"MacGregor." It was a hiss from Angus.

Galen turned away, his face ashen as his blank gaze slid over the black water filling the cavern.

Tommy peered worriedly at Galen's pallid face and tried to reassure him. "It may not be the MacGregor."

"Tommy is right," Angus said quickly, moving to his side. "What would the MacGregor have to gain in killing Scatchy?"

Galen was silent for a moment, then turned back to Lord Shropshire. "Did ye see a boat at the cottage?"

The man shook his head firmly.

"Scatchy had two boats," Robbie muttered worriedly.

"There were several horses tethered there, too," the man offered.

"How many?" Galen asked grimly. Scatchy was a poor fisherman. He had no horses.

"Six or seven."

They were all silent as the ramifications of that news sank in, then Tommy frowned and peered at Galen questioningly. "Are ye thinking he found out about this cavern, killed Scatchy, stole the boat, and came here, then snuck above stairs to steal Lady Kyla away?"

Galen shook his head. "Nay. That wouldn't explain Aelfread's absence or the missing boat."

"Aye," Robbie rumbled with relief. "The women must have snuck off on their own."

"Aye," Galen agreed, but did not look relieved himself.

"Well, 'tis all right then, isn't it?" Duncan asked now uncertainly. "I mean, if 'tis the MacGregor who killed Scatchy and took his boats, he can't have approached the island. The men on watch would have spotted them. He is most like hiding out for the day, awaiting nightfall to give him cover. So long as we bring Aelfread and Lady Kyla back ere nightfall, all should be well. Better than well since we ken his plans now."

Galen turned to Shropshire again. "Was he newly dead?"

Understanding and worry mingling on his face, the man slowly shook his head. "Nay. I would say it happened sometime early this morn. I think he had been breaking his fast."

"There!" Duncan cried with relief. "Ye see. He is most like hiding out on the mainland, waiting for dark to offer him cover."

"There was a heavy mist this morn," Galen pointed out bleakly. "That would have offered them cover."

"Aye," Tommy agreed. "And it may have aided to keep them hidden for quite a distance, but 'twas not so heavy the men would have missed the arrival of a boat once it neared shore. The watch would have seen them had they tried to land."

"Not if they approached the cliff beach," Galen pointed out grimly. "We never post a guard there."

Tommy blinked at that. "Aye, but that is because there is no way to gain access to the island from there, 'tis a dead end. He would be foolish to try to scale that cliff."

"He may have landed there, though, to wait for dark to move to another beach. 'Twould be safer than trying to make the crossing at night when a full moon and clear sky could make him visible to anyone watching."

"Aye," Tommy agreed grimly. "That *would* be the smartest move."

"But, if he did that," Duncan began with dismay. "Then Aelfread and Lady Kyla have—"

"Rushed right into his arms," Robbie growled.

Chapter 16

CAMPED on enemy ground or not, the Mac-Gregors seemed to have little difficulty relaxing. Within moments every man inside the cave had dozed off. The man left to guard the cave was still awake, but showed little interest in what happened inside. Seated with his back to the mouth of the cave, he had turned only once to peer in at them.

Deciding there would be no better time to try an escape, Kyla glanced toward Aelfread and jerked her head back toward their tied hands, then shifted until her back was to the other woman. Glancing over her shoulder then, she saw with relief that the other woman understood what she wanted. After peering down at her tied hands and taking in the knot used, she, too, turned until they were back to back. Her cold hands felt for and found Kyla's, then shifted to the rope.

Moments later, Kyla felt the rope loosen, then slip from her wrists. Releasing a sigh, she quickly shifted around, cast a nervous glance toward the guard, then set to work on her friend's bindings.

Sharing a half-triumphant, half-fearful glance as Aelfread's bindings dropped away, the two women then quickly set to work on the ropes at their ankles.

Untying them, they left them in place so that it appeared that they were still bound. Kyla then glanced at the guard once more, contemplating the next move. That, of course, was the tricky part. She had rather hoped that the man might simply fall asleep as his compatriots had done, leaving them free to tiptoe past him to the shore. Unfortunately, he wasn't cooperating; he appeared wide awake.

Frowning, she peered about the interior of the cave, searching for something for inspiration, or, failing that, something to pound him over the head with. The oars were her first choice, but they had been stacked on the floor against the one wall, with the boats then leaned over them. Inaccessible.

Her gaze narrowed on a good-sized rock half-buried beside her right foot. Leaning forward, she tugged at it experimentally, grateful when it moved. Reaching her other hand forward, she tugged it free, and hefted it to judge its weight. Satisfied, she drew it into her lap and eyed their guard consideringly.

Aye, it would do, she decided. If it landed right, it should knock the guard senseless. Now all she had to worry about was the noise such an action would make. 'Twould do them little good to knock out one man only to wake the others in the process.

Grimacing, she shook her head silently. This escape business was a tiresome chore, especially when she considered what she was escaping to. Galen would hardly be pleased to learn of their exploits. And they would have to tell him. A nudge from Aelfread drew her attention to the mouth of the cave to see that their guard was gone.

Hands tightening on the boulder, she removed her gag and got quietly to her feet, then slipped as silently as she could along the wall to the entrance. A smile curved her lips when she saw what he was about. He was standing a good twelve feet away, staring out at the ocean and whistling as he relieved himself.

She glanced at Aelfread to see amusement cover her face as she, too, peered around the entrance. Gesturing for her to wait there, Kyla took a deep breath then moved, creeping up on him as quickly and quietly as she could.

The man must have had the sight. It was the only thing Kyla could imagine. She hadn't made a single sound in her approach and had stayed well out of his peripheral vision, yet she was only halfway to him when his head suddenly whipped around. His mouth dropped open upon seeing her, and he seemed to freeze.

With no other idea of what to do, Kyla raised the boulder over her head and hurled it at him with all her might, aiming roughly for his head.

With a squeak of distress, the fellow raised his arms to protect his head, his braies immediately dropping to tangle around his ankles as he tried to jump back out of the way. He ended sprawled in the sand. Not that Kyla stood around waiting to see that. Once the rock had flown from her hands, she whirled and raced for the beach, Aelfread hard on her heels, the other woman removing her plaid even as she ran.

When Kyla peered back as she reached the edge of the water, it was to see that the guard had managed to tug his pants up and make it to the cave entrance, bleating away like a panicked sheep all the while. Even worse, the MacGregor was at the cave entrance now, ordering a boat to be brought out. He charged across the beach after her and Aelfread.

"Go!" Aelfread screeched as she reached Kyla's side. Kyla stumbled into the water, then dove under the waves. She burst back to the surface a bare moment later to see that Aelfread was ahead of her, swimming strongly toward the outcropping of rock they had to circumnavigate to reach the cave.

A glance over her shoulder showed her that the MacGregor had nearly reached the water himself. Two of his men were directly behind him and two more were following as quickly as they could with the boat between them. Behind that staggered the unfortunate Jimmy, apparently finally roused.

Turning away, Kyla struck out after Aelfread, silently praying for strength and speed. She would need the help, she knew. While she was recovering nicely from her injury and accompanying fevers, she was aware that she had not fully regained her strength and stamina. She was already tiring.

Digging down deep inside herself for whatever reserves she had, Kyla propelled herself around the outcropping of rocks. She was more than relieved to see Aelfread paused before the cliff ahead, treading water—until she realized that the tide had come in and the other woman was searching for the arrow-like rock that showed where the entrance to the now-submerged cave was. Panic welled up in her as she realized that they would have to swim the tunnel entrance underwater to reach the cave. She pushed it down determinedly. Aelfread would find it and they would make it through the tunnel. They had to.

Kyla could tell the exact moment when Aelfread found what she sought. The relief was plain on the girl's face. But it was short-lived. Panic replaced it the moment she turned to look toward her. And that was enough to tell Kyla what she had already suspected. Their pursuers were hard on her heels. She could almost feel the nearest man's breath on her neck as he pursued her.

In the next second, Aelfread's mouth opened on a shout of warning even as Kyla felt a hand close around her ankle. Water suddenly rushed past her lips as she was abruptly tugged back and downward. Whirling in the water, she swung her arms frantically in an effort to pull herself back up above the surface, instinctively kicking out at her captor. She felt her foot connect with something, then pushed with all her might, managing to break away toward the surface.

As she shot out from under the water, she saw her pursuer surface no more than one body-length behind her. Panicked, Kyla coughed out the water she had inhaled and gasped fresh air into her lungs. She struck out blindly toward Aelfread's screams, managing to keep that small distance between them out of sheer fear until she reached the other woman's side.

"Go!" she shrieked frantically and Aelfread immediately dove beneath the water. Barely managing a gasp, Kyla followed as closely as she could, her foot connecting with something firm and most definitely human as she did. It told her just how close her pursuer was. Using the man's body as an impromptu platform, Kyla pushed herself down and forward off him, her hands searching for the wall she knew was directly ahead.

Cursing, Galen turned away from Shropshire and led the men toward the stairs. Fear for Kyla was eating at him, urging him to head for the docks to follow Gavin. It was hell not knowing what was going on. Was the MacGregor even this minute creeping up on an unaware Kyla and Aelfread? Or had he already made his presence known and dragged them off?

With these questions gnawing at his nerves, awaiting news from Gavin was out of the question. Action was needed. He would take a boat to the beach. If Kyla was there, he would get her back. Even if he had to kill all the MacGregors to do it. He could not lose her. He loved her.

Galen was neither pleased nor surprised at that thought. He had been wrestling with his feelings ever since the day they had made love on the beach, the day he had realized that the fevers had not stolen her wits. He had realized a lot about her that day; she was smart, passionate, beautiful, and goodnatured. He had already known from hearing the tale of her saving her brother that she was both brave and loyal. How could he not love her? But loving her had brought him no joy. This last week had been hellish for Galen as he'd struggled to hide his feelings behind short words and a surly nature. He had to, for he knew that his wife did not love him in return. To her he was a stranger.

He would change that, he decided grimly, then paused with his foot on the first step when the sound of splashing erupted behind him. Spinning back, he stared in amazement at the woman now in the water.

"Aelfread!" Her name rumbled from Robbie's throat as they all rushed back to the edge of the rocky shelf. Whirling in the water, the woman blinked at her husband and the other men in surprise, then struck out wearily toward the shelf.

"Kyla," she gasped as she was hauled out of the water by her husband.

"Where is she?" Galen asked sharply as Robbie enfolded the woman in his bear-like embrace.

"MacGregor."

Galen stiffened at that name, his skin blanching sickly.

His own anxiety eased by the presence of the woman in his arms, Robbie frowned worriedly at his laird, then held his wife a little closer as he gently asked, "What about the MacGregor, wife? Does he have Lady Kyla?"

Frustrated at her own inability to catch her breath, Aelfread shook her head. "Picnic . . . beach . . . Mac-Gregor . . . cliff cave . . ."

"Ye went for a picnic on the beach and the Mac-Gregor was there hiding in the cliff cave?" Angus translated for her.

When Aelfread nodded, Galen grabbed her hand to get her attention, asking urgently, "Did he get Kyla?"

She nodded again. "Caught . . . both." Those words put horror on the faces of every man in the cave, until she added, "Escaped. Swam for it." That brought sighs of relief until she added, "They followed."

"But ye got away. Did Kyla?"

Before she could answer, the cave rang with the sounds of splashing again, drawing all eyes toward the water once more.

Kyla sobbed her relief as she broke through to the surface. The tunnel had seemed unending as she had used its rocky wall to both find her way and pull herself forward. Her body was trembling with effort and her lungs ached from lack of oxygen, but she had made it.

Aelfread's relieved shout hit her ears now and she struck out instinctively toward it, her eyes seeing little but the blurred shapes of the boats bobbing at their moorings off the platform. She had only taken a couple of weary strokes toward those boats however, when the water seemed to erupt behind her.

She knew without looking that one of the men had followed them into the tunnel, and apparently he was not as exhausted as herself. He grabbed her by the hair, whipping her head backward in the water and bringing her up short. She swung instinctively toward her attacker, ready to put up a fight no matter how feeble, but before she had turned halfway around, her hair was released and she was bobbing free again. Too exhausted to really think, Kyla merely struck out for the platform once more. This time she reached it unassaulted.

A hand covering her own as she grasped the slimy rock surface brought her head up to find Aelfread's face swimming into focus. The woman was crying tears of mingled relief and exhaustion as she knelt at the edge of the shelf and Kyla found her own eyes beginning to leak. Suddenly, she was grasped under the arms and lifted out of the water.

Recognizing Robbie's giant girth and thinking he had just arrived, Kyla turned back toward the water as he set her on the rocky surface of the platform, her arm lifting limply to point toward their pursuer. But that arm dropped weakly to her side when she recognized Galen was already in the water battling the man who had grabbed her. Some part of her fatigued mind realized that he must be the reason her pursuer had released her so abruptly, but beyond that she really wasn't capable of thinking. She watched him knock her attacker unconscious. Catching *him* by the hair now, Galen swam for the ledge, dragging his captive behind.

Robbie relieved him of his burden as soon as he reached the side, lifting the limp man out of the water and dropping him with little care on the rocky shelf. He turned back to offer a hand to Galen himself. Kyla couldn't even find the energy to raise an eyebrow when her husband came lunging out of the water garbed only in his shirt.

Stooping to pick up the plaid he had dropped before plunging into the water, Galen slung it over his shoulder, then turned and bent to lift Kyla away from Aelfread's supporting arms and into his own.

"See to yer wife, Robbie," he ordered, moving immediately toward the stairs. "The rest of ye stay here to be sure no one else finds the cave and enters through it. I'll send word when Gavin returns. Then ye can bring that MacGregor bastard above for questioning." With that, he headed up the steep, slippery steps.

Not having bothered to grab a torch, they were quickly enveloped in darkness. Kyla tightened her arms around her husband's neck, remaining silent during the trip.

He paused in the darkness suddenly and she heard a click as he kicked out at something with his foot. The wall on their right slid open and they were splashed with light again as Galen carried her into their room.

Sighing inwardly, she resigned herself to the verbal

blasting she more than deserved as he walked to the bed. But it did not come. He set her on the bed, came down on top of her, then pulled her into an almost desperate hug.

Kyla lay still for a moment, uncertainty rising up within her. There was nothing sexual in the embrace. She was quite sure it was not a prelude to loving. He simply seemed to need to hold her. Biting her lip, she moved her arms carefully around him, holding him in return, and that was when he finally spoke. "I'm sorry."

Kyla blinked at that, then asked uncertainly, "For what?"

"I nearly lost ye today and 'twould have been all me own fault."

"Nay, 'twas—"

"I didn't guard ye well enough," he interrupted. " 'Tis my job to guard ye. Yer me wife after all. And no' even by yer choice. I kidnapped ye and forced this marriage. The least ye could expect was for me to keep ye safe from the man I angered by such actions."

"Stop!" Amazed, Kyla pulled back to peer at his tormented face. " 'Tis not your fault. Aelfread and I snuck off again. We put ourselves in jeopardy."

"And that is my fault, too," he told her in a pained voice. "Had I seen to taking ye out sooner like I promised, ye wouldn't have had to resort to sneaking about again. Morag is right, I *have* been treating ye like a Sabine slave."

"What?" She gaped at him in amazement.

"Well, think on it. I lock ye up in the keep all the day long and only see ye at night when I use ye for me own pleasure."

Kyla rolled her eyes at that. "I seem to recall

experiencing a moment or two of pleasure in there myself, my lord," she announced dryly.

" 'Sides," he went on, ignoring her words. "Even yer escaping was me fault. Were I a better protector, ye never would have been able to slip away today."

Sighing at that, Kyla touched his cheek. "Galen—"

"I love ye."

Her mouth froze open when he blurted that, her hand stilling at his cheek.

"I do. I love yer smile, yer sweet body, and yer sassy wit. Every morn on awakening I cuddle yer sleeping body close, kiss the top of yer head, and count meself a lucky man for having married ye."

"I—"

"Nay." He covered her lips with one hand and shook his head. "I ken ye don't love me back. Ye hardly ken me. I'm still a stranger to ye. But we'll change that. And mayhap ye can come to love me?" He suggested hopefully, then added practically. "We deal well together abed, that's a start at least."

"What of Margaret?"

Galen blinked in surprise, then sighed the name sadly. "Margaret. Our marriage was arranged when we were children. We grew up together. We married," he said simply.

"Did you love her?"

"Love?" He frowned over the word. "I cared for her, but . . . nay," he admitted sadly. "I never loved her as I should have, not as I do you." A tap at the door drew Galen's irritated attention. "Aye?"

" 'Tis Gavin, me laird."

One moment Galen was reclining on the bed and the next he was on his feet, redonning his plaid as he shouted, "Did ye catch the bastard?"

There was a hesitation, then the reluctant response, "Nay, me laird, they . . ." He paused as Galen tugged the door open, his expression ferocious. Sighing, the warrior shook his head. "They saw us coming and managed to reach the mainland first. We followed, but they had horses waiting. We hadn't thought to take any. We didn't expect to find them on the beach."

"Nay, I ken," the MacDonald sighed unhappily.

"We came back and I sent the big boat over with some men and horses to track them. Then I came to see if ye wish to follow."

Galen nodded at that. "The men are in the cavern still. Shropshire and a MacGregor are with them. Fetch them and take them down to the great hall."

"Gilbert is here?" Kyla cried in amazement. She had not really even noticed the other men in the cavern when Galen had carried her out of it. Scooting off the bed, she hurried toward the chests, her exhaustion forgotten.

"Get back abed," Galen ordered, scowling when she ignored him and began tugging a fresh gown from one of her chests. "Get ye back to bed and rest," he tried again. "I'll not have ye fretting over this."

"Nay," she protested at once, tugging her gown on and quickly tying the laces. "I would speak with Shropshire."

"We'll deal with him later. After I return from hunting the MacGregor."

"Nay. I would hear news of Johnny," Kyla announced determinedly.

"Yer brother is well."

She stilled at that, relief flooding her face. "What did he with Catriona?"

"I don't ken. I'll find out, though, and let ye know."

Kyla hesitated briefly, then finished her laces, determination filling her face.

Galen glowered over this silent rebellion, then sighed. "Oh, hell! If ye must insist." Crossing to where she stood, he scooped her up into his arms again.

"I can walk, my lord," Kyla murmured dryly, clutching at his shoulders as she bounced out of the room in his arms.

"Ye've had enough excitement today. Ye'll be carried and like it."

Relief made Morag's old face glow when Galen carried Kyla below. "Oh! Thank God. I thought sure the MacGregor had ye when Gavin came back saying he was on the beach."

"Nay."

"He did," Galen contradicted, and Kyla sighed as she admitted it. "He did have us briefly, but Aelfread and I managed to escape."

Muttering under his breath, Galen set her on the bench at the trestle table, then straightened and moved to pour himself a mug of ale. He downed the first one so quick, Kyla doubted it had much of a chance to even wet his tongue. She was not terribly surprised when he immediately set about pouring himself another.

The keep doors opened then and her eyebrows rose as Robbie entered. She was not the only one surprised.

"I thought ye were above stairs with yer wife," Galen greeted the man.

Robbie shook his head as he reached the table and accepted the mug of ale Galen offered him. "Nay. I took her back to our cottage to rest. She's fair tuckered . . . Or claiming to be—to avoid me yelling at her like I should."

"Hmm," Galen muttered, tossing a glare in Kyla's direction.

"Have ye questioned the MacGregor man yet?" Robbie asked, distracting him.

"Nay, Gavin is fetching the men now. He just arrived back."

"Already? He didn't catch them, then?" Robbie sighed and downed his drink when Galen shook his head unhappily.

Spying the men starting down the stairs then, Galen set his mug on the table and straightened. Seeing his gaze move between Lord Shropshire and the other man with displeasure, Kyla could almost hear him trying to decide what to deal with first. Tommy made up his mind for him.

"He woke up shortly after ye left, me laird. He didn't feel much like talking, but we convinced him 'twould be a good idea."

Kyla raised her eyebrows at the men's wolfish grins, then glanced to the sullen-faced MacGregor who bore more than a few bruises on his countenance. Her gaze moved to her husband as he asked, "What did ye learn?"

"They did kill Scatchy. Stole his boats and rowed across under cover of the mist this morn to fetch her ladyship back as ye thought."

Galen scowled at the man. "Why? What did MacGregor plan to do?"

When the man merely tightened his lips sullenly, Galen raised his fist.

Jumping up, Kyla caught his arm, blurting, "He planned to marry me."

Galen stilled at that, his expression amazed. "He said that?"

"Aye."

"But he can't, yer married to our laird," Duncan pointed out.

"He planned to have it annulled."

"Well, he couldn't have done that . . . Could he, me laird?"

"Nay. It has been consummated," he said quietly.

Kyla flushed as the men all turned to peer at her, but said, "He said it mattered little. He could and would have it annulled and marry me himself."

The men muttered over that, Galen the only one who remained silent.

"Could he do that?"

Turning away, Galen moved to the table, then shook his head. "He may be able to. He has many friends among the English and might use them to gain what he wants." Turning back, he eyed the MacGregor man. "What will he do now?"

"I don't ken." The man gasped as Tommy twisted his arm. "He planned to take her to England, but the plan has been ruined now. He didn't get the lass."

"He'll most like stick close by to try to take her again," Galen murmured, then glanced at Angus. "Lock him up."

Nodding, Angus hustled the prisoner toward the front doors of the keep.

Galen turned to Shropshire. "Ye bring news from Laird Forsythe?"

Shropshire nodded at that and Kyla hurried to his side. "He still lives then?"

"Aye. As I told your husband, he is yet weak, but recovering."

Kyla's eyes closed in obvious relief and she swayed slightly, then stepped back to lean into her husband when he took her arm for support. "Aye, Galen said so, but I wished to hear it from you myself." The joy lighting her face was obvious and the Englishman frowned as if at something he had not expected.

"What news?" Galen prompted, when the man simply stood lost in thought.

Straightening, he sighed and shook his head. "He wishes to see Kyla."

"Of course," she cried happily. "What has he done with Catriona?"

Shropshire hesitated. "He has done nothing as of yet."

"Nothing?" She stared at him blankly. "But . . . She tried to have him killed."

"Aye. Well . . . Catriona has offered a slightly different allowance of what occurred than you. She claims that once he was down, the men turned and asked *you* for payment and that you merely laughed and refused to pay."

"What?!"

"And that, out of anger, they struck you down for trying to cheat them. That was when she escaped."

"*What?*" This time it was the MacDonald men roaring that question. Kyla had paled, her face stiff and colorless as she sagged against Galen's side.

"Well that is rot, I can tell ye!" Morag snapped.

"Aye," Robbie rumbled. "Lady Kyla wouldn't do such a thing is sure."

"She's a true lady," Tommy avowed staunchly.

Nodding, Gavin added, "Braugh."

"Honorable. Not some sly chit to . . ." Duncan's

voice faded as Kyla lifted a hand for silence and faced the Englishman.

"You have known me a long time, Gilbert. Believe you this is true?"

He hesitated, then shook his head, but to Kyla that hesitation was damning.

"Does Johnny believe it as well?" she asked unhappily, and he flushed. "I see." Turning away, she moved back to sink onto her seat in a slight daze.

"It isn't like Johnny to be so foolish," Morag murmured unhappily. "Catriona must be a witch to convince him so."

The men were muttering their agreement to this claim when Galen speared the Englishman with cold eyes. "Why would he believe it? There must be a reason."

" 'Tis the will," he admitted reluctantly.

Kyla's head raised, surprise on her face at that. "Will?"

He nodded. "Your father's will states that should Johnny die without heir, everything goes to you."

"Well that is—but I knew not about this will," she managed.

Glaring at Shropshire, Morag moved to her side to pat her shoulder reassuringly. "Of course ye didn't, child, and why would ye?"

"And then there is the fact that when you realized that your brother would not die from his wounds, you and Morag fled," he went on reluctantly.

"*Fled?*" Every single person present cried that word in disbelief together.

"Fled, did she? Half-dead on her belly in a wagon, she fled?" Morag asked sarcastically as the men voiced their own, far less polite comments on the subject.

"Johnny believes I fled the keep?" Kyla got to her feet again.

"Well . . ." His gaze slid from the others to Kyla and he sighed. "Aye."

"Well, that is just plain rot," Morag told him. "That she-witch ordered it. I told her 'twould kill the lass, but did she care? Nay."

"She claims she tried to dissuade you both from leaving, but you insisted."

"Who the Devil would believe she tried to flee with her back sliced open so deep the bone showed through?" Galen snapped, finally losing his temper at the aspersions being cast upon his wife.

"The bone?" the man murmured, eyes wide with shock.

"Aye. 'Tis a miracle she survived at all, let alone after being carted about the land like some—"

"You have seen this?" Shropshire interrupted.

"We all have," Duncan told him. "We also all heard her crying out in her fevers for her brother. 'Twas obvious she loved him and would do him no harm."

"She was fretting over him," Tommy added coldly. "She was feverish and babbling about the attack and afraid that that Catriona bitch, beg pardon me lady, would kill him ere he healed. 'Tis why Galen sent Dunc to ye."

Frowning, Gilbert peered at Kyla. "Catriona said the wound was minor."

Morag snorted at that. "Minor me arse."

"Might I see—"

"Don't even ask it," Galen muttered grimly, his hand going for his sword.

Blushing fiercely, Kyla put a hand to his arm. "But, my lord, if 'twould convince him of my innocence . . . Besides, all have seen—"

"Nay." He didn't even bother to look at her. "Yer brother may look on it if he wishes, but none other."

Sighing, Kyla let her hand drop away. "Then we must go to Forsythe."

Stiffening, Galen swiveled to gape at her in horror. "What?"

"I will not have Johnny thinking I wish him dead. We shall leave at once."

"Er . . . Now, me lady," Tommy murmured, taking in Galen's expression. "It's not the best idea to be traveling just now, what with the MacGregor about and all."

"We have no choice." Kyla moved toward the stairs. "The longer he believes me guilty, the longer he remains in the claws of that she-devil. I'll not see my brother thinking me his murderess."

"We are not traveling to England!" Galen exploded.

"Then *I* shall travel alone," Kyla announced stubbornly.

"Nay. Yer not setting foot out of this keep until the MacGregor's dead."

"Then you had best kill him quick, husband, for I shall be gone ere dawn."

Shropshire took in Galen's furious face as he glared after his wife, his lips tipping up wryly. "Lady Kyla always was fond of having her own way, as I recall."

Galen scowled at him, then stomped back to the

table and grabbed up a mug of ale. He glanced irritably toward his men who still stood uncertainly about. "Well? What are ye waiting for? One of ye get above and guard the door."

"Aye, me laird," Tommy turned toward the stairs, then paused to turn back suddenly. "What of the passage, me laird?"

Galen sighed at that, then glanced toward Angus as he returned to the keep. "Angus, go through the spare room and stand guard in the tunnel."

"Aye, me laird."

Shropshire joined Galen at the table, poured himself some ale, and stared thoughtfully at it. "Have you a window in your room, sir?"

Galen frowned at the question, but nodded. "Aye. What of it?"

"Well, I was just recalling the time they had an outbreak of the pox at Forsythe. Morag was tending the ill and Kyla insisted on helping. Johnny refused to allow it. Knowing how stubborn she was, he had her locked in her room with a guard at her door to keep her from going down to the village to help."

"And?" he asked suspiciously as his men drew nearer to hear this tale.

"Well." Grinning, he shook his head. "'Twas the damnedest thing. The chit banded her linens together, slipped out the window, and presented herself in the village as intended. Lord Forsythe was furious, of course," he added on a murmur.

Galen's horrified face rose toward his men.

"She wouldn't!" Duncan gasped in dismay.

"Nay. She couldn't," Robbie assured them. "'Tis far too far a distance to the beach. There aren't enough bedclothes in the keep to even attempt it."

"Aye." Duncan agreed, then frowned. "But 'tis her own brother thinking her a killer. And, he's in danger."

Gavin shifted uncomfortably. "She does have a lot of chests up there."

"Nay. She'd have to cut up every gown she owned to make a rope long enough," Robbie argued. " 'Sides, 'twould be foolish to try. She'd break her wee neck."

Galen was just beginning to relax a bit, assured his wife could not escape, when Tommy suddenly shouted from the top of the stairs.

"What?" Duncan shouted back, moving to the base of the stairs at once.

"Lady Kyla wishes to cut some of her old gowns into rags and needs her shears from her embroidery basket. I can't leave me post, fetch them up to me."

Duncan whirled back toward Galen at that, horror plain on his face.

Slamming his mug back on to the table top, he roared, "Tell me wife she need not cut her gowns. Tell her to pack them instead. We leave for England first thing on the morrow!"

Chapter 17

W E are almost there," Galen soothed, grimacing as Kyla lost the remaining contents of her stomach into the bucket he had positioned on the floor for just that purpose. Seated on the edge of the bed in the captain's cabin of his finest ship, he had one hand at his wife's back while the other braced her forehead as she lay, head hanging off the small cot, positioned over the pail.

Frowning as she retched again, he rubbed her back and shook his head. "Ye were the one who insisted we must travel to Forsythe."

A garbled mutter that sounded suspiciously like a curse was her reply then she began to heave again as a tap sounded at the door.

"Enter!"

Tommy stepped reluctantly in. "Gavin says we shall set anchor within a few moments," the man murmured, wincing as Kyla retched again.

"Thank God," Galen sighed.

"Hmm." A worried frown tugging at his eyebrows, Tommy hesitated at another round of rude sounds from his mistress. She had been making them nonstop since they had set sail from the island. He had never seen such a sorry case of seasickness in his life. The worst of it was, the sea was not that rough. It seemed, however, their beautiful brave mistress could not handle the slight roll.

"Will she be all right?" he asked finally.

"Once we land, aye." Galen shook his head now. "MacGregor or no MacGregor I think on the way back we'll avoid sailing until we have to cross to the island."

Tommy nodded relieved acceptance to that, then turned slightly green as Kyla's retching grew more violent. "I'll, er . . . just go and let the . . . men ken she'll survive the trip after all." He tugged the door open and hurried out.

Hearing his words, Kyla groaned and sagged wearily against her husband. It did seem she was constantly giving her people reason to view her as a weak and silly female. She could hardly blame them for their worry over whether she would survive this time. She felt fit to die. Might even welcome it. Truly, Kyla had never felt quite so sick in her life. It was all too humiliating.

"Ye should have told me ye couldn't sail."

Had she had the strength, Kyla would have rolled her eyes and asked none too sweetly how she possibly could have done that when she had not known herself. This was her first journey aboard a boat. And her last.

Considering how kind and caring Galen had proven to be during this nightmare journey, Kyla forced herself to refrain from being too irritated with what she considered to be his male foolishness. Saying they would slow them down, Galen had allowed no other women on this trip. That had left him to serve as nursemaid when Kyla had fallen ill.

Aside from a rather gruff bedside manner, he had proven himself to be most sufficient in the position. He had stayed at her side throughout, seeing to the most menial of tasks in tending her with not a single complaint, and all in such a way to minimize her humiliation over the ordeal.

"Feeling any better?"

Kyla sighed at the question, but nodded despite the fact that she did not think she would feel better until she was on dry land. Truly, he was a good man, she thought wearily as he shifted her until her head rested on his lap, his hands brushing the hair gently from her face as she dozed off into an exhausted sleep.

Galen had just realized his wife had dropped off into sleep when the second knock came. Easing her gently to lie upon the bed, he rose and moved to the door—slipping out to speak to Tommy when he saw it was him. "We've dropped anchor?"

"Aye. Shall I go ashore and rent rooms for the night?"

"Nay. Horses," Galen answered, opening his sporran to search out the necessary coins. "Purchase horses. The best ye can find."

Tommy accepted the coins, but hesitated, his feet shifting nervously before he said, "Lady Kyla has been sore ill, me laird. Do ye no' think 'twould be better—"

"Have ye forgotten the MacGregor so soon?"

"Oh, aye." Tommy sighed.

"Eight horses."

That made him frown again. "Only eight?"

"Aye. There shall only be Kyla, me, Robbie, Duncan, Angus, Gavin, Laird Shropshire, and yerself. The rest of the men can wait here."

"What of my men?" That question came from Lord Shropshire as he approached along the hallway.

Galen glanced toward the other man, irritation flickering briefly across his face. "They may follow. Ye may too if ye don't like to leave them," he added when Shropshire opened his mouth as if to protest.

The Englishman grimaced at that wryly, but shrugged. "I merely thought to point out that the more men with us, the safer Lady Kyla would be."

"Nay. The faster we travel, the safer she'll be. Small groups travel faster."

"How can you expect Kyla to travel fast when she has been so ill. She—"

"Will ride with me. 'Twill slow us down a bit, but not much if I switch horses often." He turned to Tommy. "As I said, the best horseflesh ye can find. They must be strong and fast. And purchase bread and cheese and some fruit if ye can find it. We will not stop to eat, so must do so as we travel."

Nodding, Tommy turned to hurry back above deck and Galen turned again toward the cabin. He paused when Shropshire put a hand to his arm.

"If you truly fear for her safety, why do you not just let me see her back? That way she would have no need to make this journey. I would carry the news back to Forsythe."

"And most like be killed ere ye reached there."

Shropshire blinked at that. "You think they would kill *me?*"

Rather than answer, Galen asked, "Do ye not find the timing in MacGregor's attempt to take Kyla back odd?"

When the other man stared at him blankly, he

sighed and pointed out, " 'Twas a long time between when I took and married Kyla and when the Mac-Gregor came to steal her back."

"Mayhap he simply needed time to make his plans, he—"

"Nay. Were that the case, he would have been hanging about in the area. He had just arrived. He told Kyla that he and his men had ridden through the night."

Shropshire frowned over that. "I do not see— "

"Robbie told me that one of yer men mentioned ye had traveled hard, riding long into the night and resting little? He said ye had knocked about a day off yer travels that way?"

"Aye, I thought to finish this business quickly. I have things to attend to and—" He paused suddenly. "You think he rode through the night in an attempt to arrive at Dunbar before me? That he wished to kidnap Kyla ere she could speak to me?" He looked both amazed and fascinated by the idea.

" 'Tis a possibility."

Shropshire was silent for a moment, then sighed. "It makes fascinating listening, Lord MacDonald, and I very much want to believe that Kyla is innocent in this, but the fact remains that should you simply allow me to see the injury to her back, I could carry the truth to Forsythe. Then she, at least, would not be put at risk."

Galen shrugged at that. "Aye, but Kyla will not rest easy until she sees her brother herself, anyway. So, why bother?" he asked with a wolfish smile. He turned and slid into the cabin, closing the door firmly in the Englishman's face.

* * *

It was the drumming in her head that awoke Kyla. When her eyes opened to see treetops flying by overhead, she suffered a distinct sense of déjà vu. For one insane moment she feared that the past weeks had been a mere dream, that she had dreamt those days and nights on a Scottish island in the arms of a man with flowing red hair. Melancholy was dropping about her like a cloak when a strand of familiar red hair draped her cheek and Galen's face came into view.

"Yer awake."

That growling voice was as sweet as birdsong to Kyla's poor ears. A smile suddenly split her face and she sat up abruptly as she realized that she rested not in the bottom of a wagon but across her husband's lap, his arms bracing her and holding her close. "Where are we?"

Galen frowned slightly at the croak of her voice. "England."

"We are off the boat," she commented with surprise as she glanced around and saw that they were on horseback.

"Aye and sure enough we are, me lady. We've been traveling for near a day, a night, and a day again, and ye've slept through it all."

Kyla glanced over her shoulder at that comment, slight embarrassment covering her face as she spied Tommy and recalled what she had been doing the last time he had seen her.

Catching her discomfort and guessing its source, Tommy smiled sympathetically. "Ye've roses in yer cheeks, me lady. One could almost forget ye suffered so on the ship . . . I ken I have."

Her smile returning slowly, Kyla nodded, then glanced back to her husband as Tommy dropped back to leave them alone. "Have I truly slept so long?"

"Aye." Shifting her, he reached down into a bag that hung off the side of his saddle, then straightened to produce a hunk of crusty bread for her. "Eat. You have been without nourishment too long."

Kyla reached reluctantly for the food. With memories of her seasickness still strong in her head, she wasn't eager to eat. But the moment she took her first bite of bread, the fresh yeast flavor burst inside her mouth, exciting her starved taste buds into a near-frenzy that had her quickly taking a second bite and then another. After that, she was so busy eating that she hardly noticed how dry her mouth was until Galen reached down again and produced a flask of wine.

Mumbling her gratitude around a mouthful of bread, Kyla accepted the flask and downed a good quantity of the contents before handing it back to continue eating. It wasn't until she felt his chest rumbling against her that she noticed her husband's amusement and realized that she was behaving beastly. *Ladies do not gobble their food.* She could hear that remonstrance from Morag in her head and flushed brightly, chagrin covering her face as she forced herself to slow down and nibble delicately at what was left of the loaf.

Shaking his head slightly, Galen reached into the bag once more and pulled out some cheese and an apple. Kyla managed to make her way through the bread and the fruit, but by then was too full to tackle the cheese. She returned it to Galen with regret, for it certainly looked delicious, but despite the fact that she was feeling much better now that she had something in her stomach, she was unwilling to test how strong it was just then by overfilling it.

Taking in her satisfied expression as she relaxed back into his arms, Galen smiled slightly. "Feel better?"

"Aye." Kyla produced a smile of her own for him, then sighed and said apologetically, "I am sorry to have trialed you so."

" 'Twas no' a trial."

"Oh, nay," she agreed dryly. "First you had to play nursemaid on the boat and then you have had to carry me all this way. But 'twas not a trial."

"Aye, well, mayhap 'twas," he murmured thoughtfully and Kyla's heart sank, until he continued. "Aye. In truth it *was* a trial. Especially having to cart ye about on this horse. Holding ye close. Yer body pressed against mine, rubbing against me with the motion of the horse."

"I am fair sorry, my lord," she murmured, feeling a hunger of a different sort steal through her at the husky words he spoke.

"Aye, well and sure enough ye should be, me having been neglected so long."

"Neglected?" Kyla gasped in disbelief, for it was fair shameful how much attention he had gotten before this trip. She was no expert, but felt sure to commit the bedding twice and thrice a night was fair sinful. Excess was never good.

"Aye, and have I not been poor and lonely all this time between yer being ill and then sleeping?"

"Ah, me," she said wryly. "I suppose I have been shamefully remiss of late."

" 'Tis good of ye to admit to it."

Kyla arched one eyebrow at that and suddenly sat

up straight in front of him. "I shall do better than that, my lord. I shall correct the problem," she promised silkily, mischief crossing her face briefly as she glanced about to be sure none of the men riding with them were close enough to see what she was about.

Satisfied that she was hidden from prying eyes by the curve of his arms, Kyla turned back to her husband and bit her lip as she considered how to carry out the thought that had occurred to her. She meant to tease him a bit, but modesty gave her pause for a moment before she overcame it and slid her hands to his chest to begin running them lightly over his linen-clad chest.

Galen stiffened slightly in surprise at that, but made no protest, curiosity and a queer excitement keeping him silent and still as she smoothed her hands over his body through his clothes. He truly did not believe she would do much more than that. He had noticed that until he stoked her desires, his wife was shy and reserved when it came to such matters. With that thought still echoing in his head, Galen gasped and stiffened up like a wooden doll when she suddenly delved one hand beneath his tartan, running it lightly across the sensitive skin of his hip and thigh, before closing it around his sudden arousal.

"B'Gad!" His head whipped about to be sure no one could see what she was doing. To his relief, the men all rode some distance behind.

Sucking in another gust of air, he turned back to peer at his wife sharply when she slid her hand along his swollen length. "What the Devil be ye doing?" he demanded, shocked. Was this his sweet flower of a bride handling him so? And out in the woods for all to see?

"Paying you some sore needed attention, husband," Kyla murmured innocently, sliding her hand to the base of him once again.

"Stop that!" Galen cried in dismay, grabbing at her hand and pulling it out of his tartan as he felt his desires surge within him.

"But you said I had neglected you, husband. I would—" Her words came to an abrupt halt when he turned to gesture at the men riding behind them.

Kyla straightened abruptly in his lap as the men suddenly surrounded them.

"Me wife wishes to ride her own horse."

Kyla blinked at that stern announcement from her husband, but had little chance to comment as Tommy untied the reins of the extra horse from his saddle and urged the animal up beside them. Galen then lifted Kyla and swung her onto the beast. His First then placed the reins in her hands and Galen caught her chin with one finger and turned her to face him.

"Stay close. If we're attacked, stay at me side. Understand?"

She nodded once and he bent forward to give her a quick kiss, then released her and straightened in his own saddle, urging his mount to move again.

Kyla stared after him for a moment, then shifted on her mount's back and urged him into a trot. Galen had been shocked by her brazen behavior, but he had also been aroused by it. Surprisingly enough, she had also managed to rouse her own passions and she was now looking forward to lying in his arms again. There was only an hour or so of daylight left. They would stop soon, she assured herself. Then they could wander away from the campfire and—

"Your thoughts seem pleasant."

Kyla gave a start at those words and turned to blink at Lord Shropshire. "Gilbert. I had not realized you were with us." Actually, she really had not noted any of the men with them but Tommy. Now she glanced about, taking in the fact that Gavin, Angus, Duncan, and Robbie were the only other riders with them. A frown began to pluck at her brow then, for truly it did not seem a very large party. Why, she had had an escort of some sixty men when the MacDonalds had attacked—and they had been swiftly defeated.

Reading her expression, the Englishman murmured, "I suggested your husband bring the rest of his men, as well as my own, but he refused. He seems to think that speed is more likely to keep you safe than strength."

Kyla stiffened in her saddle, aware that she was being disloyal, if not in voice, than at least in expression with her brief doubts.

"Well then, my lord, it must be so," she announced firmly with a nod. "My husband is a most successful warrior. Why, did you know that I had an escort of sixty men on the way to Scotland? 'Tis true. Catriona sent forty of her own men and twenty MacGregors met us at the border and still Galen and twenty of his men managed to defeat them. The MacDonalds are fierce warriors, know you? Why I warrant if we were attacked by twenty . . . thirty . . . even fifty warriors, these men could fight them off."

Tommy and Galen exchanged a glance as they overheard her staunch defense of his decision, then he slowed his mount until his wife's animal rode beside his own. "In truth, wife, I had thirty men with me."

"Aye, well, still, you were out-manned," she said firmly, then turned to Shropshire to add, "Catriona's men were wearing mail, and all of them on horseback, while Galen and his men were afoot." She nodded firmly to emphasize that, then smiled sweetly. "Never fear, my lord, Galen will keep us safe."

When Shropshire stiffened, looking taken aback at the suggestion that he had feared for his own safety, Galen and Tommy both burst out laughing before spurring their mounts to more speed.

Frowning, Kyla glanced from the backs of the two men as they pulled out in front to Shropshire's disgruntled expression. Then, recalling Galen's order to stay close, she shrugged her curiosity at their reactions aside and urged her horse into a canter.

Kyla shifted on her mount and glanced nervously toward the dark trees surrounding them. She had the distinct impression that they were being watched. It was the only reason she had not as yet commented to her husband that they should stop for the night. He obviously knew that they were being followed, else he would have stopped to make camp by now. It had been full dark for over an hour, the path only dimly lit by a full moon. Surely he would have stopped by now were it not for those eyes she could feel trained on her back?

Sighing, she glanced edgily around again and urged her horse up to her husband's side, nudging Tommy's mount to the side in the process. Responding to the man's startled glance with a sweet smile, Kyla turned to her husband. "Think you they will attack?"

Galen gave a start at that. "What?"

"Attack. Think you they shall attack?"

He merely peered at her as if she were mad for a moment. "Who?"

"The people following us," Kyla explained patiently, then, "Think you I am so unaware that I did not notice them as well?"

Frowning, Galen shook his head. "There is no one following us."

Kyla blinked at that. "What mean you there is no one following us? I can feel their eyes on me." Her gaze narrowed now. "Do not play me false, sir. Obviously you are aware of their presence, as well, else you surely would have stopped for the night by now?"

Galen shook his head once more and straightened in his seat. "Nay. We are not stopping for the night."

"What mean you we are not stopping for the night?"

When irritation flickered across his expression, Tommy quickly explained. "We thought it safest to travel straight to Forsythe, me lady. We can rest once we are safe within its walls."

Kyla's jaw dropped at that. It was a moment before she had regained herself enough to say, "But you said it had been two days and a night since we had left the boat."

"Aye." Both men agreed easily enough.

"But you— Did you not rest the night?"

"Nay."

"Well . . ." Kyla blinked. "What of the horses? Surely they need rest?"

"We changed horses this morn at a village."

Kyla's gaze shifted to the woods around them again before she pointed out, "But the horses have been riding through the day and now into the night. They will be tired."

"We'll change them at the next village," Galen informed her calmly.

"Aye, but if they are tired, how shall we outride our pursuers now?"

He scowled at her irritably. "There are no pursuers, wife."

"Aye, there are," Kyla responded grimly.

"I tell ye, there are no pursuers. I am a warrior. We are all warriors. We have instincts and are trained to be alert for such things and—"

"And I have rested well these past two days, while you have not, husband. Has it not occurred to you that your weariness may have dulled your instincts?"

"Nay. I—"

"I tell you we are being trailed."

Galen scowled at her, then glanced at Robbie when he said, "She may be right, me laird. I have felt fair uncomfortable for a bit now, but was too tired to place a name on me discomfort. I may have been sensing we had company."

Eyebrows rising, Galen turned toward Tommy questioningly. His First shook his head unhappily. "I don't know. I'd dozed off in me saddle. I was only startled awake when Lady Kyla moved up between us. I do sense something in the air now, but that may just be nerves."

" 'Tis the same with me," Galen muttered, peering about the clearing.

The other men shifted their gazes about now as well, then Duncan grumbled. "Well, if there is aught out there, why do they not attack?"

"They may fear we would make a break for it,"

Shropshire murmured, joining the conversation. "If they have been following us and only recently caught up, their horses may be tired as well, and unlikely to keep up with ours." He raised an eyebrow at Kyla. "How long have you sensed we were being followed?"

" 'Twas well ere dark when I first sensed them," she admitted quietly.

"The longer they hesitate, the more their horses will tire," Angus reasoned.

"Mayhap there is somewhere up ahead that they think they'd have a better chance of catching us ere we can outrun them," Duncan suggested thoughtfully. "As I recall from me trip to Shropshire when I carried Lady Kyla's necklace and yer message there, the path narrows not far ahead. Just ere a river."

"Aye, it does," Galen agreed grimly.

All were silent for a moment, then Gavin ventured, "Perhaps we are not being followed."

"We *are*," Kyla put in staunchly.

"Can we not avoid the spot to be certain?" Robbie muttered, tending to agree with his lady now. "Surely there is another route?"

"Aye," Galen murmured. "We could turn south to Stafford, but it adds a day's travel to our trip."

They all fell silent again, then Shropshire leaned forward, resting his arm on the pommel of his saddle. "Lord Stafford is an old friend of mine. He would most likely put us up for the night."

Galen thought it over briefly, then nodded. "Be ready. If we *are* being followed and their plan was to attack at the pass, they'll not be pleased at our change of direction." With that, he took up Kyla's reins and turned sharply toward the trees on their right. As quickly as that, the men closed ranks around them. Gavin and Tommy urged their own mounts into a run, taking up position at their mistress' side, Angus and Robbie closed in on Galen's flank, and Duncan and Shropshire closed in behind as they tore off the path in a charge for the trees.

They had barely crashed into the trees when Kyla's claim that they were being followed was proven true. She didn't notice at first. Unprepared for the abruptness of Galen's actions, Kyla was kept busy just trying to maintain her seat. But once she had regained her balance in her perch somewhat, she took the time to peer about, anxiety rising in her as they broke through the underbrush into the woods and she saw horsemen scattered about. Two of them were directly in their path and scrambling to get out of the way, but she spied at least a dozen more to the side who were hurrying to cut off their escape.

Of course, these men had been as unprepared for Galen's abrupt turn in direction as she herself had been and were too slow to be able to stop them effectively. However, they did manage to cut them off somewhat, in effect making a funnel, leaving only a small space open, just wide enough for Galen and Kyla's horses to slip through. Tommy, Gavin, Robbie, Shropshire, and Angus were forced to a halt, however, to confront the mounted men suddenly in their path. With Galen holding her reins and guiding her horse forward, Kyla was free to peer over her shoulder to watch anxiously as the men fought their way through the foes who had slowed them. There were only four opponents really, their comrades were a bit slower and therefore several lengths behind, but approaching quickly. The MacDonalds did not give them the chance to arrive to assist their fellows, Duncan and Shropshire assisted in making short work of their enemies, then the others turned to continue on after their lord and lady.

Kyla was just releasing the breath she had been holding when the expressions on all six men's faces warned her all was not well. Their combined dismay sent a chill through her as she turned to see that the four men they had just finished dealing with were not the only threat. A fifth man was charging from the side. Straight for *her*, she saw with a horror that doubled as she recognized him.

It was the MacGregor.

Chapter 18

FOR one second, Kyla sat frozen in her saddle. The MacGregor was charging down on her. The men were too far away to be of assistance, and Galen, half a horse-length ahead of her own mount, had not yet seen the danger. When the MacGregor's expression suddenly changed from determination to triumph as he leaned forward in his saddle to pluck her off her mount, however, she was finally moved to action and jerked her dirk from her waist to slash at his reaching hands.

He pulled back instinctively at that, barking a half-angry, half-startled yelp. Blood poured from the deep, straight wound she had given him across one palm, but his expression set into grim lines and he reached to grab for her again.

Panic welling inside her, Kyla grabbed desperately for the reins Galen held. Giving them a sharp tug, she managed to reclaim them from his startled grip and regain control of her own mount.

Gripping the ropes tightly, she slammed her heels into her mount's flanks, at the same moment pulling back hard and to the side on the reins, forcing his head back and up. The beast responded exactly as she had expected, wheeling to face the MacGregor, rearing as it did, hooves pawing desperately at the air and striking out toward the man's mount.

One moment he was reaching for her and the next the MacGregor was tugging frantically at his own reins as his horse jerked to the side, rearing in an attempt to avoid the deadly hooves that were now slashing at it.

Now aware of the situation, Galen spun his own mount back to her side. He caught her about the waist and dragged her onto his horse as she started to tumble from her rearing mount. Then he drew his sword from his sheath and raised it to meet his enemy, but, eager to avoid Kyla's still pawing beast, MacGregor's horse had already turned away and was doing its best to escape the area altogether. None of MacGregor's shouts or sawing on the reins could stop the animal's mad dash away through the woods.

Galen muttered something Gaelic as they watched their nemesis escape, then glanced at his men as they arrived and circled him and Kyla, their own gazes trained on the MacGregors who had been closing in. The men were now hesitating, unsure whether to attack or go after their leader. Unwilling to do battle while Kyla sat before him, Galen took advantage of their hesitation and swung his animal back to the south, charging off through the trees again, his men hard on his heels.

"Lady MacDonald, perhaps you would like to follow me? I shall show you to your room and you may wash up ere we sit down to table."

Kyla peered blearily at the woman holding out a hand toward her, then glanced uncertainly back at Galen who still sat his mount. She had dozed off against his chest about an hour after they had evaded the MacGregors, only to be awoken an hour later to find herself being set on the ground in the Stafford bailey. At least she presumed this was the Stafford keep. That was where the men had decided to head before leaving the path and crashing through the MacGregor party.

"Go."

Kyla frowned up at her husband when he muttered that word. It was the first thing he had said to her since dragging her from her rearing mount. He had been in a foul temper ever since the incident. It had only taken one look at his black expression to see that. She had thought at the time that silence while he worked through his anger might be the wisest approach. It seemed the passing of time had not improved his mood any.

Deciding that hauling off and punching him in the kneecap that rested directly before her eyes most likely would not improve the situation, Kyla heaved a sigh and turned to trail Lady Stafford into her castle. The men followed the woman's husband to the stables.

"Fetch a bath for Lady MacDonald," Lady Stafford murmured to a servant as she led Kyla through the keep doors, then glanced back at her apologetically. "I hope you are not offended, but I am guessing by the look of you that you have been traveling quite a while. I thought a bath might . . . refresh you somewhat."

Kyla glanced down at herself at that delicately phrased comment. She was layered with a film of dust from the ride. The lovely ivory gown Galen had dressed her in ere disembarking the ship was now somewhere between beige and tan and her skin was a most unattractive gray-brown shade. Kyla grimaced wryly. "Aye, my lady. I fear it has been several days since I have been out of these clothes, let alone seen water. I would be most grateful for a bath."

Nodding, the other woman continued up the stairs to the second level of the keep. "I did not notice any baggage with you. Is—"

"I fear circumstances forced us to leave without baggage. I believe our belongings are following, but are most likely several days behind. We have been traveling night and day since leaving Liverpool yestermorn."

Lady Stafford cast a surprised glance over her shoulder. "Yestermorn?"

"Aye. Well, we would have arrived here sooner, but we did not originally intend on putting you out so. Unfortunately we had a change of plans and had to backtrack a bit. I hope we are not too much of a nuisance?"

Lady Stafford was silent as they reached the upper hall. She led the way past two doors, to a third that she opened and ushered Kyla through. It wasn't until she had closed the door behind them that she spoke, and then it was in a quiet, earnest voice. "Lord Shropshire is an old friend. He sent word to us from Forsythe on what was occurring there. He told us all about Catriona's claims."

Kyla hesitated, uncertain how to respond to this news. "Lady Stafford—"

"Camilla," the older woman interrupted. "Call me Camilla."

"Camilla," Kyla corrected, forcing a slight smile. "I am not sure—"

"I do not believe her."

Kyla blinked at that. "You do not?"

"Nay. I knew Catriona at court," Camilla told her bitterly. "She lifted her skirts for more lords there than—" Flushing slightly, she sighed. "Pray excuse my vulgar talk. I fear I did not like your sister-in-law. I found her deceitful and overly ambitious. Catriona—" She broke off as a tap sounded at the door. Moving to open it, she stepped out of the way as the servants entered with the bath, then glanced toward Kyla once more. "I must needs see to the meal Cook is putting together for you, so I shall leave you to your bath now."

Kyla barely had time to murmur a thank-you before the woman was out the door. Wishing they had had more time to talk, Kyla sank onto the side of the bed as the servants filled the tub. They had barely finished the chore and departed when another light tapping preceded the entrance of a petite, blond servant.

"Lady Camilla sent this dress for you to don after you bathe. She thought you might like a fresh gown."

"That was very kind," Kyla murmured sincerely, peering at the lovely crimson gown the maid laid across the bed. It was not a color she would have chosen for herself, but knew it would suit her dark hair and pale skin well.

"My name is Beth," the girl announced, moving to help her undress. "I am to be your maid while you are here. If there is aught you wish, you need only ask me, my lady, and I will see to it."

"I shall remember that, Beth." Kyla sighed her relief as her gown dropped away. That sigh turned into a moan of pleasure as she stepped into the tub, and the warm liquid enveloped her aching bones and joints. She would have liked to have had a nice long soak, but suspected she did not have the time. Sighing regretfully, she quickly scrubbed away the dust from her travels, washing her back and hair with Beth's help before stepping out of the tub into a large cloth the maid held out for her.

She was dressed and seated by the fire as Beth did her best to quickly dry her hair when Galen entered. Spying them, he ordered the girl out, then barely waited for her to flee before dropping his clothes and stepping into the leftover bath water. If she had been quick in the tub, he was quicker. Bare moments after stepping into it, he was out and redonning his clothes. That done, he headed for the door once more. "Come."

Dropping the brush she had been using, Kyla scooted to her feet and scurried after him. She managed to make it to his side at the top of the stairs and he took her arm in a firm grip as they descended those, remembering his manners for all his temper.

Everyone else was already at table when they arrived. Galen seated Kyla beside Lady Stafford, then sat next to her and immediately reached for the ale.

Wondering what exactly it was she had done wrong, Kyla sighed and began to pick at the food placed before her.

"Gilbert was just telling us of your adventure on the way here," Lady Stafford said.

Feeling Galen stiffen beside her at their host's words, Kyla frowned slightly, but cleared her expression as she glanced past Lady Stafford to her husband. "Has he, my lord?"

"Aye. You may call me Stephen, Lady Kyla. I am not so much older that you need 'lord' me."

"Did you truly take your dirk to the MacGregor?" Lady Stafford asked now with something akin to amazement.

Kyla flushed at the question, but had no need to answer as her men were more than happy to brag of her exploits for her.

"Aye, she did," Angus announced proudly. "Cut him good, too. Straight across the palm." He used his own hand to show them exactly where she had got the man. "He'll feel that for a while, I can tell ye."

Lady Stafford shuddered delicately at that. "'Twas fair brave of you, Lady Kyla. I fear that had I been in your position, I should have been quite helpless."

"Not our lady," Duncan proclaimed with pride. "Naught afrights her. Why, she even took her dirk to Robbie when we attacked her escort on the way to the MacGregors. Gave him a nasty cut jest here." He gestured to his side, then shrugged. "Mind ye, she didn't hurt him much, but she did manage to make him bleed. And it isn't the first time she's given the MacGregor the slip either. He tried to take her on the island and she and Aelfread—that's Robbie here's wife—they—"

"Enough!" Galen snapped, silencing his man at once. Kyla turned to frown at her husband for his sharpness despite the fact that she herself had just been wishing she were seated closer to Duncan so that she might kick him under the table and bring his taletelling to a halt. It was not that she was ashamed of defending herself, but she was embarrassed to have so much attention directed her way. Still, now that her husband had silenced him for her, she was irritated. Mostly because she suspected he wanted the end of it for an entirely different reason than she did. It had not gone unnoticed by her that men tended to prefer women to react as Lady Stafford said that she would have in the same situation.

"What is the matter, husband? Are you ashamed of me?" she asked coldly.

"Don't be foolish, wife."

"Foolish, is it? You have been angered at me since the MacGregor attack in the woods. Think you I had not noticed? The only reason I can see for your anger is that you are shamed by my unladylike defense of myself. Mayhap you would have preferred it had I sat helpless and allowed him to take me?"

"Aye, mayhap I would," he snapped shortly.

Seeing the hurt on her face, the men glanced at each other, then Duncan cleared his throat. He murmured gently, "He doesn't mean that, me lady. He—"

"You would rather he had captured me?" Kyla asked in dismay.

"Nay, me lady." Tommy frowned at his chief. "I am sure he didn't mean—"

"Aye, I did," Galen refuted, scowling at the censure emanating from his men. "Had that happened, I surely would have saved ye—as is me place."

"Pride," Robbie rumbled now. "A man's pride is a precious thing, me lady."

"Well, damn your pride!" Kyla snapped at Galen. "I would think—"

His mug slammed down at that. "That is the problem, wife. Ye think too damn much. Don't think. 'Tis my place to do the thinking *and* the protecting."

"I see," she murmured coldly. "I do not suppose you would care to tell me my place in all of this? What task is it exactly that I am to attend to?"

Galen scowled, his mind drawing a blank for a

moment, then satisfaction crossed his face. "Yer the wife. Yer to warm me bed and bear me bairns."

Every single person present nearly groaned aloud at that as Kyla's eyes narrowed dangerously. This time it was Gilbert who tried to assuage her building temper. "I do not think he means—"

"And when I am not busy with those two things?" Kyla interrupted.

Galen shrugged irritably. "Women things. Embroidery."

"Camilla does some lovely embroidery," Lord Stafford said suddenly. Elbowing his wife, he added, "Mayhap you should show Lady Kyla some of—"

"I fear I would much rather I had been captured by MacGregor and *kept* by him than to spend the rest of my days and nights working at my needlepoint."

Every single man at the table gasped at that. Even Lady Stafford was round-eyed, though she did take a turn at trying to soothe Galen then. "She does not mean that, my lord. She is just overwrought."

"As for warming your bed and bearing your bairns," Kyla continued icily, "I fear that at the moment I do not much feel like tending to either of those things. If you will excuse me, one and all?" Without awaiting a response, she stood and strode purposefully toward the steps to the second floor.

Galen glared after her departing back until it disappeared from sight, then turned to glower at the wide-eyed people around the table, daring them to comment as he reached for his tankard of ale. Slamming it down, he turned his attention to the food before him, determined to appear unbothered by his wife's words. He had swallowed his first bite and was chewing determinedly at a second when a loud dragging, scraping sound flowed down to them from overhead.

Glancing upward, he shifted uncomfortably on the bench. These were the sounds that had emanated from his own room the night he had announced their marriage. One look at his men told him that they remembered as well.

"I believe your wife is rearranging our guest room, my lord," Stafford's wife murmured, avoiding his eyes as the men all stared at the ceiling above.

When Galen remained silent, Duncan cleared his throat and explained, "Our lady has a tendency to do that."

"Especially when she is angered," Tommy added under his breath, wondering what she was moving against the door this time. At home she used her chests. She had no chests with her now. He could only assume that meant she was now pushing furniture up against the door. Heavy furniture, too, he thought as the first dragging sound ended only to begin again a moment later as another piece of furniture was shoved determinedly across the floor above.

Pretending unconcern, Galen continued to chew, then stilled as the sound stopped again to be followed by a much louder groan of wood against wood.

His gaze slid to Lady Stafford when she uttered an incomprehensible sound then burst out with a dismayed laugh. "I believe she is moving the bed, my lord. I would wonder she has the strength. 'Tis of solid oak. . . ." Her voice trailed away into silence. Galen was no longer listening. He had fled the table, stomping determinedly toward the stairs.

* * *

It was a monster. A great behemoth of a bed. Kyla
had never seen the likes of it before. Blowing a stray
strand of hair off her forehead, she muttered something unflattering regarding its size under her breath,
then bent to the bed again, putting all of her weight
behind moving the blasted thing. She had already
moved the two chairs from before the fire up against
the door, but knew their weight was not sufficient to
keep her husband out. This great elephant of a bed
should do it, however. In fact, it alone would most
like have sufficed. She only wished she had thought
of that before wasting her energy on the chairs.

Grunting as the bed began to slide across the
floor under her influence, Kyla allowed a smile of
satisfaction to grace her face. The distance between
the end of the bed and the edge of the two chairs
before the door closed. Frustration brought a spate
of curses from her lips in the next instant when the
door suddenly pushed open and Galen slid quickly
into the room a split second before the impetus of
her push rammed the bed up against the chairs, pushing them against the door and forcing it well and
truly closed.

Straightening slowly from her bent position at
the end of the bed, Kyla glared furiously at her husband.

Galen peered back, taking in her flushed cheeks,
the disarray of her hair and the fury on her face and
could not restrain the smile that slowly grew on his
face. His own anger slipped away that easily. "Rearranging again?"

She flew at him in a fury, fists waving and ready
to do damage. Galen caught her easily before she
had even managed one blow. Pulling her forward

until her breasts rubbed against his chest through their clothes, he bared his teeth in a smile. "I like it when yer blood is hot and yer passions awakened, wife. It makes me hot, too."

Kyla's eyes widened at that, then narrowed when he dropped his mouth to cover hers. She thought of biting him. Considered bringing a knee up to do him injury, but in the end she did exactly as he accused and thought too much. While she was busy thinking, he was breaching her defenses. By the time she had decided to commit both actions, he had managed to arouse her body to the point where it was unwilling to perform either task. Instead of fighting him off, her body curved into him, her throat forcing a moan out into his mouth.

By the time he released her lips to kiss a trail along her jawline toward her ear, Kyla was sighing in defeat. She simply could not stay angry with the great oaf. On the other hand, she thought now, neither could she spend the rest of her life locked inside a castle doing needlepoint. "Husband?"

"Hmmm?" He did not stop his kisses and tender caresses.

"Husband, I do not like needlework." She bit her lip then, waiting for a response, but all she got was an unintelligible mumbling as he reached her ear and began to nibble at the delicate lobe.

Determined to make her point, Kyla said, "I mean it, my lord. I really do not like needlepoint."

"Aye, loving, I heard ye," he breathed by her ear, then swept her into his arms and started toward the bed.

Frowning, Kyla twisted her head away from the lips still nibbling at her ear and neck, and she peered at him seriously. "One might even go so far as to say that I detest needlepoint," she told him firmly.

Galen finally seemed to get the point. Slowing to a halt, he took in her expression, then sighed. "I didn't mean what I said about ye defending yerself. I was just angry at meself because ye had to. B'Gad! I didn't even sense we were being trailed. Ye had to tell me." His self-disgust over that was evident. "I should have been aware of what was going on about me. Had I been more alert, I would have tended to MacGregor right then and he would no longer be a threat."

Realizing that this was as close to an apology as she was going to get, Kyla sighed and nodded in understanding, but Galen wasn't finished.

"Howbeit, that isn't what happened. He is still a threat, and so long as he is, I can't let ye wander about on yer own. I need ye too much to be allowing the MacGregor to steal ye from me. But—" he added when Kyla opened her mouth to speak. "I promise ye this. I'll tend to the man ere we return home so that ye can run the beach again."

He sealed that promise with a kiss as he laid her on the bed. Then he dropped his plaid and pounced on her, his hands and lips giving her little chance to discuss the matter further . . . even had she really wanted to.

The earth was rumbling and shaking. Kyla's eyes popped open with dismay, her hands reaching to grasp at the bed as the room moved about her.

"Good! Yer awake."

Turning at that voice, she stared blankly at her husband, the source of all the shaking and rumbling.

Up and dressed, he was sliding the bed back across the floor with her in it.

Sighing as the bed came to a halt, Kyla sat up and peered toward the window. She could spy stars through it. " 'Tis not even morn yet."

"Aye, yer right, it isn't," Galen agreed. He gave the bed one final push to set it in place before tossing her gown and under-tunic to her and turning back to the door to grab the chairs next, moving them both at the same time.

Sighing, Kyla tugged her under-tunic on, grumbling all the while. "I do not see why you needs must wake me. Surely we will not leave ere morn? I—"

"We leave within the hour."

Kyla paused to peer at him wide eyed. "In the middle of the night?"

" 'Twill give us cover if the MacGregor followed and is waiting to pounce."

She frowned over that. "But what of the horses? Should they not rest—"

"Lord Stafford has been good enough to supply us with fresh ones."

"Oh." Seeing no escape from getting back on a horse, she finished tugging her gown on. It was a shame really, her behind was just beginning to have feeling again.

"Come along. Don't tarry." Galen started for the door. "A meal awaits ye below."

Kyla's stomach rumbled aloud at that announcement. Hunger replacing her disappointment, she slid her feet to the floor and stood, straightening her gown as she moved to follow her husband.

The Stafford great hall was dead silent when Kyla and Galen entered. At first she thought the people in the room were all immersed in some sort of prayer. Their heads were raised, their eyes turned to the ceiling as if awaiting the rumble of God's voice. Then Galen cleared his throat and all eyes turned to him.

"There were three items moved against the door last night," Tommy explained when Galen raised his eyebrows as he ushered his wife to the bench and took a seat himself.

"I moved two chairs together," was Galen's response.

"Ahh." Leaning past his lord, he smiled pleasantly at his blushing lady and nodded. "Good morn, me lady."

Kyla managed an uncertain smile, then ducked her head to the food placed before her. She hardly noticed when the men finished their own meals and left the table. She herself had barely finished and sat back to release a satisfied sigh when Galen was on his feet, hand at her elbow, urging her up. "Come. We must go."

"Oh, but—" Tossing him an irritated frown, Kyla glanced back to her hostess as her husband dragged her toward the door of the keep. "The meal was lovely. You must compliment your cook for me. Thank you for everything!" She cried the last word as Galen tugged her through the keep doors, then turned to scowl at the man. "That was most rude, husband."

"Shropshire will offer our thanks. Stafford is his friend."

"Is he not coming with us?"

"Aye. He'll be along. I just wanted to check the horses ere we leave."

"Well, surely you did not need me for that? I could

have remained behind to offer proper appreciation to—"

"Wife, have ye not noticed that when yer left to yer own devices, ye tend to get yerself in trouble?" Galen asked as he pulled her into the stables where the men were examining the horses set up for them.

"Well!" Kyla gasped. "That is simply not true, sir. 'Tis slanderous even to suggest such a thing."

"Well now, me lady, there is the time ye snuck off to the beach," Duncan piped up judiciously, having overheard Galen's comment.

"Which time?" Tommy asked dryly, and the men all laughed.

Kyla glared at them, then snapped, "Which is to be my horse?"

Without bothering to answer, Galen caught her about the waist and swung her onto the horse beside which he had brought her to a halt. Catching her wince as her bottom landed on the saddle, he cast her a sympathetic glance. " 'Tis almost over. We should be at Forsythe in another two days."

Kyla nearly groaned aloud at that. Two more days in the saddle . . . And she used to like riding. It was what she had missed most these last weeks. Access to a horse had been denied her and no amount of begging or arguing had changed that. Now she thought she could do very well were she never to ride again.

Chapter 19

GALEN peered at his wife and smiled slightly. She sat upright on her mount ... sort of. She was sleeping in her saddle, her body wavering like a willow in the wind. He could not blame her. They had been riding nonstop for well over forty-eight hours since leaving Stafford. He himself was weary enough to collapse from his saddle. In fact, he had some doubt as to whether he would be able to keep his feet beneath him were he to dismount now. He would find out soon enough, however. They were approaching Forsythe hall.

Sighing, he urged his weary mount closer to Kyla's and reached out to draw her gently onto the saddle in front of him. She hardly even stirred at the action, merely murmuring sleepily and cuddling into him.

"She sleeps the deep sleep of the innocent."

Galen glanced at Shropshire. Taking in the slightly befuddled frown on the man's face, he shook his head. "Still wondering if Catriona was telling the truth about Kyla wishing her brother dead?"

"Catriona was most convincing."

"From what I have heard ye have known Kyla all her life?"

"Aye," he sighed, nodding.

"Surely ye know then that she loves her brother? Even I have come to know that in the short time we have been together." When the Englishman's confusion and uncertainty showed on his face, Galen shook his head. "I will be interested in meeting this woman."

"What woman?"

"Forsythe's wife. She must be a real beauty to have all of ye twisted about so. That or she is most convincing in bed." Even in the dark, Galen could see the man flush at that. That, plus the fact that Shropshire did not immediately defend the woman's honor, but instead frowned, told Galen he had guessed right. "She sought comfort in her hour of need, did she? And you, as Lord Forsythe's long time friend, supplied it."

"I—" he began, but Galen cut him off.

"Never mind. 'Tis sure I am yer not the only one to have found her favors offered. In fact I ken yer not. Kyla hasn't spoken of it since awaking from her fever, but while delirious she confessed to suspecting the woman was sleeping with her brother's First."

"James?" Shropshire looked horrified at the thought, then a sudden comprehension dawned on his face.

"Damn," he sighed unhappily. "She said she loved me."

"They all say that," Robbie rumbled suddenly, joining the conversation. "At least that is what Aelfread claims. She says the ones who speak of love quickly are free to do so because they feel none, while those who truly do love, often keep such knowledge to themselves for fear the feeling is not reciprocated."

Galen glanced down wistfully at Kyla, taking in her sweet untroubled face. He would give much to believe that that was how she felt. That she cared for him, but feared saying so lest he not return those feelings. Unfortunately, he had already told her how he felt. He himself now regretted confessing his own feelings and blamed such foolishness on the stress of the moment.

His thoughts came to a halt as they reached the moat of Forsythe Castle. Bringing his mount to a halt, he shifted Kyla slightly as Shropshire raised a hand to his mouth and called a greeting to the men on the wall. Within moments the bridge was lowered and the gate lifted.

Shropshire started across it at once, Galen and his men hard on his heels, their gazes moving curiously around the interior of the bailey. It did not take more than a glance to tell that this was a prosperous estate. The people that were still about at this late hour of the night were all well dressed and obviously well fed.

"His lordship sleeps."

Galen turned his gaze forward at that to find that they were now at the foot of the stairs. Reining his mount in, he peered at the man who stood on the bottom step. The man was eyeing Shropshire with such animosity that Galen knew before the other lord introduced him that this was John Forsythe's First, James. And that Kyla was most likely right, the man had had an affair with her brother's wife. Though, judging from the soldier's bitterness, he would guess that it was now over. The man blamed it solely on Lord Gilbert Shropshire. There was nothing like a woman to make a fool of a man. And vice versa, he added when Kyla stirred sleepily in his arms.

"Should we wake him and settle this thing now?" Gilbert asked after introducing John's First.

Galen peered down at his wife's weary face and shook his head. "Nay. 'Twill keep 'til morning. They have both been sore ill. Let them gain their rest."

Nodding, Shropshire hesitated, then winced as he swung one leg over his mount in preparation of dismounting. He landed on the ground a moment later and grasped the pommel of his saddle, barely suppressing a groan. His legs shook visibly beneath him as they came back to painful life.

Galen frowned at the other man's problems, knowing quite well that he himself might suffer so and worried over the safest way to dismount while holding Kyla. He was loath to let her go for even a moment, especially here, but knew he might hurt her should his legs prove as troublesome as Shropshire's were.

"Give her to me."

Galen stiffened at that order, his gaze moving to the newcomer who now stood at the side of his horse, face solemn, arms outstretched to take Kyla.

"Who are ye?"

"He is Henry. Morag's son," James sneered, finally deigning to come forward off the steps. Approaching Galen from the other side of his horse, he added, "Naught but a serf. I shall take her."

Galen was silent for a mere moment, then turned to Henry, handing his wife down into the servant's care. Their eyes met as she passed from one man to the other, understanding passing between them, as well. Galen straightened and slid his leg over his saddle and dropped to the ground. As with Shropshire, his own legs were none too steady and he caught at his saddle when they threatened to go out from beneath him. Then they came back to pulsing, prickling life, and he almost wished they had stayed numb.

As distracted as he was by the sensations attacking his lower body, Galen did not miss the hatred that crossed James' face before he walked away, but he was surprised when the servant, Henry, commented, "You have made an enemy there."

Raising his head, Galen met the man's solemn gaze and nodded his acceptance of those words. "How fares Lord Forsythe?"

"He recovers . . . slowly."

"And I would bet you are never far from his side," Gilbert murmured. He joined them on shaky legs to tell Galen, "Henry and John were of an age and since Morag was John and Kyla's nurse, they played together. You made a good choice. Both of them are as safe with Henry as they are with his mother."

The servant smiled at that. "How is she?"

"Morag?" Gilbert shrugged. "She seems well . . . happy."

"No doubt," Henry murmured wryly. "She has ever longed to return to Scotland."

"Of course she has," Robbie rumbled. "Don't we all?"

Gilbert rolled his eyes when the Scots all murmured their agreement. "You have only just arrived in our fair country. Give it a chance ere you start crying for home."

Galen raised his eyebrows at that. "Ye and me wife lead us into a den of vipers and expect us to relax and enjoy being made a meal of?"

The Englishman grimaced at that. "Well, mayhap not just this moment, but once we clean the den out."

"Speaking of which," Galen muttered, releasing his saddle and straightening painfully. "Where is Lady Forsythe?"

"Thank Goodness!" All eyes turned toward the stairs at that exclamation, widening on a woman who could only be Lady Catriona Forsythe. She was Kyla's height, with ice-blond hair that reached past her shoulders and down to the back of her knees. It flowed out behind her like a cape as she suddenly rushed down the stairs toward them. She wore a gown of azure to match her eyes, the bodice of it cut to emphasize her generous bosom and small waist. That generous bosom came to be pressed strategically upward against a suddenly stiff Shropshire's chest as she hugged him. Peering up at the man through her lashes in a manner that was both demure and seductive, she breathed, "I feared so much for your safety on your travels, my lord. The roads can be so dangerous nowadays."

"Not as dangerous as some castles," Tommy muttered under his breath behind Galen.

Lady Forsythe peered around at that, her gaze moving sharply over the six Scots before returning to Galen. Shropshire suddenly forgotten, she reached a hand toward the MacDonald clan chief, her body seeming to flow after it.

"You must be Lord MacDonald," she murmured in a sultry half-whisper that actually sent a shiver down his back. Grasping his hand, she squeezed it briefly, then ran her smooth, soft hand along his arm, then back to slide the fingers along the inside of his wrist in a seductive manner. Her mouth made a moue before she glanced toward Henry who still held Kyla. "I see you have brought her back to us. Despite all she has done, we cannot help but love her still. Johnny will forgive her, of course."

Galen took in the feigned sadness in her expression and shook his head as her fingers slid seemingly unconsciously back and forth across his skin. She was definitely an experienced woman, he thought grimly as she shifted, her breasts brushing "accidentally" against his arm. Then her gaze shot back to his and she peered up at him through the curtain of her eyelashes, her blue eyes shining with all sorts of promises. "But we should leave that unpleasantness for the morning. Now, you are all no doubt exhausted from your travels and would wish a bath and a . . . bed."

Galen did not miss the slight hesitation and the extra meaning added to that last word. What he couldn't understand was why she was bothering with him . . . and right there in front of Shropshire. Unless it was her intention to get him away from Kyla. Perhaps to allow some injury to be done his wife?

Tugging his arm away from the woman's hold, Galen turned and scooped his wife from Henry's arms. "Aye, a bath would be appreciated. As would a bed for me wife and myself." Turning deliberately away from her, he addressed Henry. "Would ye show me to Kyla's old room?"

"Johnny is in there," Catriona snapped before Henry could respond, then regained herself enough to smile and half-whisper. "I shall show you to the room between that and mine."

Shrugging, Galen shifted Kyla slightly in his arms and fixed an uncaring expression on his face. When Catriona then turned to lead the way, he glanced at his men, his expression telling them to follow. He did *not* trust this woman as far as her hair would reach. She was trouble. Crafty. He would *not* underestimate her.

Lady Forsythe led them to a room on the upper floor, surprise showing in her eyes briefly when she opened the door and turned to see Galen followed into the room by his five men, Shropshire, and even Morag's son Henry. Vexation showed on her features briefly before she managed to smile sweetly and suggest, "There is one other free room up the hall, my lord. It is the room Gilbert used when last here but I am sure he would not mind sharing. Perhaps you would like for your men to be put there? They would be close at hand."

"Aye," Galen murmured moving to the bed to set Kyla down on it. "Have one bath brought here and another taken to the other room."

Her mouth tightened just the smallest fraction at being ordered about like a serf, then she managed another smile and left the room to pass on the order.

Gilbert closed the door behind her and shook his head. "She is like a . . . a . . ."

"Snake?" Galen suggested dryly.

"Aye. A snake. Damn, but she seems to slither right into your braies." He shook his head in bewilderment as if wondering why he had not seen it before, and Galen took pity on him.

"She has some appeal. Most men would be blinded by her sensuality."

Shropshire sighed at that, then glanced up. "What now?"

"Once they are ready, we shall bathe." His gaze slid over his men. "Ye shall take turns at it. Two of ye stand guard outside the door while the others bathe, then ye switch. Once I've tended to meself and Kyla I want ye back in here to plan out how we'll handle the night. I don't trust that woman. She plans something. She was trying too hard to get me interest."

"Aye. She was rather obvious," Gilbert muttered with distaste.

"I've the feeling she wants to get me away from this room and me wife. That means I definitely want at least two men with Kyla at all times. She'll be desperate to do whatever she plans ere Kyla can speak with her brother. That means tonight."

The men all nodded grimly at that. It seemed they had given up the peril of the journey only to land in further peril at Forsythe. No one would rest well that night. There would be no comfort until Kyla had seen her brother and straightened things out come the morn.

Galen was snoring loud enough to wake the dead. No doubt that was what awoke Kyla. Turning her head in the bed, she frowned at him slightly, then could not help but smile. Snoring or not, he looked as sweet as a babe while asleep. His face was relaxed and slack, his mouth hanging open.

Holding back a laugh, she eased the covers aside and slid carefully out of bed. They were at Forsythe. The room they were in told her that much. Kyla recognized it at once as the spare room next to her own. She did not recall arriving, however. That meant she had most likely been asleep when they had got there. Again. She had been aware that she was dozing off as they had ridden. Several times she had started awake in the saddle to find herself nearly tumbling from it. Galen had asked her at least a dozen times if she would not like to ride with him a bit and have a nap, but she had refused out of pride. If the men could manage, she could, as well. This trip was all on her insistence, after all.

She must have dozed off anyway and to the point where she had not even awoken upon arriving. Kyla grimaced to herself at that as she dressed. It was not all she had slept through. It appeared she had been stripped and bathed on arriving and had slept through it all. Galen's doing, no doubt. He was a dear man. Kind and considerate. She would have to tell him so . . . After she had seen her brother.

Renewed determination buoying her, she finished donning her clothes and moved purposefully toward the chamber door, only to pause.

Catriona.

The name was enough to make her scowl. Having slept through her arrival, Kyla had no idea what that woman was up to. She could be trouble. The woman would hardly welcome the proof of her treachery.

Biting the inside of her mouth, she paused to consider the situation. It was more than possible that Catriona would have guards at Johnny's bedroom door. She would insist it was for his own protection, but it was doubtful that they would allow Kyla inside his room to speak with him. Were Gilbert and Galen with her, Catriona could not keep her out of the room, but without them . . .

Her gaze slid around the room and a slow smile came to her lips. As with all castles, this one had its secrets; hollow walls, peepholes, and all the rest.

And it just so happened that this room had a hidden passage between it and her old one. Kyla had discovered the walkway while very young and had used it on more than one occasion to evade her parents. Today she would use it again, she decided with satisfaction. She would sneak in to see her brother, if he was still in her room. It was where Morag had placed them both on their being brought back after the attack. She only hoped he was still there.

Hurrying across the chamber, she searched briefly for the stone in the wall that when pressed revealed the passageway. She found it nearly at once. Despite the fact that so much had happened that it felt like years since she had last been here, it truly had not been that long at all. It was surprising. A matter of months really. Such a short time for so much to change. She had thwarted an attempt on her brother's life, stabbed a man while trying to flee what she thought were robbers, married, made love, escaped the MacGregor's clutches, not once, but twice, fallen in love and—

Sweet Jesu! Had she really said that? Halfway through the entrance, Kyla turned to peer back at her sleeping husband, feeling the affection and desire that immediately welled up within her. Good God, she *loved* him. She did. He had said it to her over a week ago, and she had been uncertain as to how she herself felt, but now she knew. She loved him. With all his pride, his ornery nature, his odd sense of humor, his over-protectiveness—

Come to think of it, what exactly did she love about him? she wondered with vague amusement, then sighed. The answer was easy enough. She loved his pride—despite the moodiness it sometimes caused in him. She enjoyed his fine mind and the conversations they had had, few though they might have been. She felt as light as a bird and giddy to boot when he made her laugh. She loved how he made her feel in bed and even out of it. His over-protectiveness might be annoying when he insisted she should do naught but embroider, but it also warmed her heart and made her feel cherished. But most of all, she supposed she loved him for his belief in her. Not for a moment when Gilbert had come with Catriona's accusations had he, or even any of his men, looked at her with suspicion. They had stood by her, steadfast. They, who had known her a shorter time than Gilbert and—more importantly—not even half as well as her brother. Aye, they had stood by her, just as she knew she would always stand by them.

At that moment, as she stood braced on the entrance to the passage, Kyla believed she might very well not only love Galen, but each and every one of his men. Though, of course, in a very different way. She would trust any one of them with her life at any time. An important point when she was finding trust something in short supply of late.

Sighing, she cast one last glance toward her husband, then let the panel slide closed before feeling her way along the wall to the ridge that denoted the entrance to her old room. Pressing the lever that would release the panel, Kyla eased the door open and peered inside, relieved to see that Henry was the only person present besides her brother. He, like his mother, was more family than servant. She knew he had most likely not left Johnny's side since Morag and she had been sent away. He was as faithful in his way to them as Galen and his men had proven to be to her.

Realizing that these thoughts were only pointing out that Johnny's doubts were hurtful to her, Kyla pushed them away and slid into the room, quickly raising a finger to her mouth to gesture the servant to silence when Henry spotted her and got abruptly to his feet.

Her hurt soothed somewhat by the man's open joy at seeing her, Kyla smiled and moved to the bedside to peer down at her brother. She hardly recognized the man in the bed. Johnny had always been big. As large in her memory as Galen. He had been a mighty and able warrior. Had he not been so outnumbered the day of the picnic, she knew there would never have been any danger of his dying. But his wound and the long recuperation from it had eaten away at his body. He was pale and emaciated, appearing to have shrunk to nearly half his original size.

"Kyla."

Her gaze slid to Johnny's eyes at that whisper to find them open now. The first expression to enter his eyes was joy upon seeing her, but it was immediately replaced by fear and suspicion. Kyla felt hurt, despite knowing to expect it.

"You are mending," she murmured quietly.

One short nod was his answer as doubt battled suspicion in his eyes.

"Gilbert told me so, but I would not rest until I saw it for myself."

"Thought your men had succeeded, did you?"

Kyla stilled at the dry rasp of his voice, pain swelling across her face before she hid it. She cleared her throat to murmur sadly, "He told me of your suspicions as well, but I hoped him wrong."

Johnny turned his head away at that, one hand shifting agitatedly atop the blanket and Kyla sighed. "I know you love her, but she—"

"Do not try to push your shame onto her," he turned to growl furiously. "She had nothing to gain. All would have gone to you."

"Did she know of the codicil?" Kyla asked, forcing her voice to remain calm and even. "I did not."

"You were there when the king's man told me the contents of the will."

Kyla shifted impatiently at that. "It was eight years ago, Johnny. I was a child and my heart was breaking at the loss of mother and father. Think you I heard anything that man said? Think you I even cared?"

He stared coldly past her, his expression stubborn and Kyla's shoulders straightened determinedly. "Fine. If there is no other way."

"What are you doing?" he gasped when he finally glanced over to see that she was untying the laces of her gown.

"Giving you proof," she responded coolly.

"Proof of what? What—" His gaze slid frantically to a wide-eyed Henry.

Kyla shrugged. "It matters little if he sees. The three of us used to swim naked in the river together."

"We were children then," Johnny snapped, half-sitting up on the bed. "Stop her, Henry."

Kyla turned her back to her brother to face the servant as he moved uncertainly forward. Her expression stopped him dead. "He *must* know. She will kill him yet. She will kill both of us."

Henry paused at that and nodded, then moved to stand beside the head of the bed as Kyla began to slide her tunic and under-tunic off her shoulders to reveal her back. "She said I received little but a small wound during the attack. She lied. Mayhap you should consider what else she lied about."

Dead silence was her only answer.

John stared at the wound to his sister's back in horror, a myriad of things running through his head. Not the least of which were memories his illness had taken with it until now. A rush of them. The battle with the attackers. The moment he had realized he was losing. The pain of the sword through his flesh. Kyla's scream. Seeing her running toward him as they raised a sword over his head. Shouting at her to stay back. The impact as she threw herself across him. He remembered it all now. All of it. And he cursed himself for listening to his black-hearted wife's even blacker lies. He had been a . . . "Fool."

Kyla stiffened at the whisper and immediately drew her gown back into place, fear of what it meant making her hands shake clumsily as she tried to retie the laces before turning to face him.

"Lies." He almost moaned the word as the pain of his wife's betrayal struck. Her claims of love, of passion, of happiness had all been lies. She had wanted naught but his riches. "All lies," he whispered sadly.

Each of his words striking at her heart like a dagger, Kyla swayed where she stood, then staggered toward the door. She had not convinced him. He thought her a liar. Despite seeing the injury he— Catriona had won.

"Kyla?" Johnny sat up straighter, frowning when he saw that she was leaving. "Kyla!"

Tugging the door open, Kyla hurried from the room, racing blindly down the hall she had run as a child, straight for the stairs and out the front doors of the keep.

Duncan glanced to the side when the door to Johnny's room opened, his eyes widening as a woman exited. Sobbing fit to tear a man's heart out, she raced for the stairs. Stunned, he turned to a frowning Robbie. "That looked like— Ye don't think?"

Cursing, the larger man turned to open the door of the room they had stood guard over since relieving Tommy and Gavin hours earlier. The moment he saw Galen alone in the bed, he cursed. "Wake him up. I'll go after her."

Kyla was halfway across the bailey before she realized she was running blindly with no real destination. All she wanted was to escape the pain eating at her. And she realized quite suddenly that there was only one place she could do that. With Galen. His love and faith in her would ease her troubled heart. And he would know how to set things right. She knew that as surely as she knew her name. Galen could fix it. He had to.

Turning back toward the keep, she found herself confronting her brother's First.

"Good morn, Lady Kyla."

"James," she murmured grimly, then tried to step around him only to find her way blocked again.

"I am sorry to keep you, but hoped you might have a word of advice. One of the children in the village has fallen and broken her leg."

Kyla stilled at that. "Broken her leg?"

"Aye. The bone cut right through the skin. She's bled a lot and in awful pain. If Morag were here—"

"Bertholde is supposed to tend such things now. She trained under Morag."

"Aye, but she is seeing to a birthing on the edge of the estates, so the butcher is tending the child. But he wants to bleed her and I fear the child has lost a lot of blood already, so thought—"

Cursing, Kyla pushed past the man toward the stables. "The stupid fool. Petey does not know the first thing about healing."

"Nay, my lady," James agreed easily, following her toward the stables.

"He shall kill her should he bleed her."

"I fear so," he murmured.

"Who is it?"

"Excuse me?"

"Who is it?" Kyla repeated as she entered the stables. "Which of the children? Was it little Sally? She is forever needing patching up." Her voice trailed off as she spied the wagon just inside the stable doors. Kyla slowed to a stop. "What is this? Where is the stable master?"

"I sent him on an errand."

It was more his tone of voice than his actual words that made Kyla turn. Facing the man, she opened her mouth to question him further, then cried out as she saw his fist swinging toward her head. A moment later the lights went out.

Chapter 20

"I told ye not to let her leave the room ere I awoke," Galen snapped, tugging his shirt over his head as he moved toward the door.

"She didn't come out of here. She came from the room next door."

"Well, how the Devil did she manage that?"

"I don't ken. 'Twill be all right, though; Robbie went after her. I would have, too, but he ordered me to wake ye."

"There must be a hidden door," Galen muttered distractedly, his gaze moving around the room. He cursed. "The silly wench! Doesn't she know the peril she is in? Catriona would see her dead rather than let her talk to her brother."

"Aye. Well, she has shown a distressing tendency to lack sense in such things," Duncan muttered as Galen finished donning his plaid. "Robbie will have caught her up."

"He'd better have," Galen snapped, stomping out of the room and hurrying down the hall. He was at the top of the stairs when he halted abruptly, his expression darkening as Robbie bounded up the steps toward him . . . alone.

* * *

Kyla's head was pounding when she woke up in the back of the wagon. Ignoring it, she sat up slowly and peered about, scowling at the back of the driver of the wagon she lay in. It wasn't James. Someone in cahoots with him, she thought grimly and considered her position. She recognized the land they were passing through. They were nearing the outskirts of her brother's property. She had just identified that fact when a shout drew her eyes back to the front of the wagon again to see the MacGregor and twenty men riding on the lane, headed for the cart.

Cursing, Kyla scooted quickly to the end of the wagon and leapt to the ground. She had barely regained her feet when she was grabbed from behind and lifted into the air.

Galen eyed his men grimly. They'd searched every inch of the castle and bailey, all with no sign of his wife. Kyla was missing.

"Where exactly did ye last see her?" he asked Robbie harshly.

Rather than be impatient at once again being asked that question, Robbie calmly repeated what had happened once more. "She was going out the keep doors as I came down the stairs. When I reached the doors meself she was nowhere in sight. She must have run for it."

"I thought you saw her running for the stables?" Gilbert reminded him of what he had said the first time he had told the tale.

"Aye . . . Well I *thought* I saw her run into the stables, but—"

"Ye followed at once?"

"Aye, but the stables were empty. Not even the stable master was about."

"Ye said James stopped ye?"

"Aye. He asked me what me rush was."

Frowning, Gilbert stepped closer. "Where was James coming from?"

Robbie raised his eyebrows at that. "I don't— The stables," he answered, suddenly recalling. "He came from the stables."

Galen cursed at that and turned to Tommy. "Find him. Bring him to me."

Shropshire watched Tommy leave, then turned to Robbie to ask, "Did you see anyone else leave the stables ere you entered them?"

Robbie grimaced. "Aye. A wagonload of hay."

"Hay?"

Seeing Shropshire and Galen exchange a glance, he protested, "She couldn't have been in that. 'Twas not fresh hay. 'Twas fair foul. The smell was—" He grimaced distastefully and shrugged.

They were all silent for a moment, then Tommy hurried back in. "He's gone."

"Gone?"

"Aye. The stable master said he rode out no more than ten minutes ago."

"That would not be long after Kyla went missing," Gilbert muttered grimly.

"He took an extra mount with him," Tommy added. "A white gelding."

"Catriona's horse."

They all turned to the stairs at that announcement. Johnny Forsythe stood there, Henry directly behind him, ready to catch the swaying man should he fall. "I gave it to her at my wedding."

"Catriona is locked up in her room. She would not come out when I was searching in here for Lady Kyla," Gilbert announced grimly.

Galen turned and hurried toward the stairs.

"Here we are. I fear 'tis not as nice as you are used to, but then we must all make sacrifices in this time of trouble. Besides, you shall not be long here."

Stumbling into the small, dingy room under the impetus of his push, Kyla caught at a table beside the bed and managed to stay on her feet rather than tumble into the bed as he had intended. Turning now, she faced him warily as he closed the bedroom door and began removing his sword belt. "What are you doing?"

The MacGregor raised an eyebrow in mock surprise as he set his sword aside. "I should think you would know what I am doing, my lady. You have been married to the MacDonald long enough to know when a man is disrobing."

"Why?" No matter how she tried to add force to her voice, Kyla could not keep the broken edge of panic from it as she stared wide-eyed at the man quickly removing his mail to stand clad only in braies and a top.

"You owe me a wedding night," he explained easily, then winced as he reached thoughtlessly toward the ties of his braies with his right hand. Holding that hand up now, he smiled coolly. "You owe me for this as well, do you not?"

Shaking her head frantically, Kyla pushed herself further back against the bedside table as he neared, fear eating away at her. He stopped in front of her and his hand, the injured one, moved to rest against her cheek.

"Aye. You do," he murmured solemnly. He leaned forward, then, his mouth covering hers in what she supposed he thought was a kiss, but which to her in no way resembled one. Where Galen was gentle and questing, or sometimes hungry and passionate, this man was sloppy and brutal as he alternated between almost licking at her tightly closed lips and nipping viciously at them.

Twisting her head away, Kyla felt along the table behind her until she found a nice heavy candle holder. Raising it in her hand, she slammed it into his head with all the force she could manage. Pushing him away as he cried out in pain, she made a run for the door. She had it open and was charging out into the hall before he could stumble after her, but found herself crashing into the burly chest of one of his men before she had even taken two steps toward freedom.

Cursing roundly, she spat and clawed at the man as she was dragged back into the room. Furious himself, the MacGregor barked at his man to tie her, then sat on the side of the bed, rubbing at his head irritably as his order was carried out.

Kyla continued to struggle for all the good it did. The man handling her so roughly was as large as Robbie. He had little trouble forcing her to her stomach on the floor, then keeping her there as he ripped up the top sheet of the bedclothes the MacGregor tossed him. Using those strips, he bound her hands behind her back before turning to tie her ankles together.

Once she was trussed up like a pig for the spit,

the MacGregor had the other man lay her atop the bed beside where he sat. He then ordered him from the room. As soon as the door had closed on him, the MacGregor turned to her.

"That was foolish. Where, pray tell, did you think you were running to?" He shook his head, then winced at the pain that action set up inside his skull and grimaced. "I should say, my dear, that while it is true that pain adds a little spice to the pleasures of the bed, there *is* such a thing as too much of a good thing."

Kyla glared coldly at him, then tried to roll away when he reclined beside her. Unfortunately there was nowhere really for her to roll to. She had barely rotated onto her back before he threw a leg over hers, bringing her to a halt. Kyla began cursing herself then. All she had managed to do was lay herself out like a lamb for the slaughter. With her hands bound behind her back, her body was arched upward in an entirely unintentional invitation. An invitation the MacGregor would have no qualms accepting, she could tell, as his eyes traveled over her body.

"You have a much different body than Catriona's," he mused. "Still, variety in all things has always appealed to me." With that, he reached out to grasp her gown by the neck and rend it downward, baring one breast to view.

The maid's eyes were round holes of fear as she peered through the cracked door. "Her ladyship is resting."

Growling, Galen shoved the door open, sending the servant stumbling backward with a cry of distress. One glance was enough to tell him that Catriona was not in residence. He turned furiously on the servant. "Where is she?"

"I don— My lord!" She gaped at Johnny Forsythe as he stepped into the room.

"Where is she?" he panted weakly, leaning heavily against Henry.

"I . . . She . . . I do not know."

"Yer lying," Galen snapped, taking a threatening step toward her. "She left here with Lord Forsythe's First. Where were they going?"

Panic and fear consumed her expression, but she shook her head.

Grabbing her by the arms, he shook the woman. "They've got me wife! Now where the Devil did they take her?!"

"I don't know, I don't know, I don't know!" the woman half-screamed and half-sobbed. "She told me only to say she was resting and not to let anyone in."

"Get out of my sight," Galen snarled. The woman fled at once.

"If Catriona ordered her maid to claim her asleep, she most like plans to return," Gilbert murmured as Henry urged Johnny to sit on the bed.

"Or she may have just wished for more time to get away ere we followed," Tommy pointed out.

Scowling, Galen turned to Kyla's brother. "Is there anywhere nearby that Catriona could have had Kyla taken?"

Johnny frowned over that. "Her father's estate abutts ours, but Ramsey Hall is too far away for them to use if she plans to return. 'Tis several hours' ride." He thought briefly, then suggested, "But his land ends just a half-hour from here. There is a small manor there that is usually empty."

"I thought Morrissey lived there," Shropshire murmured.

Galen's head whipped up at that name. "Morrissey?"

"One of his retainers. He used to have his own lands, but lost them through a gambling debt. Out of charity, Ramsey allows the man to remain within his old home. 'Tis the manor Johnny speaks of," Shropshire explained, then glanced to Johnny as he asked. "Is it not?"

"Aye. But 'twas a business arrangement. Aside from his gambling habit, Morrissey is a good man. A good overseer, as well, and Ramsey often has to be away at court. In exchange for allowing him to live in his family home, Ramsey has Morrissey oversee Ramsey Hall while he is away at court. But lately that has been more often than not, so Morrissey has been staying at the hall."

"Damn. That explains all."

Both men peered at Galen in surprise at that bitter murmur. "What is it?" they asked as one.

"The MacGregor's mother was a Morrissey," Tommy explained when Galen was silent. "His father married her for her dower, but he hated her because she was English. When she died giving birth to him, he sent the boy to be raised by her brother. Then he set about spending the dower and his son's inheritance ere he could come to manhood and claim them."

"Come to think of it, I do recall something being said about Morrissey having a nephew with him," Shropshire murmured.

" 'Twould explain why Lady Forsythe chose Thomas MacGregor to husband Lady Kyla," Gavin commented with understanding. "That has bothered me since hearing the tale. I couldn't figure how she came to choose him."

"Aye," Galen growled now. " 'Twas bothering me also."

"But if Morrissey was at Ramsey Hall often, the MacGregor most like would have been as well," Tommy put together now, then frowned. "Was there not some rumor that the MacGregor was to be married before?"

"He *was* married before," Angus pointed out dryly. "To Lindsay's daughter. They say he took her without her father's blessing, then beat her to death when the old man refused to pay her dower."

"Nay, I meant ere that," Tommy muttered impatiently, his brows drawn together in concentration. "It seems to me there was some rumor when he first returned from England that he would marry an Englishwoman."

"Oh, aye." Galen nodded. It had been near three years ago since what his First spoke of had happened. "Aye. One of the MacKenzies said the MacGregor had planned to marry an English lass. But the father was a wealthy English Lord and refused to allow the marriage because the MacGregor was poor."

"Catriona?" Robbie suggested in a rumble, one eyebrow cocking.

"Er . . . Johnny," Shropshire murmured uncomfortably now. "There *were* certain rumors going around court ere your marriage, that your wife had wished to marry some penniless Scot, but that her father would not have it."

Forsythe nodded. "I heard those same rumors,

but thought them the usual court tripe put out by jealous dandies. I was blind."

"Aye, well," Shropshire sighed unhappily. "All of this would explain the problem of the codicil to the will. If you died and Kyla had been forced into marriage to the MacGregor, he would inherit all."

"And if she had died after that, the MacGregor would have been free to marry Catriona," Galen said grimly.

Nodding, Gilbert turned to his friend. "This could be the evidence you needed to prove which of the women spoke the truth."

"My sister does not lie. I fear I had forgotten that for a while, but she came to me this morn. She showed me her back and I remembered all. It was as she said. I was on the ground with a sword through my belly. They were about to cut my head off, but she threw herself atop me taking the blow herself." Mouth twisting bitterly, he shook his head. "I should have never allowed that witch to whisper doubts in my ear."

Galen nodded. " 'Tis good to hear ye finally come to yer senses. But me wife may be being killed as we speak. I would go after her. Where is Morrissey Manor?"

"Take them there, Shropshire," Forsythe ordered his friend grimly.

When the MacGregor's hand moved toward her naked breast, Kyla closed her eyes and began to pray. She just knew she would be sick if he touched her.

"I hope I am not interrupting anything, my lord?"

MacGregor stilled at those arch words and glanced to the doorway.

Glimpsing her sister-in-law over the MacGregor's shoulder, Kyla sagged with relief, then nearly laughed hysterically at the irony of it. Never once, in all the time since Johnny had brought the woman home to wife, had Kyla been happy to see Lady Catriona. But she would have welcomed the Devil himself at that point if it had saved her from this man's unpleasant gropings.

Getting to his feet, the MacGregor smiled, unperturbed, at the other woman. "Now you know how I have felt knowing you shared Forsythe's bed every night." She glared at him.

"I did that for us!" Catriona snapped. "Once he is finally dead I will be a rich widow and free to marry who I wish." Softening suddenly, she hurried forward, reaching for his face with both hands. "Oh, Thomas. You know it was for you. Only you. Do not be angered at me for trying to give you all you deserve."

Kyla's eyebrows rose at that, more at the use of his first name than anything else. It was the first time she had heard his name spoken. It was amazing how one could spend so much time with a Scot and never hear his first name, she thought, then turned her attention back to the couple before her. The MacGregor suddenly caught one of the small, pearl white hands at his cheek and crushed it between his ruddy fingers, snarling. "And was James for my good as well?"

Catriona paled, but to give her credit, her expression did not change one iota. "Everything I have done has been only to further your best interests."

He raised his eyebrows at that, his hand closing even tighter around her delicate fingers before he asked pleasantly, "Will you not even ask how I knew?"

When she merely bit her lip against the pain he was inflicting, his eyebrows rose further. "Nay, hmm? Well, I shall tell you anyway. Spies, my dear. I have had someone watching you at all times. And you would do well to remember that." Releasing her, he tilted his head slightly. "Do you not wonder why I specifically ordered you to bring James here when I knew he was your lover?"

A strange glow of almost anticipation entered Catriona's eyes. "Tell me."

MacGregor leaned forward and murmured, "To kill him, my dear. My men do it as we speak."

While Kyla gasped at that statement, Catriona and her lover both smiled. Then MacGregor suddenly slapped her and barked, "Did you enjoy bedding him?"

Catriona stumbled backward a step under the blow, one hand raising to cover the mark he had left on her cheek. Anger and excitement fought briefly on her face, then she straightened, shoulders stiffening and coolly announced, "Of course not. He knows not how to treat a woman. Neither does Forsythe. They are both soft fools. Only you treat me as I should be treated." Then her gaze slid to Kyla on the bed and her expression twisted. "Have you enjoyed bedding *her*?"

Kyla stiffened indignantly at the slur to her honor, mouth tightening when, rather than deny having bedded her, the MacGregor smiled. "Certainly."

"Pig," she hissed and Kyla bit back a nervous breath, her gaze locked on the couple. She could feel the rage rolling off the man, and wasn't surprised when he caught Catriona by one wrist and twisted it maliciously behind her back, forcing her against his chest. Catriona cried out in pain at the move, but the MacGregor merely twisted her arm a little further, then reached his free hand up to the front of her gown, and tugged at the lovely material, uncaring that it ripped as he bared her breasts to his view.

"Look at yourself. You are already hard for me. Your nipples are like pebbles," he sneered and much to Kyla's amazement his words were true. The other woman's breasts were puckered with excitement, her breathing coming as short panting as the MacGregor kneaded and pulled at her flesh in a vulgar manner.

"Faith! You are probably already wet, are you not?" he growled now, snaking his hand down to jerk her skirt up and test for himself.

Much to Kyla's horror, this only seemed to excite the other woman more. She moaned as he handled her in this coarse fashion, apparently uncaring that Kyla witnessed the whole thing.

"Aye, you are," he said now with a trace of satisfaction as he delved his hand between her legs. "You are as slick as a well-used-whore with want. Tell me you want me," he ordered, laughing coldly at the way she arched into his touch. He must have pinched her flesh when she wasn't quick enough answering, because pain flashed across her face briefly, then she nodded.

"Aye. I want you," she gasped. "Oh God, Thomas. I want you." She tugged at his hair, dragging his head toward her as if desperate for a kiss but the MacGregor jerked his head away. Twisting her arm again, he sent her to her knees before him. "Beg," he ordered, smiling cruelly.

Closing her eyes, Kyla turned her head away in disgust as Catriona began to do just that, begging him to do a myriad of absolutely horrid things to her. She tried to close out what happened after that, determined to distance herself from the couple as they grappled there on the floor. She now understood the rumors circulating about this man. He seemed to like to humiliate. He certainly enjoyed hurting. Even more dismaying was the fact that Catriona seemed to enjoy being the recipient of that pain. It was all rather repellent to Kyla. She was relieved beyond expression when they both cried out their release and collapsed on the floor.

"MacGregors?" Shropshire's gaze slid over the men in the courtyard at Morrissey. There were at least a dozen of them, all excited and shouting as they watched one of their own do battle with Johnny's First. James wasn't doing too well. The battle would be over soon.

"Aye," Galen grunted, his gaze moving slowly over the men.

"They outnumber us two to one."

"That ought to about make the odds even," Tommy commented and much to Gilbert's amazement, the Scots all smiled at each other.

"I must go."

Kyla blinked her eyes open, disoriented for a moment as to where she was, until movement drew her eyes to the couple on the floor. Catriona was struggling out from beneath the MacGregor's naked weight, hurriedly drawing her clothes about her. Memory kicked in then and she realized that she, too, must have passed out briefly. After the couple's animalistic display, sleep had been a welcome relief.

"Eager to return to your husband?" the Mac-Gregor sneered, sitting up to twist one already bruised nipple as she struggled to pull her torn gown back on.

"I will be missed," Catriona answered, licking her lip as her lover leaned forward to bite down on her abused flesh. " 'Tis cruel of you to tease me so." She moaned, then, sighing reluctantly, she pulled away and got to her feet, frowning over the irreparable damage to her clothes. "You have ruined my gown."

Shrugging, the MacGregor got languidly to his feet, drawing his braies on as he did. "You have a cloak to cover it."

Exasperation crossing her face, Catriona gave up on her gown and reached for the cloak he held out. "Send word to me at Forsythe once you have killed her."

Kyla's eyes went round in horror. "You cannot do that!"

Catriona turned to her with disdain. "Of course we can."

"But I thought—"

"What?" The other woman arched her brows cynically. "That you would get to marry Thomas? You should be so lucky. Do you think I would allow that?"

"But you sent me to Scotland to—"

"Die." Catriona snapped the word. "Aye, if you had survived the journey, he would have married you, but you would not have survived your wedding night. You were to suffer an accident," she spat, then sighed. "It is nothing personal, Kyla. Truly you did at least *try* to be nice to me. I had no intention originally of seeing you dead, but then you interfered in the attack on your brother— I really must thank you for that, by the by. Had you not done so, all would have gone awry. Johnny had not informed me of the codicil to your father's will."

"That I would inherit should he die without heir," Kyla murmured.

"Aye. And, of course, since you allowed yourself to be married off to that savage MacDonald, that meant he and you would have inherited all had Johnny died from his injuries." She grimaced at that. "All would have been lost then."

"Then all is still lost," Kyla said triumphantly. "For if Johnny and I die—"

"Nay," Catriona interrupted calmly. " 'Tis all in the sequence of events. So long as you die first, all is still well. I inherit then whether there is an heir or no."

When Kyla slumped back on the bed, Catriona gave her a pitying look. " 'Tis your father's fault. Had he not written that codicil, I would have let you be." Not waiting to see Kyla's reaction to that, Catriona turned back to her lover, caressing his cheek in the first show of true affection she had actually seen between the two. "Send word once 'tis done. Make sure it looks like an accident. I will tend to her brother then and we shall be together always."

Nodding, MacGregor caught one of her fingers in his mouth, sucking on it briefly before biting down hard enough to make her start. Tugging her hand away then, she turned and left the room.

"Well . . ." The MacGregor faced Kyla. "Let us

get it done, shall we?" He suggested it as if asking her to dance rather than talking about killing her.

Pausing before her, he tilted his head and raised one eyebrow slightly. "Or do you have a last request? Your favorite meal, mayhap?" His gaze glittered as it ran over her where she lay and he reached out, grabbing the breast revealed by her torn gown and squeezing it hard as he asked. "Or mayhap there is another hunger you would like satisfied? Were you very excited by watching us?"

Kyla's mouth thinned with disgust. MacGregor sank onto the bed beside her and murmured, "I have always found such scenes stimulating."

"Aye, well . . . you obviously have perverted tastes," she muttered, turning her face quickly away when he would have pressed his lips to hers. It was a useless attempt. She had no escape and they both knew it. Perhaps that was why the MacGregor merely laughed and tugged her face back before mashing his mouth onto hers. It was the poorest excuse for a kiss she had ever experienced. He seemed more intent on chewing the lips off her face than anything else.

Kyla was just wondering if she could possibly get herself out of this mess when the man suddenly stilled against her, then lifted his head away.

Actually—she realized as his face moved further away, improving her view—he hadn't so much lifted his head away as had it torn away from her. Galen was now holding the smaller man by the scruff of his neck, fury his only expression. He shook the MacGregor in the air, then tossed him across the room where he crashed into the wall by the door. The villain slid down to sit on the floor, shaking his head dizzily.

Gilbert had followed Galen into the room. Glancing now from the dazed man on the floor to the bed where Kyla still lay half-exposed, he turned abruptly and blocked Galen's men from entering, setting up a flurry of arguing from them.

Ignoring everyone, Galen dropped his sword and bent to Kyla. "Are ye all right?" Fear and worry battled in his eyes as his gaze dropped worriedly to her torn dress and the bruises even now forming on her pale flesh. He gathered the two torn pieces of her gown together to cover her up. "He hurt ye."

"Nay. Well . . . not much anyway," she added at his expression of patent disbelief. "You came in time."

"Thank God," Galen breathed, hugging her close. "Me laird!"

Galen ignored the shout, thinking it a protest against being excluded from the room, but Kyla glanced over his shoulder, her eyes widening in horror. The MacGregor had landed on the floor beside where he had set his sword earlier. He now had that sword in hand, was on his feet, and was charging toward Galen's unguarded back.

Instinctively trying to save her unsuspecting husband, Kyla brought her knees up toward her chest, caught her feet in his stomach, and shoved Galen away to the side with all her might. The MacGregor faltered in his step as he saw his original quarry pushed out of the way, then continued forward, hatred spitting from his eyes as he rushed on toward Kyla.

Seeing the threat, Galen's men pushed by an oblivious Gilbert, bursting into the room and drawing their swords. At the same moment, Galen regained his wits enough to see what Kyla was trying to protect him from. Releasing an enraged battle cry, he grabbed for his sword, lunged to his knees, and thrust it at MacGregor even as his men rushed forward, echoing his cry.

Kyla and Shropshire both watched the outcome in amazement. Six men, six swords. All thrust at a different spot on the MacGregor as he raised his own sword to kill Kyla . . . And all of them found a home.

Eyes wide with shock, the MacGregor halted a bare step from the bed. Arms still upraised, sword hanging behind his back, he peered at her blankly.

"Damn," he gasped with a sort of startled dismay. Then the sword slid from his fingers, clanging to the floor behind him as he sank slowly to his knees. He slumped forward, his head falling in Kyla's lap where she lay on the bed.

"Damn," Gilbert echoed, sagging back against the doorframe he had been standing in throughout.

"Aye, damn." Kyla sighed wryly, then shifted a bit where she lay. She did her best to avoid looking at the swords that protruded from the MacGregor from seemingly every angle. He looked like a porcupine. A bloody porcupine.

"Could someone please remove him and untie me?" she snapped after a moment when no one moved and her saviors merely stood grimacing bashfully over the pincushion of a man that had once been the MacGregor.

Everyone was moving again at once. Galen returned to her side even as his men dragged the hapless corpse of Thomas MacGregor off her and a little away to remove their swords one by one. Doing her best to ignore what the men were doing, Kyla smiled gratefully at her husband as he quickly helped her to a sitting position, then frowned as her sister-in-law suddenly came to mind. "Catriona—"

"We caught the wench below. Henry is holding her."

"Henry? Who is with Johnny then?"

"His own men," Galen answered and when Kyla began to look worried, he soothed her. "He will be all right. We have all those who would see him hurt here . . . Unless there is someone else?" he added worriedly, pausing in untying her.

"James. He hit me in the stables and—"

"He'll not trouble anyone," Galen told her dryly. "MacGregor's men were finishing with him as we arrived."

"Oh," she murmured as he finished untying her. That done, he grabbed the linens off the bed and wrapped one quickly about her shoulders. Ordering the men to see to MacGregor's body, he carried her from the room.

Henry was waiting by the horses in the courtyard, one heavy hand gripping a sullen Catriona. The woman glared coldly at Kyla as Galen carried her past. After settling her on his saddle, he quickly joined her, then they both peered around at a sudden scream from Catriona. The men were bringing the MacGregor's body out.

Henry did his best to hold on to the woman, but her grief would not be contained. Breaking loose, she rushed forward to throw herself across the inert body. The men stopped at once and stood about, watching uncomfortably as she clutched at her fallen lover, kissing his lifeless flesh and howling hysterically.

She carried on so for several minutes before Gilbert finally moved to urge her away. He tried soothing words, then short ones, but when reason and orders failed, he glanced at Galen, shrugged, then knocked the woman unconscious with a blow to the head.

Kyla grimaced slightly at that, but said nothing. Catriona deserved that and more for what she had done. Besides, sleep, willing or forced, was most likely best for the woman just then. Her life would never be the same after today. Even Johnny would not be able to deny the evidence Galen would present to him on returning. And Galen would have to do the presenting, for she was simply too weary to face the brother who had betrayed her so with his doubts and suspicions.

On that thought, Kyla rested her head against Galen's chest and closed her eyes, not opening them again until they had reached Forsythe. Oddly enough the sight of her childhood home did not bring the sense of safety and well-being it used to. Kyla suspected she would not enjoy that sensation until her eyes rested on the MacDonald keep again.

Sighing inwardly, she smiled slightly at her husband as he set her to the ground, then turned and started wearily up the steps to the keep without waiting for him. Eager to change into a fresh gown and discard the makeshift cloak she now clutched about her, she took the stairs quickly and was several feet in front of Galen as she started across the hall.

"Kyla!"

Halfway across the great hall, she paused, her startled gaze shooting to the man seated at the table. Johnny. She had not expected him to be up. He was still unwell. Swallowing back the pain that swelled up inside her at the very sight of him, she whirled suddenly and hurried back out of the keep.

Galen's mouth dropped at her abrupt exit, then he glanced to her brother, saw the anguish on the man's face, and hurried after his wife.

The men were just dismounting when Kyla rushed down the steps toward them. Eyebrows rising curiously, they watched her start to hurry by, then she suddenly whirled and moved to the horses instead. Approaching the stallion she and Galen had shared on the way back, she mounted it with more speed than grace, the bed linens she still clutched about her hampering her actions only somewhat.

"Well?" she snapped, peering at the men standing uncertainly about. "What are you waiting for? Mount up. We return to Scotland."

Robbie squinted at that announcement and tilted his head. "Return?"

"Aye. Do you not wish to see Aelfread?"

"Aye, but—"

"Then mount up."

"Wife." The gentle tone of Galen's voice, added to the touch of his hand on her knee, drew her eyes reluctantly down to him as he reached the side of the horse.

"Come," he ordered gently, holding his hands up to her.

Kyla hesitated, then shook her head. "I want to go home."

Galen nearly smiled at that. She sounded like a frightened child. It was the first time since meeting this courageous woman that he had seen any evidence of vulnerability in her at all. It was a bit reassuring to him just then. "Ye must say farewell to yer brother first," he told her gently but firmly.

"Henry can tell him farewell for me. Give him my love, Henry," she ordered, glancing at the man holding the limp Catriona.

"Yer afraid!" Duncan blurted the realization the moment it struck him.

"I am not!" Kyla snapped, then her lip trembled. "He thinks I tried to have him killed. Even after I showed him my back—"

"Nay!" Henry dumped Catriona into Robbie's startled hands and moved to stand beside Galen. "He remembered all the moment he saw your back."

"Do not lie to me, Henry. He called me a fool, said it was all lies."

"He called himself a fool and said all Catriona had said were lies," Henry corrected gently. "You misunderstood him."

She hesitated at that, hope coming to life in her eyes. Galen smiled at her reassuringly, holding his arms up to her once more. "Come. I'll stand by ye."

"So will I," Robbie rumbled, turning to shove Catriona at Tommy so that he could move up to stand beside his laird and offer his support to his lady.

Frowning at the burden he held, Tommy unloaded her on Gavin. "And I."

"As will I," Gavin murmured, tossing the woman to Angus who immediately turned to Duncan, but Duncan was swifter and hurriedly stepped forward adding his own vow of support.

Frowning, Angus discharged the woman on Shropshire, then stepped forward himself with a firm nod.

Amusement tugging at her lips, Kyla peered from

the hapless form of the unconscious Catriona to Shropshire's unhappy face. Meeting her gaze, he hesitated briefly, then in a most unchivalrous move, dumped the woman on the ground and stepped forward. "We shall all accompany you."

"My brave saviors," Kyla murmured, stifling her amusement as she swung her leg back over the pommel and dropped into her husband's arms.

"Aye, well . . . *He* didn't really do any of the saving," Duncan grumbled, jerking a thumb toward Shropshire. "Fact is, he tried to stop us from saving ye, if ye'll recall. The footsy scunner."

"Now, see here . . ." Gilbert snapped, turning on the man.

"It's true," Duncan defended. "First ye wouldn't let us in the room, then yer blade never left yer sheath."

"My back was to the room, I did not see that he was up. Besides, 'tis better that than for there to have been seven bloody swords in the poor blighter."

"At least *we* ken that we saved her," Angus snapped.

"Which one of you?" Shropshire snorted with distaste.

"You are all my saviors," Kyla interrupted smoothly. "Every single one of you rushed to my aid when I needed you. Even Gilbert. I shall never forget that. Now, shall we go in and say our farewells to my brother?"

Shropshire hesitated, his gaze on the woman he had set on the ground. "*I* had best stay with this one until Johnny decides what to do with her. You go ahead."

Smiling a thank-you, Kyla nodded and turned

back toward the stairs. With Galen's hand at her arm, she started back up the stairs, only to hear the discussion continue behind her even as the men followed her up the stairs.

"Never fear, we ken the truth of the matter," Angus muttered.

"Aye, the English are a bunch of wee, sleekit, cow'rin, tim'rous beasties," Duncan murmured back.

Pausing, Kyla whirled to face her men at that and Duncan's face twisted with dismay as he realized that he had just insulted his own mistress. "Not ye of course, me lady." When she continued to frown at him, he swallowed audibly. "Nor yer brother, either. I mean, yer only half English anyway, the two of ye and . . ."

When his voice faded to silence Kyla rolled her eyes, shook her head, and turned to continue up the steps.

Chapter 21

"So. Do ye get seasick like yer sister?"

Lord Forsythe raised his eyebrows at Tommy's question, but merely shrugged. "I do not know. I have never been aboard a boat before."

When his First groaned at that response, Galen smiled with amusement and shook his head. No doubt the warrior was fearing having to tend to the man as Galen had had to tend to Kyla on the way over. The memory of that hellish trip was enough to steal the amusement from his face and set him to frowning again. He had intended on traveling back to Scotland by horseback to save her the trials of a return journey by boat, but she had insisted on taking the boat when she had learned that it made it a much shorter journey.

"If 'twould be shorter, 'twould surely be easier on poor Johnny, who is still healing," she had reasoned. " 'Sides, I have most like gained my sea legs now," she had assured him naively. "I will manage the trip well enough."

In the end, Galen had given in to her wish to take the boat. Just as he had given in to her other wishes of late, he thought sourly, his mind returning to the day he had brought her back safely from Morrissey Manor.

Once persuaded to face her brother, Kyla had marched grimly into her brother's castle as if walking to meet the hangman. Two minutes later she was crying and hugging her repentant brother and assuring him she forgave him all. Of course, once that had happened, her wish to return home had immediately fled.

"Nay, Galen, I would stay and visit Johnny. He is still recovering," she had said. "Surely a short visit to get to know your brother-in-law would not hurt you?"

A "short visit" had turned into two weeks. During that time, Kyla had seen to replacing her brother's First for him, cleared out the last of Catriona's men, and generally set things to right in her old home. She had also managed in that time to convince her brother that he should return with her to Scotland for a visit.

"Morag would be glad to see you on the mend and I would surely enjoy the visit. We could play chess by the fire at night," Galen mimicked her words to her brother in his head, then sighed, realizing with not a little bit of shame that, of all things, he was jealous of the attention his wife had been bestowing on her own brother. It was a sad case and that was the truth, he decided grimly, but could not help himself. His feelings for her were so strong and all encompassing, it hurt his heart that she did not return them. It was a torture to watch her bestow the easy affection he hungered for on others, even her own brother.

Sighing, he glanced over his shoulder at his wife. She had started out between him and her brother, but had fallen back a ways after the first two hours of travel. Seeing her thoughtful expression, he slowed his mount until he was at her side. "What has ye so pensive, wife?"

Kyla smiled slightly. "I was just thinking, my lord."

"About what?"

"You."

Galen blinked at the forthright answer, then peered at her curiously. "And what exactly were ye thinking about me, wife?"

Kyla shrugged. "I was recalling how you tended me when I was ill. . . . First from my injury, then on the boat."

"Aye, well. . . ." He shifted uncomfortably on his horse. "And sure enough ye needed tending."

"Hmmm," Kyla murmured. "I was also pondering over how you promised me you would tend to the MacGregor ere we returned home. And you did. 'Tis now safe for me to picnic on the beach with Aelfread."

Galen grimaced at that, for his idea of tending the man and what had actually happened did not exactly merge well in his mind. All he said was, "Somehow I fear ye will have a bit of trouble getting Robbie to agree to that."

Ignoring that suggestion, Kyla murmured, "You also told me that should I be taken, you would rescue me back and you did."

"Aye, well, as I recall it, I said that ye should have allowed yerself to be taken and that I *then* would have saved ye. Or some such rot," he reminded her with some embarrassment.

"And you did," Kyla repeated. "Save me, I mean."

Galen was grimacing over his foolish pride the night he had made that statement to her when her next words brought his breathing to a halt.

"I love you." She had barely said the words when she spurred her horse from a walk to a run and sent him racing up the path past the other men.

Galen stared after her in amazement for a moment, then dug his heels into his horse's sides and charged after her. Catching her up, he leaned out and caught her about the waist, dragging her onto his own mount.

"What did ye say?" he demanded, drawing his own mount to a halt.

"You heard me," Kyla murmured, settling comfortably against his chest.

"Say it."

"I *love* you."

"Saints preserve us," Galen breathed. "I never thought to hear words so sweet. Say it again."

"I would rather show you," she murmured shyly, and he caught his breath again. He lowered his lips to capture hers in a soul-searing kiss that left them both oblivious as the men caught up to them and reined their animals in, grinning as they watched the intimate embrace. Well . . . Most of them were grinning. Johnny was a little less than amused.

"Ahem."

Recognizing who was making the noise, neither of them paid much attention to his feigned throat-clearing, so he tried again . . . a bit louder. "Ahem!"

"Go away, Johnny," Kyla murmured as Galen kissed a trail to her ear.

"For the love of God, Sister! Show some decorum! We are out in the woods for all to see."

"Just as you were when you and Catriona were dallying by the river?" she suggested, reminding him of a day shortly before the attack when he and Catriona had slipped away to make love in a clearing in the woods by the river. Unfortunately, Kyla had been restless that day and decided a walk along the path would lift her spirits. Instead of lifting her spirits, she had got an eyeful of her brother lifting his wife's skirts.

"You saw us?" The horror in his voice was obvious.

"As you said, 'Out in the woods for all to see.' "

He sputtered at that and the men chuckled. Kyla stilled at once. In her passion-dazed state, it had not occurred to her that the men would have reached them also. It was one thing for her brother to come upon them engaged so, but quite another for her men to see her in such a state. Flushing brilliant red, she tugged away from her husband. "Please, husband. 'Tis unseemly to behave so out in the open."

Galen blinked at her embarrassed face, then at the men surrounding them. Understanding dawning on his face, he swung her into his arms and abruptly dismounted. "We'll camp here tonight."

"Here?" Tommy peered around at the inhospitable setting with doubt.

Galen nodded firmly. "Aye. Here. See to it."

"But 'tis only just past the nooning hour," Duncan protested. "We have many hours of travel left to us."

" 'Tis making up for the lack of rest on the way out that I'm about," Galen explained drolly as he carried Kyla off the path and started into the woods. " 'Sides, we must no' wear out Kyla's brother. He's still no' fully recovered."

Stung at the suggestion that he was not up to par, Johnny straightened in the saddle. "The hell you say! I could ride the rest of the day and well into evening!"

"So could I, but no' in the saddle," Galen murmured under his breath and Kyla gasped and glared at him.

"Husband!"

"He didn't hear," Galen defended himself.

She relaxed slightly in his arms at the truth of that, but was looking worried now. Galen sighed inwardly, already knowing what was troubling her.

"Mayhap we should not leave him alone, Galen."

"He is no' alone, wife. My men will tend him."

"Aye, but he is still suffering over Catriona's betrayal."

"A suffering he well deserves for getting tangled up with that she-snake to begin with," he responded with no sign of sympathy. "The man should have used his head in picking a wife, rather than what was between his legs."

"As you used your head?" Kyla suggested archly, and Galen paused to peer down at her as she pointed out, "You did not even know what kind of wife you were getting when you attacked our party. As I recall, 'twas revenge you were after when you carried me off to wed."

"Aye. And had I known how sweet revenge could be, I would have come to claim ye sooner," he said with a wolfish grin, then added more seriously. "Besides, I didn't lose me heart to ye because of yer fair looks and yer hot body in me bed. I gave me heart only when I knew ye were worthy of it."

"Oh, Galen," Kyla breathed, love filling her eyes. "Those are the sweetest words I have ever heard."

Galen grinned widely at her approval, then kissed her quickly before moving on again. "I've a passel more of those that I would tell ye, wife. And I'll whisper each one of them against yer naked flesh just as soon as I find a comfy spot to do it in."

"Is that a promise, husband?" Kyla murmured, running one finger along the rim of his ear. "You have always kept your promises to me."

" 'Tis no' just a promise but a vision that has been haunting me o' late."

"A vision?" Kyla's eyebrows rose, the day he had loved her on the beach coming immediately to mind. He had exercised a couple of visions there that day, she recalled with a shiver. Her voice was husky as she murmured, "I do so enjoy your visions, husband. Pray hurry and find a 'comfy' spot."

Keep reading for a peek at

THE IMMORTAL WHO LOVED ME,

Lynsay Sands' next Argeneau novel

Available Spring 2015 from Avon Books

Sherry's gaze slid from the girl to the dark-haired young man now sliding into the seat across from her in the booth, wondering briefly if he was this Basil person. If so, he wasn't her type. Dressed in black jeans and T-shirt with a leather jacket, the guy looked like the stereotypical bad boy. Not her scene at all, she thought with something like relief. Stephanie was wrong; she was not a life mate to this man. But even as she began to relax, Stephanie gestured and said, "Sherry, this is Justin Bricker."

Sherry swallowed and nodded in greeting, her entire focus shifting to the heat emanating from the man settling into the seat beside her. "And that's Basil Argeneau," Stephanie added.

Taking a deep breath, Sherry forced a smile and turned to peer at the man who was supposedly her life mate. She stared at him silently for a long moment, drinking him in.

Basil had blond hair, but golden blonde, not the dirty blond of Leo and his boys. It was also cut short. The man had full lips, chiseled cheeks and chin, and the most incredible silver blue eyes she'd ever seen.

Her gaze dropped to what she could see of his body, where he sat beside her, and she noted the wide shoulders under the dark designer business suit and that his stomach appeared super flat. But that was all she could tell with him sitting so close. It was enough. The guy was . . . well . . . jeez, he was a hottie.

"Definitely the pepperoni," she muttered.

"Excuse me?" Basil Argeneau said uncertainly.

Realizing what she'd said, Sherry flushed and shook her head. She had no intention of explaining that he was hot and spicy like Stephanie's pizza pepperoni. And he was. Certainly, he was hotter than any guy she'd ever dated, and she had dated a lot of guys over the years. She'd even lived with one fellow for a bit. She was thirty-two after all, not a child. This guy, though, looked younger than her. Maybe twenty-five, she thought with concern, and then recalled Stephanie's claim that these vampires or immortals stopped aging at about twenty-five. Before she considered how rude the question might be, Sherry blurted, "How old are you?"

His eyes widened slightly and then he simply said, "Old."

Sherry frowned at the vague answer and pressed, "Older than thirty-two?"

For some reason that made Justin Bricker snort with amusement.

When she glanced his way, he slid a cell phone out of his pocket, set it on the table, and grinned at her as he suggested, "Try adding a couple of zeroes behind the thirty-two and you'll still be three hundred and forty some years off."

Sherry frowned at the suggestion, not sure she believed him, but before she could question him on the matter, the brush of fingers along her arm made her glance quickly to Basil. His touch had sent a shiver of sensation down her arm, leaving goose bumps in its trail. Sherry unconsciously rubbed her arm in reaction and stared at him wide-eyed.

"Are you thirty-two then?" Basil asked.

Sherry nodded.

"And you own your own store?" he asked. "A kitchenware store, I understand."

"Yes." Sherry sat a little straighter, reminding herself that she wasn't a breathless teenager but a grown-up, successful business woman who had worked hard and was now reaping the rewards . . . which she got to pay half of to the government. The thought made her scowl again, which made Basil sit back slightly. Noting that, she smiled wryly and said, "Sorry. I was just thinking about my taxes."

If she'd thought that would reassure him, she'd thought wrong. If anything, it made him frown, and that was when Sherry realized it probably wasn't flattering to be talking to him and thinking of her taxes.

"Are you single?" she asked, to distract him from her momentary faux pas.

"Yes. You?" he asked politely.

"Mostly," she answered at once.

"Mostly?" he echoed, frowning even harder.

"Well, it's . . . I've been dating a guy, but it's just casual; dinner, a movie, the occasional business function. We aren't exclusive or anything," she assured him.

Basil nodded solemnly. "I am."

"You are what?" she asked uncertainly.

"Exclusive."

It was a simple word, but somehow carried the finality of a judge's gavel, and Sherry was trying to sort out what it meant exactly and how she should respond, when a chime sounded from the phone Justin had set on the table. She glanced his way as he picked it up, thumbed the screen, and then stood.

"Well, kids. You'll have to finish this 'get to know you' thing in the SUV. Nicholas says the street is clear at the moment and we have to get you out of here before Leo and his boys come back around."

Sherry glanced to Stephanie and then to Basil as he stood, noting the hand he was holding out to help her up. So gentlemanly, Sherry thought. She took the offered hand, startled by the tingle it sent through her fingers and up her arm. The man seemed to be full of static electricity. Probably didn't use Bounce in the dryer, Sherry thought absently as he released her hand to take her elbow and usher her toward the front door of the pizza joint.

Sherry glanced over her shoulder as they went, relieved to see that Stephanie was right behind them with Justin on her heels. Sherry had started out trying to keep the girl safe, but suddenly felt like she was in over her head and Stephanie was the only lifeline she had. Weird.

"Here we are."

Sherry turned forward again as Basil urged her out of the pizzeria and to the back door of an SUV illegally parked in front of it. She allowed him to usher her inside, then settled in the far seat and busied herself doing up her seat belt before risking looking at the man again. He'd settled next to her and was doing up his seat belt as well, so she glanced to the front of the vehicle where Stephanie was doing the same in the passenger seat.

"Do we know if everyone was okay at the store?" she asked no one in particular as Justin Bricker got into the driver's seat.

"My daughter and Drina were headed there to take care of matters," Basil announced quietly. "They'll report when they are done, but I'm sure everyone is fine."

Sherry stared at him blankly. "Your daughter?"

"Katricia," he explained.

"Katricia who's getting married?" Sherry asked slowly.

He nodded and smiled faintly. "She met her life mate at Christmas."

"Teddy the police chief where Stephanie lives," Sherry said, recalling the girl's words from earlier.

"Yes." He smiled. "She's settled in Port Henry with him and helping him police the town."

"Right," Sherry murmured, but she was trying to wrap her mind around the fact that this man—who looked no more than twenty-five—had a daughter old enough to marry anyone. She didn't care what Justin had said about adding two zeroes and so on, this man *looked* twenty-five. Clearing her throat, she asked, "And how old is your daughter?"

He paused and squinted toward the roof of the SUV briefly. "Well, let's see. She was born in 411 AD so that makes her—"

"What?" Sherry squawked with amazement.

Basil blinked and glanced at her with surprise.

Forcing herself to calm down, she asked uncertainly, "You're kidding, right?"

"No," he said apologetically.

"Right." Sherry peered out the window. 411 AD.

So if she got together with Basil, she'd have a step-daughter who was . . . what? Sixteen hundred and some years old? Cripes. This was crazy.

"Do you have any children?"

"Good God, no!" Sherry blurted, jerking around in her seat to look at him with horror for the very suggestion. She wasn't married, for heaven's sake. Although she supposed that wasn't necessary now-adays, but the very idea of having children was kind of terrifying. She spent most of her time at the store working ridiculously long hours. She couldn't imagine trying to raise a child, let alone more than one, with the schedule she kept. Maybe someday . . . when things were more settled . . .

Sighing, she shook her head and decided a change of subject was in order. "So how did you get named after a spice?"

Basil's lips quirked with amusement, and he explained, "Stephanie mispronounced it. My name is Basil."

"Basil," Sherry echoed, pronouncing it Baw-zil as he had.

Basil nodded. "It's short for Basileios."

A car horn had honked as he spoke and she wasn't sure she'd heard right. Tilting her head, she asked, "Bellicose?"

"No, not bellicose," he said with a chuckle. "That is a temperament, not a name. My name is Basileios." He spoke slowly and loudly this time to be sure she heard.

"Basileios," Sherry murmured and then pursed her lips briefly as the name tickled her memory. "So you weren't named after a spice, but some big snake from Harry Potter? Nice."

He blinked. "A snake? What the devil are you talking about?"

"I think she's getting Basileios mixed up with basilisk," Stephanie said helpfully, turning in the front seat to grin at them.

"Basilisk, right," Sherry said with a smile and then shrugged. "They sound very similar."

"They are *not* similar," he said grimly. "My name is Baw-sill-ee-os. Basileios."

"Well, you said it fast the first time and it sounded kind of like basilisk," she said apologetically.

"It did kind of, didn't it?" Stephanie agreed.

"It did not," Basileios said indignantly.

Feeling herself relax a bit, Sherry teased, "Well, if you're going to go and get all bellicose about it, maybe we should just go with the spice and call you Basil after all," she said, pronouncing it like the spice. And then she muttered, "Or Pep."

Apparently, he had excellent hearing. Expression blank, he asked, "Pep?"

"Short for pepperoni," she explained with embarrassment.

"As in you're the pepperoni in her pizza," Stephanie said and burst out laughing.

Basileios stared from one to the other blankly, and then asked Stephanie, "You're quite sure this woman is my match? There is no mistake?"

Stephanie laughed even harder at the question, but Sherry wrinkled her nose at the man. "Be nice, spice boy. I woke up this morning on earth. Five hours later I've stepped into the twilight zone. Cut me some slack here. I was just teasing you to let off a little steam."

"Hmmm," he murmured, and then allowed his

eyes to rake down over her figure as he offered, "There are many much more pleasant ways to let off steam."

Sherry went completely still. Images were suddenly flashing through her mind of some of those more pleasant ways. They were hot and sweaty flashes of them naked, her head thrown back, neck exposed as his mouth and hands traveled over her naked body.

Cripes, the flashes were so real it was like they were doing it right then. Sherry's body actually responded as such, her breathing becoming low and shallow. Much to her dismay, her nipples even hardened and liquid pooled low in her belly and then rushed down to dampen her panties.

Flushing bright red, she shifted uncomfortably in her seat, then turned to peer steadfastly out the window as she tried to banish the images and her body's reaction to them.

Jeez, she'd never experienced anything like that before. She just wasn't the sort to imagine things like that about a virtual stranger. Heck, she'd never even had such powerful imaginings about anyone she'd ever dated. Truth be told, she hadn't known it was possible to turn yourself on with just a thought. And having them now, in the backseat of an SUV, with Stephanie, Justin, and Basil there . . . well, it was just embarrassing as all hell. It made her glad Stephanie couldn't read her thoughts. She hoped Basil and Justin couldn't either.

UNFORGETTABLE ROMANCES FROM
NEW YORK TIMES BESTSELLING AUTHOR

LYNSAY SANDS

An English Bride in Scotland
978-0-06-196311-7

Annabel was about to become a nun, when her mother
arrived at the abbey to take her home . . . to marry the
Scottish laird who is betrothed to her runaway sister!
From the moment Ross MacKay sets eyes on Annabel,
he is taken with his shy, sweet bride. And when an
enemy endangers her life, he'll move the Highlands
themselves to save her.

To Marry a Scottish Laird
978-0-06-227357-4

Joan promised her mother that she would deliver
a scroll to the clan MacKay. But traveling alone is
dangerous, even disguised as a boy. When Scottish
warrior Campbell Sinclair lends his aid, she is more
than relieved . . . until he surprises her with lingering
kisses that prove her disguise hasn't fooled him.

Sweet Revenge
978-0-06-201981-3

Highlander Galen MacDonald is on a mission of
revenge: kidnap his enemy's bride and make her his.
When he realizes Kyla is delirious with fever, he
wastes no time in wedding her. While Kyla is grateful
to the Scottish laird for saving her from marrying a
loathsome man, she is just as furious that Galen has
claimed her for his bride.

LYE7 1214